THE PRICE OF PASSION

"What would it take to get you to turn me loose?"

He raised one eyebrow at her and said nothing.

She rushed on. "Suppose I . . . suppose I let you make love to me in exchange for freeing me?"

He threw back his head and laughed. "Have you ever had a man before?"

She felt her face flame. "You know I haven't!"

"Then you might not be skilled enough to make it enjoyable."

She was incensed. "You're turning me down?" She lunged at him, scratching and clawing. If she could sink her nails into those arrogant blue eyes . . . !

Cougar caught her wrists and they went down in a heap as they struggled. He came up on top. He lay there, both of them breathing hard as he pinned her hands above her head.

"You little vixen! I ought to . . ."

He bent his head suddenly and covered her mouth with his. He kissed her deeply, thoroughly. For a long moment, she surrendered to his seeking mouth, her body molding itself against his.

Oh, God, no man had ever touched her like this, and the way her eager body responded scared her.   .

Books by Georgina Gentry

APACHE CARESS
BANDIT'S EMBRACE
CHEYENNE CAPTIVE
CHEYENNE CARESS
CHEYENNE PRINCESS
CHEYENNE SPLENDOR
CHEYENNE SONG
COMANCHE COWBOY
ETERNAL OUTLAW
HALF-BREED'S BRIDE
NEVADA DAWN
NEVADA NIGHTS
QUICKSILVER PASSION
SIOUX SLAVE
SONG OF THE WARRIOR
TIMELESS WARRIOR
WARRIOR'S PRIZE

Published by Zebra Books

APACHE TEARS

Georgina Gentry

Zebra Books
Kensington Publishing Corp.

http://www.zebrabooks.com

ZEBRA BOOKS are published by

Kensington Publishing Corp.
850 Third Avenue
New York, NY 10022

First Printing: December, 1999
10 9 8 7 6 5 4 3 2

Printed in the United States of America

For my Apache friend, Irma Kitcheyan, who took me out to all the historic Arizona sites I needed to see and shared with me so many authentic Apache stories;

for my writer friend, Janis Reams Hudson, who first gave me some Apache Tears and told me the tragic legend;

and finally, for the Indian scouts who served so bravely and were, for the most part, unappreciated and unsung.

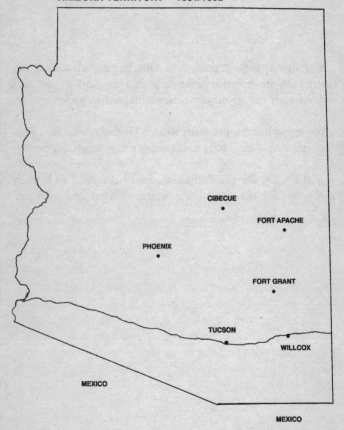

ARIZONA TERRITORY   1881/1882

CIBECUE

FORT APACHE

PHOENIX

FORT GRANT

TUCSON

WILLCOX

MEXICO

MEXICO

Prologue

Apache Tears. It is the name for the black, sometimes tear-shaped obsidian gemstones found in the sun-splashed wilderness of Arizona. An ancient Apache legend goes with the gem. Some of the tale varies, depending on who is telling it, but here is the basic story: A small band of courageous Apache warriors came up against a superior force of either soldiers or enemy braves. They fought valiantly, killing many of the enemy. However, eventually trapped on the top of a cliff, more than half the Apaches were killed as they held off the larger enemy group. Rather than surrender, the few brave survivors leaped off the cliff to their deaths. The grieving Apache women wept copious tears that fell to the ground and were turned into black stone. Today, Apache Tears still signify a great and undying love.

Indian scouts. The U.S. Cavalry of the Old West used a lot of them from many tribes. Among the best of these were the Apaches, who were brave in battle, relentless on the trail and expert at tracking their quarry. Only once in the entire history of the West did Indian scouts ever turn against their white masters. When it happened in August of 1881, those mutinous scouts were Apaches.

That much is recorded history. And maybe, just maybe, there might also have been a romance between a red-haired temptress and an Apache scout who desired her with such passion, he would give her a necklace of Apache Tears and risk everything to possess her. . . .

Chapter One

Near Fort Grant, Arizona Territory
August, 1881
Dawn

"But I'm not sure I *want* to marry the lieutenant!" Elizabeth Winters pouted as she leaned back against the bouncing seat of the stagecoach and brushed a stray red tendril away from her face.

Mrs. Everett, her gray-haired guardian, mopped her sweating jowls and glared at her. "My stars! Libbie, don't be difficult. Of course you're going to marry young Van Harrington! Must I remind you that your inheritance is almost gone? Now, let's hear no more—and put a smile on that pretty face! We're about to arrive at the fort."

She would have to do as she was told, Libbie thought with a frown of despair as the stagecoach pulled through the gates in a cloud of dust. What other options did she have? Her parents had spoiled her and granted their only child's every wish, but they were gone now and her fortune seemed to have melted away. Since her mother's old friend had become her guardian, Libbie seemed to have a voice in almost nothing. Now even her heavily mortgaged California mansion had been sold to pay expenses. With increasing frustration, Libbie had reacted by becoming as difficult as possible.

Now she forced herself to smile as she peered out the window at the passing action on the parade grounds, soldiers coming and going, the orderly rows of adobe buildings shimmering in the early morning heat. "I must say I like what I've seen of Arizona Territory."

"Pah!" Mrs. Everett wiped dust and sweat from her beefy face with a dainty handkerchief. "It's a savage land, fit only for savages! Lieutenant Van Harrington must have been out of his mind to request an assignment like this. Thank the heavens we're on to Boston tomorrow!"

The sun was just rising over the hills to the east, painting the scene all red and gold and purple. Libbie caught her breath at the distant beauty of the untamed landscape surrounding the fort as the stagecoach pulled to a halt with a jangle of harness in the square of the parade grounds. Libbie brushed the dust from her green silk gown and felt the confining heat of her corset and long petticoats. Like it or not, it had already been decided that she would marry the wealthy young blue blood late next spring when Libbie graduated from Miss Priddy's Female Academy in Boston only two weeks before she turned eighteen.

At least, marriage would get her out from under Mrs. Everett's thumb. Although she'd only met him a couple of times, she remembered that Lieutenant Phillip Van Harrington was handsome and he did write lovely letters. Maybe she could make the lieutenant dance to her tune; men had always been smitten by her beauty.

The rangy old driver swung down from the seat and

came around to open the door, slapping his Western hat against his leg, dust billowing as he opened the stage door. "Here we are, ladies."

"My stars! What a godforsaken place!" Mrs. Everett snapped as he helped her down from the coach. Then she turned sternly to Libbie. "Don't forget your parasol! You mustn't take a chance on that sun ruining your skin."

"But I like the feel of the sun on my face," Libbie argued with a haughty shake of her fiery hair.

"Libbie, ladies do not have sun-tanned skin, and the Lieutenant expects to get a lady. Need I say more?"

Feeling both angry and helpless, Libbie sighed with frustration and snapped open the lace parasol. In the times she had seen the sun-drenched skies of this wild, fierce land as she passed through from California to Boston, she had come to love the desert and the vast landscape she had seen from the train window. But of course, her guardian was right; ladies were admired for their pale, delicate skin, and with her fair complexion, she tended to freckle anyway.

Damn! Someday, she thought, and gritted her teeth, *someday I'll be of age and then I'll defy Mrs. Everett and do as I wish. No you won't,* she thought as she stepped from the coach, *the wedding is planned for a few days before your eighteenth birthday. After you marry Phillip, he will make all your decisions for you. Well he might boss me, but he won't make me like it.*

Even as she thought that, there was the lieutenant striding toward her; mid-twenties, tall, handsome, and broad-shouldered with blue eyes under sandy hair and a square, mannish jaw. It was only his pale mustache, his thin, tight lips, and his manner that made him seem a little prissy, she thought.

"Ah, Mrs. Everett, and Elizabeth, my dear! Did you have a good trip?"

Mrs. Everett wiped her beefy face and grumbled about

the heat, but Libbie nodded as he bent to kiss her hand. "Yes, Phillip, actually, we did, although it is a long way from the train."

"Beastly country!" Phillip snorted. "Snakes and savages! I can hardly wait to return to Philadelphia and civilization." Now he turned his warmest smile on her pouty guardian. "Ah, so glad to see you again, dear lady! I'm sorry about the heat! Arizona is hell for civilized people."

Mrs. Everett simpered at him like a schoolgirl. "It was made agreeable only by the knowledge that you were waiting for us, dear boy. Isn't that right, Libbie?"

"What?" Libbie barely heard her. A man had caught her attention; a tall, big-shouldered, dark-skinned savage who leaned against the corner of a nearby adobe building and watched her with startling blue eyes in his dark, square-jawed face. More shocking was that he was bare-chested, wearing only a skimpy loincloth, knee-high buckskin moccasins, and an interesting necklace of silver and turquoise beads set off by tear-shaped black gemstones that hung against his massive, muscled chest. His black, straight hair reached almost to his shoulders and a red headband held it in place. She studied him carefully. He was perhaps three or four years younger than Phillip, but already much more of a man than the lieutenant would ever be.

The savage stared at her in a bold, impudent way that sent a chill of either fear or anticipation up her back; Libbie wasn't sure which.

Ndolkah leaned against the building and studied the haughty white girl who stared at him with such frank curiosity. So this was the future wife of the arrogant lieutenant. Everyone at the fort had been saying she would visit as she passed through from California on her return to school back East.

She was very beautiful and very young, Ndolkah forced himself to admit, noting the early morning sun glinting off the red hair that peeked from beneath her expensive hat with its sweeping plumes. The lace parasol partially shaded the pale complexion. Her green eyes matched her fashionable dress, and the bustle only accentuated her small waist and the creamy swell of her bosom. *Libbie,* the lieutenant had called her. A better name for the flame-haired beauty would be Blaze, Ndolkah thought. Yet she was more than beautiful; there was something about her that hinted that behind that ladylike manner, she was also as rebellious and headstrong as a wild mustang filly. One thing was certain—this beauty was too much woman for the prim tenderfoot lieutenant to tame. Ndolkah smiled ever so slightly at the thought.

"Elizabeth," Phillip scolded, "what are you looking at?"

She knew she shouldn't stare, but she couldn't take her eyes off the virile, half-naked man leaning against the adobe building. "Who is that?"

Phillip turned to look. "That half-breed savage?" he snorted. "Ndolkah, one of my Apache scouts; old Mac McGuire's son. Hey you, Cougar!" He shouted and made a gesture of dismissal, "haven't you got work to do?"

Ndolkah nodded to the English translation of his Apache name, gave the lieutenant a mocking half-salute, and looked boldly into Libbie's eyes before turning and saun-tering away.

Libbie took a deep breath, unnerved from the frank appraisal of his gaze, but she watched him go, his long-legged stride accenting the hard muscles of his tanned, naked back. The nerve of that scout! His blue eyes had seemed to taunt her; almost seemed to undress her with his look as he left. "Ndolkah," she murmured, "what does it mean?"

Phillip made a gesture of annoyance. "Cougar, or so the Apache tell me."

Cougar. Yes, that name fitted him, Libbie thought, watching him saunter away with easy grace; tawny skin, muscular as a wild animal, moving with a powerful gait.

"He's an arrogant devil," Phillip snapped, "if he weren't so darned good as a scout, and old Mac's son, I'd let him go, and I may have to have him whipped yet."

"I wouldn't try that if I were you, Phillip," Libbie blurted without thinking, "he looks like he could take you in a fight."

"What did you say?" Phillip asked.

Mrs. Everett's fat face paled. "Libbie said she's really looking forward to tonight, didn't you, dear?"

Libbie sighed at her prompting. "Yes, of course."

Phillip beamed at the pair as he barked orders to some enlisted men about handling the ladies' luggage. "Oh, yes, I did write you that we'd planned a ball in your honor?" He took Libbie's elbow and they walked along the wooden sidewalk, her guardian puffing in their wake. "There's not much excitement out here at Fort Grant except trying to keep the savages from attacking settlers. I'm still hoping to get into a real battle and avenge my father's death." He smiled at Libbie and pulled at the sandy mustache above his thin, tight lips. "I'm sure you'd be pleased if I won a medal or two. If I'm lucky, I might get assigned to the President's staff."

"Isn't it tragic about the shooting?" Mrs. Everett asked, puffing along behind them.

"Yes," Phillip flung over his shoulder. "If Garfield doesn't survive his wounds, I guess I can kiss that promotion good-bye."

"Really, Phillip," Libbie said before she thought, "you might show a little compassion for the President! After

Lincoln, I'm sure the country thought we'd never have another assassination attempt."

Mrs. Everett poked her in the back again—hard. "We'd be thrilled if you won some medals, wouldn't we, Libbie?"

Libbie gritted her teeth and smiled prettily at him from under her parasol. "Of course, Phillip; every woman loves a hero."

Behind her, Mrs. Everett said, "And they'd look so good on your uniform in the wedding."

He threw a smile at the woman over his shoulder. "By then, I hope to be transferred back to Washington, whether the President survives or not."

"My stars! How exciting!" The dowager fanned herself as she puffed along. "Isn't that exciting, Libbie?"

"Hm? Oh, yes," Libbie said, stifling a yawn. "Somehow, I was hoping we'd stay out here. This is beautiful country; wild and untamed and savage." In her mind's eye, she saw the half-naked scout and the intimate way his blue eyes had assessed her. His bold gaze had said: *I want to possess you; to strip away all that civilization along with that green silk dress.*

"Ye gods, my dear, you must be joking!" Phillip snorted and patted the hand looped through his arm. "No civilized person would want to live out here; only the Apache feel at home in this wild country."

In her mind's eye, she saw the Apache scout galloping across this sun-splashed wilderness—uncivilized, untamed and free. In her imagination, he reached for her, swung her up on his pinto stallion, and galloped away with her.

"Elizabeth, are you all right?" Phillip peered anxiously at her as they paused on the sidewalk. "Your face is flushed."

Oh, dear God, if he should even guess at what she'd been thinking . . .

"It's this blasted heat," Mrs. Everett said behind them,

"and Libbie is such a delicate, high-strung lady. Thank goodness I brought some smelling salts!"

Smelling salts? What she needed was to get out of this corset and long petticoats. "I'm fine." She gave her escort a haughty shake of her head.

"Here we are." Phillip paused in front of an adobe building and opened the door. "I'm afraid this is the best we have to offer—not good enough for real ladies, but I'm afraid it will have to do." He stepped aside so they could enter.

Mrs. Everett beamed up at him, still fanning herself with a lace hankie. "You're such a dear boy! I knew I was making the right decision when I introduced you two at that Christmas ball!"

Phillip took her beefy hand and kissed it. "And let me assure you, sweet lady, that I will never forget the favor you did me in doing so! When I marry Elizabeth, there will always be room for her guardian at our home."

"Go along with you, Lieutenant." Mrs. Everett giggled like a schoolgirl as they entered and looked around.

It was much cooler inside the thick adobe walls. The room was primitive in its furnishing—a pair of beds, a chest, several chairs, and a Navaho rug spread on the wood floor. There was a big tin tub in the corner and Libbie looked toward it with longing.

The soldiers had followed and now put the luggage down. The lieutenant dismissed them curtly and they saluted and left. Libbie had a distinct feeling that the lowly soldiers didn't like the young aristocrat any better than Cougar did, but they weren't arrogant as he had been.

"Now, Elizabeth, dear," Phillip said as he bustled about opening the windows, "I'll have a girl sent over with food and bathwater. You two can rest until this evening."

"Oh, but I don't want to rest," Libbie protested as she

closed her parasol with a snap. "I want to see as much as possible; maybe go riding."

"But there's nothing to see!" Mrs. Everett looked aghast.

"Damn it. You don't have to go," Libbie said. Her patience with the woman was wearing thin.

"Libbie!" Her guardian gasped. "What on earth will Phillip think about a girl who swears? Can't you say 'darn it,' or 'drat,' or something?"

"I say what I mean," Libbie answered with a toss of her fiery curls.

"Never mind, dear Mrs. Everett," Phillip's thin lips forced a smile. "I'm sure when we're wed, I can tame the lady and teach her proper behavior."

Tame the lady. Damn it, she didn't want, didn't intend, to be tamed. Libbie looked at Mrs. Everett's stricken face and remembered their financial situation. With a sigh, she turned her most charming smile on the wealthy young officer. "I would love to go riding. I do ride very well, Phillip."

He took out his handkerchief and mopped his face. "Ye gods! Really, my dear, Mrs. Everett is right; there's nothing to see but desert and hills and savages."

She favored him with her most pretty pout. "I must warn you that I'm quite spoiled, Phillip; Daddy did that. I usually get what I want."

"I can indulge you a little now, my dear," Phillip frowned, "but of course, when we're married, I'll expect unquestioned obedience, as any husband would."

When we're married. Libbie sank down on a chair and took off her hat. She barely understood what it was a married couple did in bed, but she was certain it was awkward and embarrassing. The more she thought about Phillip taking off her nightdress and kissing her breasts with his thin, prim mouth and that wispy mustache, the more she was sure she wouldn't like it at all.

"My stars!" said Mrs. Everett, "Libbie looks faint."

Phillip came over to her chair. "My dear?" He took her hand and rubbed it anxiously. "Are you sure you'll be all right?"

His hands were as pale and delicate as her own, Libbie thought and imagined the Apache scout's dark, big hands. They would be strong and hard. She had a sudden vision of his full, sensual lips kissing her breasts. She felt an unexpected surge of excitement and took a deep breath. "Mrs. Everett is right, Phillip, I'm tired and need some rest."

"Fine." Phillip backed toward the door.

"However, I'd still like to go riding later this morning." Libbie stood up. "I wish I didn't have to use a sidesaddle."

"Libbie!" Mrs. Everett rolled her eyes. "You mustn't shock young Phillip with your jokes."

"I'm not joking," Libbie pouted.

The lieutenant paused at the door. "Of course you are, my dear." He used the smug tone of a condescending father to a not very bright child. "Very well, I'll bring horses over about ten and we'll go riding. However, we won't get too far out of sight of the fort. There's a lot of unrest among these savages right now, and you'd be a delicious prize to any of those bucks."

Mrs. Everett gasped at the image his words presented, but Libbie felt an unaccustomed thrill run through her. "Thank you, Phillip."

He smiled and bowed. "Ten o'clock it is then. I'll send a girl with food and bathwater."

Libbie watched him walk away from the door. He might be handsome, but even the way Phillip walked was prissy.

Mrs. Everett sighed with relief and closed the door. "My stars! What on earth were you thinking, young lady?" she snapped as she turned on Libbie. "The Van Harringtons have a high position in Philadelphia society; Phillip will marry a girl only if he thinks she is a real lady and as blue-blooded and proper as he himself.''

"He's a prissy prig," Libbie frowned as she began to unbutton the green silk.

"But he's a *rich* prissy prig," Mrs. Everett said as she came over to help Libbie with her dress. "I went to a lot of trouble arranging to come by here on the way back to Boston so he could be reminded of how pretty you are. Phillip Van Harrington is quite a catch, my dear, and the only son of a prominent Philadelphia society leader."

"I don't care," Libbie sighed and stood up so her guardian could unhook the back of the green silk gown and begin to unlace her corset.

"You will care when you're out of money, Elizabeth Winters," the dumpy lady huffed as she struggled with the laces. "Now that we've sold your parents' home in California, that money should last less than a year, considering the fancy wedding we'll have to put on. But by then, we'll be into the Van Harrington wealth and won't have to worry anymore."

"I'm not worried," Libbie protested. "Money isn't important to me; freedom is."

"Easy to say when you've always lived in the lap of luxury," the other scolded, "but I haven't. As your mother's close friend, I'm trying to look after your best interests."

"My inheritance seems to have just melted away in the six years since their deaths in that railroad mishap," Libbie thought aloud. "I thought Daddy told me I would have plenty to keep me in the lap of luxury the rest of my days."

"Well, your father misfigured." She didn't look at Libbie as she began to unpack their luggage. "Expenses are higher than expected. Besides, it costs a fortune to keep you in that fancy Boston school." She sounded defensive and angry.

Why was the plump woman so upset?

"You didn't even ask me if I wanted to go to Miss Priddy's Academy. You just enrolled me." Libbie stepped out of her dress.

"You are not only spoiled, you are unappreciative!" Mrs. Everett took the gown, shook it, and hung it up without looking at Libbie. "Besides, it takes a lot to live the way we live; that's all."

"That's your choice, not mine," Libbie complained. "Except for horseback riding, my life is dull, dull, dull! And I don't care a fig about fine clothes and society balls— and I hate living back East!"

"You could at least think of me," her guardian complained as she fanned her damp face with a kerchief, "and if you weren't so silly and immature, you would care about all the good things money can buy. Don't let young Phillip see how spoiled and headstrong you are, or even your beauty might not be enough to cinch this deal. Remember, you might not get another chance at such a fine catch!"

Libbie whirled around. She started to answer that Mrs. Everett seemed more interested in her own comfort than Libbie's happiness, but decided she was wasting her time.

"Now what are you pouting about?" her guardian demanded.

"Nothing," Libbie said, and bit back a torrent of anger. At seventeen, she was underage and helpless; Mrs. Everett had complete control and would until she handed her ward over to Phillip on their wedding day. Libbie would never get to make any decisions on her own; she was powerless to do anything but sulk and make life difficult for those who commanded her life.

"That's more like it." Mrs. Everett brushed a wisp of gray hair back into her bun and began to shake out clothes and hang them up. "By the way, I saw the way you stared at that half-naked savage with such boldness. It's a wonder your fiancé didn't take offense."

"I wasn't staring."

"Yes, you were. Proper ladies keep their eyes downcast."

"Then it's a wonder more of them don't collide with walls and furniture," Libbie snapped.

"Don't get smart with me, young lady!" Her voice was as stern as her plain face as she returned to her unpacking. "We came by the fort just to dangle you like a carrot in front of the lieutenant's nose to remind him what a prize he's going to get next spring when you graduate."

"Damn it, I don't want to be a prize!" Libbie complained, flopping down on the bed, "I want to laugh every time I think of what it will feel like on our wedding night when he takes my nightgown off. His mustache will tickle."

Mrs. Everett paused and gasped, plump hand to her throat. "My stars! Such thoughts from an innocent girl! I'm frankly appalled! Remember that a woman is expected to do her duty in her husband's bed. Give him some heirs as quickly as possible and think of the money and prestige that goes with the union; that's the most a girl can expect."

"But I want more than that," Libbie insisted, "I expect him to make me want him to take off my nightdress, to thrill me with his kisses—"

"You must stop reading those trashy romance novels those naughty girls hide under their mattresses at Miss Priddy's," the lady scolded, shaking her finger in Libbie's face. "What's really important is making a secure match so we'll both have comfort the rest of our days."

"But I want love and excitement, and most of all, freedom!" Libbie's green eyes blazed.

"Then you expect too much"—the other shrugged—"especially for women of your social class—"

They were interrupted by a knock at the door, and Mrs. Everett turned and called out, "Yes?"

"Your breakfast, *señora*," a woman's voice called, "and some bathwater."

The plump matron opened the door and gestured. "Bring it in."

A pretty Indian girl entered with a tray. Libbie rolled over on the bed to stare at the girl and smiled. "Hello."

But the girl glared at her. "I am Shashké, your maid."

Libbie nodded and watched her. The Indian girl was about Libbie's own age—maybe seventeen or so, but dark, and her drab clothes hid a voluptuous body. A bright red flower was tucked in her black hair. *Now why would the girl frown at her?*

Libbie watched the girl set up a breakfast tray. "Is Shashké an Apache word?"

"Yes." The sultry girl did not smile. "I am named for the month I was born; whites call it January."

"You are very pretty." Libbie smiled.

The girl scowled. "My husband thinks so."

Mrs. Everett hissed at Libbie under her breath. "Don't be so democratic to the help; it isn't seemly for a lady. You," she addressed the Apache girl in a loud command, "get on with your work."

Libbie was embarrassed by her guardian's behavior, but she kept silent. She sat on the edge of the bed and Mrs. Everett drew up a chair. There was steaming strong coffee, fresh oranges, and warm tortillas with scrambled eggs and fried pork covered with spicy hot sauce. Libbie thought the food delicious and dug in with gusto, while her guardian complained about the peppery fare. The hostile Apache girl said nothing as she filled the tub with buckets of hot water carried in from a cart outside.

Libbie finished her food and pushed her plate away, curious about the Apache girl. "Have you worked at the fort long?"

The girl paused, eyeing her sullenly. "Not too long. My people are camped to the south of the fort."

"Libbie," Mrs. Everett reminded her, "you shouldn't

talk to the servants. You're interfering with the girl doing her job."

"No, I'm not," Libbie said.

The Indian girl finished filling the tub and frowned at Libbie. "You are as Ndolkah said, very beautiful," Shashké admitted grudgingly and her dark eyes shone with anger.

"Thank you," Libbie answered, still puzzled by the dark beauty's hostility. Why would the Apache girl be discussing Libbie with the scout? Was it only idle curiosity or was there more here than met the eye? Could the pair be a couple? A feeling passed over Libbie at the thought of the virile scout holding Shashké, touching her with the hot intimacy his gaze had hinted at as they swept over Libbie in such frank appraisal.

She had a sudden vision of the pair locked together in a torrid embrace and shook her head to chase the image away. To clear her thoughts, she asked, "Will you be at the dance tonight?"

The girl hesitated, then smiled, but there was no mirth in her face. "Of course. Someone has to serve the punch and clean up after the white people's dinner."

"You arrogant wench!" Mrs. Everett rose to snap at the Apache girl, "Get out of here before I report how uppity you are!"

Shashké turned and fled out the door.

Libbie frowned at the other. "There was no need to do that."

"That Injun wench was forgetting her place!" The guardian shrugged as she went over to the luggage and began to arrange Libbie's fancy soaps and delicate undergarments on a chair. "Almost as arrogant as that Injun buck this morning. How dare he stare at you that way!"

"I didn't notice," Libbie lied. "I'm sure you misread his intentions."

"Hah! An idiot could have seen what he was thinking

as he looked at you. Imagine the effrontery of that savage thinking about you with lust—"

"Oh, please, you exaggerate." Libbie took off her corset and lace pantalets, then slipped into the tub of steaming water with a satisfied sigh. She closed her eyes and leaned back in the tub, feeling the warmth against her skin and remembering the way Cougar's eyes had caressed her with heated emotion. If he truly belonged to Shashké, Libbie felt guilty about her strong attraction to the scout.

"Everybody knows Injuns can't be trusted," the other woman said as she bustled about, getting out fresh lace underthings for Libbie.

"Don't be silly, Mrs. Everett, these Indians work for the whites."

"That one scout looks like he wears no man's collar," the other predicted dourly.

That was what had been so fascinating about him, his arrogant independence and his rugged masculinity, Libbie thought, but of course she dared not say that. Instead, she began to take down her long, fiery hair so she could wash it and wondered idly what it would feel like to have a man tangle his fingers in her locks and pull her hard against him while his hot, demanding mouth dominated hers and his strong hands covered her breasts.

Libbie closed her eyes a long moment, trembling with excitement. Mrs. Everett was right; Cougar signified danger and forbidden excitement. Libbie wondered suddenly if he would be at the dance. Abruptly, she began to look forward to the night ahead.

Chapter Two

After her bath, Libbie put her hair up and slipped into a pale blue broadcloth riding outfit, complete with perky feathered hat and fine leather boots.

Mrs. Everett scowled at her charge. "Put some rosewater on your face and see if you can protect it from the sun."

"I will not!" Libbie flung up her head and strode to the door. "It's about time you stopped giving me orders!"

"You should learn not to be so sassy," the plump dowager warned. "Men don't like headstrong women."

"Would you believe I don't care?"

"You will care if you lose young Harrington and we're both out on the street begging!"

"I think you're more worried about your own future than mine!" Libbie snapped.

Before her irate guardian could reply, there was a knock at the door and Libbie rushed to open it, glad for the interruption.

Phillip stood there, looking dapper in his blue uniform

and holding the reins of two horses. "I'm here to take you riding, madam." He made a low, exaggerated bow.

She was almost glad to see him—any excuse to be away from the stern older woman and out into the fresh air. "Wonderful! I'm ready to go." She gave him a warm smile and went out, calling back over her shoulder, "We'll be back in a couple of hours."

Mrs. Everett followed them to the door. "Lieutenant, just the two of you? No chaperon?"

"Oh, for heaven's sake!" Libbie stormed.

Phillip seemed to force a smile, but he was plainly annoyed as he stroked his mustache. "Surely, dear lady, you aren't implying that I would take advantage of an innocent, respectable—"

"No, of course not," the woman backtracked, "it's just that with only the two of you, I thought the Indians might present some danger—"

"With me along?" Phillip gave her a self-assured look and patted the pistol at his side. "I'll protect her if some savage gets in our way. I'm an excellent shot you know; you should see my hunting trophies."

Reassured, Mrs. Everett closed the door.

Libbie turned from patting the dainty sorrel mare. "You know, Phillip, I'd almost swear you'd like a chance to shoot some Indians."

He shrugged. "That's what I came out to Arizona for—revenge. An Apache war party killed my father almost a quarter of a century ago when he was stationed in this miserable Territory."

"Oh?" Libbie mused, "I've read a lot of history, but I didn't realize there was any Indian trouble in this place about that time."

"It was one of those small, isolated incidents, the army said," Phillip answered. "Ironically, he was to have been sent back to Philadelphia the very next day."

No wonder Phillip hated Apaches. Her heart softened a little toward him. "I'm truly sorry," Libbie murmured. "It must have hurt you a great deal."

Phillip made a gesture of dismissal. "I was only four years old at the time. I don't even remember him. My dear mother and her unmarried sisters who live with us raised me."

A mama's boy. Libbie had suspected that.

"Here, my dear, let me help you." He put his hands out for her small, booted foot and lifted her up to the sidesaddle.

Libbie arranged her skirt and frowned. "I wish you'd brought me a regular saddle."

He paused as he was about to mount his own bay gelding. "I had thought you were joking. Ladies don't—"

"I know all about what ladies don't; it's been drilled into me enough. Just once, I'd like to grip a horse between my knees and gallop away with my hair flying in the wind."

Phillip grinned as he swung into the saddle. "Elizabeth, my dear, your exuberance is so refreshing!"

They turned and rode out at a walk, Phillip studying the outline of her ripe body in the fine blue riding habit as they started away from the post. *You sassy, spirited little bitch,* he vowed, *you need to be broken and trained into being a subservient and dutiful wife, and I'm just the man to do it. Once I control you and your fortune the only thing you'll ever get between your pretty thighs is me.*

Libbie adjusted her perky plumed hat and looked over at him. "A penny for your thoughts." She gave him her most winsome smile.

He grinned back at her. "I was just looking forward to our marriage, my dear. I think you are going to make me very happy and give me many sons."

Libbie flushed and looked away, as the image of his pale mustache on her breasts came to her mind again. Strange, he hadn't said anything about making her happy. "So where shall we ride?"

They were heading off the fort grounds at a lazy trot.

"We can't get too far away," Phillip cautioned, "there are bears in the area and some unrest among the Apache right now; some crazy medicine man is stirring them up, telling them the whites are going to disappear and they'll have their own land back again."

"Bears?"

"Don't worry, my dear." He patted the rifle hanging on his saddle. "I've killed dozens of them. The Apache don't like it, though."

"Why not?"

Phillip shrugged. "Who knows how a savage's mind works? Something about bad spirits or some such. Crazy people. If we don't kill all these Apaches, we ought to cage them."

"You can't blame them for wanting to be free," Libbie murmured, "that's a basic hunger of everyone."

"Ye gods! You sound almost sympathetic to the red devils," Phillip answered in a cold voice.

"Phillip, you can't hate all Indians because of something that happened so long ago."

"They're all alike," he snapped. "Because of savages, all my mother had to remember my father by was a couple of medals and a glowing letter from his commanding officer."

Libbie reached over and touched his hand. "It was a very long time ago, Phillip. For your own sake, you need to put it in the past."

"Never. Not until I have my vengeance," he murmured. However, he brightened at her touch and smiled. "Let's speak of happier things, shall we? Mother has been making grand plans for our wedding."

She didn't want to think about the wedding, even though

it seemed inevitable. "Where shall we ride to? Isn't there any friend of yours we can visit—maybe some ranches I can see?"

Phillip hesitated, looking over at her as they rode. "I suppose we might go out to Mac McGuire's ranch; I've only seen him a couple of times since I arrived six months ago. We don't really mingle, of course; different social class, you know."

He was as big a snob as his mother. Libbie had only met that remote, frosty socialite twice and hadn't liked her any better the second time. Well, if she must marry him, maybe she and Phillip would build their own home some distance from Henrietta Van Harrington.

The morning was warm, the breeze gentle. She didn't care where they rode as long as she could drink in these magnificent views of desert, buttes, and distant, shadowy hills. "Who's Mac McGuire?"

"Mac was my father's striker—you know, sort of an officer's Man Friday. He loved this wild country and after Father was killed, Mac retired out here and started ranching."

"Oh?"

Phillip's handsome face scowled. "Too sympathetic to the Indians, I'd say, for an old cavalry man. And I'm a little annoyed with Mac—he's got my father's ivory-handled Colt and won't give it to me."

"Did you ask him?" She was intrigued.

"Yes, and you know what he told me? Said it was bad medicine for the son to carry a dead man's gun. Old coot's been hanging around Injuns too long; beginning to think like them. Sometime, I think I'll just sneak in and steal it; he doesn't see or hear very well, so it would be easy."

"Why, Phillip, you wouldn't!"

He looked annoyed. "Well, why not? It's mine by rights anyway, and I surely don't want his half-breed son inheriting my father's pistol. Imagine a white man marrying an Apache girl!''

She shrugged. ''So what?''

''Ye gods, Elizabeth, I hope you're joking! Lots of white men take up with pretty Indian girls, but they don't *marry* them; it's unthinkable.''

''Why?'' Libbie asked.

''Oh, Elizabeth,'' he scolded, ''don't be so naive. A soldier doesn't have to do the honorable thing by a redskinned squaw; just give her a few beads or trinkets and she'll believe anything.''

Libbie winced. His comments didn't make her like Phillip any better. They rode a moment in silence, and a thought crossed her mind. ''So Mac McGuire is Cougar's father?''

Phillip nodded and frowned. ''Most arrogant scout I've got; speaks English and Mac's taught him to read and write. That half-breed thinks he's good as any white man. If it weren't for the friendship between Mac and my father, I would have booted Cougar from my outfit months ago.''

Cougar. In her mind, she saw the big, wide-shouldered rogue and remembered the way he had looked at her with banked passion in those startling blue eyes. There was a subtle challenge there and in the way his muscles gleamed in his naked back as he'd turned and sauntered away, as arrogant as the mountain lion for which he was named.

''It certainly fits him,'' she thought aloud.

''What?'' Phillip's head jerked up.

Damn it, she was going to have to be more discreet. In a few months, she wouldn't even be allowed to think freely. She didn't like to lie, but she didn't want to incur Phillip's wrath, either. ''Nothing. I—I was thinking of the little ring bearer we'll have in the wedding—a close friend's younger brother. His satin suit is so cute on him.''

''Hmm.'' Phillip yawned.

Libbie had noted before that unless the conversation centered on him or his family, the young aristocrat wasn't terribly interested.

They rode a number of miles in silence; Libbie enjoying the ride and the wild landscape, even though the heat was building in the late morning.

"Elizabeth, my dear, you're awfully quiet. What is that silly little head of yours thinking?"

She gritted her teeth. "Not much, Phillip, just silly little girl thoughts."

He smiled, missing the sarcasm in her tone. "Just as I thought! You're very much like my mother and sisters after all; nothing in your mind but fashion and parties. Philadelphia is already talking of the grand wedding your guardian is planning."

And it will take the last cent of my inheritance to do that, Libbie thought. She watched the rocky trail ahead of them, wondering how shocked Phillip would be if he knew that what she had really been thinking was how it would feel to be pulled into the half-breed's embrace and kissed with all the heat she'd seen in that sensual mouth?

The images set off such an unexpected storm of feelings in her soul that she succumbed to a wild urge to gallop across the desolate country, feeling the warm wind against her face.

"Let's race!" Libbie said abruptly and urged her mare into a lope across the rocky landscape, leaving the surprised Phillip behind in a cloud of alkaline dust as she galloped down an arroyo and through the silver sagebrush ahead.

"Watch out, my dear. You'll get hurt!" She heard his bay gelding clattering across the rocks behind her.

But instead of stopping, she threw back her head, laughed, and rode harder still. Libbie didn't stop until she had reached a plateau where she reined in, her mare hot and blowing. "I beat you!" She wheeled the mare around to shout with triumph.

He galloped up to her and she saw fury in the blue eyes and the set of the square jaw. "Really, Elizabeth, it's not seemly to try to compete with a man."

She raised her chin in defiance. "Why not?"

"It just isn't, that's all!"

"Not good enough!" she flung over her shoulder as she turned back up the trail. "I'd hoped you'd be pleased that I can be an equal partner."

He rode along beside her, his mouth under the wispy mustache drawn into a grim line. "Elizabeth, I don't want an equal partner; I want a wife."

"It could be the same thing." She had angered and embarrassed him by beating him and she knew it.

"You *are* frightfully spoiled, my dear," he said and he bit off his words, looking straight ahead. "However, I suppose that's to be expected, being an only child and then an orphan. But of course that will have to change."

He was really upset. Her first reaction was to tell him what a spoilsport he was, but then she remembered her financial situation. Libbie forced herself to duck her head and assume a humble tone. "I'm sorry, Phillip. I'll try to be more circumspect in my behavior."

He didn't look quite so annoyed. "It's all right. You're very young, Elizabeth, and I know you just need a firm hand and some discipline."

His smug tone rankled her. Libbie forced herself to laugh. "Daddy used to say I was untamed and untamable."

"We'll see about that," Phillip snapped under his breath.

"What did you say?"

"Nothing, my dear."

However, she had heard him and it rankled her. "Phillip,

I'm a modern woman; I don't expect to live in submission like a slave. Lincoln freed them, remember?"

He didn't answer, but his jaw was set. "Let's not fuss, shall we?" His thin smile looked forced. "It's a nice day, despite this horrid countryside. Mac will certainly offer us some lemonade."

"All right." She decided she would not pout or argue that this was wonderful, beautiful country. "Look," she pointed, "there's an adobe house in the distance and a horse tied up at the hitching rail."

Phillip cursed under his breath as they rode closer, staring at the big paint stallion. "Cougar's here; I've a good mind to ride on."

Cougar. She felt her hands tremble on the reins and was surprised at her own reaction. She wasn't certain whether she looked forward to or dreaded seeing him again. "Nonsense!" she pouted. "I—I'm feeling a bit faint and you promised me a glass of lemonade, remember?"

"I shouldn't have taken you out in this August heat. I hope you aren't about to swoon." He looked anxious.

"Perhaps if I got in out of the sun a moment . . ."

"Yes, let's ride on over to the house. Perhaps Mac will have some smelling salts, or at least some cold water." They rode into the ranch yard and three spotted mongrels came out of the barn, barking and wagging their tails. The big half-breed and a short white man with graying hair and beard came out on the covered porch as the pair rode up.

"Hello there! Good to see ye," the older man yelled in a Scottish accent as they reined in.

Phillip nodded in return as he dismounted and came around to help Libbie down. "I've brought my fiancée by to meet you, Sergeant."

"I'm no longer that, young man, but I'm never too old to entertain a pretty miss!"

Libbie smiled as they approached the porch, trying to ignore the bare-chested scout, who leaned against a porch post watching with a stony expression. She noted he still wore the unusual turquoise, silver, and ebony gem necklace. "Delighted to meet you, Mr. McGuire. I've heard so much about you."

"Hey? What's that?" He craned his head. "Ye'll have to speak up, lass, me hearing's gettin' as bad as me eyes."

"Nothing important." Libbie smiled at the old man.

Mac motioned for them to come up on the porch out of the sun and peered at her with age-dimmed dark eyes. "Ah, lass, 'tis good of you to come. The whole post's been abuzz with news of your arrival, but I wasn't expecting a personal visit from such a feisty girl!"

Libbie laughed. "What makes you say that?"

The other man filled his pipe, his dark eyes twinkling. "Cougar told me about the last half of that horse race he just witnessed from my window."

"You're a good rider," Cougar said to her with grudging admiration.

Phillip's face flushed. "It's not seemly for a woman to gallop madly like that, trying to beat a man. My mother would have been shocked if she'd seen Libbie's behavior."

"That so?" Cougar said coolly. "*My* mother would have liked it."

Damn it, Libbie thought, *they seem likely to start throwing punches right here on the porch.* She looked helplessly at the old man.

Even Mac McGuire must feel the tension between the two men, for he said, "It's hot, lass. Won't you sit down and I'll get us some lemonade? I've made it with water from the well; good and cold."

"That would be wonderful," Libbie answered, but she couldn't take her gaze off Mac's big, virile son and the way he stared at her. Looking up suddenly, she realized the old man must have seen it, but he said nothing as he went inside. Then she realized that Phillip was watching them both and she looked away.

Cougar motioned toward some chairs made of unpeeled branches. "Your face is flushed, miss. You'd better sit down."

"I'll look out for the lady's welfare." Phillip's voice was as cold as his azure eyes.

She was embarrassed about his bad manners. "I can look out for myself, thank you both."

Phillip said to the other, "I told her ladies didn't have any business out in this heat, but she insisted."

Cougar looked her up and down with a searching gaze as they took a chair while he continued to lean against a porch post. "Somehow, I suspect the lady will do as she pleases."

"Not after we're married!" Phillip declared.

Libbie started to make a remark, then remembered she must not push Phillip too far. She lowered her gaze in the awkward silence that followed.

Her fiancé cleared his throat. "Cougar, have you found some new scouts for our outfit?"

The Apache nodded, but Libbie was only too aware that he continued to watch her as he fingered his necklace. "A bunch of White Mountain Apaches. They're young and green, but eager to learn."

Phillip frowned. "You think they'll do?"

Cougar shrugged. "Like I said, Skippy, Deadshot, Dandy Jim, and the others are very young and new to the service."

"What funny names for them," Libbie smiled at the scout, but he didn't smile back.

"White men's names," Cougar explained. "They don't try to learn our Apache names. Anyway, it will take a while for them to get used to taking orders and build some loyalty to the army."

Phillip took off his hat and mopped his face and mustache. "Discipline's probably what they need; a few strokes across the back with a quirt would teach them."

The half-breed frowned. "A little kindness and some extra food for their families would do a lot more."

Libbie moved to defuse the tension. "Why does the army need more scouts?"

Phillip said, "Because a bunch of our regular Apache scouts are off in New Mexico Territory right now on the trail of Nana and his war party that crossed the Rio Grande a few days ago."

"Is the army expecting trouble here?" she asked.

"The army goes looking for trouble," Cougar retorted. "Haven't you heard the drums echoing through the hills? If the whites would just be fair to the Apache—"

"Judging from the letters he wrote home, my father tried to be fair with the Apache," the lieutenant snapped, "and they murdered him. An iron hand is the only way to deal with savages!"

Cougar started to say something, but seemed to reconsider. She watched that square jawline as he took a deep breath and gritted his teeth.

She had a sudden feeling he was about to pull back his fist and hit the officer. Both these men were tall and broad-shouldered, but the half-breed was younger by maybe three or four years and he had more muscle. She had no doubt which one would win the fight.

"Uh," she gulped, "Cougar, why don't you see how your father is doing with the lemonade?"

Instead, Cougar went down the steps, every line of his big body hostile. "I've got duties back at the fort; tell Mac I had to go." He swung up on the paint stallion and rode off.

"Ye gods!" Phillip cursed under his breath. "Damned

arrogant savage. He didn't even wait until I dismissed him.''

Libbie watched the scout gallop away. He sat like he was part of the horse, a study in grace and speed. His back muscles rippled as he rode, and he gripped the stallion with strong thighs. There was something about the way he mastered the horse that excited something deep within her. She took out a handkerchief without thinking and fanned herself. ''If that Apache's so hard to deal with, why don't you fire him?''

''Because he's the best scout we've got,'' Phillip admitted grudgingly. ''He knows every redskin in the area and every rock and canyon for hundreds of miles. Funny though— he hadn't been so hard to deal with until today.''

It had started with her arrival, Libbie realized with abrupt clarity.

Mac came out just then with a tray of tumblers and stood watching the dust disappearing over the horizon.

''Your son said he had business at the fort,'' Libbie said.

''Hey?''

Libbie repeated her words.

''Oh?'' He looked at her a long moment, a question in his dark eyes. ''Here''—he set down the tray—''a pretty lass like you deserves better than this poor place has to offer. Help yourself, Lieutenant.''

''She'll get a lovely party tonight,'' Phillip said as he took a glass. ''Are you coming, Mac?''

''Of course; biggest happening this year.'' The old Scotsman handed Libbie a glass and she gulped it gratefully, savoring the tart, cold taste.

''Delicious!'' she declared with her warmest smile.

''So what do you think of the Territory?'' Mac sat down in his chair and sipped his drink, then reached into his shirt pocket for a worn old pipe. ''Do ye mind if I smoke, lass?''

"Not at all," Libbie answered. "I love this country; all wild and free like the mustangs and the Indians."

Mac leaned closer to catch her words, then sighed and lit his pipe. "But not for long, I'm afraid; settlers pouring in, the army trying to corral the Apaches. Eventually there'll be no refuge for either mustangs or Apaches except maybe in the mountains of Mexico across the border." He nodded toward the south.

"I can hardly wait to get back to Philadelphia," Phillip grumbled, "I came out here on a fool's errand, I guess."

Mac puffed his pipe and frowned. "Young man, I was your father's best friend, even if I was only his striker. Bill liked this country and these people."

"So they killed him for it!" Phillip's face flushed with anger.

There was a tense moment in which Libbie bit her lip, embarrassed for Phillip's bad manners.

The old man hesitated and sighed. "Forget the past, Lieutenant. My advice to you is to request a transfer far away from here and never come back."

Phillip stood up. "You were his best friend, and yet you tell me to forget it without attempting to take revenge? I don't even really know the details of how he died."

Mac combed his fingers through his beard and looked away. "I—I wasn't there when it happened. You got an official letter from his commander, didn't ye?"

Phillip nodded. "Yes, but it was pretty vague; he just told me what a hero Father was, dying in a skirmish with the savages. I always meant to ask him for more information, but he died several years ago, you know."

"I know." Mac didn't say anything else for a long moment. He smoked and stared into space. Or perhaps the old man hadn't heard all Phillip's words.

Mystified, Libbie enjoyed the rich scent of his pipe and waited.

"William Van Harrington was one of the finest men I ever knew," Mac said finally, looking up, "a man of principle with a great sense of honor; that should be enough for you. Be proud of him and let his spirit rest in peace."

"I will have my revenge," Phillip promised, "that's what I came out here for."

"Even if you start an Indian war?"

"Then I can kill even more of the red devils." The muscles in his square jaw clinched.

Damn Phillip for his rudeness to this nice old man. In the awkward silence, Libbie cleared her throat. "Well, now, Mr. McGuire, aren't you going to show me around the place?"

Mac nodded, seemingly relieved to change the subject. "Aye, lass, would ye like to see the house?"

"I certainly would." Libbie stood up.

Phillip took a deep breath and seemed to regain control. "Did I see some new horses out in the corral as we rode up?"

"Mustangs; broke 'em myself, me and Cougar," the old Scotsman said in his thick brogue. "The army looking to buy new mounts?"

"Yes. I'd like to see them. Maybe I could make recommendations."

Mac smiled. "Lieutenant, you head on down to the corral. I'll show the young lady the house."

Phillip started off the porch and Mac opened the screen door for Libbie. "I'm afraid it's pretty messy; I live alone, except for Cougar dropping by when he's not gone on a trip with the soldiers."

"Your wife has been dead a long time?" She followed the old man inside, speaking loudly so he'd hear.

"Aye, since Cougar's birth; died in my arms; didn't seem to want to live anymore. She's buried on a hill not far from here, where I can go up to put flowers on her grave."

Strange. For most women, a loving husband and a new son should have given her everything in the world to live for. Libbie wanted to ask questions, but decided it wasn't polite. Mac's sad expression spoke volumes. "You must have loved her very much."

"I did." He paused, his dark eyes wistful. "She was so spirited and so very beautiful; you remind me of her a little, young lady, except she had dark hair and eyes."

Libbie's gaze grew accustomed to the cool dimness of the room. It was a masculine place: leather chairs, a big stone fireplace, rifles hanging over the mantel and deer antlers on the wall, Navaho rugs on the wood floor. There was a big gun cabinet against one wall full of weapons, and shelves and shelves full of books, worn with wear. The room smelled of wood smoke, leather and tobacco. It looked comfortable, the kind of place rugged men called home. "I like it," she said.

"It's not fancy," Mac apologized. "I'm sure you're used to much finer and grander houses."

She shrugged. "Such things aren't very important to me. I'm getting awfully tired of civilization, too. That's why you stay out here, isn't it?"

He nodded. "Aye, lass. The West gets in some folks' blood. Some can't stand it; some of us can never leave it."

She picked up a small, faded daguerreotype off a table. In it, a much younger uniformed Mac McGuire smiled back at her standing next to a tall, broad-shouldered officer who was handsome, square-jawed and sported a fine mustache over a warm smile. "Major Van Harrington?"

Mac nodded.

"His son looks like him."

"What?" Mac looked startled.

She raised her voice. "I said Phillip looks like him."

"Oh, yes, of course." He took the photo from her hand,

staring at it a long moment, then sighed and put it down. "Such a tragedy."

"But you don't hate the Apache as Phillip does?"

The old Scotsman shook his head. "I understand them. Never expected young Van Harrington to show up out here; he belongs back East. This country is too hostile for him."

"He says he never really knew his father; maybe he's searching for answers."

Mac McGuire stared at the picture. "Sometimes a man should let well enough alone."

She waited for him to continue, but he only stared at the picture. Mystified, she studied the weathered old fellow. "You served with the major a long time?"

The other nodded and seemed lost in memories. "Aye, lass, why I remember a time . . ." Abruptly, he shrugged and smiled. "You're being polite, I know, listening to an old, deaf, half-blind soldier who rambles on and bores a young lady."

"I'm not bored," Libbie protested. "I'd like to hear more about Arizona and your experiences."

"Ah, no. Ye'd best be getting back so you can get ready for the ball."

They went out on the porch.

"I like you, Mac McGuire," Libbie said. "I'll save you a dance tonight."

He looked at her, a twinkle of admiration in his eyes. "I like you, too. You're frank and feisty—refreshingly different for a woman."

She felt herself blush to the roots of her red hair. "Will—will your son be coming to the dance?"

"Cougar?" Mac cleared his throat and looked embarrassed. "Miss, you don't understand how things work out here."

"Then enlighten me."

"The soldiers consider Cougar a savage; he won't be welcome at the party."

"But he's half white," Libbie protested.

"Actually, he's more than half white; his mother had a little French blood, courtesy of some passing trapper a couple of generations back. However, he's spent much of his life among his mother's people, so the army thinks of him as Apache."

"Oh." Libbie started down off the porch.

Behind her, Mac McGuire asked, "You're leaving tomorrow?"

"Yes, going back to school in Boston."

He came down the steps, and together they walked toward the corral. "And you'll be married back there?"

"Yes, next spring, as soon as I graduate. Phillip hopes to be promoted and transferred back East by then."

"In case we don't get another chance to talk, I want to wish you happiness and good luck, young lady."

She smiled at him. "Thank you."

"Hey, you two!" Phillip came out of the barn and waved. "Mac, you do have some fine horses; I'll talk to the quartermaster about them."

Mac nodded.

"Are you about ready to go, Elizabeth, dear? You look very tired."

She was tired; tired of Phillip's fussing over her. "All right."

They walked back to the house and mounted up.

"Good-bye, Mr. McGuire. See you tonight."

"Good-bye, miss." The old man nodded and said to Phillip, "She's a beauty, Lieutenant. Bill would have been pleased. May you have many children."

Phillip smirked. "I'll make sure of that!"

Libbie flushed at the mental image his words evoked.

She closed her eyes and bit her lip as they rode out. "Phillip, please. You embarrassed me."

"And that half-breed undressing you with his eyes didn't?" He sounded jealous.

"I don't know what you're talking about." She kept her gaze on the trail ahead.

"I don't know how you could have missed it; old Mac was certainly aware of it. Just looking at Cougar's face told me what he'd like to do to you. I had a good mind to thrash him soundly!"

"I don't think I'd try that if I were you," she murmured under her breath. The half-breed could probably kill the prissy officer with his bare hands.

"What?"

"Nothing," she snapped. "Damn it, I'm tired, Phillip. Let's go back to the fort so I can get a bath and some rest before the ball tonight."

"I'll overlook both your peevishness and your unladylike language," he said smugly. "After all, you're just a woman and it's dreadfully hot in this horrid place, not fit for civilized people at all."

Libbie gritted her teeth to hold back a rejoinder. She'd better learn to be as meek and mild as most women; Phillip expected it. On the other hand, she'd met Mrs. Van Harrington, and Phillip's mother seemed anything but meek and mild. A cold and stern dowager, Henrietta Van Harrington didn't seem like a match for the officer in the old daguerreotype at all. Well, maybe the lady had been a beauty in her day and maybe she'd been sweet and vulnerable before her husband was killed. Libbie looked about for some safe topic of conversation. "Tell me about Shashké."

"Who?"

"The Apache girl who brought our breakfast this morning. Did you know she's named for the month in which she was born, January?"

"Never was interested enough to inquire." Phillip snorted. "She's just an Injun wench who works as a maid around the fort. I've never given her a second thought; I don't know why you should."

"She seemed to take a special dislike to me."

"Oh?" He looked at Libbie a long moment. "What did she say?"

"Nothing much; it was her attitude, that's all."

"I suppose as far as an Injun wench is concerned, you've got everything and she resents it. Life is hard if you're not white in this country."

Libbie remembered the girl's faded dress. "I thought I'd give her a little gift or something when I leave."

Phillip yawned. "That would be a nice gesture; whatever you think, my dear, although the greedy little wench would probably rather have money to give her man for booze so he won't beat her."

"Beat her?"

"Don't be so shocked." He glanced sideways at her as they rode, evidently enjoying Libbie's dismay. "I hear it's commonplace among the savages."

She couldn't believe Cougar would beat anyone small and helpless, but what did she really know about him? She wanted to ask more, but decided it wasn't wise.

No, she couldn't imagine Cougar beating a woman, but she could imagine him making passionate love to one. With sudden clarity, in her mind, Libbie saw the big, virile savage wrapped in the sultry Shashké's arms while they made love together on the grass in the moonlight . . .

Abruptly, Libbie faced the truth; she wished for a love like that of her own, and she wasn't likely to find it with Phillip!

Chapter Three

Mac McGuire smoked his pipe and watched the pair ride away from his ranch. He stood there until they were out of sight; then, with a sigh, he started up the nearby hill to where his beloved was buried. He was sitting there on a rock by her grave pulling a stray weed from the flowers he so carefully tended, when he heard a step and turned.

Cougar came out from behind some scrubby trees, leading the paint stallion. "If I'd been an enemy, you'd be dead."

Mac nodded. "Aye, me hearing is gettin' as bad as me eyes, and that's a fact. Good thing I'm on good terms with all the tribes."

"They think of you as one of them."

Mac didn't look at him; his mind was busy with the conflict between the two younger men. "I thought ye had business at the fort?"

"I just wanted to get away from the lieutenant before I hit him."

"Cougar, listen to me," Mac ordered. "Grit your teeth and let him be. He'll be gone next spring."

"What did you think of the girl?"

Mac looked at him sharply. "Don't ye be thinkin' of her at all."

"She's leaving tomorrow." Cougar fingered his necklace absently, staring into the distance.

Mac sighed. He had once felt that same hopelessness over an unattainable woman. There was no way to make the younger man feel any better; he could only try to talk some sense into him. "Forget about that red-haired lass. She's high society, the same as him."

"You think I don't know that?" Cougar's voice was as anguished as his eyes.

"So don't be thinkin' about how her lips might taste or how soft her skin might feel under your hands."

"I can't help it; she was made to pleasure a man, give him sons."

Mac frowned and lit his pipe, shook out the match. He had never felt as much empathy for Cougar as he did now. "She was made to pleasure a wealthy *white* man."

"She's too much woman for the lieutenant; he'll never tame her."

"That's not your concern." Mac stood up and blew a cloud of fragrant smoke. "Stop what you're thinkin'. You know it's no good; red and white can never find happiness together." He looked down at the grave, remembering while his dark eyes misted.

Cougar reached out and put his hand on Mac's stooped shoulder very gently. "My head tells me you are right, but my heart—"

"Listen to your head, boy," Mac scolded. "There are some obstacles too great for love to overcome. Your own past should have taught you that."

"But not if it's a very great love," Cougar protested.

"You're dreaming, lad." Mac shrugged his hand off and turned to walk down the hill. "Just stay away from her; she'll bring you nothing but trouble."

"I've already got trouble," Cougar grumbled as he led his horse and fell in alongside Mac.

"That Shashké again?" Mac glanced sideways at him.

He nodded. "She's cheating."

"Damned silly little fool! Doesn't she know what the Apache do to unfaithful wives?"

"Sure she knows, but she's too vain and foolish to care."

"That's bad." Mac shook his head as they walked back to the house. "She's got such a pretty face."

Cougar shrugged. "If she doesn't stop, she won't have it long."

"Have you tried talking to her?"

"Yes, but she's like a bitch in heat; one man isn't enough for her."

Mac smiled as he remembered another, more delicate Apache beauty so many years ago. "Unlike Shashké your mother was a one-man woman. I'm sorry you never got to know her."

"You break Apache taboos in speaking of the dead," Cougar reminded him uneasily. "To do so calls them back from the Happy Place where the dead go."

"Sorry, sometimes I still think like a white man and as such, she's often on my mind. I wish she could have lived to see you grown up."

Almost absently, Cougar's hand went to the necklace he wore. "I wish it, too."

They walked the rest of the way in silence, Mac remembering the dark beauty he had loved so very much, but it hadn't been enough. He didn't want the same tragedy to happen to her son. "Maybe I won't go to the dance tonight. Maybe I'll stay here and we'll drink some *tiswin* and smoke and tell of hunts and battles; all the good old stories of the Apache. Bring along your friend, Cholla."

"Cholla's scouting for the troops in New Mexico," Cougar reminded him. "Don't know when they'll be back. Old Nana and his warriors have crossed the border and are setting that Territory ablaze."

"Then you and I will drink, and stare into the fire and listen to the drums."

"No." Cougar shook his head and gently put his big hand on the other's stooped shoulder. "Go to the dance; you'll enjoy it. Maybe I'll ride along."

Mac frowned. "You'd be better off if you didn't. The lieutenant was well aware of the way you were looking at his lady."

"A woman like that is wasted on him," he said again.

"She must see something in him or she wouldn't be marrying him."

"Funny, she doesn't look at him like she loves him."

There was no reasoning with the boy. Mac turned and looked back up the hill, remembering that the heart never listened to reason. "That's not for you to decide. The lieutenant has wealth and a fine family."

"You think I'm not aware of that?" Cougar snapped as he walked up on the porch, took out his makin's, and rolled a cigarette.

A long way off in the hills, a drum began a slow rhythm. The wind picked the sound up and carried it across many miles of hills and desert to all the Apache people.

Cougar listened a moment, then said, *"Noch-ay-del-Klinne* is telling the people that if they dance the dance and do the ceremonies, the white people will disappear."

"I know. The Apaches tell me things they don't tell other whites."

"That's because, in your heart, you are one of them. You loved an Apache girl; *really* loved her."

Mac smiled, seemingly lost in a past memory. "And always will," he whispered.

They both turned to listen to the drums echoing faintly in the distance.

Mac said, "The drums have been talking all summer. If the soldiers will just be wise and patient and let that medicine man alone, the warriors will lose interest when nothing he predicts comes true."

Cougar took out a small metal match safe and struck a match, cupping his big hands around the flame as he lit the cigarette. "Have you ever known white soldiers to do the wise thing?"

"Mostly not." Mac frowned.

"The Holy Man says he will bring the dead chiefs I must not name back to life; the Apache need only believe that it is possible."

Mac watched him smoke, loving him more than any man could love a son. "Mangas Coloradas Victorio, and Cochise," he thought aloud, then peered at the younger man. "Do you believe that?"

Cougar smoked and slowly shook his head. "Some things Apache I believe; some things I am too white to believe. It is hell to be caught between two worlds."

"For that, I am truly sorry. When a man loves a woman, *really* loves her, nothing else matters. He doesn't think about how it will be for a mixed-blood son in a white world."

"Yet I'm beginning to see how a man could want a woman that badly." Cougar knocked the ash off his cigarette.

Mac winced. The sooner that flame-haired girl was away from the fort, the better. He didn't want Cougar to do something so rash, he would end up in trouble with the army.

"In the olden days," Cougar mused, "when a warrior

saw a woman he wanted, sometimes he just fought for her and took her."

"These are not the olden days," Mac reminded him.

Cougar gave no sign that he had heard. He smoked and they both listened to the echoing drums carrying messages across many miles from the north.

"The soldiers may do something foolish," Mac said.

"They do that often." Cougar tossed his cigarette away.

"I meant I just hope they don't start a new Indian war."

"You'd be safe enough. The Apache like and respect you; you speak their language."

"I'm not thinking about myself, lad." Mac shook his head. "I was thinking of all the women and children, white and red, who'll suffer if there's an outbreak."

"Maybe you can talk to the colonel at the dance tonight; urge him not to do anything rash."

Mac nodded. "Aye, I'll at least try; my conscience won't let me do anything else."

"And I'll ride along." Cougar's rugged face was set and stubborn.

There was no use arguing with Cougar when he had made up his mind. "All right, but stay away from the lieutenant's woman."

"I know my place." His voice was as melancholy as his blue eyes.

"Good. I love you too much, lad, to let you repeat that tragedy."

Cougar didn't answer, staring out at the rough terrain while the drums echoed faintly through the hills.

He's too much like his mother to listen, Mac thought with frustration, *and Libbie Winters can only bring him trouble and heartache. Thank God she'll be gone tomorrow!*

* * *

That evening, Libbie dressed for the party with mounting excitement.

"My stars!" Mrs. Everett said with a smile, and mopped her wet brow. "You're certainly in a much better mood! You and the lieutenant had a lovely ride?"

"Ride? Oh, well, of course." Libbie looked through her jewelry case for her fine gold earrings. It unnerved her to realize she hadn't been thinking of Phillip at all.

"Wonderful!" Her guardian wheezed as she walked around the room, shaking the wrinkles from the pale pink sateen ball gown Libbie would wear tonight. "Thank goodness, then, you had the good sense to remember the wisdom of making a good marriage?"

Libbie merely murmured something noncommittal and tried to focus on Phillip, but her mind remembered instead the big half-breed scout and the way he had looked at her while they were all on Mac McGuire's porch. She could tell from his expression that he was mentally taking her clothes off very slowly and deliberately. She had been both shocked and fascinated by the virile maleness of him.

You're playing with fire, Libbie, she warned herself as she began to brush her hair until it shone. *Nobody knows what I'm thinking so what's the harm? And after all, I'll be leaving tomorrow and I'll never see him again.*

"Here, you need help putting your hair up." Mrs. Everett seemed in a rare good mood now that things were going according to her well-arranged plans. "Let me send for that sulky girl who was here this morning."

"I think we can manage," Libbie answered. "She probably has too many duties already." She didn't want to have to deal with the sullen Shashké. She dabbed a few drops of a faint lilac scent on her wrists and behind her ears. "Who all do you suppose will be there?"

"Well, everybody," Mrs. Everett gushed as she began to put up Libbie's hair.

"Everybody?"

"Yes, the officers and their ladies, and all the respectable white people," the other said as she put Libbie's hair up in elaborate curls on top of her head. "The Indians and the Mexicans won't be invited, of course."

Libbie's spirits fell a little. Damn. Well, what had she expected? Of course a half-breed Apache scout wouldn't be invited. Toying with Cougar was like playing with the wild animal he was named for—dangerous and forbidden. He couldn't be turned into a lady's obedient pet. She must keep her mind on Phillip and the fine marriage she would be making.

"You look beautiful!" Mrs. Everett put her hands on her plump hips and surveyed her handiwork. "Now all you need is for me to lace your corset a little tighter."

"My waist is small enough," Libbie protested with a pout.

"No, it isn't!" The other scolded as she reached for the laces. "A gentleman likes a woman to have a waist so small, he can touch his fingertips around it."

"He'd have to have awfully big hands," Libbie protested, but grabbed onto a bedpost so Mrs. Everett could lace her small waist even tighter. In her mind, she saw a pair of big, dark hands and imagined them encircling her bare waist.

"Lieutenant Van Harrington has a gentleman's hands; small and fine," the other woman remarked as she pulled the laces tighter still.

"Damn, stop it! I can hardly breathe!" Libbie protested.

"Tsk! Tsk! Will you never behave and talk like a lady? Now pinch your cheeks to put some color into them."

Libbie couldn't breathe and her tiny slippers hurt her feet. Mrs. Everett straightened Libbie's bustle and surveyed her handiwork with satisfaction. "You look beautiful; every man there tonight will want you."

But the man who interested Libbie would not even attend, Libbie thought with resignation and tried to focus her thoughts on the dapper young officer to whom she was engaged. It didn't work.

Finally they were ready—plump Mrs. Everett in no-nonsense dark gray faille, and Libbie in her pink sateen with ribbons and tiny flowers down the bodice and matching ones in her red hair. Libbie put on the fine gold earrings.

Mrs. Everett looked her over and nodded. "You'll turn a few heads tonight, I'll wager, and the lieutenant will want you more than ever. We can stop worrying about money."

"I never worry about it," Libbie snapped.

"I guess not!" her guardian scolded, "but I worry enough for both of us. Bargain with your beauty and youth, my dear, while you've got it to bargain with."

"I feel like a prize filly at an auction," Libbie complained.

"Now don't be acting spoiled and sulky on me," Mrs. Everett warned. "You be so charming, the young heir will be trying to move that wedding up to Christmas."

"With the kind of elaborate wedding you and Phillip's mother have planned, it'll take 'til next summer to make all the arrangements."

"What do you expect for the biggest society event Philadelphia has seen in years?" the other challenged. "It must be done right, with plenty of expensive pomp and ceremony. We don't dare let important people know you're almost penniless."

"Why not?" Libbie snapped. "You think it will matter to Phillip?"

"With your beauty, maybe not, but"—and the lady lowered her voice conspiratorially—"we wouldn't want him to suspect you might be marrying for money."

"Which I am. It isn't honest." The whole facade sickened Libbie.

"Honest!" Her guardian sneered and fanned herself. "Only the young think about honor and true love. Think instead about losing our present lifestyle, both of us working as shopgirls or governesses."

A loveless marriage terrified Libbie more than poverty, but there was no point in arguing with the older woman. "I'll leave all the details in your capable hands, Mrs. Everett; I've still got a whole year of school ahead of me."

Mollified, Mrs. Everett reached for her wrap, and about then there was a rap on the door. When Libbie opened it, Phillip was outside with a buggy.

"My!" he said, and his blue eyes widened with pleasure as he stared at Libbie, "don't you look splendid!"

"Doesn't she, though?" Mrs. Everett beamed at him. "I'll wager there'll be other young officers tonight who'll try to monopolize her time."

"Well, I don't intend to let them!" Phillip offered Libbie his arm and they went outside to the buggy, Mrs. Everett bringing up the rear. "It's not far, really, but I thought you wouldn't want to get dust on your dress."

They got in and drove the few hundred yards to the meeting hall. The Arizona night was hot with a thousand fireflies and the scent of flowering cactus. From the distant hills echoed a rhythmic beat.

Libbie cocked her head as they drove. "What is that sound?"

Phillip cursed under his breath. "Ye gods! They're at it again!" To Libbie, he said, "I thought I told you we're having a little trouble with some Injun medicine man over near Fort Apache. He's got this fool idea that he can bring dead warriors back to life and run all the whites out of his land with his magic. I'm one of those who've been urging the colonel to get tough and abide no nonsense. Might as well nip this in the bud."

Libbie's green eyes widened. "Is there liable to be trouble?"

He gave her his most charming smile and ran one finger over his pale mustache. "If there is, my dear, you can just wager I'll be in the thick of it and kill me a few savages!"

Mrs. Everett made a sound of approval. "Good for you, Lieutenant! Some medals across your chest would look mighty fine at the wedding."

Phillip reached over and put one of his delicate hands over Libbie's. "They would, wouldn't they?"

His hand felt moist and as dainty as a woman's, Libbie thought, but she couldn't pull away. "I don't think killing people should be treated so lightly."

"I'm a soldier, Elizabeth, that's what I do." Phillip's tone was condescending and lofty.

"Oh, really? How many battles have you seen so far, Phillip?"

She heard Mrs. Everett gasp. "Libbie! That wasn't polite! You must forgive her, Lieutenant; her parents spoiled her terribly."

Her parents. Their tragic deaths in that railroad incident had left her so lonely. But never had she felt so alone in the world as she did at this moment, riding along with these two people who now controlled her life.

However, Phillip shrugged and tightened his grip on Libbie's hand so hard it hurt, but she was determined not to cry out.

He said, "That's what I find so appealing about our Elizabeth—her youth and innocence. She simply needs a husband's strong guidance so she will behave like the proper lady she is."

Mrs. Everett breathed a sigh of relief. "I'm so glad you understand, young man."

Libbie jerked her hand from Phillip's and flexed it. It ached from his crushing her fingers together. She wanted to lash out at him, but remembered again how financially dependent she and her governess were on this union and bit back her words.

"I know your parents spoiled you, Elizabeth," Phillip said with an indulgent smile, "and they could afford to. Everyone back East knows the Winters were one of the wealthiest families in California before their unfortunate deaths."

But not anymore, Libbie thought, and then she wondered—would that make any difference to Phillip if he knew? Why should it? The Van Harringtons had plenty of money of their own.

The drums still echoed faintly through the hills as Phillip tied the buggy to the hitching post and came around to help the ladies out. Instead of offering Libbie his hand, he put both hands on her trim waist and lifted her down. His fingers felt hot and moist through the pale pink sateen and Libbie shuddered at the thought of them on her bare skin.

"Are you cold, my dear?"

"What?" She jerked up, disconcerted, her mind still on the distasteful images.

Mrs. Everett fluttered nervously, obviously upset by Libbie's inattention. "She's just so high-strung and delicate, like most ladies, you know."

"Of course." He was staring down at Libbie in the moonlight, puzzlement in his cold blue eyes. "Shall we go in, my dear?"

Libbie nodded, mentally scolding herself that she must remember to act like a ninny and giggle while hanging on Phillip's every word. Somehow, such silliness went against her nature.

They entered the crowded hall. It was hot inside, although all the windows were open. A large crowd of military men and their ladies milled about, the women fanning themselves delicately. There was a long table to one side with a punch bowl and refreshments, and at the front of the ribbon-festooned hall, a small band, composed of soldiers in blue, were tuning up their instruments. Now they broke into a lively, if slightly off-key rendition of "Camptown Races."

Phillip looked around. "I must introduce you to the commanding officer," he said above the music. Libbie let him lead her through the dancing crowd toward where the senior officers had formed a receiving line.

"Miss Winters, allow me to introduce the commander of Fort Grant."

The gray-bearded officer bowed deeply as Libbie extended her hand. "Charmed, Miss Winters. We've all heard so much about you."

Libbie smiled. "It was good of you to have a party in my honor. I'm very pleased."

"There's not much to entertain us out here," the senior officer said. "Any diversion is a welcome one, and a beauty like you is more than a diversion."

"You flatter me!" Libbie smiled, fluttered her eyelashes, and fanned herself daintily.

Phillip's chest puffed with pride and he took her down the line, introducing her to the other officers and their ladies. All commented on her beauty and the ladies were eager for news from the outside and what fashions the ships were bringing in to San Francisco.

However, most of the officers were unaccompanied. She commented on that as she and Phillip turned toward the dance floor.

Phillip shrugged. "Can't expect most white women to live in this hellish place. We'd all like to leave as soon as possible and give Arizona back to the Apaches and the rattlesnakes."

Mac McGuire joined them about that time. "Well, not all of us," he said by rejoinder, "some of us like it here."

"Mr. McGuire!" Libbie took his hand warmly. "I'm so glad you decided to come!"

He grinned and combed his fingers through his beard. "Well, as I remember, lass, you promised me a dance later."

"I certainly did." She looked around, not daring to ask. "Did—did you come alone?"

"Ah, lass, I did. I'm a widower, ye know."

The big half-breed hadn't accompanied his father. She tried to cover up her disappointment. "I—I thought you might have a lady friend."

Mac shook his head and his face saddened. "I only loved one woman, lass, and she'd not have been welcome in this fine company anyway."

Libbie's curiosity was piqued, but seeing Phillip's disapproving look, she kept silent. She liked the rough frontiersman, but she did not dare ask more about his personal life and his son without raising Phillip's ire.

The lively pace of the music changed as the band began a slow waltz.

"Ah," Phillip smiled, "if you'll excuse us, Mr. McGuire, I'd like to dance with my fiancée."

"Of course."

Phillip swept Libbie into his arms and they whirled out onto the floor. Phillip had a firm hand on her waist, his eyes trying to look directly into hers, but she looked away. "It's even better than I expected, Elizabeth," he said triumphantly. "Everyone here is looking at you and commenting on your beauty. You look like a vision in that pink dress and fiery hair. Those gold earrings must have cost a pretty penny."

She only nodded and smiled at the compliment, thinking that most rich men wouldn't be concerned with the value of a lady's jewelry. Libbie felt like a prize filly being trotted out for a horse show, but she tried to behave as was expected of her, nodding to ladies on the sidelines who were talking among themselves. They returned her nod with warm smiles. The officers looked at her wistfully as Phillip danced her around the floor.

They danced past the refreshment table about the time Shashké came through the kitchen door carrying a tray of dainty cakes. The Apache girl had an apron tied around her waist, and she scowled at Libbie as she carried her tray over to the table and began to place the tiny cakes on a platter.

Libbie saw the longing and the anger in the girl's dark eyes and felt sorry for her. "She'd give anything to be out here on this dance floor in a pretty dress rather than just working in the kitchen."

Phillip shrugged. "Ye gods, Elizabeth, whatever can you be thinking? It's a matter of birth, my dear; she's just an Apache wench. Everyone would be scandalized if someone like that actually attended the party."

Libbie watched, mystified at the girl's angry glare. Shashké put out her tray of cakes and went back into the kitchen.

As Phillip whirled her about, a movement outside an open window caught Libbie's eye. Cougar stood outside watching her. Libbie purposely looked away and whirled Phillip around so he wouldn't notice the scout.

"Elizabeth, dear." Phillip frowned. "I'm the man, remember? I'm supposed to lead."

She felt herself flush and she looked up at him with her most becoming pout. "I'm sorry, Phillip, I was just enjoying myself so much, I forgot."

He actually grinned at her. "It may take a little while for me to unspoil you, but I'm sure you are going to make me a wonderful, dutiful wife."

The thought of the meek, mild creature Phillip expected her to be almost made her groan aloud. Past Phillip's shoulder, she could see Cougar still standing outside the window staring at her. The frank, appraising way he looked at her made her feel warm and dizzy. If he didn't get away from that window and any of the soldiers noticed him, there might be trouble!

Cougar watched the white beauty as she danced with the prissy lieutenant. She had seen him, too. Her green eyes had widened and her expression had changed. Then she had whirled away so that Phillip did not see Cougar. Or maybe the move had been merely accidental.

He would be in trouble with the soldiers if they caught him out here spying on the dancers, but he couldn't bring himself to turn and walk away.

He was mesmerized by the red-haired vixen in a shiny dress the color of a new sunrise, with darker pink flowers and ribbons in that fiery hair. Golden earrings caught the lamplight as she whirled, but it was her hair that hypnotized him. If she belonged to him, he would give her a more suitable name: *Blaze.* Yes, that name fit her. Cougar gritted his teeth as the lieutenant pulled her even closer. It was mostly the possessive, smug way the lieutenant held the girl against his body that annoyed Cougar.

Even though he did not know how to dance the white man's dances, he closed his eyes and imagined himself out on the floor, whirling the girl about, holding her slender body close to his big one. He would dance her out a side door and into the darkness. Once outside, he would hold her so close, she could scarcely breathe while his mouth kissed her as he had yearned to do since the first moment he saw her stepping down from that stagecoach. From that moment on, he had known there could never be another woman for him.

He had a vision of carrying her out into the hills where he could make love to her the way she needed to be loved— totally, intently, and without interruption. He would take the pins from her hair so he could tangle his fingers in those fiery silken locks while he kissed her lips and eyes. Then, very slowly, he would unbutton that lacy pink dress so he could reach those full, creamy breasts and caress them the way she had never been caressed. And after he had made love to her, gently and completely, he would take her in a possessive embrace and hold her and protect her until the dawn. His manhood came up hard and insistent at the thought of holding the white girl in his arms.

He heard a step behind him and whirled to find Shashké standing there. "I saw you through the window," she purred. "Why do you look at her with such wanting when you have me here and now?"

Before he could protest, the sultry girl slipped her arms around his neck, pressed her full breasts against his naked chest, and kissed him. Oh, it was so tempting! Cougar needed a woman badly; he had not lain with one in a long time, and then it had been only a drunken Mexican whore in a border cantina.

For a moment, he weakened; then he took a deep breath and pulled away from Shashké's hot mouth. He glanced toward the window. Libbie Winters had seen it all!

Angry now, he pulled Shashké away from the window and into the darkness. "You little fool, anyone inside could have seen that if they'd been looking."

She threw her head back and laughed. "Who would care among the white people? You think that girl cares?"

"Keep her out of this!"

She looked up at him, beautiful and passionate, the scarlet cactus bloom in her dark hair scenting the night around them. "I want you; I've always wanted you; you know that." Her voice was low and husky with need as she slipped her arms around his neck again and rubbed herself against him.

He could feel every inch of her ripe body through the faded cotton dress even as her mouth sought his again, and she slipped her tongue between his lips.

Oh, it would be so easy to take what she offered. Shashké was hot and passionate; his for the taking with no obligations. Everything in him urged him to pick her up and carry her into the darkness where he could get his hands and his mouth on her eager, willing body.

"No, Shashké. I have a warrior's honor."

She ignored him, sliding enticingly down his body until she was on her knees, pressing her big breasts against his thighs. He could feel every tempting inch of her as her hands went to his breechcloth.

He wavered in his resolve and gasped aloud as her hot, wet mouth tasted him.

For a split second he trembled, fighting an overpowering urge to tangle his big hands in her hair and put his manhood deep in the sweetness of her lips, letting her please him until he was sated.

He wavered a long moment, wanting to let her take his seed in a long kiss, then steeled himself and caught her black hair in one big hand, pulling her away with a curse. "You slut! Have you no shame? You are a married woman, yet everyone at the fort knows you sleep with a white man."

She stood up, laughing easily, not at all offended. "So what? I can easily please more than one man."

Cougar leaned against a tree, trembling with anger and need. "Then you should go back to the village and please your husband."

"Him?" Her lips curled into a sneer. "Beaver Skin is

old; old enough to be my father, and there's no sap left in him for a young woman's lusts."

"He was once a great warrior who rode with Victorio," Cougar reminded her.

"So what?" She shrugged, her dark eyes defiant. "I got little say in choosing him, and I'm tired of living like a reservation squaw in a wickiup made of branches with me wearing a threadbare dress and no shoes. I'm pretty; I intend to use that to better my lot."

Cougar snorted in disgust. "You won't be pretty long if your husband catches you with another man. You know what the Apache custom is for cheating wives."

"I'm not worried." Shashké yawned. "My stupid husband trusts me. Besides, my white lover is going to buy me pretty dresses and take me far away from here."

Cougar shook his head. "You are the one who is stupid. The white man will not marry you; he will use you for his pleasure and then throw you away when he tires of you."

"I'm already tired of him," she admitted, playing with the scarlet cactus flower in her ebony hair. "He is not much of a lover and his manhood is small compared to yours. Pleasure me, Cougar; no one need ever know."

However, he drew himself up proudly and shook his head. "I respect the old warrior who is your husband and I value my own honor."

"But you do not mind lusting for the fire-haired girl who is promised to the lieutenant!" Her voice rose in anger. "Listen to me, Cougar! You will never lie between her thighs and put your son in her belly, so bring that hunger to me. Should you get me with child, I might convince my old husband it is his and he would be pleased."

"You play a dangerous game, Shashké," he warned with calm dignity, "take care and remember old Apache customs. You are vain about your pretty face; protect it with faithfulness.''

"Oh, you honorable fool!" She raged as she turned and ran back inside the kitchen.

With a sigh, Cougar returned to watching the dancers through the window, and this time he was careful to stand so that those inside could not see him. Libbie Winters still whirled about the dance floor, a vision in a cloud-pink dress of some filmy soft fabric, with her red hair catching the lamplight.

Absently, he fingered the necklace he wore that had been a token of love from his Apache mother to his white father. If it had belonged to his mother when she died, it would have had to be buried with her or destroyed, as was the custom of her people. However, now it was his. *Apache Tears.* What a tragic legend.

His mind returned to the fire-haired girl. Shashké was right. He was a fool because there was nothing Cougar wanted so much at this moment as to stride inside, pick up the arrogant white girl, throw her across his shoulder, and carry her off into the desert night, where he could possess her completely; body and soul. And pity the white man who tried to stop him!

Chapter Four

Libbie sneaked another glance at the window as she and Phillip waltzed. She had seen Shashké embrace Cougar, kiss him, and then Phillip whirled her away. When she turned her head again toward the window, she could no longer see the pair. Evidently they had faded into the night to make love.

Well, so what? That wasn't her business. Yet she found herself craning her neck, hoping to see something and absently stepped on Phillip's foot.

"Elizabeth, what is wrong?" he snapped and led her off the floor. "You seem totally distracted."

Oh, damn. "I—I'm just a little breathless," she answered, knowing she must not anger him, "shall we have some punch?"

They headed for the refreshment table, where officers and local ranchers and shopkeepers stood about sipping something stronger than punch and discussing the state of the country.

"They say the President is still alive after that assassination attempt," one said.

"Maybe he'll make it then," another replied. "I hope they hang that anarchist!"

"Speaking of hanging," a third remarked, "maybe it's time we hung a few redskins! Tiffany, you're the Indian agent, what do you make of it?"

Mr. Tiffany cleared his throat importantly and twirled his mustache, obviously pleased to be the center of attention. "I keep warning we need more troops. Can't expect much from savages."

A rancher put in, "Have you heard those drums?"

"They're driving us all loco," a stout civilian complained. "Just what the devil do you suppose those heathens are up to out there on Cibecue Creek?"

Mac McGuire had just walked up. He nodded to Libbie and then said, "It won't amount to much of anything if the army will just leave them alone. When *Noch-ay-del-Klinne* doesn't live up to his promises, the Apaches will lose faith in him and things will settle back down. I've told the colonel as much."

Phillip bristled as he handed Libbie a cup of punch. "Well, I for one am tired of doing nothing! I think we should go out there, bring that crazy medicine man in and lock him up! Force! That's the only thing these savages understand!"

There was a murmur of agreement around the circle of men.

Libbie blurted, "I think what Mr. McGuire says makes sense."

All the men turned and stared at her, evidently unused to women who spoke their minds. Phillip reddened and frowned. She had embarrassed him by speaking out, she could see; only Mac McGuire smiled at her.

Phillip cleared his throat in the sudden silence. "You

gentlemen must forgive Miss Winters. She's only a woman, after all, and doesn't understand about such things.''

"Phillip, don't treat me like an idiot!'' she snapped, setting her punch cup on the table with a bang. She'd done it now; most of the men were staring at her aghast, but she was too annoyed to care. Phillip's face had turned a dull, ugly scarlet.

"Anyway,'' one of the others said to cover the awkward silence, "Colonel Carr up at Fort Apache will probably be the one to go on that campaign; I'm glad it's not me.''

"They may need help,'' another grumbled, "which means some of us might get transferred up there. In this August heat, it'll be a miserable trip.''

Libbie asked, "How far is Cibecue from Fort Apache?''

Mac considered a moment. "Maybe forty or fifty miles to the northwest.''

A bewhiskered settler chewed his lip and considered. "Will the army trust its Apache scouts in this fight?''

Phillip frowned again. "I suppose we'll have to. We've got a bunch of fairly new, young ones. Maybe they'll do all right; or at least as good as Injuns get.''

The other men guffawed and Mac frowned, obviously straining to catch all the words. "That isn't fair; the scouts have always been loyal.''

A thin, arrogant lieutenant looked down his nose at Mac. "Of course you would say that, with a half-breed son—''

"I hope ye're not about to insult him, Lieutenant Dudly,'' Mac warned; he seemed to be gritting his teeth.

"Here, here,'' said the minister, gesturing to everyone to lower their voices, "this is no place to start a fight, gentlemen; there's ladies present.''

"Don't mind me,'' Libbie said before she thought, "it's just getting interesting.''

She heard some gasps and knew she should have stifled her comment.

Mac took a deep breath, as if calming himself. "For myself, gentlemen, I'm going to discourage the army from attempting to arrest the Apache holy man. There's no point in deliberately starting an Indian war."

The music struck up again, the band playing a newly popular tune: "My bonnie lies over the ocean; my bonnie lies over the sea . . ."

Mac put his punch cup on the table and bowed gallantly to Libbie. "Miss Winters, may I have the honor?"

"Of course!"

They swung out onto the floor and Libbie breathed a sigh of relief. She remembered to raise her voice so he wouldn't have to strain to hear her. "I just couldn't keep quiet. Thank you for rescuing me!"

Mac smiled. "Thank you for giving me the excuse."

"My fiancé is furious; his eyes look like blue ice."

Mac glanced over at the simmering lieutenant and grinned. "Aye, Cougar was right about you."

She didn't want to ask, but she couldn't help herself. "What—what did he say?"

Mac laughed. "He said ye were too much woman for the lieutenant; he'd never be able to tame you. I'd say Cougar judged ye pretty well!"

She didn't know whether to feel complimented or insulted. "I'm not sure I want to be tamed! At any rate, Phillip is from a fine family and everyone says it will be a very good match."

"Yes, of course, lass." His tone was overly polite, but he didn't sound as if he meant it.

The doubts rose up deep within her all over again. She didn't seem to have any options, so she must not think about changing her mind. "So," she mused as they danced, "you seem to know the Apache better than anyone in the Territory. Is there going to be trouble?"

Mac frowned and blinked his faded old eyes in the lamplight. "Miss Winters, I'm afraid some of our young officers are bored and would like to win some medals."

She thought about Phillip. "Is there any real danger?"

"We're about to bring the Apache wars to a close here in the Territory, even though Jack Tiffany is as crooked an Indian agent as ever drew breath—he and his accomplices back east. But trouble could easily break out again if the army does something rash and foolish. The Apaches' loyalty is with their own people."

"Does that include Cougar?"

His dark eyes questioned her interest in his son, but he said only, "Cougar is a son of both worlds, but I think he would be loyal to the army, as long as his mother's people are treated fairly."

As they danced, she looked toward the window again, but there was no one there. She wanted to ask Mac McGuire a million questions about his half-breed son and Arizona Territory, but about that time the music ended.

"Thank you so much, lass." Mac smiled. "It's been a long time since I've held a pretty girl in my arms."

Libbie blushed, and in her mind she saw the image of a young Scotsman making love to an Apache girl and producing the big half-breed son.

They started back toward the refreshment table, where the young officers still gathered. Shashké came out of the kitchen just then and refilled the punch bowl, glaring all the time at Libbie.

"I just don't know," Libbie said, thinking aloud.

"What?" Mac asked, straining with one hand to his ear.

"That Apache girl." Libbie shook her head. "I haven't done anything to her, yet she acts like she hates me."

Mac seemed to be choosing his words carefully. "Envy," he said finally in his thick brogue. "You're white and have everything as far as she's concerned, and she doesn't have much to look forward to."

Libbie remembered the girl embracing Cougar. "I wouldn't say that."

"What?" Mac asked.

"Nothing."

As the pair reached Phillip's side, Mrs. Everett waddled over, fanning herself. She looked like a great, gray whale, Libbie thought.

Mrs. Everett said, "I'm tired. I think I'll leave early and go back to our room."

"Oh," Libbie said, "if we're to leave—"

"My stars! Not you, my dear." Her plump guardian held up a restraining hand. "You stay and have a good time. I'll just get someone to walk me back, and you two young people can come later."

In a flash, Libbie realized the older woman was deliberately plotting to get her ward alone with Phillip. Then it would be up to Libbie to enthrall the officer, make amends for her rash sassiness. Libbie realized all this, and yet she didn't want to be alone with the lieutenant.

"Madam," Mac said politely to Mrs. Everett, "I'll be happy to escort you back to your room before I join some of my old cronies for another drink."

"Come along then," the plump matron said with frowning disdain. Evidently, she felt herself a cut above the old man socially.

Everyone said their good-byes and Mrs. Everett left, accompanied by the rancher.

Libbie danced with several more young officers and then the band began to play, "Good Night, Ladies."

Phillip took her in his arms and held her close as they danced this final dance. "It's been a wonderful evening," he whispered against her ear.

Libbie stiffened at his touch, then remembered that, after all, he had the right to be affectionate toward her. "Yes, it has, hasn't it?"

The dance broke up. Libbie said her thanks to the ladies and senior officers, and then she and Phillip went outside into the hot night.

Phillip said, "Let's walk back. It isn't far and we can talk."

"All right." She looked around, wondering where Cougar was. Probably having a drink somewhere with Mac McGuire and his old cronies. No, more likely lying under a bush making love again to the sultry Apache beauty. Around them, couples were leaving in their buggies or walking back to their quarters. Now that the music had ended, she could hear the drums again, carried faintly on the summer breeze.

"Ye gods!" Phillip cursed under his breath. "Damned savages!" Then he apologized for swearing before a lady. "I can't help it, dear; I'm concerned about your safety tomorrow. I wonder if I should ask for a military escort for your stage?"

"Oh, Phillip, don't you think you're overreacting?"

"When you've heard as many tales as I have about how bloodthirsty these savages are in battle, you wouldn't think so. Remember, this is their country and they're as much at home in it as tarantulas and rattlesnakes and just as deadly. Even their name, *Apache*, given to them by the Zuni tribe, means 'enemy.' "

She was only interested in one Apache, but she must not mention his name. "Hmm," she said.

"Elizabeth, your behavior tonight was abominable." Phillip's tone was cold. "I thought young ladies from Miss Priddy's Academy had better manners."

She resisted the urge to slap him, but of course, she must make amends so this marriage would go through. She ducked her head as if abjectly chastened. "I didn't mean to upset you and embarrass you in front of your friends."

He took her hand as they walked, evidently mollified. "I know you've been terribly spoiled and are a little head-strong, but a wife must never contradict her husband."

"Even if he's wrong?" Libbie said under her breath.

"What?"

"Nothing. Of course you are right, Phillip. I must remember you are *always* right!"

"Of course." He sniffed with satisfaction, evidently missing the sarcasm of her tone. "It isn't wise in this Territory to come to the defense of Injuns; sneaky, untrustworthy devils that they are."

"Mac McGuire seemed more worried about what the army was liable to do than the Apache," Libbie said.

"Well, what do you expect from an old Injun-lover like Mac?" Phillip snorted in derision as they walked back toward her quarters. "He's still talking about what happened here ten years ago when this place was known as Camp Grant."

"So what did happen?" She glanced over at him as they walked through the moonlight.

He shrugged. "Nothing much. Some troops and settlers from Tucson lured a bunch of Apaches here with food and liquor, then slaughtered them."

"Women and children, too?"

"Yes, but so what? After all, they were Apaches."

"Why, Phillip, that's terrible!"

"I'd expect a woman to think that," Phillip said with arrogant amusement, "but not an old soldier like Mac. As close friends as he and my father were, I find it incredible Mac could be so forgiving of his killers!"

"It's been a long time, Phillip," Libbie suggested, "maybe it's time to forget the past."

"I made a vow to my mother," Phillip said, "that I would avenge my father's death."

Libbie didn't say anything. She had found Mrs. Van

Harrington difficult to like—a cold, proud, snowy-haired dowager who seemed overly possessive of her only son. Her house was a shrine to William Van Harrington's memory; portraits of him hung everywhere, and the widow still dressed in black after all these years. Libbie hoped she wouldn't be expected to move into the Van Harringtons' mansion where Phillip's mother ruled with an iron hand over her old-maid sisters and a timid group of servants.

Undesirable option that that would be, it still wasn't as bad as being out on the street, homeless and penniless. Mrs. Everett was right; Libbie had no alternatives. That didn't make Libbie any happier about the wedding.

She would not think of that now. It was a lovely night; the breeze carried the scent of blooming flowers, and night birds called. From a distant hill, a coyote wailed. In this exotic, sultry atmosphere, her thoughts inevitably turned to that most primitive of passions. In her mind, Libbie imagined Cougar and Shashké together under the stars. She took several deep breaths, attempting to stifle her rising passion as she pictured herself in his arms instead.

"Elizabeth, are you all right? The way you're breathing, perhaps I've overtired you walking from the dance."

"No, I—I'm fine." She was embarrassed at her forbidden thoughts.

The moon went behind drifting clouds and Phillip paused, almost to Libbie's door, and pulled her under a vine-covered arbor.

"Let's talk a moment here where no one can see us," he said.

"All right." She sighed and let him take both her hands in his. She knew she should flutter her eyelashes and flirt with him, but she just didn't care that much. Phillip bent his head and kissed the backs of her hands. His wispy mustache tickled as it brushed against her knuckles. "My dear."

She managed to stifle laughter at her thoughts about the mustache. "Yes, Phillip?"

He looked down at her, his blue eyes bright and earnest in his handsome face. "Mother was right; you are the perfect choice for me."

His mother again. "Oh?"

"Elizabeth, I'm crazy to possess you! I can hardly think of anything else but our wedding night!" He kissed her on the mouth then. Libbie stiffened in protest, then remembered and let him kiss her. It was as uninteresting as she feared it would be, his mouth prim and dry, his mustache tickling her skin.

She must think of the positive things, she thought as his lips moved feverishly across her face. Yet she instinctively tried to pull away from him. He was breathing hard and pressing his body against hers. She could feel his rigid maleness through her pink dress. "Phillip, please! This is highly improper—"

"I can't help myself. I want you, Elizabeth, even if you are spoiled and too headstrong! I think of nothing else but marrying you and the sons you will give me!" Phillip tightened his grip, molding her against his tall figure as he kissed her again. His passions became more heated and his hands roamed up and down her back while he breathed harder.

Libbie started to protest again, but Phillip's mouth covered hers as he tried to force his tongue between her lips. His hand came up and tore at her bodice.

She struggled to pull her face away. "Phillip! Please!"

"Let me, Elizabeth, please let me!" He was panting hard, trying to rip her bodice open, leaving a trail of wet kisses across her face. "We're engaged. It's only a matter of time before we do it anyway."

"Phillip, no—!" But he blocked her protests with his

mouth, tearing at her bosom while dragging her toward a grassy area in the secluded shadows beside the building.

She managed to get her mouth free. "Phillip, please, what will people think?" Libbie struggled with him, but he was a tall, big man. He was going to take her whether she consented or not.

"Ye gods, Elizabeth, we're engaged! In only a matter of months, I can take you any time I want!"

The thought horrified her. "But we should wait until we're wed—"

"You'll not put me off!" he whispered in a fever against her mouth while he pulled her toward the shadows. "By God, I'll have you now!"

She dared not scream for help; it would be too humiliating. Instead, she struggled with him, her common sense telling her she should submit. In only a few months, he'd have the legal right to her body anyway. Still she didn't want Phillip's kisses or his touch and she tried to push him away, but he panted out loud, his sweaty hands reaching inside her bodice to paw her breasts.

A full moon came out from behind a cloud, and a sudden shadow fell across them both.

They jerked apart, Phillip cursing. "What the—?"

"Excuse me, sir," Cougar said, "I was wondering if you had any orders for me before I go to my quarters?"

Phillip glared at the big scout, then seemed to gain control of himself as he straightened his uniform.

Libbie took a deep sigh of relief, rearranging her mussed bodice. "Good night," she said, then turned and fled the few yards to her quarters. Once inside, she shut the door and carefully locked it. Mrs. Everett was sound asleep; Libbie could hear her snoring. She leaned against the door and tried to hear the conversation outside, but to no avail. Thank God Cougar had happened along and interrupted Phillip's ardor. She frowned as she realized the scout had probably been lying in those nearby bushes with the eager Shashké and had heard the disagreement.

No doubt tomorrow Phillip would be contrite and apologize for his ungentlemanly conduct and want her even more. She would be wed by the time she was eighteen without ever having really tasted life or been in control of her own destiny. With a sigh of resignation, Libbie slipped into a lightweight cotton nightdress, crawled into bed, and lay there sleepless.

Outside, Phillip glared up at the big half-breed. "What the hell do you mean, sneaking up on us like that?"

The scout's face was as expressionless as stone. "I'm sorry, sir. I was in the neighborhood and thought I'd better check with you."

Phillip considered the possibility. Maybe it was an accident that Cougar had walked up just as Phillip was about to overwhelm the cold beauty. If the savage had waited just another ten minutes, Phillip would have taken her virginity, and the girl would have felt obligated to go through with this marriage. Phillip had a strong feeling that Elizabeth Winters was having second thoughts. Even though she was only seventeen, she was headstrong enough to change her mind.

After tonight, Phillip wanted Elizabeth with a lust he had never dreamed possible. Well, he would have her and he would break her spirit until she was a meek and obedient wife. He dared not let her change her mind or Mother would be terribly displeased with her only son. Henrietta Van Harrington desperately wanted this marriage to take place.

"Sir, did you hear me?" Cougar asked.

"Damn it, yes, I heard you!" Phillip came back to the present and how much he disliked the half-breed. It occurred to him suddenly that if there were an expedition out to capture that Apache medicine man at Cibecue Creek, maybe in the confusion, a stray shot might kill Cougar and no one need ever know. Phillip was an excellent shot. His plan made him smile. "Let's just both call it a night."

"All right, Lieutenant." The scout saluted and they both turned, walking in different directions.

Shashké put away the last of the dishes in the big kitchen and blew out the lamps with a sigh as she took off her apron. Such a lot of work for this party honoring the elegant Miss Winters!

Her lip curled with a jealous sneer as she left the hall and went out the back door. The post was deserted, everyone long gone to bed except some distant sentries. The night wind carried the rhythmic beat of drums. She paused and brushed back her ebony hair, fingering the red cactus blossom behind her ear and thinking about the men in her life. She dreaded going back to her wickiup and her old husband, but of course, she must. Perhaps he would be drunk on *tiswin* and asleep so that he wouldn't try to make love to her when she crawled between the blankets.

She grimaced at the thought as she started away from the building. Old Beaver Skin wanted a son, but most of the time, he couldn't perform the act, leaving his young, hot-blooded wife frustrated and needing a man. She smiled with longing as she thought of Cougar. If she could ever persuade him to make love to her, no doubt the virile half-breed would give her a son on the very first try, and the child would look enough Apache to fool her husband.

The problem with Cougar was that he had an old-fashioned warrior's sense of honor. She smiled to herself as she walked. Tonight she'd managed to touch him and rub against him. After he'd thought about that a couple of hours, maybe he'd need a woman badly enough that he'd come looking for her. The thought of mating with him made her take a deep breath, and a warmth spread through her ripe body.

A tall, broad-shouldered man stepped out of the bushes in front of her. *Cougar?* Her heart beat with anticipation.

The shadowy silhouette said, "I know I shouldn't, but I've been thinking about you."

Her spirits fell as she recognized the voice. "It took a while to clean up after the party. The way you looked at the white girl, I didn't think you would want me."

"She's just a girl; you're a woman," he murmured and began to unbutton her faded dress.

"And I know how to please a man." Shashké caught his hand and guided it to her full breast; then she reached up to kiss him.

He squeezed her breast. "You're trouble; nothing but trouble."

"But such pleasant trouble, no?" she whispered against his lips.

"Yes, you slut!" He jerked her hard against him, kissing her again, thrusting his tongue deep into her mouth, his hand ripping at her bodice. "I told myself I must not see you again, but I can't help myself!"

"You won't be sorry." Pleased with his confession of need, she led him to the shadow of the bushes and they lay down.

"Suppose your husband wakes and finds you not there?"

She threw back her head and laughed, exposing her throat to his feverish, seeking mouth. "Let me worry about him; he is old and stupid." She opened her bodice for his eager hands and let her thighs fall apart.

"I need you!" he whispered urgently again as he positioned her. "I'm going to take you more than once tonight!"

"I need you as many times as you can do it." She pulled him down on her and raised her hips to meet his thrusts as he came into her. She knew the white girl had aroused this need in him, but Shashké was the one who could fill that need.

"Tell me you love me," she pleaded as he thrust into her.

He didn't answer, his mouth on her breast, his breath hot against her dark skin as he rode her hard.

"You'll make me your woman so I can leave my old husband?"

"Shut up!" he ordered, breathing hard as he rode her. "Ye gods, shut up and let me finish!"

Maybe he might love her a little, Shashké thought, but she had a sinking feeling that she was only satisfying the lust that the beautiful white girl had created in Lieutenant Phillip Van Harrington.

Libbie lay sleepless and restive in her bed as the hours passed. Through the open window of the hot night, she could hear the faint beat of drums carried on the desert wind.

She was still shaky from her unexpected ordeal, knowing she had come very close to being raped. *Well, no, when it's done by your fiancé,* she thought ruefully, *it would probably only be considered compromising a young lady. Had Phillip sensed that she was having second thoughts and was trying to put her in a position where she would be obligated to marry him? The raw lust in his blue eyes had scared her. If Cougar hadn't happened to come along . . .*

Libbie twisted restlessly in her bed, listening to Mrs. Everett snore. What had the half-breed been doing out and in that area? Then she remembered the scene she'd witnessed through the window. Of course he'd been out in the nearby bushes coupling with Shashké and was on his way back to his quarters. She remembered the way the two had looked in their embrace and imagined what it would feel like to go into the arms of a man who knew how to please a woman.

She felt her face burn. Damn! What on earth was she thinking about? She was having primitive, uncivilized yearnings about a man who belonged to another woman. How shameful! Libbie felt a sheen of perspiration on her body. Good heavens, this room was hot!

Quietly she got up, slipped on a light wrap over her sheer cotton nightdress, and opened the door. The breeze felt cool and inviting. Libbie hesitated a moment. There was no one around; not a soul stirred nor a dog barked. The whole post must be asleep. Maybe she would just go stand outside in the cool air a moment and then go back to bed; no one need ever know. Mrs. Everett would be shocked, but then, Mrs. Everett was snoring away like a beached whale; oblivious to everything.

Libbie took a deep breath, surprised at her own daring, and stepped outside, closing the door behind her. It was quiet out here except for the distant beat of drums. The primitive sound seemed to blend into her heartbeat.

Abruptly, a tall, wide-shouldered figure loomed up out of the shadows. Startled, Libbie opened her mouth to scream, but the figure clasped one big hand over her mouth.

Oh, dear God! Phillip had come back to take her, whether she liked it or not.

Libbie tried to break free, but he jerked her up against his powerful body, fighting to keep his hand over her mouth. "Stop it! I won't hurt you!"

She froze in surprise and blinked up at him. It was Cougar!

Chapter Five

Libbie looked up at Cougar, her heart pounding with shock.

"Will you please not scream?" he whispered.

She nodded, and very slowly he took his hand from her mouth.

"How dare you!" She slapped him hard.

His head snapped back and his expression turned as dark as thunder. He rubbed his jaw. "If you were a man, I'd kill you for that."

She realized suddenly that she was standing outdoors in a very flimsy nightdress and wrap. Her nipples must be visible to him, judging by the way he was staring at her. Self-consciously, she crossed her arms over her breasts. "What are you doing lurking out here?"

He smiled and leaned against a post. "I wasn't lurking; I was guarding your door."

"Guarding my door! You have to be the most arrogant man I've ever met. I've got hundreds of soldiers to guard me."

He smiled faintly. "That's who I was guarding you from; I half expected the lieutenant to come back in the middle of the night and sneak into your quarters."

She was almost speechless. "Lieutenant Van Harrington is a perfect gentleman."

"Uh-huh." In the moonlight, she could see the intense emotion of his blue eyes. "He looked like a perfect gentleman when he was about to rape you a couple of hours ago."

Libbie felt her face flame. "Phillip is my fiancé. He—he might have gotten a little carried away."

Cougar regarded her with thinly veiled amusement. "You're spirited, but you're naively innocent, Miss Winters. If I hadn't stepped out of those bushes, he'd have had you flat on your back like some two-bit whore."

"Damn you! I don't have to listen to this!" She whirled, grabbing for the doorknob, but Cougar reached out and put his hand on the doorjamb next to her, blocking her entry.

"I didn't mean to offend you," he said softly, "I just wanted to warn you about the lieutenant."

She should go in; everything in her told her that being here was highly improper and her reputation would be ruined should anyone see her. She should push his hand off the door and run inside. Yet the magnetism of this man was enough to hold her. In the moonlight, she could see the necklace gleaming around his brawny neck and the sinewy muscles in the brown arm that blocked her escape. Very slowly, she turned around to face him, but he didn't step back.

He was close enough that she could feel the masculine heat from his half-naked body. "You're wasted on the gutless lieutenant," he murmured.

"My choice is hardly your concern."

"I know that." His big hand reached out and brushed

a dainty tendril of red hair from her face. His fingertips brushed across her forehead, his touch was so gentle and so tender that it surprised her.

His bare chest was close enough that she could touch him if she reached out, but of course she did not. In the moonlight, she noted the scars here and there on his virile frame and the way the moonlight shone on the striking necklace he wore. The tension felt like lightning crackling across a hot desert sky.

Looking up at him, she studied the curve of his sensual mouth. She must not look at that mouth and think of it covering hers. "Where—where is your woman?"

He looked mystified. "I have no woman; I have not chosen yet."

"But isn't Shashké—?"

He threw back his head and laughed, exposing white teeth. "When I choose a woman, it will be one who is faithful, not one who exchanges her favors for money and gifts."

He still had her entry blocked with one big arm, standing so close that it made Libbie tremble. *He had no woman,* Libbie thought. *Why should she feel such relief?*

"Are you cold?" He seemed amused by her discomfort.

"No." What should she do? She could scream for help and bring everyone running—at the cost of her reputation.

"Are you afraid?" His voice lowered to a soft, soothing whisper.

"No!" she lied, looking up at him defiantly.

"Don't ever be afraid of me," he said, "I would kill the man who hurt you; this I promise."

She stared deep into his eyes and knew he meant it. "You arrogant rogue! What gives you the right to be my protector?"

"It is a decision I have made," he answered, his voice firm, "but of course, I can only protect you in my own country." He stepped back with a sigh. "You will leave tomorrow, Blaze?"

"My name is not Blaze; it's Libbie."

"What does that name mean?"

"I don't know," she snapped, thinking how ludicrous it was to be standing out here all but naked, discussing her name. "I was named for my grandmother."

He reached out to touch her fiery hair. "Blaze would be a more fitting name for you." She didn't pull away from his hand, and he ran his fingers through her tangled curls.

"Phillip would kill you for that," she said, jerking her head away from his hand.

"Are you going to tell him?"

"I might."

"I think not. A fire-haired hellion with a name like Blaze would not go whining to a cowardly lieutenant."

She must not admit even to herself that she had liked the way his fingers felt in her hair. She must not; she must not. She let her arms fall helplessly to her sides. "I—I must go in now. It's late and I leave in the morning."

"I'm not stopping you." He kept stroking her hair.

"Are you going to stay outside my door all night?"

He nodded. "I told you I was going to protect you." He frowned and reached up to finger the massive necklace he wore. "You may be in danger if the trouble with the Apache grows worse; a war party might attack stage routes."

The thought shook her. "Should I ask for an army escort? Phillip has offered—"

"The Apache are as silent as rattlesnakes when they strike, and like the rattler or the tarantula, this is their country. Many an army troop has been wiped out by warriors they never saw."

"Then what should I do?"

He looked down at her a long moment, his blue eyes troubled and uncertain in his dark face. Then slowly, his hands reached up and took the necklace from around his neck. "This necklace was given by my mother to my white father. Do you know the legend of the Apache Tears?"

She shook her head. "No, but I've admired your necklace."

"Once, a long time ago, a large number of enemies attacked my people."

"Were they soldiers or other Indians?" She didn't want to ask, but she was as fascinated by the mysterious black stones as she was the Apache.

"No one seems to know for sure. Our warriors were outnumbered, but they fought bravely until the enemy backed them to a top of a cliff. Our women watched from the valley. Finally, wounded and at a loss for weapons, our warriors leaped from the cliff to their deaths rather than surrender or give the enemy the satisfaction of killing them."

"And the women?" Libbie looked up at him, fascinated by the legend.

"The Apache women wept great tears for their fallen heroes and where the tears touched the ground, they were turned to black stones. They have been known ever since as Apache Tears."

"What a beautiful, tragic story," Libbie whispered.

For a long moment, Cougar did not answer, staring down at the magnificent silver, turquoise, and black gemstone necklace in his big hand. "My mother wept enough tears to fulfill the legend," he said. "In this country, white and red cannot love without causing tragedy, and no one knows that better than I." Very slowly, he reached out and put the necklace around Libbie's neck, but he didn't move his hands away. The silver was still warm from his body, as warm as his fingers on her throat.

"What are you doing? I can't accept this!" She couldn't retreat any farther. Libbie reached up to touch the black, tear-shaped stones, and her fingertips touched his, causing her to take a deep, ragged breath.

Now it was his hard hands that trembled as his fingers moved to cup her bare shoulders. "I give this to you, Blaze, for the same reason that my mother gave it to my father; it will protect you."

She wondered when Mac had given it to their son, but she didn't ask. Too aware of the feel of his hands on her shoulders, she glanced down at the necklace. Its silver gleamed in the moonlight against the curve of her breasts above the sheer nightdress. "Protect me from what?"

She looked up at him and felt his big hands tighten on her shoulders. For a second, she had the oddest sensation that he was about to sweep her into his arms, hold her against his scarred, naked chest, and kiss her with a passion that she could only envision in her dreams.

"If your coach is waylaid by any Apache, Blaze, show them this necklace. As long as you wear this, no Apache will harm you."

"Why?"

He looked down at her, confident in his masculinity. "All will recognize it, and none will dare to touch a woman Cougar protects."

How very arrogant of him! He was looking down at her possessively. If she gave him the slightest sign of surrender, she had a feeling he was going to swing her up in his arms and carry her away. His nearness was creating such a heady sensation that she wondered if her legs might give way under her. She took a deep breath and shook her head defiantly to break the spell. "I—it's your dearest treasure, I can't—"

"Yes, you can." He caught her hand as she reached up to take the necklace off. "Trouble may break out at any time, and it's a long way back to Willcox and your train. Wear it, knowing I want you safe."

"You have a lot of nerve making yourself my protector. Phillip would be furious!" She must go in before he jerked her into his embrace and she couldn't stop him from doing what her heart hungered for him to do. With a confused and angry cry, she tore out of his grasp, turned blindly, groping for the doorknob, and went in. Slamming the door behind her, she shot the bolt. She leaned against the door, gulping for air and watching her guardian anxiously, but Mrs. Everett snored on.

Libbie was shaking as she climbed into her own bed and lay there looking at the ceiling. She reached up to touch the necklace and remembered the feel of Cougar's strong hands as he placed it around her throat, his fingertips touching the swell of her breasts. She had felt a terrible need for his hands to go lower still in the sheer nightdress and cup her breasts and caress them.

Was she out of her mind? She had a sudden impulse to jerk the necklace off and throw it against a wall. No, better yet, she would open the door and throw it in his face if he were still outside. Breathing hard, she sat up in bed and considered that. The necklace was as warm as his hands about her throat. *The thing was a mark of possession,* she thought, *like a dog collar . . . or a wedding ring.*

Phillip. Oh, God, what would Phillip think if he saw the necklace? How could she explain how she'd come by it? It would mean trouble for Cougar, she knew.

A shadow crossed the window, a shadow that she recognized from the long hair, the width of the powerful shoulders, and the square-jawed silhouette. Cougar was keeping his word about staying near her door all night. It both touched and infuriated her that he should take on the role of her protector when she had a fiancé. She ought to get up, open the door, and throw the necklace in his arrogant face.

However, as she started to rise, she reconsidered. Somehow, she was half-afraid that if she opened that door, neither of them would be in control of what might happen next. So she lay there, sleepless and angry, for a long time before she dropped off into a troubled sleep.

In her twisted dream, her name was Blaze and she wore nothing but the necklace, her long red hair blowing in the wind. She rode naked on a galloping mustang and a big, dark warrior came riding in pursuit. Just as he was about to pull her from her pinto, Libbie awakened, gasping for air.

Outside the window, a pale pink dawn kissed the distant hills while in the next bed, Mrs. Everett snored blissfully away. Libbie glanced down, remembering last night, and reaching up to touch the necklace, she took it off. It was a thing of beauty. *Apache Tears.* She remembered the legend of great love that time and death could not conquer.

What was she to do with the thing? She must not let anyone see it; it would be too difficult to explain how she had come by it. Quickly, she got up and hid it under some clothing in her valise. She would decide what to do with it once she got away from the fort. After all, in a couple of hours, she would be on her way back to the train and would never see the half-breed again. She was startled at how troubled that knowledge made her feel.

She poured some water in the bowl, washed, then dressed in a no-nonsense peacock-blue bouclé traveling costume. She buttoned the fitted jacket and put up her hair. Finally, she awakened Mrs. Everett so the two could breakfast and get ready.

Later, while they were packing, there was a knock at the door.

Mrs. Everett was out of sorts and grumpy. "Now who could that be?" she asked as she waddled to the door to open it.

Libbie held her breath. She half expected it to be Cougar, wanting his necklace returned.

"Oh, it's you; about time you got here," Mrs. Everett snapped.

Shashké entered, wearing an old cotton dress and a fresh scarlet cactus bloom in her dark hair. She looked at Libbie with cold eyes. "I was sent to help you pack."

Mrs. Everett frowned at her and motioned. "Well, don't just stand there, girl, get busy!"

The plump lady returned to her own luggage as Shashké picked up Libbie's valise and began to fold long lace petticoats and put them inside.

"I can do that," Libbie said and rushed to take it from her hand. "I think Mrs. Everett needs your help more than I do."

"I certainly do!" grumbled the stout lady. "You're not much of a maid; you'd never hold a job back East."

The Apache girl scowled and opened her mouth as if to reply, then shrugged and began to help Mrs. Everett.

Libbie held her breath, watching the girl. Had Shashké seen the necklace when she opened the valise? She had made no sign if she had. Libbie drew a great sigh of relief and continued packing the bag. Then she hesitated. As Cougar had said, it was a long way back to Willcox, where they would catch their train. The necklace would do her no good if she weren't wearing it should their stagecoach be attacked by a raiding party. Worse than that, suppose someone like Mrs. Everett or a maid found the necklace during their train trip? There'd be hell to pay. What to do?

"Here, girl," her guardian snapped at Shashké. "Help me get these trunks packed so the soldiers can load them."

"Yes, *señora.*" The girl sounded resentful, but she went to help. They were both bending over a trunk, trying to find room for an extra bustle and Libbie's riding boots.

Libbie took advantage of their diverted attention to slip the necklace out of her valise. She hesitated only a moment before placing it around her throat under the high collar of the peacock-blue jacket she had selected. Quickly, she buttoned the traveling outfit so the jewelry could not be seen. When Libbie reached a place where no one would notice, and she was safe from marauding Indians, she would toss the necklace away. *How dare that half-breed scout put his collar of ownership on her?*

Without thinking, she reached up to touch the hidden jewelry. Libbie was all too aware of the feel of it. If she closed her eyes, she was once again standing out there in the night with his big hands gently touching her throat.

Another rap at the door. "It's Phillip, my dear, here to see you off."

Was she crazy? There was no telling what would happen if Phillip saw the necklace. Libbie reached up to touch the neck of her jacket again, making certain it was buttoned so that it hid her throat. "Just a minute; we're almost ready."

She opened the door as Shashké closed Mrs. Everett's trunk. Phillip smiled, extending both hands as he entered. "Well, my dear, it's a lovely day for travel; not hot yet."

"Well, thank God for that!" Mrs. Everett puffed. "This place has the heat of Hades. I can hardly wait to go!"

"Nonsense!" Libbie protested, "I love Arizona! I wouldn't mind coming back someday."

Phillip laughed as he motioned the servant girl to leave and directed the two soldiers who were waiting outside to gather up the luggage. "Surely you jest! This country is as wild and untamed as the Apaches who inhabit it; no place for civilized people at all!"

"Libbie," Mrs. Everett scolded, snapping open a parasol with a flourish, "here you must remember to protect your delicate skin from that sun. As hot as it is, I don't know why you chose such a high-necked dress."

Phillip frowned. "She's right, my dear—you really should change."

In a panic, Libbie thought fast. "I—I was protecting my delicate skin from the sun, just as I've been told."

Phillip shrugged, but Mrs. Everett smiled at her suddenly obedient charge as she handed Libbie the parasol.

She took it with a sigh, wondering what the stern dowager would think of her erotic dream of galloping naked across the desert wearing nothing but a savage's necklace and with her bare bottom exposed to the relentless sun?

The travelers started out of the room, the soldiers burdened down with luggage. Phillip offered Libbie his arm, and she hesitated only a moment before she took it as they exited into the bright desert morning. She hardly heard him as he chatted about how much he would miss her until he saw her again next spring. "Hopefully, I'll be permanently transferred by then—unless a big Apache war breaks out."

She gave him her most appealing smile from under her parasol while looking past his shoulder, searching the area for Cougar. "Is that likely?"

"Not if we go up to Cibecue Creek and nip this thing in the bud. I have asked to be sent on the campaign— good chance for promotion and some medals."

She nodded at the appropriate places as he talked, but her mind was on the gemstones around her throat, as warm as a man's fingers. She imagined trying to explain to Phillip how she had come by the necklace, but of course, he would never know she had it. They strolled slowly toward the stage stop while the soldiers and Mrs. Everett hurried ahead with the luggage. As they reached the waiting stage, the regimental band was gathered there and began to play the old army tune, "The Girl I Left Behind Me."

The elite and the curious had gathered around to see the ladies off. The unkempt old driver frowned and spat tobacco juice from his perch on top of the stage as the soldiers loaded the luggage.

"Oh, dear," Libbie said.

"What's the matter, my love?"

"Phillip, I meant to give a small gift to that Apache girl." Libbie looked anxiously back toward her quarters.

Phillip stifled a yawn. "Don't worry about it; she's not used to having much. Apache women are treated like horses around here, kept for a man's convenience."

"That's terrible!" Libbie dug in her reticule. "Here, here's the pair of gold earrings I wore last night. I could tell she admired them." She put them in Phillip's hand. "Tell her I thank her for her help."

"Libbie," Mrs. Everett scolded, "that's too nice a gift for some little Injun squaw."

"Listen to your guardian, Libbie," Phillip said.

But Libbie shook her head. "I felt sorry for her; she doesn't seem to have much of a life. Promise me you'll give them to her, Phillip, and tell her I said thanks?"

"Oh, all right; I'll humor you in this. I suppose you can afford to give away gold earrings." He put them in his pocket.

Mrs. Everett opened her mouth, then seemed to think better of it. "Well, of course she can. She has lots of jewelry, don't you, Libbie?"

The necklace seemed to burn into her throat. "Uh, yes, I do."

"All aboard!" the driver yelled. "Or you ladies will miss your train."

There seemed to be no other passengers. Even with the music, the sound of distant drums echoed faintly on the early-morning air.

Mrs. Everett frowned. "Don't the savages ever stop?"

"I'm sorry they disturbed you," Phillip said smoothly as he helped the plump lady up the step and into the stage. "We'll kill a few Apaches and take care of that little problem."

The soldiers put the valise in the boot and the big trunk up on top of the stage. Now Phillip paused before Libbie. "Well, I guess this is good-bye, my dear." He took her by the arms and she realized he was going to kiss her.

"Phillip, please, people are watching."

"Oh, you're so proper! Let them watch; after all, we are engaged. We'll correspond, my darling, and spring will be here before you know it."

Mrs. Everett leaned out of the coach, fanning herself with her kerchief. "That's right, Lieutenant, and there's a million things to be seen to with a big society wedding."

"Right." He was looking into Libbie's eyes. "About last night . . ." He lowered his voice to a whisper.

Libbie looked past his shoulder, remembering the violent way he'd torn at her clothing and put his hands on her. "You needn't apologize, Phillip."

"Oh, but I do. It's just that I want you so much, Elizabeth. Men have earthy appetites and I got carried away."

"I said I understand, Phillip." She did not look at him, wondering what marriage to this man would be like, yet certain she had no alternative. Abruptly, in the shadow of the buildings, she saw Shashké watching, her mouth a hard line, her arms folded defiantly across her full breasts. What was upsetting the girl? Perhaps she had expected Libbie would leave her a coin or two. Shashké was in for a pleasant surprise when Phillip gave her the fine gold earrings.

Libbie looked in another direction. Under a lone cottonwood tree, Cougar sat his paint stallion. When he caught her eye, he reached up slowly to touch his neck and nodded to her. Libbie pretended not to see either of them.

"All aboard!" The driver shouted again. "If we don't get a move on, you ladies will miss the train."

"Good-bye, my dear." Phillip kissed her. It was little more than a dry, passionless peck, but after all, a crowd was watching.

"Good-bye." She could hardly wait to get out of his embrace. "We'll write."

"By next spring, I hope to have a chest full of medals," he bragged as he helped her into the coach.

To cover the awkward moment, Libbie laughed, perhaps a little too heartily. "Of course, Phillip!"

Now she nodded and, lifting her full blue skirts, climbed in. She pulled out a handkerchief and leaned out the window to wave as the coach started with the crack of a whip and a jingle of a harness. They pulled away in a cloud of dust. Libbie tried not to look back at either Shashké or Cougar, but they both watched her stoically. Instead, she laughed and waved at Phillip, who blew kisses until the stage rounded a curve in the road and Fort Grant disappeared from view.

Libbie leaned back against the plush horsehair seat with a sigh and touched the neck of her dress. She could feel the silver against her throat like a reminder of Cougar's touch.

Phillip watched until the coach was out of sight, then smiled and felt the gold earrings in his pocket. What an extravagant gift for an Injun squaw! Well, the silly little heiress could well afford it. He intended to put these earrings to good use. Right now, he had a meeting with the fort commander to see what action he intended to take about the heightened tension up in the northern part of the Territory. He could hardly wait for the chance to kill a few Apaches. That wouldn't bring his father back, but it would feel damn good!

The drums beat all day. When Phillip ran into Cougar in the stables, he asked, "Don't those damned things ever stop? They're getting on everybody's nerves!"

The big half-breed didn't smile. "I think that's the purpose."

"How good are those new scouts if we need them?"

Cougar considered. "I wouldn't suggest the army use them against their own people yet. Some may still have old loyalties."

Phillip swore under his breath and wiped the sweat from his patrician face. "The devil wouldn't claim this country."

The Apache looked back at him impassively from blue eyes under the scarlet headband. "Lieutenant, this place is disturbing you; you ought to ask for a transfer out."

"Not yet! I came for revenge; my dear mother has talked of nothing else my whole life."

Cougar lowered his voice almost gently. "The major found only a grave in this country; that should be a warning to you."

Phillip laughed without mirth. "They're the ones you should be warning." He jerked his head in the direction of the distant drums. Then he took a sudden closer look at the big man before him. "What happened to that necklace you always wear?"

Cougar touched his own neck and shook his head. "I seem to have lost it somewhere since yesterday."

"You don't seem too upset," Phillip snapped. "I thought it was your finest possession. You lose it gambling?"

Cougar hesitated. "You might say that."

Phillip snorted with scorn. Who could understand how the minds of careless savages worked? Once again he marveled at how Mac McGuire could have loved and married an Apache girl. Lusted after, yes, keep one as a mistress, of course—but make her respectable by *marrying* her? Preposterous!

"Anything else, Lieutenant?"

Phillip shrugged. "The commander's calling a meeting tomorrow morning for all of us who are being transferred to Fort Apache."

"That include me?"

"He said the top scout, and your name was mentioned," Phillip said in a grudging tone.

"Fine. I'll be there." He turned to go.

"Aren't you forgetting something, Injun?"

Cougar paused, gave him a half-hearted salute, and sauntered away, leaving Phillip glaring after him. *If there is action,* he thought with a malicious grin, *I'm going to see that damned scout gets a bullet in the back and let the hostiles take the blame for it.* With a sigh, he returned to his duties.

That night, Phillip lay on his bunk, watching the deepening shadows and thinking about Elizabeth. In less than a year, she was going to belong to him, and he could do whatever he wanted with her fortune and her body. He licked his lips at the thought. Last night, he'd gotten impatient and almost ruined it all. Well, he probably wouldn't see her again until right before the wedding, so all he had to do was keep writing sweet letters and poetry to her.

Phillip smiled. Women were such stupid ninnies—all but his dear mother. It was Henrietta who had helped set up the introduction at the ball, which Phillip had attended to look over the available heiresses. Elizabeth's beauty had been an extra bonus, because even if Libbie hadn't been pretty, his mother would have insisted he court her and marry her because of the fabled Winters wealth.

He needed that wealth. The Van Harringtons had lost plenty in some bad investments Phillip had made a couple of years ago and some gambling debts he'd run up. Now they were all but penniless!

Chapter Six

The rattle of gravel against his window brought Phillip up off his bed. About time! He'd been expecting his visitor, so he was only partially dressed. He went to the door, opened it, and peered into the night. Shashké beckoned to him from the nearby shadows of a Joshua tree, the cactus blossom in her black locks scenting the air. He smiled with pleasure and looked in both directions to make sure no one was around before motioning her over to him in the doorway.

"Sweet, I've been thinking about you." He reached out and grabbed her breast. "Come on in."

Shashké brushed his hand away and shook her head. "Hah! You've been thinking about that red-haired white girl, and now that she's gone, you want me again."

Ye gods! Spare me from a stupid, jealous slut. "Now, sweet, you know you're really the one I love. However, my mother is going to insist I marry her because of her social position and because she's inherited lots of money."

"Has she? She didn't leave me even a small coin to show her appreciation as her maid."

He had the gold earrings Elizabeth had left for the Apache girl in his pocket. "Ah, but I have something nice for you, something I took from Elizabeth's purse when she wasn't looking."

The girl's greedy dark eyes brightened. "A gift for me? Give it to me!"

"Later. Come on in." He gestured. "It's more comfortable in my quarters than in that old barn."

Shashké shook her head. "I can't come in there. You have dead bears in there; it's a taboo place."

"Dead bears?" Phillip looked over his shoulder, then threw back his head and laughed. "It's a bearskin rug and a head mounted over the fireplace. I like to hunt."

She scowled at him, pretty with the exotic blossom in her hair. "You break Apache taboos in killing bears. We believe the spirits of our dead inhabit the animals' bodies."

Damn stupid Injuns. He caught her hand and tried to pull her inside, but she resisted.

Shashké shook her head. "I have to be most careful of offending the bear spirits because of the month I was born."

Phillip didn't want to hear about ignorant Injun beliefs and he didn't give a damn what month she'd been born in. All he wanted was to get her under him for a few minutes. "Aw, sweet, come on in and I'll give you that present."

She backed away, shaking her head. "Bring the present. I'll meet you in the usual place." Shashké disappeared into the night.

Oh, hell. The barn was clear across the parade grounds. Phillip scowled and stared after her a long moment before he shut the door and walked across the pine floor, wondering where he'd left his boots. His bare foot came in contact with the bearskin rug's head and he stubbed his toe, cursed, and kicked the head hard. "Apache superstitions, bah! I'll kill all the bears I want!"

This was probably the last time he'd enjoy the lusty Apache girl. Rumor was that his unit was being transferred up to Fort Apache to put down the unrest at Cibicue Creek. He was getting tired of Shashké anyway and maybe there'd be plenty more like her around the other fort. He made sure he had the gold earrings in his pocket and smiled to himself as he went out the door and sauntered through the darkness to the barn, humming to himself with satisfaction.

It was ironic, really, that Elizabeth's gold earrings were about to buy him an evening of lust. But on the other hand, it was going to be her money that paid for the pretty white mistress he would choose when he returned to the East. Even if his new wife did find out he was unfaithful, there wasn't much she could do after they were wed and Phillip had control of all her wealth.

Shashké was waiting in the hay of the cavalry barn. "Give me the present," she demanded.

Greedy little bitch. "Let's make love first," he bargained, sitting down on the hay.

"No, present first," she insisted.

"Okay." Phillip pulled the gold earrings from his pocket and held them out. The moonlight gleamed through a broken plank of the barn and reflected on them. "Here, do you like these?"

"Oh, the white girl's earrings! They are beautiful!" Shashké grabbed them from his hand. "I saw her wearing them at the ball."

He grinned. "They'll look better on you, sweet. You're much prettier."

"She gave them to me?" Shashké put them on.

Phillip considered. So what if his fianceé had asked him to give them to the girl? Shashké would never know, nor would Elizabeth. The Apache girl would be very free with her favors for the brief time left before he was transferred. "She doesn't know you have them," he lied. "Like I told you before, I stole them out of her purse to give them to you."

"You really love me after all." She was all smiles now, the gold earrings gleaming in the moonlight when she turned her head.

"Why, sweet, could you ever doubt it?" He took the cactus blossom from her hair and tossed it aside. "Now show me just how grateful you are." He pulled her to him and kissed her long and hard while she pressed her big breasts against his chest until his manhood came up rigid and throbbing.

She lay back, her ebony hair spread like smudged ink on the yellow hay, gold earrings reflecting the moonlight. He reached to pull her blouse to her waist, knowing she wore nothing beneath that would discourage his seeking hands. Nor pantalets either, he thought with a smile as he ran his fingertips up her bare, warm thigh.

"I've thought of nothing but you, sweet," he whispered, "my gift proves that, doesn't it?"

"I love you, Phillip. You'll take me back East with you when you go?" She reached up and began to open his shirt.

"Yeah, sure." He almost smiled at the ridiculous idea. What would Mother think if he showed up with an Injun slut in tow? Shashké was a stupid, trusting wench. His body ached with the thought of taking beautiful Elizabeth's virginity. Soon, she would belong to him and he would have her at his mercy in the marriage bed. Now he closed his eyes, pretending those were Elizabeth's fingers tracing circles on his bare chest.

"I run a terrible risk if my man ever catches me sleeping with you before we leave Arizona."

"You won't get caught; stop worrying about it," he breathed as he bent to her breast. He didn't care whether she was in any danger or what Apaches did to cheating wives. Passionate, pretty Shashké was only entertainment to while away the long, dull nights until he found another more interesting slut or got transferred out. He sucked her nipple into his mouth while he stroked her lush body, and she responded by running her hands inside his shirt, digging her nails into his shoulders, and pulling him down on her.

"No," he gasped and pulled away from her, "you know what I want." He reached to unbutton his trousers, and even as she protested, he grabbed her by the back of the neck, forcing her face down into him. "Do it!" he demanded. "You know what I want!"

She hesitated, but as he pressed her face against him, she opened that hot, sweet mouth and caressed him with her tongue. He made a sound of pleasure and relaxed, letting her play with him. When he was Elizabeth's husband, he could force her to do this to him whether she liked it or not. As his wife, she would be almost powerless legally. Phillip fully intended to humble that spoiled little bitch!

Now, as his passion built, he wanted more. "Take it!" he demanded. "Take it all!"

She struggled just a moment, but he had one hand on the back of her neck, forcing her. After a moment, she surrendered to his will until he reached a pinnacle of pleasure. Then he lay there a long time, breathing hard.

"What about me?" Shashké demanded.

"What about you?" Phillip yawned. Satisfied now, he was ready to return to his quarters. He sat up and began to button his shirt.

"I still need a man." She was sulky.

Phillip shrugged, bored now with the stupid, illiterate girl. "So go home to your husband."

"He's old and can almost never do it," she fumed, combing the straw out of her tumbled hair with one hand. "You could at least tell me you love me when we do this."

"I love you," he repeated automatically. "I need to be getting back now."

"I'll wager if you had that redhead here with you, you wouldn't be in such a hurry to return to your bunk."

He paused in pulling on his boots and thought about the elegant Miss Winters lying naked and defenseless on silken white sheets, her long red hair in complete disarray as she awaited his pleasure. When he thought about her, his passion began to build again. He intended to keep her on her back until he got her with child. Elizabeth's wealth and an heir would please his mother. By then, he'd probably be tired of the lady and could return to his wild, whoring ways. Mama wouldn't care, and his wife couldn't stop him.

Shashké put her hand on him, began to stroke him. "Make love to me," she demanded, "or I'll scream that you attacked me and bring everyone running."

"Is that a way to thank me for the nice present?" If he didn't satisfy the slut, she was just vengeful enough to do it. Shashké had become a real problem for him. With a sigh, he rolled over on top of her.

She took his full weight gladly, thinking the lieutenant wasn't very virile, or skilled at lovemaking, or nearly as big as she would have liked, but he would have to do. Her lusty appetite might have been satisfied by Cougar, but the big half-breed would not give in to her; he had too much respect for her old husband. Yet here in the moonlight, with his broad shoulders and square jaw, the lieutenant looked enough like Cougar that with a little imagination, she could pretend that at last she was mating with the man she really wanted.

"Can you do it?" She locked her thighs around him and offered him the feast of her breasts as she dug her nails into his hips and broad shoulders.

It took him a few minutes to build up enough rigidity to please her, and then he rode her hard while she tore at his chest and back with her nails, using him for her pleasure until she was satisfied.

With a tired sigh, he rolled off her and sat up. "Okay, now I've really got to be getting back."

"You never stay and hold me and tell me you love me," she complained.

He was truly sick of her. Phillip stood up and brushed the hay from his clothes. "Maybe next time."

"There is a rumor around the fort that some in your unit might be transferred up to Fort Apache."

He was counting on it to get away from the tiresome girl. "Maybe; I don't know."

She stood up and grabbed his arm. "Take me with you when you pull out."

"Now, sweet, you know I can't do that. I'll send for you later." He brushed her hand off his arm.

"But later might be too late!" she protested. "More and more of the Apaches know about us. My old husband might hear that I have been betraying him."

Phillip didn't care what happened to the girl now that he was going to be moving on. "I'll send for you later," he lied.

Shashké looked up at him, knowing he was lying, yet powerless to do anything about it. Her husband truly loved her, she ought to go home to him, but the young white officer could offer her dresses and more jewelry, all the things that fine white girls had. If she could only get Phillip to stay a little longer here with her, maybe she could convince him. Yet he was even now starting for the door. "Come back, Phillip; it's not late."

He scowled. "I told you I have to go."

How could she make him stay? Then she remembered and slowly smiled. "I know a secret you would like to know."

"I doubt that." He yawned as he turned to go.

"I know something about your white girl," Shashké whispered desperately, "something you would want to know."

It had the desired effect. He stopped and looked at her. "Elizabeth? What about her?"

Shashké shrugged and playfully poked with one bare toe at the straw. "Oh, just something."

He stared at her as if attempting to decide whether she was bluffing, then grabbed her arm and twisted it. "Tell me, you stupid slut!"

"Oww, Phillip, you're hurting me!" She had never seen this side of him before.

"I'll hurt you more," he promised between clenched teeth, "if you don't tell me!"

She was weeping now, but he only tightened his grip. "I—it wasn't anything."

"Tell me and I'll decide that." He twisted her arm harder.

"Stop, you're hurting me! I'll tell!"

He didn't turn her loose. "So tell."

"Jewelry," she sobbed. "It's about the necklace." She wished she hadn't mentioned it now. She didn't mind bringing trouble to the hated, stingy white girl, but she truly cared for Cougar. "Maybe she—she stole that, too."

"What necklace? Elizabeth wouldn't steal anything. Tell me!" He twisted her arm again.

If she screamed, would anyone come before he could really hurt her? Shashké struggled to pull her arm away, but he didn't let go. He seemed to be enjoying her pain. This was a side of the aristocratic officer she had never seen before. "The necklace; she has the necklace."

Phillip didn't let go. "What necklace? She's got lots of those, pearls, diamonds, gold lockets—"

"Cougar's Apache Tears necklace!" She almost screamed it.

To her relief, Phillip gasped and his blue eyes widened in surprise as he turned her loose. "What the hell—?"

She sobbed, favoring her injured arm, but Phillip didn't seem to notice. "I—I don't know how she got it, but I saw it in her luggage when I helped her pack this morning."

"Cougar's necklace?" Phillip scratched his head slowly, his handsome face puzzled. "How—? Does she know you saw it?"

Shashké looked up at him and shook her head. "I don't think so; I didn't say anything."

"How the hell did she—?" His voice trailed off and he seemed to be trying to figure it all out.

Shashké backed away, shaking her head. "I only know she has it."

The officer's face was a mask of fury. "I'm going to get to the bottom of this!"

She was afraid of his anger. "You don't want to challenge Cougar. He is a skilled warrior; he would kill you and then you would never take me away from here so I can live like a white girl!"

He didn't even seem to hear her. "Maybe it wasn't his necklace, maybe it was another like it that she bought at the trading post."

Shashké shook her head. "There is no other necklace in all Apache country like that one. They say Cougar's dead mother gave it to his white father as a sign of her love."

She didn't like the jealous fury she saw on the lieutenant's face.

"Why would that damned Injun buck give it to Elizabeth?"

"I don't know." She looked away, wishing she had never told him.

"What else do you know? Tell me, you dirty Injun bitch!" He grabbed her and slapped her hard.

She cried out and put her hands to her face, tasting the warm, coppery blood from her cut lip. All she had for her fortune was her pretty face. Without her beauty, she would never escape from her poor, dull life. "Maybe—maybe she liked it and bought it from Cougar."

"Don't be a fool! Everyone on the post has admired that necklace and tried to buy it, me included. Cougar said there wasn't enough gold in all Arizona to buy it, so why would he let Elizabeth have it?" He grabbed her by the shoulders, digging his fingers into her flesh, and repeated his question through clenched teeth. "Why would he let her have it?"

"Didn't you see how he looked at her?"

Phillip heard nothing more. A red rage began to blur his sight as he imagined anything, everything. He threw Shashké to the ground and strode away, oblivious to her sobbing entreaties behind him. Yes, he had seen the way that big breed looked at Elizabeth—as though he'd like to pick her up and carry her away someplace so that he could ravage her virginity.

The image of the big Apache lying between his fiancée's thighs angered him past all reason as he strode toward the barracks. Then he pulled up short and smiled. What was he thinking of? Prissy little Elizabeth was so frigid, she would hardly let Phillip kiss her; there was no passion in the society miss. He could not say the same for the virile scout. Phillip had seen the banked fire in the Apache's blue eyes as he looked at the lady. The gall of that breed! Phillip would teach that savage to lust after a white woman!

He aroused four of his biggest, meanest troopers, men who owed him favors for lending them money at cards or getting them out of the guardhouse when they'd run into trouble fighting or slacking off. He put his finger to his lips as he awakened each of them, motioning them to dress and come outside. They joined him, half-dressed and yawning.

"Don't ask any questions," he snapped. "I've got someone I need to get information from!"

"At this time of night, sir?" Jones scratched the tattoo on his massive arm.

"I said no questions!" Phillip barked and started walking. "We're going to pay a little visit to Cougar."

Behind him, the men faltered.

"Beg your pardon, sir," Hans, the big blacksmith volunteered, "he's not an easy man to—"

"There's four of you!" Phillip swore. "And this is important!"

"The lieutenant's right," Corrigan argued. "I don't like that big breed; he thinks he's as good as a white man!"

Rollins had been a teamster before he enlisted. Now he flexed his rippling muscles. "There's five of us. We can take him!"

The five of them began walking again toward where Phillip knew Cougar camped when he wasn't at his father's ranch. The scout liked to sleep under an open sky in a grove of trees at the edge of the fort. Phillip told the four rogues his plan, and they faded into the underbrush near Cougar's camp. Phillip himself walked boldly in.

Alert as the animal he was named for, Cougar heard just the slightest sound of a boot on gravel before he came up out of his blankets, grabbing for a rifle.

"Whoa." The lieutenant laughed, holding up his hands. "It's just me! Nobody could ever sneak up on you, could they?"

Cougar frowned and relaxed, throwing his weapon to

one side. "I'm an Apache, Lieutenant, we live on the edge of danger. What do you want at this time of night?"

Phillip shrugged. "I just wanted to know if you've heard any rumors from the Apaches. Every soldier I've talked to is jumpy."

The drums had begun beating again in the background.

"At this time of night? Can't you wait until morning to see what the commander has to say?"

Phillip shrugged. "Why don't you make some coffee and we'll talk? Maybe we've had our differences in the past, but we're maybe going into a difficult campaign up north, and I thought you might have heard some rumors."

"All right." Frankly puzzled and still a little sleepy, Cougar got up and knelt by the ashes of his fire to stir it to flames. "You'll be disappointed in how little I know. Most of the Apaches don't tell me much because I work for the army and am loyal to it. Believe me, though, there's no plotting going on. If everyone will keep their heads, this will all blow over, and—"

With his head down as he poked at the fire, he heard a sudden noise and came up fighting even as he felt a terrible blow to the back of his head. He went to his knees, struggling to stay conscious through a haze of pain. He heard running feet and then he was pinned to the ground.

"We got 'im, Lieutenant!"

Someone was holding his arms and legs.

Even with the blinding pain, Cougar fought to break free and almost succeeded, lashing out with one powerful arm.

"Hang on to him! He's a strong devil!"

The next few seconds were a blur of pain and confusion, but finally Cougar found himself tied up and propped against his saddle.

The lieutenant looked down at him, grinning, but there

was no humor in the cold blue eyes. "Thanks, boys," he said to the four men in the shadows. "You can leave now."

Cougar tried to bring his vision back into focus as his assailants fled. He never got a good look at those who'd attacked him. "What in the hell is this all about?"

"Call me sir," the lieutenant commanded and kicked him hard in the groin. "And I'll ask the questions, you dirty savage!"

Agony exploded through Cougar's lithe body and he doubled up, but he did not cry out, even though he was numb with pain. He would not give the other that satisfaction.

Phillip glared down at him. "What's happened to that necklace you always wear?"

A warning shiver went up Cougar's muscular back. "I— I lost it."

The officer sneered and kicked him again, sending agony through every nerve. "For something that meant so much to you, you don't seem very concerned that it's lost."

Surely the lieutenant couldn't know the truth. Cougar gritted his teeth against the red haze of pain. "What— what is this all about?"

Abruptly, the officer bent and struck him hard across the face. "You red heathen, you know what this is about!"

Cougar looked up at him through a murderous haze, his own scarlet blood coppery warm in his mouth and dripping down his chin. He said nothing, thinking instead how he would kill the officer, slowly, painfully, if he got a chance. No, of course he could not do that; he would be breaking an old Apache taboo.

Phillip squatted before him, caught Cougar by the hair, and raised his head, twisting Cougar's hair until the pain made him gasp.

The lieutenant smiled at his pain. "You arrogant son of a bitch! You gave the necklace to Miss Winters."

He must protect the white girl; she was fragile and innocent. "No, I—I lost it. If she's got it, maybe she found it. How—how did you know—?"

"Because she told me about it, you ignorant bastard!"

He couldn't imagine the flame-haired beauty doing that. "No." He shook his head. "No, I did not give it to her!"

"You lie!" The lieutenant struck him across the face again.

He fought against the blind rage building in him. No matter what Mac said, no matter the Apache taboo, he yearned to kill Phillip Van Harrington. Cougar pulled hard at his bounds until his strong muscles rippled and knotted, but he couldn't break the ropes.

The lieutenant grinned, seeming to enjoy his struggles. "Elizabeth told me you gave it to her and she laughed about it. You hear me? She threw back her head and laughed at the ignorant savage who'd taken a shine to her. She thought it was so amusing! We both had a good laugh about it before she got on the stage this morning."

Cougar winced. The lieutenant's words hurt him as the harsh blows never could. Could he have misjudged the spirited beauty so badly? Could the white girl have been so shallow and so cruel? Would she have made a joke about the sacred gift he had bestowed on her? He remembered watching from a distance as she got on the stage. Phillip had kissed her. Cougar remembered watching that, wanting to be in the lieutenant's place, imagining what it would feel like to hold her. He tried to remember every detail. Yes, she and Phillip had been laughing together. He couldn't believe Blaze would take his gift so lightly, and yet, there was no other answer, no other way that the officer could have known about the necklace. "What—what did she do with it?"

"She threw it away! What do you think she did with a worthless thing like that? She's a rich white girl with lots of jewelry, and she took it as a big joke!"

In his mind, Cougar imagined the fiery girl throwing back her head and laughing, tossing away his most precious possession. The image hurt him as no battle wound ever had. And in his heart began to burn a fierce anger for the arrogant Elizabeth Winters. At that moment, he had never hated anyone as much as he hated the red-haired white girl.

"I see by your face that you're a little upset!" Phillip sneered, striding up and down before him. "I just wanted you to know this is what you get for trying to cross the color line—ridicule and punishment. How dare you offer a gift to my fiancée!" The officer kicked him hard between the thighs and Cougar doubled over with a strangled moan. As he lay writhing in the dirt, Phillip kicked him in the face with his riding boots.

"Remember this every time you think of even approaching a white woman now, you lusty savage!" Harrington snarled through gritted teeth. "Stay in your place! You'd better learn that lesson, or by God, next time I'll figure out a way to hang you!" At this, he turned and strode into the darkness.

Cougar lay there half-conscious, his big muscles stiffening and aching from the blows and beatings. He tried to untie himself, but he'd been well bound. He lay there with the dew falling on his aching body and the hate in his soul growing stronger with each beat of his heart.

Libbie Winters. Blaze. He had given her the necklace in good faith, trying to protect her from any Apache attack on the stage and she had made a joke of it, shared the ridicule with the uppity lieutenant. Mac had been right; Cougar could not cross the invisible barrier. It brought only the heartbreak and tragedy it had brought his parents. He had thought a very great love would make color and social position unimportant, but he'd been wrong.

Strange, he would not have believed the white girl would

do this thing; she had seemed so touched by his gift. It showed that he had been mistaken in his judgment; she was as cruel and shallow and arrogant as her fiancé.

Cougar lay there in pain through most of the night, his anger at Elizabeth Winters growing as he planned his revenge should she ever return to the fort. Toward dawn, he heard a step and, still struggling to free himself, looked up with alarm. The lieutenant might be having second thoughts about Cougar filing a complaint with the commander and come back to silence the scout permanently.

Shashké came out from the shadows of some mesquite trees. "Cougar?"

He didn't want anyone to see him this way; bloody and injured. It was too humiliating for a warrior, but he needed help. "Over here."

Her dark eyes widened with shock as she ran to him and bent down. She said a curse in Apache. "Oh, Cougar, how bad are you hurt?"

"Bad enough, although I don't think any bones are broken. Untie me. How did you know I was here?"

She was busy untying him so he couldn't see her face, but he felt her start. "I—I let the lieutenant make love to me. He bragged about what he was going to do, but I didn't believe him. What was this about, anyway?"

He considered his answer as she untied his arms and he rubbed his raw wrists. Shashké would probably throw back her head, laugh, and ridicule him for being so naive as to give a gift to the high-born white girl. "Just a difference of opinion between me and the officer." He began to untie his legs.

She stepped back and winced as she surveyed his injuries. "It must have been a big difference of opinion."

"Forget it; it was something between men." He managed to stand up, but every sinewy muscle in his big body ached.

She seemed to be struggling with a decision, her pretty face troubled.

He paused and stared at her. "Where'd you get those earrings? Those belong to the white girl. Did you steal them?"

"No, she—he gave them to me. After all, she has plenty." Shashké seemed both angry and defensive, but he dismissed her attitude as petty and unimportant. After all, he had more important things on his mind right now. He picked up his rifle.

Shashké caught his arm. "Cougar, you won't kill him? The lieutenant is my only chance to get away from here."

He groaned aloud as he straightened up. "Little Bear Tracks, you're a fool; the lieutenant uses you for his pleasure until he leaves. He cares nothing about you. Go home to your husband and be a good wife."

She shook her head. "The lieutenant has made me promises. I want to live like a white girl."

Cougar sighed. There was no reasoning with her. "You know what will happen to that pretty face if you are caught cheating. The gossip already spreads among our people."

"It is worth the risk!" She glared back at him stubbornly, the gold earrings glinting under the late night stars. "You will not kill the lieutenant?"

He could not kill the lieutenant, even though he hungered for revenge. To do so would break an Apache taboo, and his soul was more Apache than white. All he could do was hate the man, yet he hated the arrogant Elizabeth Winters even more. If she ever dared to return to this country, Cougar would take his revenge; there was no taboo against killing her. No, humiliating her would be even more satisfying, if he ever had her at his mercy.

"Your lieutenant is safe, Shashké," he assured her, "the army would hang me if I killed him. And thank you for coming out here to see about me."

She did not meet his eyes. "It's all right. If you ever change your mind about us—"

"No." He shook his head. "I've got an Apache heart, Shashké. I cannot do that which is dishonorable to our people."

"And I have done much to dishonor our people, haven't I? I should tell you—"

She hesitated, then abruptly turned and fled. He stared after her in puzzlement. She acted as if she were guilty of something. Well, of course he had just shamed her for dishonoring her husband, but he had more important things on his mind right now than a foolish, ambitious girl.

It would be dawn soon. With a sigh, he reached for his saddle. He'd ride out to the ranch and let Mac patch him up. What he hated most was that the old man would scold him and say, "I told you so."

It was hopeless for Cougar to yearn for that which he could never possess, and his passion for the fire-haired girl could bring him nothing but trouble and pain. Only a very great love could withstand crossing that forbidden line between their two peoples, and she felt no love. Elizabeth Winters had betrayed him and laughed at him. So now Cougar's love had been replaced by a burning hatred!

Chapter Seven

Cougar rode out to the ranch. As he reined in, Mac came out on the porch. Cougar dismounted slowly and painfully. "Don't even ask!"

The dour little Scot stared in shock, then hurried down the steps to assist him. "All right then, I won't, but I can guess."

Cougar leaned on him as Mac helped him up onto the porch where he collapsed in a chair. Mac pursed his lips, combing his fingers through his gray beard and surveying him. "Can ye not avoid trouble?"

He had expected such a lecture, but Cougar only grunted and shrugged. "I've tried. The lieutenant's taken a special dislike to me."

"Do you think he suspects—?"

"No, it's not that," Cougar assured him with a tired sigh.

"Aye, and I knew he'd be trouble the first time I saw him here at the fort. He's already been here, you know, wanting the major's pistol." Mac's brow furrowed with worry.

"He wouldn't if he knew—"

"I hope he never finds out," Mac said. "Some things are better left alone."

Cougar rolled and lit a cigarette with an unsteady hand. "Among the Apache, everything a dead person owns is buried with him."

"Aye." Mac nodded. "But whites buried the major and they brought back those two things."

Cougar blew smoke and thought a long moment. "I hope they don't both bring bad luck."

"Enough of this uneasy talk," Mac said. "Wait here; I'll get some liniment." He went inside.

"Bring me a drink, too," Cougar yelled as he leaned back in the chair with a sigh. He knew he must look as bad as he felt; bruised and battered.

In moments, Mac returned with ointments, rags, and a bottle of good Scotch whiskey. "This ought to fix things." He poured the other a drink and then cleaned the cuts on Cougar's face with a gentle, gnarled hand. "Reminds me of when you were a lad; always gettin' banged up, you were. What started this?"

Cougar winced. "He brought some toughs and came looking for me."

Mac paused. "Why?"

"Same thing you used to ask me when I was a kid." There was a long silence as Cougar sipped his whiskey and looked away. He didn't want to bring trouble to Mac by getting him involved. "Nothing much; just a disagreement. Forget it."

"Ye have never been a good liar, lad." He put a comforting hand on Cougar's broad shoulder. "Are you sure he doesn't suspect—?"

"No." Cougar shook his head. "It wasn't that. It was about the girl."

"Ahh." The other nodded as if that explained everything.

"I hope you're not going to say 'I told you so.' " Cougar gulped the rest of his drink and wiped his mouth with the back of his hand.

" 'Tis tempting," Mac admitted. "She was a beauty, all right, but out of your reach."

Cougar scowled and stood up. "Don't you think I know that?"

"What happened to your necklace?"

Cougar didn't answer. His hand went automatically to his neck.

The older man peered up at him a long moment as if in disbelief. "You've never taken that off in all these years."

"I lost it."

The other looked troubled, shook his head, and filled his pipe. "I know ye too well, lad; don't lie to me. You gave it to that girl." It was a statement, not a question.

"And the spoiled little bitch threw it away and laughed about it with Phillip!" Cougar made an angry, dismissing gesture.

"Hmm." Mac scratched his gray beard. "Somehow, she didn't seem like that type."

"I was a fool!" Cougar started down off the porch, then paused. "I should have listened to you."

"A man listens to his heart," Mac said gently. "I did, even though it brought me heartache, as I knew it would."

Cougar paused by his big paint stallion and smiled at the other. "Thank you."

He shrugged. "For what?"

"For everything; you know."

Mac snorted and tried to make light of the words, but his brown eyes misted. "No more than any man would do for a son." He looked toward the hill where Cougar's mother slept forever. "Loving women causes most of the world's troubles, I think."

"Then why don't we smarten up?"

"Ah, lad, because we can't live without them; and because any man worth his salt listens to his heart, not his head." Mac wiped his eyes. His mind seemed a long way off, as if he were lost in memories.

"You miss her, don't you?" Cougar blurted, not caring that he must not speak of the dead.

"Every hour of every day; but she left me you."

"I was not your obligation; the Apaches would have raised me."

Mac shrugged. "Aye, and they helped. But I wed her so I could protect her." He looked into Cougar's eyes. "You've been the best son any man could want. Be careful, boy. I promised her as she took her last breath, and you took your first, that I'd always look out for you."

Cougar smiled gently at him as he stood up. "You've kept that promise, but I'm a grown man now. You can't protect me forever."

The other cleared his throat awkwardly. "I would if I could."

"Sooner or later, all eagles must take to the air, even if they take a chance on falling," Cougar said gravely as he went down the steps and swung up on his horse. "I don't want to worry you, so I'll try to stay out of the lieutenant's way. It will be tough; he's got it in for me."

In the background, the drums began to beat again.

Mac turned and peered toward the distant hills, blinking with his poor sight. "Looks like you both may soon be too busy to carry on a personal feud."

"I know." Cougar, too, stared off into the distance and frowned. "I think some of us may be transferred up to Fort Apache, so I may not see you for a while."

"They nervous about a possible Apache outbreak?"

Cougar nodded.

Mac scowled. "Aye, and well they should be, the way that crooked Indian agent, Jack Tiffany, and his cohorts are cheating them. White men just never care enough to understand Indians." Mac's weathered face creased into worried lines.

"Only you." Cougar nodded affectionately. "You understand, and they trust you."

Mac acknowledged the praise with a nod. "I've tried to do right by them and keep my word; that's protected me all these years while ranches around me were burned and raided."

"The Apaches always remember their friends," Cougar promised, and as he turned his horse, he muttered to himself, "and their enemies." He nudged his paint stallion into a walk.

"Take care, boy!" Mac called after him.

Cougar waved acknowledgment as he rode away, heading back to the fort.

Behind him, Mac McGuire watched him leave. At that moment, the grizzled old Scot almost called out to him that he loved him, then hesitated and the moment was lost forever. Men did not say such things to each other, and yet the boy meant more to him than his own life. One woman Mac had loved in all his many years, but she had not loved him. Still, every time he looked into Cougar's face, he saw her dear face and remembered. In a way, he still had the mother through the son.

Cougar rode back to the fort and dismounted at the stable. A passing young private stared at him, seemed to be about to ask, then thought better of it. "They're in a meeting; rumor is it's important."

The meeting. He had forgotten about it after what had happened last night. Cougar cursed under his breath and nodded to the young Apache scout who came out of the stable.

Dandy Jim looked up at him earnestly and asked in their language, "You have had trouble?"

Cougar touched his bruised face absently. "Since the day I was born."

Dandy Jim turned and looked toward the distant hills, where the drums echoed. "We will not have to fight our own people? The others worry—"

"I will try to reason with the white man." Cougar put his hand on the young Apache's shoulder. "Maybe they will just send us up there to warn the Apaches. Take care of my horse."

Cougar handed over his reins and hurried toward headquarters. He dreaded facing those curious white men, but there was no help for it; he was a head scout and he had to be there. He came in late and stood near the door, ignoring the curious stares at his cut and swollen face. Phillip smiled ever so slightly and pulled at his mustache.

"Well," said the commander, pausing in mid-speech while pointing at a big map, "I'm so glad our head scout has finally graced us with his presence."

Quiet titters went around the room, but Cougar ignored them and snapped a salute. "My apologies, sir."

The officer took a good, long look at him. "You braves been guzzling *tiswin* and fighting over squaws again?"

More laughter. Cougar took a deep breath to control his temper and looked at the lieutenant. Phillip lounged in his chair, completely at ease. He knew the Apache brave wouldn't complain or tattle on him. "I suppose you could say it was over a woman, sir."

The colonel shrugged and turned to the map behind him. "So as I said, a few of you are headed up to Fort Apache. Lieutenant Van Harrington has volunteered, even though the mission may turn out to be dangerous." He beamed at Phillip.

Phillip colored modestly. "It's in the blood, sir; my father was much decorated."

Cougar stifled a groan, and the other men in the room frowned. Young Van Harrington was not too popular with the other soldiers.

The senior officer cleared his throat and tapped on the map with his pointer. "My guess is Colonel Carr will have orders from headquarters to go out to Cibecue and arrest that damned medicine man before he stirs up any more trouble."

"If you please, sir," Cougar blurted, and everyone turned to stare at a lowly Indian scout who would dare interrupt the colonel's briefing.

"Yes, what is it?" The colonel scowled blackly at him.

"I think the army's making a mistake," Cougar said without thinking, then realized he'd made a second blunder. "That is, sir, if they will just leave that Ancient One alone, soon his followers will realize that his omens are false and the trouble will fade away."

There was a silence that seemed to echo. It was so quiet, Cougar could hear the distant, faint commands of soldiers marching on the parade grounds and the buzz of a horsefly through the window in the simmering August heat.

The senior officer's face reddened with anger. "This meeting is adjourned!" he snapped. Men saluted and began to file out. "You, Cougar," he called, "you and Lieutenant Van Harrington stay here."

Now what?

Phillip looked worried, running a nervous finger around his collar. He needn't sweat, Cougar thought with contempt. It was beneath Cougar's dignity to report what had happened between them.

The room was empty now except for the three of them, and the old man was scowling at Cougar.

He had committed a great mistake, Cougar knew, blurting out opinions unasked before the cavalry officers. Cougar had no idea what the commander would do to him for being rash enough to comment, but at least his conscience was clear. Riding out to arrest *Noch-ay-del-Klinne* could only lead to a major rebellion and bloodshed across the Territory.

The commander gestured Cougar and Phillip forward. "At ease," he muttered, scowling darkly at Cougar but smiling warmly at Phillip. "Your father was a great man; he helped me when I was a green young pup, fresh from West Point. All the men who served with Bill loved him."

Phillip beamed. "Thank you, sir. I hope to follow in his footsteps. Perhaps you could put in a word for me in Washington about an assignment back East?"

The other nodded. "Well, yes, of course; least I can do. I intend to do good things for you, Phillip; I owe it to your father. You can win some medals on this Cibecue thing; look good on your uniform."

"Thank you, sir. I'll see you're invited to my wedding next spring."

"I met the young lady, remember?" The colonel smiled again. "My wife's already looking forward to it. She says it will be the social event that has all Philadelphia talking."

Blaze. In only a few months, she would belong to Cougar's hated enemy. The thought of Phillip making love to the fiery-haired beauty tore at Cougar's heart. Then he reminded himself again that the arrogant girl had ridiculed and laughed at him, then thrown away his most prized possession.

The colonel returned to poring over his maps. He seemed to have forgotten about Cougar. Cougar was used to that. White men often treated Indians as if they were invisible. Cougar cleared his throat. The officer looked up, frowned, and motioned him forward. "You're old McGuire's boy, aren't you?"

He hoped there weren't going to be any snide comments on that. "Yes, sir."

"I remember him, too; good man. Mac's legendary for his fierce devotion to Major Van Harrington. That's why I'm cutting you some slack."

An alarm went off in Cougar's mind. "Were you—were you in this area when the major died, sir?"

The other shook his head. "No, I'd been transferred out. Real tragedy; ambushed way out in the hills by a war party, the troopers said. Don't know what Bill was doing out there without his striker; he hardly went anywhere without Mac riding along."

"Damned murdering savages!" Phillip said. "The commander wrote my mother that they buried him where he fell. I would have liked to put a fine stone on the grave, but that commander is dead now and the soldiers either dead or scattered, so I'll never be able to find it."

Cougar fidgeted, but he knew the others wouldn't notice. He wasn't of any importance to either of them.

"Yes, it's too bad we'll never know the details." The colonel sighed and went to the window, absently watching a cavalry squad riding past toward the barns. "But what matters is that Bill was well loved and well thought of by the men he served with."

"Yes, sir, my mother treasures the letter his commanding officer sent—and of course, the medals."

Cougar stirred uneasily and looked away. Yes, the major had been well loved. Cougar knew about the major's death—Mac had told him—but the secret was to be kept forever.

The commander continued to stare out the window. "I am in the devil's own country," he said softly, "not a place for civilized men. I don't know why we insist on trying to hang on to this blasted land. We ought to give it back to the Apaches."

"Sir!" Phillip gasped, evidently shocked.

"Forget I said that," the senior officer snapped as he whirled around.

"The Apache think it's a very good idea," Cougar said.

Phillip glared at him. "No one asked you."

The senior officer ignored Cougar's comment.

Cougar frowned. "Permission to speak, sir."

"Yes, what is it?" The officer rubbed his jaw impatiently.

"Everyone knows the Indian agent is crooked and has partners back East. Between them, they are making big profits from selling off the supplies the government sends for the Apache."

"I'll pretend I didn't hear that, scout." The senior officer frowned and dismissed him with a curt nod. "I'm not responsible for the agents or the government program. I'm only responsible for keeping the peace."

"But, sir—"

"Dismissed!" the officer snapped. "Ready your scouts to accompany Lieutenant Van Harrington and his patrol up to Fort Apache."

"Yes, sir." Cougar saluted, ignoring Phillip's pleased grin. It was a long way to Fort Apache. He'd have to be careful and keep an eye on Phillip. He was certain the older man would not be above shooting Cougar in the back—or getting some of his bully boys to do it.

However, the long ride north to Fort Apache was uneventful, although there was Indian sign all along the hostile buttes and ridges, while the drums still echoed without ceasing across the lonely desert. Cougar stayed alert and saw more than one lookout watching the little group as it rode north in the late August heat. The scouts noticed, but Cougar shook his head at them to remain silent. The white men seemed to see little, but then white men missed much of nature and the things that happened around them. As the patrol traveled north, Cougar kept a keen eye on the Apache lookouts who came and went from one bluff to another, fading like ghosts in the shimmering lavender gray of dawns and crimson sunsets.

Cougar kept an eye on Phillip, too, certain that the officer intended to get the scout killed if he had half a chance. For his own part, Phillip ignored him.

They reached Fort Apache and were immediately called into Colonel Carr's office.

The senior officer greeted Phillip warmly, only nodded to Cougar. "At ease, men." To Phillip, he said, "How was the trip up?"

"No trouble," Phillip assured him, pulling at his wispy mustache. "Didn't see a single Indian. I think this whole thing's overblown."

Cougar started to speak, but thought better of it.

Colonel Carr stared at him. "You have something to say, scout?"

"Begging your pardon, sir. I hate to contradict the lieutenant, but the hills were full of lookouts and smoke signals. The soldiers just failed to see them."

Phillip turned an angry red. "Now, see here—"

"He's probably right, Lieutenant." Colonel Carr ran his hand through his graying hair. "That's why the army relies on Indian scouts. You know, about a dozen years ago, I was fighting Cheyenne Dog Soldiers. A bunch of Pawnee scouts led me right to Tall Bull's camp. Because of those scouts, we ambushed the Dog Soldiers and almost wiped them out completely."

Phillip brightened. "Killing Indians; yes, I'd like that! Where was that, sir?"

"Summit Springs, Colorado Territory. Buffalo Bill Cody was along."

"I've heard of him," Phillip said grudgingly. "But surely the army could have handled those Dog Soldiers without Indian scouts—"

"I don't think so." Colonel Carr shook his head. "I always respected my scouts' opinions, so pay attention to what your scouts tell you; they know this country better than you."

Phillip looked furious. "Begging your pardon, sir, I wouldn't put it past these murderous Apaches to lead us right into a trap!"

Cougar's first impulse was to hit Phillip; then he remembered where he was and let his doubled fists drop to his sides.

Colonel Carr stared at Cougar keenly, judging him, but when he spoke, it was to Phillip. "I've heard of your father, Lieutenant, a legend in his time. I hope you can someday fill his shoes."

"I hope so, too, sir, but I'm beginning to wonder if I'll ever be able to live up to everyone's expectations." Phillip frowned. Perhaps he was weary of living in his father's shadow.

"Oh, I'm sure you will; maybe with this next assignment."

"Sir?"

The senior officer smiled and brushed his gray hair back. "Unfortunately, Gatewood is on leave, so you'll be working with Lieutenant Cruse."

Cougar almost groaned aloud. The Apaches all knew and respected Lieutenant Gatewood, whom they called *Bay-chen-daysen*—Big Nose. He did not know this Lieutenant Cruse. He hoped Cruse wasn't as vain and inexperienced as Phillip.

"Lieutenant," Colonel Carr continued, "we are riding

up to Cibecue Creek tomorrow to arrest that old medicine man who's raising such a ruckus."

Phillip smiled. "Excellent!"

Cougar felt the hair rise on the back of his neck. "Sir, the army intends to enter *Noch-ay-del-Klinne's* stronghold?"

"What's the matter—scared?" Phillip sneered.

"Lieutenant, remember your dignity as an officer in dealing with underlings!" Carr chided. Then, in a patronizing tone, he said to Cougar, "I take it that you are questioning my orders?"

Cougar shook his head. "No, sir, I'm questioning the wisdom of whoever gave that order—"

"Of all the audacity—!"

"Silence, both of you!" the senior officer stormed. He looked at Cougar as if he couldn't quite believe Cougar's foolhardiness. "You may continue, scout. I'd like to know why you think West Point's best are such idiots."

Cougar took a deep breath. "Sir, attempting to arrest the holy man might set the whole Territory ablaze. If you could force that Indian agent to give the Apaches their supplies instead of stealing them, and just be patient, the Apache will settle back when none of *Noch-ay-del-Klinne's* visions come true."

"Hmm." Carr chewed his lip thoughtfully. "Then you don't think there's anything to this Ghost Dance thing?"

"Not unless the army tries to put a stop to it," Cougar said.

"Nonsense!" Phillip blurted. "We'll take some troops, ride out there and nip this uprising in the bud!"

The colonel took out a handkerchief and wiped the sweat from his gray mustache. He looked at Cougar. "Can I count on the Apache scouts' loyalty?"

Cougar considered. "Some of our men are brand new and idolize the holy man. It would be best if they weren't put to the test that soon."

"Ye gods," Phillip grumbled, "he's trying to keep from going into battle."

"I've survived more fights than you'll ever see," Cougar snapped, "and I don't ask others to do my fighting for me."

"Silence!" the senior officer thundered. He turned to stare out the window again, his shoulders slumped with the weight of decision. Outside, the soldiers still marched in the late August sun, and the scent of dust and horse sweat rose on the hot air. "I need the scouts," he said finally, "but I'm hesitant to have a troop with me that I'm not sure I can depend on."

"Some of the scouts are very young yet, sir," Cougar said by way of apology, "but they are brave and good fighters."

The colonel paced up and down, his face furrowed with indecision. "And maybe someday they'll get a chance to show that, but I think this is not that time. I've got to talk to Lieutenant Cruse about this, but my heart tells me not to take newly enlisted scouts."

"A man should always listen to his heart." Cougar remembered Mac's words aloud. "Now if I could convince you not to go out to Cibicue at all—"

"You are dismissed, Cougar!" the colonel roared. "The last time I checked, I was still commanding officer here!"

"Yes, sir." Cougar kept his face immobile as he snapped a salute and turned to go. Phillip smiled with pleasure as Cougar turned and strode from the building.

Phillip watched him go, more than a little pleased with himself. "If I may say so, sir, a civilized man should listen to his brain, not his heart. I know you will make the right decision."

The other frowned. "I wish I could be so sure, Lieutenant. Will you take a message to the telegraph for me?"

"Certainly, sir." Phillip reached for a pad and pencil.

The senior officer paced up and down as he considered. "It's to Major General Orlando Willcox, Whipple Barracks, town of Prescott. Stop. Going to Cibecue Creek tomorrow to arrest the medicine man known as *Noch-ay-del-Klinne*. Stop. Question some of my new Apache scouts' loyalties. Stop. Ask permission to leave most of them behind. Stop. Will await your approval. Stop. Best Regards, Eugene Carr." He paused and looked at Phillip. "You get all that?"

"Yes, sir."

"Good. Get it on the wire immediately. Unless I get orders to the contrary, I'll expect I'm supposed to take the scouts."

"Yes, sir." Phillip picked up the pad, saluted smartly, and left the building, snickering as he went. That damned Injun had looked like a fool and Phillip couldn't be in a better position with the colonel. Unlike the senior officer, Phillip had little regard for the fighting abilities of this bunch of scruffy savages, and he intended to win some medals on this campaign. He went immediately to the telegrapher and stood and watched as the soldier sent the message.

"It may take a while, sir, to get an answer back."

Phillip scowled. "It better not take too long," he grumbled, "we're riding out tomorrow, whether we get an answer or not."

"Yes, sir. I'll let you know as soon as I get a reply."

"Do that!" Phillip ordered and strode out of the office. He smiled as he thought of Cougar's bloody and bruised face. This campaign was a perfect time to rid himself of the savage who had dared to look at Phillip's future bride with lust. Indeed, if a battle broke out, who was to say from which direction a bullet came?

Thinking about Elizabeth made him want a woman, any woman. Tomorrow, maybe he would have a chance to kill that impudent Injun. Tonight, maybe he could find a

Mexican whore or an Injun girl working as a maid here at the fort.

He found one, not as pretty as Shashké or as desirable as the red-haired vixen, but available. He met the new slut behind the barracks to slake his lust. And while he took her fast and brutally, he imagined she was Elizabeth Winters and he was enjoying her while Cougar watched in helpless frustration.

At the army post near the town of Prescott, the telegraph key chattered, and the soldier at the desk grabbed a pencil and began to write, then yelled at the man in the outer office. "I've got an urgent message from the commander over at Fort Apache." He handed the young man the paper. "Get this to General Willcox at once and get me an answer."

General Willcox looked up from his meetings with his staff officers as a knock sounded at his door. "Yes?"

The soldier entered, saluted. "Message from Fort Apache, sir."

"At ease." The general took the note and read it. "Hmm. Let me give this some thought." He reread the message, tossed it across the desk to one of his officers. "What do you think?"

The other man read it and shrugged. "Well, Eugene Carr has worked with Indian scouts before; Pawnee, I think. If it's his gut feeling not to trust those green scouts, it just makes sense to leave them behind."

"That's what I thought, too." He turned to the waiting soldier. "Take a message and get it out right away."

The other whipped out a paper and pencil.

"To Colonel Eugene Carr, Fort Apache. Use your own

judgment about including the Apache scouts on your mission. Stop. Signed Major General Orlando Willcox.''

"Yes, sir." The man finished writing, saluted, and left. The senior officer leaned back in his chair and sighed. "Damn, I hope we're not about to get into another Apache war."

"Oh, I don't think so; not once they go out there and arrest that crazy medicine man."

The other nodded and fanned himself with the telegram. "Damned worthless country! Fit only for Apaches and rattlesnakes. We ought to give it back to them and get out."

"I'll pretend I never heard you say that, Willcox." The other man laughed. They both stared out the window at the soldier striding across the parade ground to the telegraph office with the reply.

At that moment, somewhere deep in the wild country between the two locations, an Apache brave climbed a straggly pine tree. The drums had been speaking for days, saying that the white men were increasingly uneasy and afraid. All knew that when white men were unsure, they called to each other on the talking wires to send more troops. If the wire no longer talked, the bluecoats were helpless.

The Apache reached for the sharp skinning knife at his side, cut the humming line, and smiled to himself as it fell. Now the soldiers could not use its magic to send messages. If the white men took to the warpath, they could not call for more soldiers.

The warrior grunted with satisfaction as he climbed down the tree, quick as a bobcat, swung up on his swift spotted pony, and rode back to the Apache stronghold.

* * *

At Fort Apache, within the hour, the telegraph operator was back in Colonel Carr's office. "Pardon me, sir, but for some reason, the telegraph's down. I'm not sure whether our message got there, and I'm not getting anything from them."

The old officer swore under his breath and ran his hand through his gray hair. He wasn't prepared to take the responsibility of making that decision alone, not when he had doubts about the dependability of some of the younger, more inexperienced Apaches. On the other hand, the campaign needed those scouts. If his troop was undermanned and rode into an ambush, he'd catch hell from the big brass for not taking them along. Without an agreement from Willcox, he couldn't share the responsibility; he'd have to make the decision alone.

He clasped his hands behind his back and paced the floor. "I wish Gatewood was back from leave," he muttered. "Cruse and Van Harrington are so inexperienced with Indians."

"Sir?"

He paused. "Never mind. How long will it take to get the wire fixed?"

"We've got to find the damage first, sir."

Oh, hell. He'd have to send out a patrol to find and repair the break. Had it been an accident or a deliberate prelude to a major Apache offensive?

His common sense told him it would take days to repair the telegraph and get authorization. He didn't have that much time before events appeared to be headed for an all-out Indian war. If there was a major outbreak, there'd be hell to pay when the politicians and the newspaper started looking for someone to blame. "Well, keep trying, soldier. Maybe we'll get lucky."

"Yes, sir." The soldier saluted and left.

Colonel Carr paced up and down, staring out at the merciless sun pasted against a still, faded sky. "Damned hot, godforsaken country," he muttered. "Whether I take the scouts or not, I've got to ride out to that Apache stronghold tomorrow!"

Monday, August 29, 1881

It was the palest of lavender dawns, before the sun had even risen above the eastern rim of the hills, when Cougar stuck his head in Colonel Carr's office and saluted. "We're still riding out to Cibecue today?"

"Yes." The officer looked as if he hadn't gotten much sleep. "I haven't heard whether I'm supposed to take the new scouts or not; so I guess I'll take them."

Cougar frowned in disapproval, but it was not his decision to make. Some of the Apache scouts were under twenty years old and had only been with the army a few weeks. "I'm not sure how the green ones will react if there's a fight."

"I have no choice unless I get approval from General Willcox to leave them behind. Besides, not knowing what we're riding into, we may need the extra manpower." His expression said the old officer was troubled, but was weary of discussing it. "We'll be leaving as soon as we can get mounted. You're dismissed."

"Yes, sir." Cougar hesitated, but decided there was no point in arguing with the officer. All he might do was get himself thrown in the guardhouse and he needed to be along on this campaign to see if he could keep the peace and save lives on both sides.

In less than thirty minutes by the sun, Cougar had his

men gathered up and his big paint stallion ready to go. Now he wheeled his horse and cantered toward the white troops. He passed near where Lieutenant Van Harrington was assembling his cavalry and pretended not to see him. Cougar rode back to his troop of scouts and dismounted.

There were twenty-three Apache scouts, a few experienced ones like Sergeant Mose, many of the others new to army life.

"Cougar," the young one called "Skippy" by the whites asked softly, "where are we going?"

"Out to Cibecue Creek." He saw the men exchange doubtful looks and there were expressions of disapproval on some of the brown faces, but no one said anything.

Listen to his heart or his brain? Cougar wished Mac was there to advise him. Well, it was not his decision to make, and he had warned the colonel; he could do no more. It wasn't fair to put new scouts' loyalties to the test this soon, when they might be going up against their own blood kin.

He shrugged and reined in his dancing, restless stallion. Cougar still felt sore and stiff from the beating Phillip and his bullies had given him, and he wasn't at all certain that if Phillip got the chance, he wouldn't put a bullet in Cougar's back. In the meantime, they were facing a long ride, about forty-five miles to the northwest under a broiling August sun.

The sun was just beginning to rise as the troop rode out—Colonel Carr and his Sixth Cavalry, including five officers and seventy-nine enlisted men as well as the twenty-three Apache scouts.

From Cougar's viewpoint as a seasoned scout, this action had "disaster" and "danger" written all over it. He wasn't afraid of the fight—he had numerous battle scars over his muscular body—it was just that he had no confidence in the whites' judgment. He reached up out of long habit to touch his necklace for luck, then remembered. Cursing himself for a fool, he nudged his big horse forward and fell into the line of march over the hot and rocky terrain.

The sun beat down on them pitilessly as they rode, heat waves rising off the barren land. Cougar licked his dry lips and watched the horizon in all directions, wary of a trap, and more wary of Phillip Van Harrington. With all the broken promises the whites had made them, and the way the Indian agent had been cheating them, the Apaches were angry and suspicious.

The troop camped halfway, and the next day rode into the Apache camp on Cibecue Creek, to be greeted with cold and distrustful faces. The colonel signaled Cougar to ride up beside him. "Act as my interpreter. Tell them we have come to arrest *Noch-ay-del-Klinne.*"

"If you please, sir," Cougar cautioned, "it is not good manners to be so abrupt. You should bring out gifts and food, sit down for a long parlay."

At the colonel's other side, Lieutenant Van Harrington said, "If I may be so bold, Colonel, why should we go through all this ceremony? We're just dealing with ragged savages, not Queen Victoria."

"Watch your tone, Lieutenant," Cougar snapped. "They can sense scorn even if they don't understand English. There's respect involved here."

The colonel seemed to think it over even as he looked around the circle. Cougar could tell he had just realized the troop was in the middle of a sizable Apache force. "All right, we'll parlay with them."

Cougar breathed a sigh of relief. Maybe they would get back to the fort with their skins intact after all. Damned if the lieutenant didn't look disappointed. Cougar turned and began preparations for a long parlay.

The two sides talked all afternoon, with the Apache leaders and the frail medicine man protesting that he did not mean to start a fresh war. The soldiers insisted that they only wanted to take him back to the fort and discuss the problem with him. Cougar had second thoughts as he translated.

The old medicine man asked him in their language, "Can I trust the whites?"

Cougar hesitated, torn between loyalties. These were his mother's people, but the other half of him was white. "I am not sure," he said truthfully. "I do not know the one called Carr well, but he wants to avoid bloodshed and war."

Finally, *Noch-ay-del-Klinne* agreed to go back to the fort with the soldiers. Cougar breathed a sigh of relief, but he heard angry muttering among the distrustful Apache.

"What are they saying?" The colonel leaned over to Cougar.

"They don't like it, sir. They're afraid something bad will happen to their holy man once he's in custody."

Phillip snickered. "Now wouldn't that just be too bad."

"Watch your mouth, Lieutenant," the older officer snapped. "I remember when the army tried to take Crazy Horse into custody and killed him right there on the grounds of Fort Robinson. Then we had a Cheyenne war on our hands. I'd like to avoid that here, if possible."

"Yes, sir." Phillip glowered at Cougar; his wispy mustache trembled in rage.

The frail medicine man mounted up and rode out with the soldiers, the watching Apache grumbling louder.

"Whew!" Phillip said to the colonel. "I thought we were going to have to fight our way out of that."

"It isn't over yet," Cougar cautioned. "They might still send a war party after us."

"Oh, they won't do that," Phillip sneered. "They're cowards and they can see how well armed we are."

Cougar gave him a cold look as they rode out. "Lieutenant, believe me, if they come after us tonight, you won't know it until you feel that cold blade slicing through your throat.''

Phillip turned pale and swallowed hard.

Cougar's gut feeling hung over him that whole afternoon as the troop started back toward Fort Apache. Though most of the soldiers seemed oblivious to it, the scouts were aware that they were being trailed by warriors.

That night, as the soldiers made camp, as Cougar had feared, all hell broke loose.

Chapter Eight

Just as Cougar had feared, when the troops bedded down for the night on their way to Fort Apache, the warriors following them attacked, trying to free their medicine man.

Captain Hentig looked about wildly. "What's happening? I thought Apaches wouldn't fight at night?"

"Only in desperation!" Cougar yelled. "A rumor has spread that *Noch-ay-del-Klinne* will be murdered at the fort as Crazy Horse was up north!"

Then there was no more time to talk or reason as the Apaches began firing from the bushes and bluffs around the camp. Yelling confusing orders to the troops, the officers tried to rally the soldiers to make a stand and keep from being overrun, but in the darkness and the noise, no one could bring order to the chaos as they were attacked. Gunfire echoed from both sides, and horses whinnied and reared in terror, throwing their riders. Men ran helter-skelter in the noise and dusty darkness. All about Cougar, men fell bloodied and screaming.

He had to at least get his scouts into a defensive position! Cougar fought his way to his horse while yelling orders to the Apache scouts. Some didn't seem to hear him above the hellish din and echoing gunshots. Others, suddenly thrown into their very first fight, ran about, seemingly confused as to what to do, and loath to fire at their relatives and friends.

As he watched, Captain Hentig clutched his chest and fell with a shriek. Cursing under his breath, Cougar swung up on his paint stallion and galloped into the fray, trying to organize his men to provide cover for the soldiers as they retreated. In the flickering firelight and flashes of gunfire, alkali dust clung to bloody, sweating faces, both white and brown. An Indian scout shouted in pain and went down, caught in the deadly crossfire.

Dirt seemed to grit between his teeth from the clouds of dust, and he could smell the warm blood on the chilly desert night. As Cougar watched, a soldier screamed and fell with bright blood bathing his shiny brass buttons. On the other side, too, warriors chanted war songs that were cut off abruptly as bullets found their mark.

Terrified, Cougar's horse reared and whinnied at the strong scent of blood, gunpowder, and swirling dust. However, Cougar himself was cool and brave under fire, assessing the situation, noting that the troop was surrounded and outnumbered. Maybe if they would free *Noch-ay-del-Klinne* and make an orderly retreat, the Apache wouldn't follow them.

Even as he thought that, he saw Phillip raise his rifle and aim it at the bewildered medicine man. "Damn that Injun for causing all this trouble! I'll fix him!"

"No!" Cougar yelled in protest, knowing that to kill the holy man might seal all their fates, but his shout came seconds too late. *Noch-ay-del-Klinne* clutched his chest, stumbled, and fell in the sand.

Cougar swore loudly, but under the barrage of echoing rifles, he couldn't hear his own words, much less the commanding officer who was out there somewhere in the middle of this firelit hell. At least, maybe he could save a few lives. "Retreat!" he yelled. "Get back where there's more cover!"

However, the soldiers' lines had been breached. In the confusion, instead of a solid line of troops and scouts facing off the warriors, hand-to-hand fighting had broken out, and the young Apache scouts paused uncertainly, looking about. Their relatives and friends were fighting to save the medicine man, who lay on the ground, seemingly wounded but still alive, and they didn't seem to hear Cougar shouting orders.

He groaned aloud as he realized that as he had feared, some of the greenest scouts were now joining up with their kinsmen, enraged over the shooting of the holy man. He still might manage to bring them back to the army's side; the young scouts liked and trusted Cougar. Even as he spurred his horse to ride forward to rally his men, he saw the sudden glint of a rifle barrel and glanced over to see Phillip's grinning face as he looked directly at Cougar, aimed, and pulled the trigger.

For a split second, Cougar's brain denied the action, refused to believe that a cavalry officer would turn his weapon against one of his own men. Even as his brain denied it and he froze in horror, the bullet tore through his right shoulder and almost tumbled him from the saddle. Agony washed over him, causing his own rifle to drop from his nerveless fingers. Cougar managed to hang on to his horse as it reared and snorted. He saw the smile and the glint of triumph in the other's blue eyes and realized, as the lieutenant raised his rifle again, that this time Phillip would kill him!

"No!" Pain almost overpowered him as he clung to his

saddle and fought to stay conscious. In that heartbeat, Cougar realized how badly he'd underestimated both the officer and how much Phillip hated him. And now Phillip was aiming at him again and Cougar was without a weapon, unarmed and defenseless. In that second, he did the only thing he could do to save his life; he urged his horse forward, galloping straight toward Phillip.

His big paint stallion leapt over the lieutenant, and Cougar kicked his weapon aside as he passed him and galloped across the perimeter of the circle. Hostile Apaches were between him and the army lines now, and there was no way to get back through the gunfire to rally the scouts. Worse than that, Cougar was bleeding badly; he felt the warm blood running from his useless arm, dripping onto the saddle, and staining the stallion's spotted coat scarlet.

Now the soldiers were retreating, losing men at every step.

Amazingly, *Noch-ay-del-Klinne* still lived. He crawled forward on his belly, trying to reach safety.

"Ye gods, the bastard's still alive! I'll fix that!" Before anyone could stop him, Phillip grabbed a hatchet, ran forward, and killed the wounded man. Then Phillip stumbled to his feet, shouting and gesturing wildly. "Look, men, Cougar's gone over to the enemy! Get him! Somebody get him!"

Even as Cougar opened his mouth to shout a denial, he saw the glint of rifle barrels as terrified and confused bluecoats turned their weapons toward him. Reeling in the saddle, near fainting from pain and loss of blood, Cougar acted instinctively. Spurring his horse, he turned and galloped out of the melee, many of the confused younger scouts following him. He wasn't certain where he was going; he only knew he had to get out of rifle range!

He could barely sit his horse, and his eyes were almost blinded by a haze of pain and swirling dust churned up by galloping horses and running men. He had to return to his scouts, help save them, let the colonel know he was loyal, that he wasn't a traitor or a deserting coward. Dimly, he clung to his saddle as the paint carried him away from the confusion and bloody battle. Some of the scouts had followed him out of the fray; others were still back there in the fight, Apaches on both sides, some breaking that most ancient taboo, brother killing brother.

He was several hundred yards out into the darkness now, the firing growing dimmer as he struggled to stay conscious. Just what he had warned about had happened with his inexperienced scouts and their divided loyalties. The realization hit him as he fought to stay in the saddle; then darkness claimed him and he knew no more.

When he awakened, it was dark and one of the other scouts had put some herbs on his wound and tied it up to stop the bleeding. In the distance, he heard occasional gunfire. "What—what happened?"

"The army is retreating back to the fort under cover of darkness, with the warriors harrying them," the other said. "There are many dead on both sides."

Cougar groaned aloud. "What about *Noch-ay-del-Klinne?*"

The men around him scowled. "Did you not see the lieutenant finish him off with an axe as one would kill a wounded dog? It is only fitting now that the lieutenant die at the hands of an Apache!"

"Phillip!" Cougar gasped as he struggled to sit up. "He has tried to kill me."

One of the very young runaway scouts, Dead Shot, peered at him hopefully. "Would the colonel understand? Some of us lost our heads in the excitement."

Another asked, "What will the army do to us?"

Cougar didn't speak. He knew what the answer would

be, but yet he could hope. "Maybe the colonel would listen. None of us meant to desert the soldiers and become traitors."

It was ironic, he thought; he, who had tried to help, who had remained loyal, was now a deserter along with these young, green scouts. If only Mac were here to give counsel, Colonel Carr might listen to him.

A scout held a canteen to his lips, and Cougar drank long and deep, relishing the cold, clear water, trying to think of his men's welfare. "When word gets out, the army will send reinforcements. They will hunt us down like coyotes and kill us without mercy."

"You are gravely wounded," a man said. "Shall we take you to the ranch?"

Cougar shook his head. "No, that's the first place the bluecoats will look."

His friend, Turtle, agreed with a nod. "It would bring trouble to the man called McGuire, who is a friend of our people."

"I must ride to the fort and explain to the colonel," Cougar gasped.

Another caught his arm as he tried to stand, keeping him from falling. "You are too weak to ride. We all need time to rest; many are hurt."

There was nothing Cougar could do but agree as the men lowered him to the ground.

"It was the lieutenant who started this," said another, "I saw him shoot our holy man. I saw him try to kill Cougar."

"I doubt the whites will believe that," Cougar whispered with a growing anger.

"Why does the officer hate you so?" one asked.

"I made a gift to his woman and she told him," he admitted bitterly, automatically reaching up to touch the necklace that no longer hung around his massive neck. He had been betrayed by both the red-haired beauty and his own heart. A blind fury began to build in him, fueled by his own stupidity at giving his heart to a white seductress who had laughed and thrown his most precious possession away. Because of the haughty Elizabeth Winters, he could not go back to the bluecoats; no one would believe him. Even if he returned, Phillip would plot to kill him again; he would have to watch his back continually. At the moment, it was a moot point; he couldn't even stand, much less ride.

In the distance, the shots echoed across the barren land as the cool night deepened and the soldiers fought their way back to the fort. Cougar could do nothing but lie there and listen, gritting his teeth against the throbbing pain of his wound. After a while, he drifted into unconsciousness, and in his tortured dreams he saw her face and those bright green eyes. A hatred for the fiery-haired beauty crowded out the passion he had felt for her, and he imagined his big hands on her fragile throat. If he had her at his mercy, there was no end to the things he would do to her!

Days passed as Cougar drifted in and out of consciousness in the cave. Old Owl Woman, the wet nurse who had raised him, came to care for him and brought him news.

"Our warriors harried the soldiers all the way back to the fort, surrounded and attacked it, but the bluecoats sent for reinforcements."

Cougar groaned aloud. "I knew it! A new Apache war is starting!"

The old woman nodded. "Many of the Apaches are on the warpath or have fled the reservation and headed for the old stronghold deep in the mountains of Mexico, where they will be safe from soldier attacks."

"What about my scouts?" He tried to sit up, but she restrained him.

"Some of them went in and surrendered to the soldiers. They are sorry for their actions in the heat of the moment, but the soldiers would not listen and threw them in jail. It is said they will put them on trial."

"By Ussen, if I could only get to that trial to make the whites listen—"

"You think they would?" Her brown face furrowed as she shook her head. "You know the man called McGuire will try to help, but all say it will be useless. Besides, the soldiers are looking for you, too. They call you a traitor."

A traitor. For many years he had faithfully served the white man's soldiers—and now this! If only he could talk to Colonel Carr, if only . . . No, he was still too weak to ride. There was nothing he could do for now. Phillip. Phillip had had a large part in this, and it was all over that red-haired temptress. Cougar's life had been turned upside down and destroyed for love of the girl he called Blaze. As he lay helpless and recuperating, his hatred for the white beauty built until it glowed like a hot flame that consumed him.

Things were very dull in Boston, Libbie thought as she left French class at Miss Priddy's Academy and went to check her mail. It was chilly now that it was late September. President Garfield had died in mid-September after lingering for weeks from the assassin's bullet that felled him in July, and of course plans were under way for a big trial; there seemed to be little else in the newspapers.

Her thoughts went to Arizona, and she wondered what was happening out there. She had written Phillip a polite note when she got back to school, thanking him for a lovely visit. She tried to think of something to say about their coming marriage that was enthusiastic, failed, and finally didn't mention their wedding plans at all. On the other hand, she hadn't received a letter from Phillip since she'd left Fort Grant, and she was torn between relief and worry. *Had she said something to offend him? Did she care?* With Mrs. Everett reminding her often that her inheritance was almost gone, she supposed she should be concerned, but maintaining their present lifestyle seemed much more important to her guardian than to Libbie.

Now here at last was a letter from Phillip in her mailbox. Libbie sighed and stared at the envelope: then she took it up to her room to read.

My Dearest Elizabeth:
    I'm sorry I haven't written sooner, but there has been a terrible outbreak with the Apache here. . . .

Libbie's interest picked up when she saw Cougar's name. By Phillip's account, there had been a mutiny while the army tried to arrest some evil medicine man. The troops had killed lots of savages. Eight soldiers, including a Captain Hentig, had been killed or died later from wounds. He himself had barely escaped with his life while, of course, saving the day for the army. There was some talk of a medal, and wouldn't it look splendid on his dress uniform for the wedding?

Damn Phillip for his shallow arrogance. Libbie sighed and scanned through the rest of the letter quickly. Cougar, that cunning half-breed, had helped lead the rebellion. The medicine man was dead, and some of the scouts who had mutinied had given themselves up or been captured. Of course there were going to be trials for the traitorous Apaches.

Traitors. Libbie reread the whole thing, but the last part was rather vague, and Phillip veered off the subject, talking about a hunting trip he was planning. He hoped to kill another bear and maybe a wolf to stuff for his library back home.

Libbie read the letter again. *Was Cougar one of those being held in jail for trial?* She couldn't be sure. The memory of the man came back to her as if they had met just last night—the touch of his hands on her skin as he placed the necklace around her throat, the torment she'd felt when he stood so close. *Was she out of her mind to be having such fantasies over a half-breed scout in a faraway place?*

Tears came to her eyes as she hurried to take the necklace from where she had hidden it in a box under her bed for safekeeping and away from the curious eyes of her schoolmates. For a long moment, she held it, remembering that night, that man. He had seemed so honorable and protective. *Could he possibly be guilty? What did they do to traitors? Did they hang them?*

Quickly she reached for pen and paper and began to write a note to Phillip, asking for more information about the mutiny. But then she paused and considered. What would Phillip think if she wrote and asked about Cougar? He might be suspicious and jealous. Very slowly, she crumpled the letter and began again in a very casual manner, commending him on the possible medal and asking for further details of the event.

After she mailed the letter, she began watching the newspapers, searching for every scrap of information on that faraway Territory. Arizona might as well be on the moon as far as civilized Boston was concerned, Libbie decided, or at least, it was all being pushed off the pages by earthshaking events such as the death of President Garfield and the coming trial of his assassin.

There was almost no mention of events in Arizona Territory, except that several days later, Henrietta Van Harrington did send her a friendly note telling her Phillip had been transferred back to Fort Grant, along with a clipping from the Philadelphia paper about Phillip's heroism, and how much young Van Harrington was like his father, who, the paper reminded its readers, had been slain in battle by that same tribe of savages almost a quarter of a century before.

Phillip lay back on the straw in the dimly lit barn and reread Elizabeth's letter, then laughed aloud. "Ye gods! She's trying to be so casual, but damn her, she doesn't fool me!"

"Doesn't fool you about what?" Shashké rolled over on him, rubbing her naked breasts against his bare body.

He reached up and caught one of her big breasts in his hand absently. "Nothing that concerns you, my pet."

Her pretty face turned into a pout. He did have to admit she was very arousing with her black hair in a tumble and the fine gold earrings gleaming in the light.

She put the scarlet cactus blossom between her white teeth, playing with it. "It is that red-haired lady again, isn't it? I thought you were going to tell her about us?"

"I am; I am," he lied. "This just isn't the right time yet, that's all." Damn, he was tired of this stupid Injun slut. She was getting too possessive and jealous, threatening to tell the commander and anyone who would listen of their relationship.

"When is the right time?" the slut insisted.

"I don't know. Maybe after the holidays—January, or maybe later."

She brightened. "January, the month of bear tracks. A good omen for me."

He hardly heard her. All he knew was that she was smiling again, which meant maybe she'd let him vent his lust on her nubile body. He pulled Shashké to where he could get his mouth on her breast, and his manhood began to build to hardness again. Yes, he was weary of the slut, but he hadn't figured out how to dump her yet. In the meantime, Elizabeth must think he was pretty stupid himself not to see through that letter. He could read between the lines; she wanted more information about that damned scout's fate. Phillip didn't have any intention of relieving her anxieties. After all, when the army did capture the elusive scout, they were going to hang him, along with those other scouts who had come to the fort after Cibecue to surrender. But first, there had to be the formality of a trial.

Hell, let Elizabeth stew a while and get over her attraction to the scout. After he married her next spring, he'd control her and her fortune. He was looking forward to the use of her beautiful body. He'd do what he damned well pleased with all her wealth, too, and if she complained about anything, he'd beat her senseless.

Shashké nuzzled his ear. "I shouldn't keep meeting you in broad daylight," she murmured. "It makes it easier for my old husband to find out."

What did he care? He rolled her over on her back and made ready to enter her ripe body.

"You don't ever tell me you love me," she complained, trying to wiggle out from under him.

He wasn't going to be stopped now, not when he felt ready to explode with lust. "I love you," he whispered, frantically forcing himself into her before she could change her mind. He had a rich fianceé, a lusty Injun mistress, a possible medal, and his bitter enemy, Cougar, was on the run, being hunted down like a hapless coyote.

"Life can't get any better than this!" he assured himself as he rode Shashké hard and brutally, pretending that it was the genteel Elizabeth Winters. Well, next spring, it would be!

* * *

In the bright moonlight, Cougar noted that the desert nights were turning colder with the coming of autumn. Soon, in the mountains to the north, there would be snow. Cautiously, he rode through the night and reined in, checking for an ambush. Now he whistled a bird song, waited for the answering call. He had to give the signal three times; the old man's hearing was getting worse. When the answering signal came, he nudged his horse through the dark night toward the secret meeting place—his mother's grave.

"Boy? Is that you?"

His heart warmed at the familiar voice. He dismounted and threw his arms around the old man's shoulders. "I've missed you!"

"And me you!" The other stepped back, wiping his eyes awkwardly in the moonlight. "Ever since Turtle came out here to bring me the message that ye were still alive, but wounded, I've been worried to death."

Cougar sat down on a rock. "Have the soldiers been here?"

"Aye, many times. That was why I was afraid to come to ye, afraid they would follow. My eyes and ears aren't what they used to be, I'm afraid."

"Thanks for sneaking us the supplies through Turtle. I knew the lieutenant would watch the ranch, and I did not want to bring you trouble by coming here too soon."

The other man smiled warmly as he lit his pipe. "Ye've been bringing me trouble since the day ye were born, but I wouldn't have traded a minute of all these past years."

Cougar felt his own eyes tear up, and he cleared his throat awkwardly. "What is the gossip at the fort? What has happened to those scouts who surrendered?"

Mac puffed his pipe and avoided Cougar's eyes. "There

was a quick trial, not much of a defense. The poor devils didn't even seem to know what was going on, since none of them speak English."

"Did you speak in their defense?" Cougar asked.

"Ye know I did." Mac nodded and smoked. "But the army thinks of me as the father of the most traitorous half-breed scout, so no one listened."

Cougar swore under his breath. "You know I was no traitor! The lieutenant tried to kill me at Cibecue and my horse bolted, so I ended up outside the army's lines."

Mac shook his head. "I told ye you'd make a bitter enemy of him over that girl."

"Don't even mention that red-haired bitch to me!" He spat to one side with contempt. "So what of my scouts?"

Mac sighed. "Some are being sent away to prison—three of them, unless the new President, Arthur, commutes their sentences, which isn't likely. The army will hang Skippy, Dandy Jim, and Dead Shot at Fort Grant next March."

"Aiyeh!" Cougar agonized for a long moment. "Maybe if I went in, gave myself up, tried to explain—"

"No!" Mac said. "They'd hang you for sure! You dying won't help those poor devils. The whole territory's aflame now with a new Apache war. The only safe haven for any of you is Mexico."

"Those scouts are my men. I've got to try to save them."

"Cougar"—the old man laid his hand on the broad, scarred shoulder—"ye can do nothing more for them. I'll try to send messages by Turtle if anything changes. I'd advise ye to get yourself a woman, cross the border, and try to make a new life for yourself."

He thought of the flame-haired beauty who had scorned his humble gift. "There's only one woman I want."

Mac sighed. "Aye, and you're a fool to want what ye can never have! Don't waste your heart on a girl whose love belongs to someone else."

"You're a fine one to be giving advice," Cougar said pointedly. "I'm only doing what you did."

"Aye, and you see what it brought me." The old man smoked and peered with dimmed eyes at the grave.

"Would you do any differently if you had it to do over again?"

Mac smiled slowly and blinked back the sudden moisture in his eyes. "You know I wouldn't. The little time she was mine was worth the heartache." He stood up and handed Cougar a bundle. "Here, I've got a few supplies for you. Not much—a little meat, some matches, a blanket."

"Thanks." He took the bundle and they embraced one last time. "May Ussen look after you."

"I'm not the one in danger," Mac cautioned. "You be careful now. Phillip's at Fort Grant and there's talk of a big promotion for him next spring for his gallantry at Cibecue."

"Gallantry?" Cougar snorted. "He caused the trouble."

Mac shrugged. "You know how the army works; they're very good at covering up their mistakes."

Cougar stared at the grave. "So you've told me."

"Sometimes there's no harm in it if the truth would cause pain."

Cougar looked at him a long moment, loving him so much that for a moment he could not speak. "You have an Apache heart, you know that?"

Mac blinked rapidly and cleared his throat. "So your people tell me. Good-bye, boy. I'm not much on religion, but I'll pray for you."

"Pray for Phillip," Cougar said through clenched teeth, "he's going to need it!"

Mac shook his head. "You can't."

"I know." Cougar nodded as he swung up on his paint stallion. "But such evil cannot go unpunished."

"Then let Ussen punish him," Mac said.

Cougar nodded. "But if that arrogant white girl ever comes here again, I will have my revenge! There is nothing I wouldn't do to her for the way she has scorned and humiliated me!"

"Then I'll pray she never comes to Arizona again."

Cougar didn't answer as he wheeled his horse and galloped away.

Mac waved and watched Cougar ride out, wishing he could take the burden of a broken heart from him. He watched until the silhouette was swallowed up by the night shadows. Then Mac turned to the grave and remembered the past. "Ah, me gentle beauty, how I miss you! He's grown up now; you'd be so proud!"

Somewhere in the darkness, a night bird called as if answering his lonely voice. Mac swallowed the big lump that threatened to choke him as he recalled the terrible, terrible night she died. It hadn't been his name she had called out in her last moments.

Chapter Nine

As autumn deepened, the days and weeks seemed to crawl past for Libbie in Boston. As Christmas approached, her guardian and Mrs. Van Harrington corresponded frequently about wedding plans and met several times, although Libbie seemed so casual about it all to her guardian that Mrs. Everett reprimanded her privately when Libbie went to her town house for tea. "We must hook this young man! I'm going to be spending the last of your inheritance on this big wedding!"

"What would happen if I changed my mind?" Libbie said idly, looking out the window at the barren trees swaying in the icy wind and remembering the golden warmth of Arizona.

"My stars! Bite your tongue!" Her plump guardian paled and wheezed hard. "You'd have to go to work like some shopgirl, and then what would happen to poor me?"

"You might have to go to work, too," Libbie said.

The other drew herself up proudly. "I am a lady!" she

announced with a superior sniff, "I wasn't cut out to be some parlor maid or seamstress; that's for immigrants and the lower classes!"

Libbie bit her lip and didn't say anything. She looked out the window at the cold, feeling very much alone as she remembered other holidays with her parents—and the warmth of Arizona and a big man's arms last summer.

Obviously taking silence for meekness, the older woman changed the subject. "Have you been writing Phillip regularly so he won't forget you?"

"Some," Libbie murmured. "I've been so busy with my studies."

"Hmm." The stout lady looked unimpressed. "And have you heard from young Phillip lately?"

"More than I've written him. He's terribly busy, I suppose. There's trouble with the Apache attacking outlying posts and ranches ever since that Cibecue thing. He's gotten a commendation for that and is hoping to be promoted to captain, as well as getting a medal."

"Well, I've got a surprise for you!" Her guardian fanned herself briskly. "We've been invited to spend the Christmas holidays at the Van Harrington mansion. You know, we've hardly seen their home; she's always come here to work on wedding plans."

"Oh." *Damn. She hoped Phillip wasn't coming in on leave.* On the other hand, if he were, she might hear details of a certain big half-breed.

"Well!" Mrs. Everett huffed, "you don't seem very excited about the prospect."

"It's just that Phillip surely won't be there." Libbie tried to cover her lack of interest. "With all that trouble with the Apaches, I'm sure he can't get leave right now."

"Arizona. Apaches. My stars! Do you realize how often you mention that horrid place and those half-naked savages?" Her guardian snapped.

"I was just thinking of Phillip," Libbie said, reaching for her coat. She hadn't realized until now just how often that faraway place was on her mind. And Phillip was her only link to that place. She wondered suddenly if she might have a letter in her box at school. "I must be getting back," she said, "to work on my needlework and knitting." Libbie hated doing fancy needlework, but all genteel young ladies were expected to be accomplished in it.

"Just make your plans for Philadelphia," the plump lady reminded her, "and for heaven's sake, be sweeter to Mrs. Van Harrington and more enthusiastic about the wedding."

"Yes, of course." Libbie straightened her hat and hurried out the door to the carriage. With any luck, there might be a letter from Phillip. His last letter had said the traitorous Apache scouts had been sentenced to hang, but there was a possibility of appeal. Mac McGuire would do something, she thought—surely he wouldn't let his half-breed son go to the gallows!

The holidays at the Van Harrington mansion turned out to be a disaster as far as Libbie was concerned. The weather turned especially cold and miserable, and as she and her guardian alighted from the carriage at the mansion, Libbie's heart sank. "It looks like a dreary old castle," she muttered, staring up at the gray stone turrets.

"Behave yourself, young lady!" her guardian snapped. "It's a fashionable mansion that has been in the Van Harrington family for several generations. They are old Philadelphia society, you know, and very, very respectable."

Libbie gathered up her skirts off the dirty snow as the coachman came around to help them with their luggage. Possibly she would become mistress of this dungeon upon her marriage to Phillip, but she wasn't looking forward to it.

The door opened and Mrs. Van Harrington came sweeping out, lean and grim, still dressed in widow's black, although Major Van Harrington had been dead a quarter of a century. "Ah, my dears! You're here earlier than I expected! Do come in!"

She bustled about, snapping orders to meek and trembling maids who came out the door to help with the luggage. Libbie tried to smile and let her future mother-in-law embrace her and plant a dry, cold kiss on her cheek. Mrs. Van Harrington's thin lips smiled, but her cold gray eyes did not. Again, Libbie was certain that she would be making a mistake to marry into this family.

She must stop thinking like that; of course she was going to marry Phillip. Her inheritance was almost gone and what would a genteel lady do without money? Somehow, the idea of going to work didn't frighten her as much as it did her plump guardian, but then, what kind of position could Libbie hold with a knowledge of French, playing the violin and not very good needlework? Perhaps a governess? With a sigh, she followed the two other women into the house and prepared her mind for a long, dull holiday.

She was not disappointed. Inside, the house was as grim and foreboding as Mrs. Van Harrington herself. The lady ruled the mansion with an iron hand, and Libbie had a feeling she wasn't about to give up control to a very young daughter-in-law. The assorted nieces, nephews, old-maid sisters, and cousins who came for the holiday were as hostile to her as possible, except they did seem to have an unusual interest in Libbie's financial holdings, which puzzled her. She brushed all questions aside with vague answers, hoping the women of that family didn't suspect Libbie was almost broke and marrying Phillip for the security of the Van Harrington fortune.

Even a Christmas tree didn't seem to cheer up the grim, dreary mansion as the holiday progressed. Looking about, the place seemed a trifle threadbare to her, but perhaps they were only old-fashioned and very conservative with their spending. Mrs. Everett was delighted with everything, already picturing herself ensconced in cozy large rooms of her own in the mansion, no doubt enjoying ordering the maids about and living a life of ease.

On the second afternoon she was there, Libbie discovered the library. On its wall were dozens of pictures of the late major at various stages of his life. Libbie studied the photos, wondering about the man. In the earlier ones, he looked fairly happy, but as the photos aged, there was something sad and haunting about those bright blue eyes.

Mrs. Van Harrington came into the library. "Wasn't William a handsome man?"

Libbie nodded, still looking at the photos. "He looks like Phillip with those wide shoulders and that strong jaw."

"Doesn't he, though?" she said proudly, picking up a small, silver-framed photo from the desk. "You'll have such handsome sons, my dear."

Sons sired by Phillip. She pictured herself naked in bed with Phillip . . . No, she didn't like that thought at all. She stared at the photos again, then blinked. *Was she out of her mind?* The thought that had just crossed her mind was simply too outrageous. To banish it, she turned and smiled at the lady. "You must have loved him very much."

"I did. Oh, we had some problems, as all young couples do, but we adored each other. Now I lavish all my love and attention on our son."

A mama's boy. Libbie had sensed that from the first.

Henrietta still stared at the old photo. "William died a hero, you know, killed by those terrible savages out there where Phillip is now. I've seen to it that my son doesn't forget he must avenge his father's death. He was only four when his father was murdered."

"Yes, I know," Libbie said softly, "Phillip told me." She looked around at the other pictures. In them all, Henrietta Van Harrington was smiling; William was not. There was something tragic about his expression. Maybe the marriage hadn't been as happy as Mrs. Van Harrington thought.

"Well, enough of these sad thoughts." The lady put the photo back on the desk. "I shan't wear black to the wedding, of course, but you know, I've spent my whole life mourning William. Now his son, my precious boy, is my whole life, my only reason for living."

A warning bell went off in Libbie's head. She was going to have to compete with her mother-in-law for Phillip's love and attention. She realized she didn't much care. "I think I hear guests arriving." She turned, relieved to be able to exit gratefully.

"Yes, we must join them." The other woman lifted her skirts and started for the door. "All my dear friends want to meet you. I've been in such deep mourning, my dear, I haven't redecorated in many years. Since you'll be living here, after the wedding, we must redecorate. I've already chosen the wallpaper and fabrics."

Libbie set her jaw. *Damn. So she wasn't to have a home of her own. Well, what had she expected from a mama's boy?* "As the future mistress of this house, shouldn't I do that?"

The other turned and smiled ever so slightly, but there was no warmth in the cold gray eyes. "I'm sure you will like what I've chosen."

Her tone was almost a challenge, and Libbie was about to rise to it when she remembered Mrs. Everett's dour warning about how close they were to being penniless. "Of course," Libbie managed, swallowing a protest, "I'm sure I shall."

With a sinking heart, Libbie realized what she'd always

suspected was true; Mrs. Van Harrington did not plan to give up control of either the money, the house, or the son. She expected—no, would demand—a pliant, meek daughter-in-law to produce heirs for the Van Harrington fortune. She felt like the proverbial lamb being led to the slaughter. But that was not a good comparison; Libbie was anything but meek!

Mrs. Everett dropped her powder keg in late February. First, Libbie received a hastily written note from her by messenger saying there was something very important to discuss. Mrs. Everett asked her to please come to tea that afternoon and make herself as beautiful as possible. Libbie stared at the note with a sigh.

Was Phillip in town? If so, wouldn't he have let her know? Maybe his mother was visiting to finalize all the nuptial plans. Libbie had a beautiful, extravagant wedding dress, bought with almost the last of the inheritance. If this wedding didn't go through, Mrs. Everett had warned her, they were both going to be selling apples on the street. That, Libbie thought as she began to dress, seemed more and more desirable rather than becoming mistress of that graystone dungeon.

Libbie put on a beautiful green-velvet walking suit that brought out the color of her eyes and added a wonderful matching hat with perky feathers as she made ready for the visit to her guardian's town house. She had been saving a little money here and there since before the Christmas holidays, but it wasn't much; certainly not enough to finance her escape from this straitlaced school and that very respectable marriage. All the other girls had been congratulating her on her nice catch.

Now she called for a carriage and arrived on a snowy, cold afternoon at her guardian's place. *I'll wager it's warm in Arizona, and I hate the cold,* she thought as she stood shivering on the doorstep and rang the bell.

"Do come in." Mrs. Everett, wearing an oppressive dark-olive dress, opened the door and caught her hand. "Something terrible has happened!"

"Phillip's changed his mind?" She tried to sound worried as she entered, but felt relief instead.

"My stars! No, worse than that!" She closed the door against the cold wind and motioned Libbie to a chair. "Sit down. Let me get you some tea." The plump woman waddled away and returned with a tray of dainty cups, steaming with the hot brew, and a plate of sugar cookies.

Libbie sipped the steaming tea gratefully, savoring the bracing warmth. "I am so tired of the cold weather; too bad the Van Harringtons don't live farther south."

"Are you not listening to me?" Mrs. Everett scolded. "I said something terrible has happened!"

"Are you ill? Has someone died—?" Libbie began.

"Worse than that! The Van Harringtons have no money!" The lady leaned back in her chair and reached for her smelling salts, fanning herself all the while.

"What?" Libbie paused with her tea cup halfway to her lips.

"That's what I said!" The lady warmed to her tale, evidently pleased at catching Libbie off guard. "When we were there at Christmas, I became suspicious because everything seemed so threadbare, so I began making inquiries. The Van Harringtons have gone through their fortune— bad investments and Phillip's wastrel ways before he went off to the army. That's why he went out of his way to get an introduction to you at that ball; he's a fortune hunter!"

Libbie paused and let the words sink in. Then she put down her cup, threw back her head, and began to laugh.

"Libbie, what is the matter with you? Have you taken leave of your senses?"

"Don't you see?" Libbie wiped her eyes and laughed some more. "The joke's on us; we were after money, too."

"This is not funny!" She fanned herself rapidly. "I can already see us both working as shopgirls. I've contacted Mrs. Van Harrington and broken the engagement in no uncertain terms."

"It might have been nice if someone had let Phillip and me make the decision," Libbie said sarcastically. "Do they know we're broke, too?"

"No, thank goodness, so we can start looking for a more suitable match right away."

Libbie began to laugh again, partly from sheer relief. "I don't have to marry Phillip Van Harrington?"

"Stop laughing! This is serious! We'll be out of money by this summer, and if you aren't engaged by then—"

"Suppose I say no?" Libbie snapped.

"Of course you can't say no." The other looked at Libbie as if she'd lost her mind. "What is a well-bred young lady to do except marry well?"

"I just might decide to go West; I really liked it there."

"Now I know you've lost your mind." Her guardian looked sympathetic. "Poor child, I know this is a great shock, but I've been thinking ahead."

"For just once, I'd like to make some of my own decisions."

"Don't get sassy with me, young lady!" Mrs. Everett shook her plump finger in Libbie's face. "I promised your dear mother I'd look after you—"

"Why have I always had the feeling that you were really looking after the Winters fortune?" Libbie was annoyed enough now to say what she'd been thinking for a long time. "And I'm sure Daddy left plenty of money; I can't imagine why we've run out."

Mrs. Everett's heavy jowls turned a mottled red. "How

dare you? Are you suggesting I've wasted or misappropriated your inheritance?''

"You tell me!" Libbie glared back at her.

Her guardian did not meet her eyes, hesitating uncertainly. "Why, you ungrateful, spoiled—!"

"So it's true!" Libbie fired back.

"So I played a little whist and tried to make a few investments; I was only trying to help," Mrs. Everett said self-righteously.

"So you've helped me right to the poor house!"

"This is no time to panic," the stout lady declared, fanning herself. "There are other fortunes to be had."

"What? Whatever are you talking about?"

About that time, the doorbell rang and Mrs. Everett looked relieved as she stood up.

Libbie blinked. "Are you expecting someone?"

"A possible suitor." Mrs. Everett smiled and waddled toward the door. "That's why I asked you to look beautiful."

"Damn! You've made all these arrangements without even asking?" Libbie was aghast.

Her guardian paused with her hand on the doorknob. "Well, we've got to do something drastic before the money runs out."

Libbie stood up. "I don't want to meet another suitor. I'll go out the back door."

The doorbell rang again.

"Sit still and behave yourself like a proper lady!" Mrs. Everett commanded even as she opened the door. "Well, Mr. Higginbottom, so nice of you to come!"

Higginbottom? She wasn't about to marry someone named Higginbottom, but it was too late to escape the introduction.

"My dear lady," she heard a quavering voice from the front porch say, "I was so pleased to be invited to meet your ward."

The two came into the room and Libbie stared, speechless.

"Libbie, my dear, may I present a dear old friend, Mr. Ebenezer Higginbottom."

Old was right. He was balding, very plump, and bandy-legged. He could easily have been Libbie's father. Or maybe even her grandfather. Suddenly, being penniless didn't seem like such a bad alternative after all.

"Charmed, my dear." He took her limp hand in his and kissed it. "Mrs. Everett didn't exaggerate your beauty."

Mrs. Everett glared at her. "Where are your manners, Libbie?"

"I'm pleased to make your acquaintance," Libbie said automatically, staring at him. His false teeth didn't fit well and they clicked when he opened and closed his mouth. However, there was no doubt he was prosperous; a big gold watch chain hung across his brocade vest, and his clothes were of the finest fabric.

"I am sorry to hear of your broken engagement," he said with great sympathy, but his nearsighted vision seemed to be focused on her breasts.

"That young cad misrepresented himself!" Mrs. Everett sniffed. "He was only a cheap fortune hunter, after my ward's inheritance."

Mr. Higginbottom leaned even closer to Libbie, absolutely leering at her. "You won't have that problem with me, my dear. I am one of the richest men in Boston; only the Shaws and the Van Schuylers are as substantial as I am."

Mrs. Everett beamed. "Yes, we met your partner in Arizona. You remember Mr. Tiffany, the Indian agent, don't you, Libbie?" she prompted.

Tiffany? Oh, yes, the crook who was getting rich cheating the Apaches with the help of dishonest partners back east. So this was one of the partners.

Her guardian took the caller's hat. "Do let me get you some tea, Ebenezer. Would you like something more substantial than a cookie? Perhaps a sandwich—?"

"Oh, dear me, no." He dismissed the offer with a shaky hand. "Too much meat is bad for my gout."

He was still staring at Libbie's bosom as Mrs. Everett poured his tea. "Yes, she is as lovely as you told me, Mrs. Everett."

Libbie crossed her arms over her chest and looked about as if to escape. She wasn't quite sure what she was expected to say.

"And she plays the violin and does needlework," Mrs. Everett volunteered.

"Good! A wife in my social position needs skills like that. Of course, I certainly would like some heirs." He grinned wickedly and Libbie stared back at him, imagining herself in bed naked with this old man. It was a worse image than sleeping with Phillip.

"I really need to be getting back to school," Libbie said and stood up.

Her guardian shot her a look like a dagger. "Must you, my dear? I'm sure Ebenezer would like to know more about you."

He was looking at her breasts again. "I think I know all I need to know," he lisped as his teeth clicked. "My dear, you're evidently a lovely young lady very soon to graduate from a good school, and I am a man in need of a wife. At my age, I don't see any reason to be coy about this."

Mrs. Everett smiled. "It might be a little unusual, but perhaps we could plan something for this summer."

"I must be getting back," Libbie said, a little desperately now.

Mr. Ebenezer Higginbottom stood and made a courtly bow. "I am at your service, my dear, and hoping to know you better soon."

"Perhaps you can take Libbie driving this weekend," Mrs. Everett suggested, "and show her your estate."

The old man's false teeth clicked as he nodded. "Splendid idea! I have a fine coach and the best matched set of carriage horses in town."

"I'll think about it." Libbie said and, grabbing her coat, hurried out the door.

Mrs. Everett called after her. "I'll send you a note, my dear."

Libbie didn't look back as she fled back to Miss Priddy's school.

What to do? She was out of the frying pan and into the proverbial fire. Or rather out of Phillip's bed and into Ebenezer's. Libbie shuddered at the thought. Phillip seemed almost appealing by comparison with the rich old geezer Mrs. Everett had found to replace him. She stopped to check her box for mail and found a letter from Phillip. She couldn't help but smile at the irony of it all; two penniless people trying to marry a fortune, and they had both been outfoxed.

She went to her room, sat on her bed, and read the letter. Evidently he hadn't heard that his duplicity had been discovered, because he opened with "Dearest Girl" and told her how much he and Mother were looking forward to the wedding this summer.

What caused Libbie to stop smiling was his last line:

. . . They'll be hanging three of the traitorous Apache scouts at Fort Grant the first week of March. Two others have been sent to prison. I'll be at Fort Grant as part of my duties to witness the executions, of course. The army is beefing up security, expecting that all these savages on the warpath might try to rescue the condemned men. I hear hanging's an awful death; you'll be fortunate not to have to watch. . . .

She paused and reread the letter, searching for the names of the condemned scouts. They hadn't seemed important enough for him to mention. Libbie dropped the letter from nerveless fingers.

Why did she have a terrible premonition that Cougar was thinking of her, as she was of him, at this very minute? Was it because their souls had seemed to speak to each other in that brief moment when he had bestowed his necklace on her? Was the army going to hang the scout who had put the beautiful Apache Tears on her throat and touched her so gently?

"Oh, please, no!" With a cry, she retrieved the necklace from its hiding place and sat holding it with tears dripping down her face. She touched each stone, remembering the warm caress of his fingers on her throat, and the sudden scary desire she had felt as he stood close to her. She had never felt that emotion before.

Now they were going to kill him and Phillip was going to watch; no doubt eager to give her the details later, even though gentlemen never told anything gory or shocking to a lady. She had a sudden feeling Phillip would relish telling her the details; he had seemed to dislike the scout so.

What could she do to help Cougar, especially thousands of miles away in this dreary frozen city? She rose and searched out the small purse she had hidden in her chest. After she counted the money in it, she sighed. There were only a few dollars, perhaps enough for a train ticket and a stagecoach one way. If she made this trip to Arizona, she couldn't get back.

Abruptly, she raised her chin and took a deep breath. She was tired of the life she was living and weary to death of her greedy guardian. Money had never mattered to Libbie. At that moment, she decided she wasn't coming back, not ever, no matter what happened. She'd rather take her chances in that exciting new Territory, taking charge of her own life rather than live a meek, safe existence as the rich Mrs. Ebenezer Higginbottom. Libbie shuddered at that thought.

She began to pack, making sure she included the necklace of Apache Tears. She wasn't taking much and she wasn't sure what she was going to do when she got to Fort Grant except try to save the Apache scout from the gallows. How she might accomplish that, Libbie hadn't the faintest idea; but she was desperate enough to try anything. She didn't look back as she grabbed her small valise, her reticule, and ran out the door. If nothing else, she wanted to see Cougar one last time before they hanged him!

Chapter Ten

February 28, 1882

Phillip felt happy as he crossed the parade grounds at Fort Grant. It was still chilly, but soon it would be spring. Because of his gallantry at Cibecue he had been offered a reassignment to an important post in Washington, D.C., where he might further his political ambitions. Then, with his bride's wealth, family prestige, and beauty, he was certain his future had nowhere to go but up!

However, he hadn't yet gotten his full measure of revenge against the damned Apaches, especially the one called Cougar, so he had delayed accepting the new post until late spring. Besides, he wanted to be present at the hangings. Phillip grinned with anticipation at the thought.

Yes, he was going to get to see that red-skinned trio dancing on air! His only regret was that Cougar wasn't among the condemned men. He scowled at the thought of the hated half-breed, who had gone on to leading war parties all over the Territory, raiding for food and supplies for those damned starving Apaches. He and his warriors struck like lightning, took horses and cattle, and then were swallowed up by the vast desert and buttes of this godforsaken land.

Well, with new reinforcements now combing all of northeastern Arizona Territory, it was only a matter of time before the red devil was captured, and Phillip hoped to be the one to pull the trap when they hanged Cougar, so it was worth it to delay his assignment to Washington.

Phillip's biggest problem now was Shashké who was making more and more demands on him, perhaps suspecting that he would soon be leaving and had no intention of taking her with him. He was tired of the sulky girl, and besides, he'd just noticed a sergeant's lusty daughter and was hoping to make a new conquest.

As he sauntered across the parade ground, a soldier ran up to him and saluted. "Telegram, sir, from your mother."

Phillip saluted carelessly and walked toward his barracks reading the wire.

Problem has arisen. Stop. Secret discovered. Stop. Engagement broken and Libbie has disappeared. Stop. Letter following. Stop. Love, Mother.

Ye gods! What could have happened? Maybe Elizabeth had found out about Shashké. Phillip crumpled the paper in his hand and considered. *Secret discovered.* Oh-oh. That high-and-mighty little society bitch had found out the Van Harringtons were penniless! Now he would never get his hands on the Winters fortune or get that temptress in his bed and at his mercy. He had planned all sorts of erotic pleasures once she was legally his.

Where could Libbie have gone? More important, could he find her and sweet-talk her out of breaking the engagement? To lose both her money and the pleasure of taking her virginity was unthinkable! However, with the hanging only days away, he couldn't get a furlough right now to deal with this. He wished he had more details, but with the Injuns harassing the mail and attacking supply caravans, it might be weeks before he got his mother's letter. He considered sending a telegram, then immediately shook his head. He certainly didn't want to wash the family laundry via the telegraph where all the fort would find out about it. *What to do?*

Phillip started walking again, thinking hard. Until he knew more, he couldn't plan a course of action. He paused and pulled at his skimpy mustache. Whatever it took, he was looking forward to bedding the beautiful redhead, and he wasn't about to lose all that dowry!

March 3, 1882, dawned cold and gray at Fort Grant. Phillip Van Harrington snapped to attention in front of his line of troops as the senior officers came out of the building and walked down the line of soldiers lined up on the parade ground. They paused before him and Phillip saluted.

"At ease, Lieutenant." The older man looked up and down at Phillip's troops. "Any sign of trouble?"

"No, sir, we've got plenty of reinforcements; the Apaches won't try to rescue them."

The other sighed and pulled out his pocket watch. "Damned sorry business."

"If you say so, sir." Phillip wasn't shedding any tears over three stupid Apaches. He looked toward the new gallows standing starkly against the coming chill dawn.

"I was hoping for a last-minute reprieve from the President," the senior officer muttered, following Phillip's gaze toward the gallows.

Phillip didn't say anything. He was delighted they were going to hang those three Injun scouts. He only regretted he could not witness hanging a lot more Apaches—particularly Cougar.

The senior officer looked around at the assembled troops and the civilians and dignitaries assembled on the parade ground in the cool morning wind. "Then we'll get on with it." The officer strode toward the jail behind the gallows.

Phillip yawned and wished this thing was over so he could go have another cup of coffee. He had already asked for a furlough to go help in the search for Elizabeth, but the senior officer had seemed preoccupied and waved Phillip out of his office.

He shifted his weight from one foot to the other as they all waited for the condemned men to be brought out. Damn the stubborn, spoiled little red-haired wench! He could only hope to find her and sweet-talk her into marriage. If so, once the knot was safely tied, he'd wear out his quirt on her little backside to turn her into a subservient and obedient wife. He listened to the flag on the parade ground flap in the cold wind and wished the officers would get it over with.

From the top of a distant hill, Cougar and his warriors sat their horses and watched the parade ground with its soldiers and crowds of curious white settlers. "We must attack the fort and save them."

"Are you mad?" asked Turtle. "Look at the number of extra bluecoats today. Not one of us would get out alive."

Cougar frowned. "What you say is true, but we must do something!"

"The three would not want our whole band wiped out in a rescue attempt," said the old warrior to his left.

In helpless frustration, Cougar clenched his fists and watched the scene below. The three scouts were being led from the jail in chains, armed soldiers surrounding them. Out on the parade ground, extra soldiers from other forts stood in formation with weapons at the ready. Cougar reached for his rifle.

Another warrior frowned. "What is it you do?"

"They would rather die by a friend's merciful bullet than be strangled like puppies with a string."

"The distance is too far."

Cougar brought his rifle up to his shoulder and sighted. The other brave was right; the condemned trio was out of rifle range. Dandy Jim, Skippy, and Dead Shot walked with dignity toward the gallows, heads high. Such silly names, soldier names, for three good warriors. Even Cougar couldn't remember their Apache names, he thought now as he watched with a heavy heart. He could see the heavy chains on the scouts' wrists and ankles, and the wind carried the faint clang of metal to his ears. *Did he only imagine he saw Phillip Van Harrington in that formation of soldiers standing at attention on one side of the parade grounds? He couldn't be sure.*

The trio of hapless Apaches stumbled as they walked, their heavy chains dragging as they were led toward their deaths. There seemed to be hundreds of bluecoats standing in the parade ground, their brass buttons and rifles catching the first faint light.

As Cougar and his men watched from their hilltop, the condemned men trudged up the steps to the gallows and the padre stepped forward. The three looked confused as they surveyed the huge crowd that had come to watch. One stared stoically straight ahead; one watched the ropes swing in the wind. One glanced up toward the hilltop, and his gaze seemed to lock on Cougar's.

That silent appeal wrenched at Cougar's heart. He

shoved his rifle back in the scabbard. "We must do something to stop this!" He spurred his horse forward.

However, even as he did so, old Beaver Skin reached out and hit him across the back of the head with the butt of his pistol.

With a groan, Cougar slid from his horse. The big paint snorted and reared, then settled down and nuzzled his fallen master.

The old warrior looked down at Cougar's prone form with a sigh. "You are a very brave man, Cougar," he said, "but we cannot save our three friends today. We must leave them to our god, Ussen. Our warriors will live to fight another day and woe be to the bluecoats!"

Phillip had the most uncomfortable feeling that he was being watched by silent eyes, but the parade ground was quiet except for the jangle of the leg chains on the condemned men and an occasional cavalry horse stamping its hooves. The priest had stepped forward to speak to the three Apaches. To Phillip, the three looked confused and bewildered, as if they weren't quite sure why they, who had scouted for the bluecoats, were now going to be killed in this most horrible manner.

Ye gods, why did they have to drag this out? Couldn't they just hurry up and get it over with so everyone could go have a nice breakfast? Phillip shifted his weight impatiently and stared at the scouts. He had forgotten how young the condemned Apaches were, not much more than boys. They looked pale but composed as the ropes were put over their heads and adjusted. Phillip imagined slipping one of those same nooses over Cougar's head and smiled at the thought. Now the black hoods were going over their heads and the minister was praying aloud.

Phillip glanced around in curiosity. Some of the soldiers

who had liked the three scouts looked grim and pale. He wondered for a moment if any of the three had wives and families. Injuns bred like animals with no more attachment to each other than coyotes; the wives would find other mates. Phillip wondered idly if any of the about-to-be-widowed Apache girls was pretty. Maybe he could fill in the void for the grieving widows.

The officer on the platform was reading the official verdict and sentence. He was reading in English, of course. No doubt the condemned men couldn't understand a word of it. The wind carried away the words, and they could hardly be heard anyway over the flag snapping in the early morning wind. Finally the officer stepped back.

Damn, that wind was cold for this part of the country! Phillip shivered and watched the gallows, willing this thing to be over so he could retreat inside for some coffee. There was a long pause, broken only by the cold March wind and a horse shaking its head, rattling the metal on its bridle.

Then an official stepped forward and sprang the trap. Around him, Phillip heard a collective gasp from some of the soldiers who were seeing men die for the first time. For less than a heartbeat, the bodies fell, then hit the end of the ropes with loud thumps.

Phillip smiled to himself as he watched the limp bodies swing at the ends of the ropes. Settlers were turning away, their faces pale and sick. Around him, he heard soldiers swallowing hard, as if they were nauseated. Phillip felt only a grim satisfaction. This would teach other Injuns not to revolt against their white masters. Three wasn't much of a payback for Major Van Harrington's death, but Phillip intended there would be more before he was finished. Next time, he vowed, it would be that damned Cougar. Who was it who said that the only good Indian was a dead Indian? Well, there were three mighty good Indians at Fort Grant this morning!

To start your membership, simply complete and return the Free Book Certificate. You'll receive your Introductory Shipment of 3 FREE Zebra Contemporary Romances, you only pay $1.99 for shipping and handling. Then, each month you will receive the 3 newest Zebra Contemporary Romances. Each shipment will be yours to examine FREE for 10 days. If you decide to keep the books, you'll pay the preferred subscriber price (a savings of up to 20% off the cover price), plus shipping and handling. If you want us to stop sending books, just say the word… it's that simple.

FREE BOOK CERTIFICATE

Yes!

Please send me 3 FREE Zebra Contemporary romance novels. I only pay $1.99 for shipping and handling. I understand that each month thereafter I will be able to preview 3 brand-new Contemporary Romances FREE for 10 days. Then, if I should decide to keep them, I will pay the money-saving preferred subscriber's price (that's a savings of up to 20% off the retail price), plus shipping and handling. I understand I am under no obligation to purchase any books, as explained on this card.

Name _____

Address _____ Apt. _____

City _____ State _____ Zip _____

Telephone (___) _____

Signature _____

(If under 18, parent or guardian must sign)

Offer limited to one per household and not to current subscribers. Terms, offer and prices subject to change. Orders subject to acceptance by Zebra Contemporary Book Club. Offer Valid in the U.S. only.

Thank You!

CN093A

THE BENEFITS OF BOOK CLUB MEMBERSHIP

- You'll get your books hot off the press, usually before they appear in bookstores.
- You'll ALWAYS save up to 20% off the cover price.
- You'll get our FREE monthly newsletter filled with author interviews, book previews, special offers and MORE!
- There's no obligation — you can cancel at any time and you have no minimum number of books to buy.
- And—if you decide you don't like the books you receive, you can return them. (You always have ten days to decide.)

lll..l..lll...lll.....llll.ll.l.l..l.l..ll..l.l.l.lll..lll...lll...l

Zebra Contemporary Romance Book Club

Zebra Home Subscription Service), Inc.

P.O. Box 5214

Clifton , NJ 07015-5214

* * *

Cougar had stumbled to his feet even as the traps of the gallows were sprung.

"No!" he cried out, but the wind carried away his words. He tried to run forward, as if he would rush down to the parade ground and stop the execution, but Beaver Skin reached out and caught his arm.

"They go with Ussen to the Happy Place," the old warrior said.

The war party watched in sadness from the hilltop.

Young Turtle said, "Let us be gone from this cursed place."

But Cougar continued to stare at the bodies of his friends swinging from the gallows in the distance. They let them hang there a long, long time while the whites watched in silence.

Cougar's skull was throbbing with pain as he stumbled to his stallion and mounted up. He knew Beaver Skin had saved him from folly and did not hate him for it, but he hated the soldiers he had once served. "We will make them pay for this," he said solemnly as they turned their horses and rode out. "Sooner or later, we will make them pay!"

In the early dawn, Libbie got off the train at Willcox and smoothed the rumples from the soft-pink velvet dress she wore. Then, picking up her reticule and her small valise, she hurried to the connecting stage office. The door was locked. She rattled it and cursed under her breath.

Leaning on a post near the door was a rough-hewn, weathered man in faded jeans and shapeless western hat. "It's locked up."

"I can see that! I need to get the next stage out to Fort Grant," she said.

He looked her up and down and spat tobacco juice on the worn wooden porch. "Lady, the stage stopped running a week ago because they're expecting more trouble with the Apache."

Damn. She hadn't counted on this after she'd come all this way over the last several days. She was exhausted, almost out of funds, and now she was stranded in a strange town. However, Libbie wasn't one to give up easily. "Look, I must get to Fort Grant today."

"Wantin' to see the excitement, huh?" He grinned. "Half the folks in the Territory is headed over to watch the hangin'."

She didn't dare ask any details. "I—my fiancé is assigned there." Maybe she couldn't stop the army from executing Cougar and the others, but if she could save Cougar's life, she was bound to try. "Do you know where I could rent a buggy?"

"Maybe." He pushed the battered hat back and spat tobacco juice again. "What kind of man would let his sweetheart make that dangerous run across Apache country?"

"It's a matter of life or death." Libbie gave him her most winsome look while she calculated the last of her little hoard of funds. "I could pay very well."

"Lady, who can put a price on your life?"

She smiled at him. "You look like a mighty brave man to me."

He colored and kicked his boot toe against the floor. She could see by his expression that he was thinking it over. Finally he said, "I reckon since no stages have run for days, the Apaches wouldn't be expecting travelers; so maybe there'd be no ambushes."

She got her money out of her reticule so he could see

it. He appeared to be looking at her clothing, possibly judging whether she or her fiancé could possibly come up with more.

"My fiancé is Lieutenant Phillip Van Harrington," Libbie said, "of the Philadelphia Van Harringtons."

"Important galoot, is he?" He looked at the money in her hand with greedy eyes.

"Some would say so."

He spat again. "I might could get a horse and buggy, miss; but it'll cost you. If I'm gonna risk my life, I expect to be well paid."

She didn't even ask, just handed him what money she had left. "Just get me there. There'll be more if we make it." She wasn't sure where she'd get any more, but she was desperate to try to stop this hanging or at least see Cougar one more time. "Can we leave right away?"

"Soon's I can get the harness on." He disappeared out the back door. Libbie sat down on her suitcase and waited. What had she let herself in for? This man could be a robber or a killer, or he might take her money and run. On the other hand, he looked greedy enough that if he thought there'd be more at the end of the trip, he'd drive her.

In a few minutes, the man returned driving a worn and very creaky buggy pulled by an old chestnut horse. "Is that the best you could do?"

"It'll get us there. Get in, lady."

"All right." She threw her little valise up on the seat beside him and climbed up onto the back seat so she wouldn't have to sit next to him. Besides the fact that she didn't feel much like talking, she was also afraid that with all his spitting, he might get tobacco juice on her pale pink dress.

She reached up to touch the Apache Tears necklace she wore under the high collar of her dress. Would it indeed protect her from harm if they ran into Apaches along the way? Somehow, she had faith in Cougar's promise.

As they drove out of town, he took off his hat and scratched his tangled hair, looking back at her. "Lady, you must love that soldier a whole bunch to make this trip with the Apaches on the warpath."

"You're going, too," she pointed out.

"I'm doin' it for the money, and I'm thinkin' I must be loco. Them Apaches is all het up over that Cibecue thing. The army's hangin' some of them over it."

Her heart seemed to stop. "So you said. When?" She wanted to beg for more information, but she knew that if she acted too interested, the driver would wonder why.

"Don't know for sure; telegraph lines been down. Injuns keep cuttin' them. I thought today, but it might be tomorrow."

Today. Cougar might already be dead. No, she would not consider that possibility. "Can't you drive a little faster?"

In answer, he slapped the horse with the reins and it broke into a trot. He tried to keep up a conversation, but Libbie didn't encourage it. Her mind was too fraught with worry.

It was warmer now, the sun covering the landscape by mid-morning. The driver stopped the buggy once to water the horse. "We'll be there in a couple more hours."

"Can't we do any better than that?"

He grinned. "You must be awful eager to see that soldier boy."

Libbie made a noncommittal sound. She hadn't given Phillip a thought. If she ran into him, what was she going to do? It might be delightful to see his face when she told him she was as penniless as he was, but right now her mind was riveted on only one thing—Cougar. "Can we go on now?"

The driver got back up on the seat and whistled to the

horse. "No sign of Injuns yet," he threw back over his shoulder, "but I can almost smell 'em in the area. 'Pears to me that fancy lieutenant of yours should give me a nice bonus for gettin' you there safely."

"We'll see." Libbie frowned and wiped the alkali dust from her face, looking up at the sun moving relentlessly across the sky. If she couldn't stop the hanging, she wanted to at least tell Cougar good-bye. Where she would go or what she would do after that, she didn't know.

The driver spat off the side of the buggy as it clipped along the road, throwing up dust behind it. "I'd like to see that hangin.' Them scouts is guilty of treason. Onliest man who don't think we ought to hang the whole Apache nation is that rancher, Mac McGuire. He's been trying to save them redskins from the gallows."

Mac. Yes, maybe he'd give her shelter and help her figure out what to do. Libbie sank back against the seat and closed her eyes. In her mind, she saw Cougar walking tall and proud to the gallows even as she drove toward him. "Can't you drive a little faster?"

The driver snapped his little whip at the horse. "I tole you hit was gonna be a long ways, ma'am. You shoulda waited 'til the stage begins to run again."

That would have been too late, Libbie thought. Her heart sank as she thought, *Even now, I may be too late.*

The buggy moved down the road at a fast clip and into a little valley. Libbie reached up to touch her necklace and prayed that she wasn't too slow to intercede on the scout's behalf, even though she had no hope the commander would listen to her. Phillip would be furious if she tried to save Cougar, but what did she care? She could hardly wait to see his face when she told him she was as penniless as he was!

She was jolted out of her thoughts by the driver's startled cry as he glanced off toward the east. "Oh, my God!"

Libbie turned to look at what had caught his attention. In the distance, at the top of a butte, a large war party of Indians sat their horses and watched the moving buggy.

The driver swore and began to whip the horse. The startled chestnut set off at a gallop.

Libbie took a deep breath and grabbed onto the seat to save herself from tumbling off. "Maybe they haven't seen us," she said.

Even as she said that, the tiny, distant figures pointed toward the moving buggy and then began a slow, single-file descent of the butte.

The driver cursed and whipped the horse to run faster. The buggy moved now at breakneck speed, churning up dust. Libbie felt it clinging to her fair skin and tasted the grit of it as she gasped for breath. She coughed and hung on. "Can't you do something?"

"I've got a rifle, ma'am!" he flung back over his shoulder, "but you can't hit nothin' from a movin' buggy, and I ain't about to stop and take on a whole war party!"

The Indians were coming at them full speed now, although with the dust they were churning up, it was difficult to make out anything but bright war paint and running horses.

It was too terrifying to contemplate. Libbie closed her eyes in the choking dust, but from a distance, she could hear yelping cries as the Apaches hit the bottom of the butte and started after the buggy at full gallop. "We—we aren't going to be able to outrun them, are we?"

"Not with a buggy! We ain't got a chance!" There was terror in the driver's voice, and she could smell the fear sweat on him. Libbie reached up to touch the necklace under the collar of her dress. *Damn, why had she taken off on this foolhardy jaunt?*

Libbie glanced back over her shoulder, choking on the

swirling alkali dust. It was apparent their pursuers were gaining on them. All she could see was running horses and brown bodies. "What do we do?"

The buggy slammed to a halt as the driver pulled hard on the reins. She had to grab the seat to keep from falling out.

He grabbed his rifle and jumped down from the seat.

"You're going to make a stand?" Libbie asked.

He had his knife out, cutting the lathered horse loose from the rig. "Sorry, ma'am, I got no chance against that whole bunch! I—I'll go for help!"

Even as she watched in disbelief, the man swung up on the horse.

"You're leaving me here?"

He avoided her eyes, but she saw the ashen terror on his face. The man didn't answer as he whipped the lathered horse and galloped away toward the fort.

"Wait! Come back!" Libbie screamed in protest, but he was rapidly disappearing as the war party galloped toward her. *What to do?* She had no weapon and no horse. Well, she certainly wasn't going to sit here and wait for them to kill her! There were some brush and cactus a few hundred yards up the road—maybe she could hide there!

Libbie clambered down from the buggy, lifted her skirts, and began to run up the road. She didn't even know how far it was to the fort, but at least she would die trying to save herself.

They were gaining on her. She stumbled and fell, got to her feet, and ran on, cursing the tight corset that restrained her breathing. Libbie glanced back. In the swirling dust, most of the warriors had stopped to vandalize the buggy, but one was galloping toward her, bright paint across his dark face, his horse decorated for war. He was almost upon her, galloping as if to ride her down. She stumbled, got to her feet and ran on, heart pounding with terror.

When she glanced back again, the rider was almost upon her—and she could see that he had bright blue eyes, and those eyes were full of vengeance!

Chapter Eleven

She looked up at him in astonishment as he loomed over her on his galloping horse. "Cougar?"

He hesitated, pulling on the reins, causing the paint to rear and whinny. In the swirling alkali dust, she saw only his war-painted face and bright blue eyes. Those eyes widened now with surprise and hatred. "You!"

Hatred? His eyes were like glacier ice in that painted brown face. Instinctively, Libbie scrambled to her feet and took off running; she stumbled, fell, got up, and began to run again, breathing hard. Behind her, she heard the thunder of hooves. She glanced over her shoulder. The big stallion was coming at her in a dead gallop. He was going to ride her down!

Even as she screamed out a protest, he leaned from the saddle and swung her up before him on the saddle.

"Cougar!" she kicked and shrieked. "Don't you remember me? Put me down! How dare you run off my driver!" She beat her small fists against his bare chest.

He paid no more attention to her blows than if she were a child. Instead he threw back his head and laughed, but there was no warmth in that laughter. "Remember you? How could I forget? So we meet again, lieutenant's lady!"

So they hadn't hanged him after all—or maybe he had escaped. She was only too aware of the strength and the warmth of the arm gripping her through the pale pink dress. She had forgotten how big and male he was. Terrified by his tone and the fury in those cold blue eyes, she looked up into his face, but saw no warmth there. Past his broad shoulder, she saw the other warriors tearing into her luggage, throwing her things in the air. "Make them stop! They're destroying my things!"

"You're in the hands of savages, and yet you worry about fine clothes and jewelry," he sneered, but he didn't yell at his men to stop. Instead, he hung on to her, ignoring her struggles as he rode back to the buggy and spoke to his men in his own language. It was apparent to Libbie that he was urging them to hurry. Now he turned his own mount toward the south. "We will leave now," he informed her in English, "before your brave driver reaches the fort and brings a bluecoat rescue party."

"How dare you! I'm not going anywhere with you!" She struggled, but he held her against him firmly, paying not the slightest notice of her protest. Instead, he kicked his magnificent stallion into a gallop and pressed Libbie against his warm, naked chest.

And to think she had come to Arizona hoping to save this wretched half-breed from an army hanging. The ingrate! Now she wished he was on the scaffold and she was being given the privilege of pulling the trap.

"Listen to me!" she demanded, but he didn't even look down at her as he galloped south, surrounded by his warriors.

Soon Phillip will come to the rescue with a bunch of soldiers, she thought. Or maybe not. Phillip wasn't all that brave, and maybe he'd found out by now that Libbie was as penniless as he was. "Cougar, listen to me!" she screamed.

But his jaw was set, his mouth grim, and he looked ahead as he rode, paying no more attention to his captive than if she'd been a bundle of clothing he'd salvaged from the wrecked buggy.

What to do? There didn't seem to be anything she could do until they stopped and he was willing to listen to reason. Then she would show him the necklace she wore and demand that he respect his promise. Could she count on him remembering that promise, or was he only a heathen savage after all?

She didn't know how long they rode south. Her mouth was dry, and the sun scorched her delicate skin. Once the group stopped to rest in the shade of a mesquite tree and Cougar poured a little water in his hands and offered it to his horse, which drank gratefully.

She was scared, but she wasn't going to show it. She drew herself up haughtily. "If the horse can spare it, I would like a drink, too."

He glared at her darkly. "I need to keep the horse in shape so it can run. Perhaps if you do without until you are more humble, I will give you water, too."

If he thought she would beg for a drink, he was sadly mistaken. "What about the Apache Tears necklace?" she asked. "You told me—"

"Hush!" His face turned angrier still. "Don't remind me of my foolishness!"

The fury in his blue eyes silenced her. She wasn't certain why he was so angry, but now she was afraid to pursue it. Obviously, he regretted giving the necklace to her, or maybe it didn't mean anything after all. He had lied to her, perhaps in the hopes of seducing her. He was as bad as Phillip. And to think she had made this long trip hoping to save his neck from a noose! What a fool she had been!

The warriors mounted up again, the others paying no more attention to her than if she'd been a rifle or a saddle pack. Their expressions said she belonged to Cougar, and they were not interested in what he did with his possessions; that was his decision.

"You, get back up on the horse," he ordered with an arrogant gesture.

"I will not! I'm tired and sore," Libbie yelled back. "I demand that you return me to the fort."

"You are a captive, and as such will demand nothing." He picked her up unceremoniously and threw her up on the stallion in a swirl of white lace petticoats and pink velvet. For a split second, she wondered if she could urge the stallion into a gallop and escape, but at that moment, Cougar swung up behind her and slipped his arms around her waist. He pulled her back against his strong, half-naked body. The sensations that coursed through her at the feel of his flesh startled her.

"How dare you handle me so familiarly!"

"I dare because I own you," he snapped and pulled her closer still. "Now shut up before I throw you across a pack horse like a load of flour and tie your hands and feet under the horse's belly."

The others must speak a little English, or at least they understood the clash of wills, because the warriors broke into laughter.

She was furious. Cougar's hands were hot on her waist and she could feel his maleness as she sat in the vee of his thighs. "Perhaps you didn't understand me. I demand—"

"You will demand nothing," he said coldly and nudged his horse forward again. "You are my slave."

"Slave? But you don't understand—"

"No, it's you who doesn't understand," he snapped. "I

will decide what is to become of you. You are at my mercy, arrogant white girl!''

What was he so angry about? Whatever it was, this was no time to argue with him. When they finally got wherever they were going, maybe he would have controlled his temper and would listen to reason. And if not, surely that cowardly driver had made it to the fort and a cavalry troop was on its way to save her.

It was late afternoon and Libbie was so exhausted, she was reeling in the saddle. She tried to stay awake, but she kept falling asleep in Cougar's arms. She could feel his breath against her hair, the beat of his heart, and he was cradling her almost gently. She wanted to pull away from him, knowing this was not proper, but she was too weary to care.

Finally, the group reached a small camp of wickiups in some hills. Where were they? There was no way to know. Libbie had a sinking feeling that the Apaches had been careful to cover their trail so that army trackers would have a difficult time following the raiders.

Indians of all ages came running out to meet the group as they rode in. Libbie tried to ignore the hostile glares by sitting up as proudly as if she were a queen and these riders were her servants.

Cougar dismounted and held up his hands for her. She glared down at him and wondered if she could possibly turn the horse around and make a run for it.

"Get down!" he demanded in a voice that brooked no argument.

"I will not!" She put her chin up proudly. "You take me right back to the nearest white settlement and—"

He reached up, caught her arm, and jerked her out of the saddle. She fell in a heap at his feet while the surrounding Indians laughed. Her hair had come loose from its pins, and now it fell around her shoulders. "I am your owner now," he said, "you will do what you are told."

She looked up at him, defiance blazing in her green eyes. "How dare you treat me like this? How dare you—?"

He reached down without a word, picked her up, and tossed her across his shoulder like a sack of flour. She could feel the heat of his big hands across the back of her bare legs and her face pressed against his bare, muscular back. She had never met a man this strong. Even as she puzzled over what to do next, he turned and strode across the camp, followed by a curious crowd of Indians.

Cougar walked quickly, acutely aware of the warmth and softness of her body hanging over his broad shoulder and the silky feel of her legs under his hands. He had never felt such mixed emotions toward a woman—wanting to kiss her and kill her at the same time. Then he remembered how the lieutenant had said she'd laughed at Cougar, and his heart hardened. Now that he had taken her captive, he wasn't sure what he was going to do with her; let the rich lieutenant ransom her, probably. The Apaches could use the money for food and supplies. Cougar had stolen her on impulse because from the first moment Libbie Winters had walked into his life, he had wanted her as he'd never wanted another woman. A pity, since she was such a cold, arrogant bitch!

He strode toward his wickiup, ignoring her small fists beating on his bare back. Maybe he would use her to lure a soldier patrol into a trap. With his friends hanged just that morning, fury and grief still controlled his emotions. Or maybe he would use the girl for his pleasure before he let the hated lieutenant ransom his future bride. It would be a good joke on Phillip for Cougar to take her virginity and then toss her back to him as used goods. Probably Phillip wouldn't want her back if another man had touched her.

He could feel her small fists beat against his bare back as he walked with her. Her red hair had come loose from its pins and hung almost to the ground, brushing against his bare flesh like fiery silk.

"Stop that!" He slapped her hard across the rear.

"How dare you! How dare you touch my person!"

Libbie was suddenly afraid. Cougar didn't say anything, only kept walking. Damn! She was in a hostile camp many miles from any whites who might help her. Cougar had evidently forgotten his promise. Or worse yet, never intended to keep it.

Now he paused and carried her through the door of a thatched wickiup and dumped her unceremoniously on a pile of furs; then he stood glaring down at her.

Libbie shook her hair away from her face and glared back. "Return me to the fort at once!"

"So, Blaze, we meet again." He stood, hands on hips, frowning down at her.

"My name is not Blaze—it's Libbie."

"Blaze suits you better." He shrugged. "And since I own you at the moment, I choose what to call you."

"Like a pet dog?" She was livid.

"Exactly."

Oh, he was so arrogant!

He picked up a canteen from the floor. "Now, Blaze, would you like some water?"

She hesitated, watching him open the canteen and take a long drink. The water ran down both sides of his mouth and dripped onto his bare, muscular chest.

"Do you expect me to beg for it?"

He considered a long moment, then handed it to her. "That's not a bad idea. Slaves should be submissive."

"Submissive I am not!" Libbie grabbed the canteen and turned it upside down, letting the water run out on the ground.

He only smiled thinly. "Your arrogance is both challenging and annoying. But I will soon take that out of you. Very well, now do without!" He turned on his heel and started to leave.

"Wait, where are you going?" She was more afraid of the other warriors than she was of him. At least he spoke English; maybe she could reason with him.

"I have to report to the council." His blue eyes were cold as glacier ice. "Then I'll be back."

She glanced around furtively, wondering what the chances were of slipping away.

He must have read her mind because he said, "I wouldn't try it, Blaze. It's a long way through hostile country."

She didn't say anything as he turned and strode out.

Damn, why had she made that proud, silly gesture and poured out the water? She grabbed the canteen and turned it up to her lips, but there was only a drop or two in it. Maybe when he came back, she'd humble herself and ask for water. Or maybe not.

Mercy, she was smothering in this corset. She managed to unhook her dress, take the corset off, and put her dress back on. Now she had nothing on under the pink velvet except a long, lacy petticoat and the necklace, but who would know or care? She hesitated. He had grown so angry when she mentioned the necklace, maybe she should take it off and throw it away. Her hand went to her throat under the pink velvet. There was no place she could throw it or hide it that he might not find it.

Libbie amused herself for the next few minutes imagining the army coming to her rescue and capturing Cougar. Maybe they would hang him for kidnapping her. She took off her shoes and wiggled her toes, considering. Maybe they would offer to let her pull the trap that dropped him. That sounded very appealing right now.

After a few minutes, Cougar reentered the wickiup. "We're moving on after dark; less likely to be seen that way."

For the first time since her capture, she took a good long look at him. He wore nothing but the skimpiest of breechcloths and a pair of tall moccasins. She was both fascinated and shocked by his almost naked body. It was brown, muscular, and scarred. "Who is we? Surely you aren't planning on taking me—"

"I will take you wherever I want to take you, Blaze. You have no say in it. Eventually, we'll be crossing the border and into the Sierra Madre."

"Mexico?"

He nodded. "Out of the reach of pursuing soldiers. We can't go too far until we hook up with the gun runners who bring supplies."

She licked her dry lips, uneasy at the way his blue eyes were devouring her slim body. "Suppose I don't want to go?"

"Are you as deaf as old Mac? I told you, you are a pet with no choices in what I do with you. You are also a nuisance that will slow us down. Some of our people are not pleased that I brought you here."

"So why did you?" she challenged him.

He hesitated, not looking her in the eye. "Because you are worth a lot of cartridges and supplies to us in ransom money. I'm sure rich Phillip Van Harrington will pay well to get you back."

"Phillip isn't . . ." She paused. If the Apaches found out Phillip wasn't rich, then what? "Suppose he won't or can't ransom me?"

Cougar squatted and looked her over slowly with those hard eyes. "Any man who ever saw you would want you, Blaze. The lieutenant will come up with the money, believe me; I would."

She was unnerved by the frank passion in Cougar's eyes—passion and male need. She wasn't at all sure Phillip cared that much; but he might try to help her if he hadn't found out that she was penniless, too. She needed a plan.

Don't panic, Libbie, she told herself. That was what the average silly girl from Miss Priddy's Academy would do. *You're braver and more resourceful than that.*

What she had to do was stall for time and try to keep the Apaches from crossing the border until either the army could catch up to them or she could figure out a way to escape. Cougar was evidently a leader and gave orders. What would delay him? She saw the way he was looking at her, and she knew exactly what it would take. A shiver went up her back, and she wasn't sure whether it was fear or excitement. She had never believed she could be so daring, but then, she'd never been a prisoner of Indians before. "Suppose I—I offer my body as ransom?"

His eyebrows went up, and then he threw back his head and laughed sardonically. "You offer to bargain with what I can already take? Blaze, you disappoint me!"

She backed away from him, her trepidation growing. "You'd—you'd just—take me, even if I said no?"

"Does the thought of being loved by a savage terrify you so much then?" He seemed to be enjoying her discomfort hugely.

"No, I mean yes. I—I don't know what I mean."

"Then let's find out." He advanced on her, and she stumbled backward, knowing he was toying with her.

She was as angry as she was scared. "Damn it, stop that!"

"Stop what, Blaze? I haven't done anything." He wasn't smiling now as he advanced on her.

At this point, she tripped over a blanket roll and went sprawling backward. She lay there looking up at him, a confusion of red curls, pink velvet skirts, and a swirl of lacy white petticoats. "Don't you touch me!"

He threw back his head and laughed. "Spoken with all the ferocity of a cornered kitten. Do you bite and scratch too?"

"Try me!" She looked up at him towering over her. There was no way to get up and no place to retreat.

"Maybe I intend to, lieutenant's lady."

Libbie shrieked and crossed her hands over her breasts. "Don't you touch me! Phillip will shoot you—"

It had been the wrong thing to say, she realized that the minute she saw the added fury on the Apache's handsome face.

She could fight and scratch, but she didn't have a chance against this man. Still she intended to give as good as she got before she was raped. She lay there breathing hard and glaring up at him.

The big Apache stood staring down at her, an expression of aroused passion on his rugged face. She had never seen such desire in a man's eyes. "I am going to have you, Blaze, if it costs me my life. Taking your virginity is something I have dreamed of."

She desperately struggled to get to her feet. "It's just a woman you need; any woman, not me."

"I wouldn't be too sure. You underestimate your charms."

She shook her head. "No, it's just that you hate Phillip so much, you want his woman."

"And I will have her." With one big hand, he reached down and caught the front of her pink bodice and ripped it open even as she tried to strike his hand away. When the fabric tore, her full, pink-tipped breasts spilled out and he gasped and paused as his gaze took in the vision of her half-naked breasts. In that skimpy loincloth, his arousal was most evident and his eyes were afire with banked passion; and then they widened with surprise.

In that moment of silence, with both of them breathing

hard, he began to curse softly. "The necklace. You are wearing my Apache Tears necklace."

She scrambled to a sitting position, her hands going up to touch the necklace she had forgotten she was wearing. "You told me it would protect me."

Cougar was almost shaking with his need, standing looking down at her. With her hands at her throat, her beautiful, rose-tipped breasts were naked for him to see, her fiery hair in a tousled tumble over her shoulders. She was the most desirable woman he had ever seen, and he had never needed a woman as much as he needed one at this moment. No, not any woman—*this* woman.

The silver, turquoise, and Apache Tears stones lay against the swell of her creamy bosom. He reached out ever so slowly, tangled his fingers in the necklace, and pulled her closer to him. She dared not breathe, feeling the heat of his fingers against her naked breasts. No man had ever touched her so intimately before. The sensation was both exciting and scary. For a split second, she wondered if that strong hand was going to rip the necklace from her throat.

Instead, he gradually turned loose the necklace. "Take it off!" he commanded.

"I will not!" She straightened and glared back at him, fire in those green eyes, her bare breasts forgotten. "You said it would protect me!"

"You are a cold-blooded bitch to use that promise as a safe passage during an Indian war."

Her courage returned at his hesitation. "You didn't say there were limitations on it."

"What in the hell are you doing out here anyway?"

"I came because of the hangings," she blurted, "I thought you—"

"You thought I was being hanged?"

She was too annoyed to be truthful. "Of course. I wanted to see the army stretch your neck."

She saw the anger in his hard face. "Sorry to disappoint you."

"It isn't over yet," she reminded him, "and in the meantime, is your word good? Does the necklace protect me?"

"By Ussen, you know it does!" He had given her his oath, and he could not touch her or harm her as long as she wore that necklace of Apache Tears. Nor by custom could he forcibly remove it.

He gave her a black look, turned, and stalked out, leaving her trembling at her close call. Libbie realized suddenly that she was sitting here half naked and that he had seen her breasts.

He came back with a canteen and she crossed her arms over her breasts.

"I've already seen them," he said without expression as he handed her the water, "there's no need to hide them from me."

"All right then!" She was just scared enough to be defiant. She took her hands from her breasts, grabbed the canteen, and tipped back her head, drinking long and deep.

Cougar watched her, envied the droplets running down both sides of her mouth, dripping on her breasts. He had a terrible urge to sweep her up, kiss the cold water from her throat and nipples, but he did not move. If he touched her, he was not sure he could keep from throwing her down across those furs and taking her virginity, and rape was an Apache taboo. His people thought the raped woman's bad spirits would haunt a warrior. He had felt desire for women in the past, but never with this mindless, burning passion he was feeling now. "I'll get us some food."

She shook her hair back and tried to pull the torn edges of her bodice together, fastening them with a hairpin.

Cursing under his breath, Cougar went out. He couldn't bear to be within reach of Libbie Winters without wanting her lithe, creamy body. Damn her for keeping the necklace—not out of sentiment, but for safe passage to come see him hang. He walked to the big stew pot boiling in the center of the village. Someone had stolen a rancher's steer, and the tribe was eating well tonight. He got two gourds full, returned to the wickiup, and thrust one at her. "Eat and get some rest; we've got a long road ahead of us."

"All right." She ate slowly and watched him from under her lashes. She would delay this move as much as possible, she thought, so the army could catch up to them. Or maybe when Cougar dropped off to sleep, she could steal a horse and escape.

"Hurry up!" he ordered, "the camp is packing up to move out."

"I'll have you know I'm not used to gulping my food like some—like some—"

"Savage?" he suggested.

"I didn't say that."

"No, but you were thinking it. Let's go." He stood up.

"But I'm not finished."

"Yes, you are." He reached over, grabbed the gourd, and tossed it away. "I'm not so stupid, Blaze, that I don't know you're trying to delay us."

She was still hungry and furious. "So what if I am?"

He was gathering up weapons and canteens. "Apaches sometimes kill captives that can't keep up."

His words sent a chill up her back. He was bluffing. Wasn't he? "Why—would they do that?"

"Because trigger-happy soldiers are usually on our trail and we won't get our women and children killed over an enemy captive."

"I'm not going anywhere." She sat down in the middle of the wickiup.

"Yes, you are." He picked her up, flipped her over his shoulder again, and strode from the wickiup. "Don't try my patience, Blaze. I can't protect you if the council decides you're more trouble than you're worth."

That thought hadn't occurred to her. She didn't want to get herself killed trying to delay the march so that the soldiers could catch up. She hadn't realized how strong he was until he tossed her up on the horse. At that point, for the first time, she noticed the livid scar on his shoulder. He seemed to see her notice it.

"Compliments of your dear Phillip at Cibecue." His tone dripped sarcasm.

"Phillip? But you're on the same side."

"*Were* on the same side." Cougar swung up on the horse and pulled her against him familiarly. "He saw a chance to kill me and tried to take it."

"Phillip wouldn't do such a low-down—"

"Wouldn't he, though? You don't know your fiancé very well."

Something in his voice hinted there were many things about Phillip Van Harrington she did not know, but Cougar said no more, only spurred his horse to join the line of march to the south. A stretch of desert and low hills lay around them in a purple haze.

Mexico; they were going to Mexico, she thought in desperation. Once they were across the border, the army might never find her!

Chapter Twelve

Only an hour after the hanging, Phillip was in the colonel's office.

"What is it?" Colonel Carr snapped as he halfheartedly returned Phillip's salute.

"Sir, I'm requesting a furlough—"

"Are you out of your mind?" The other man slammed his fist down on his desk and stood up. "In case you've forgotten, Lieutenant, we hanged three Apaches this morning, and I feel rotten about it. Now I'm waiting to see if war parties attack the fort or set the whole Territory ablaze."

Damn the old man. Phillip cleared his throat. "Yes, sir, I realize that, but I've got important business back East—"

"We've got important business here!" The other paced irritably. "I don't understand you, Lieutenant. You were offered a chance to transfer and didn't take it. Now you come in wanting a furlough. Well, with all this Apache trouble, none of us are going anywhere. Your business can wait!"

"But—"

"Did you not hear me, Lieutenant? Now get out of my office!"

"Yes, sir." Phillip saluted and fled. When he looked back over his shoulder, the commander had poured himself a whiskey and was staring out the window at the gallows.

Ye gods! What was he to do? Because of those damned Apaches, Phillip was stuck out here, maybe for years—at least until the Apaches were all corralled. Or killed. He thought of his father. *Yes, killed would be better.*

In the meantime, Elizabeth would never warm his bed and he would lose all her beautiful money. Maybe Mama would have some ideas, but he hadn't gotten a letter from her yet, and the telegraph wire was down half the time because of those cursed savages.

At this point, getting drunk seemed like a pretty good idea. Phillip headed for his quarters. To hell with assignments. If anyone needed him, they'd have to search him out.

He'd had about three or four drinks when he heard a shower of gravel against his window. He peered out, then scowled. Shashké stood outside, looking about nervously as if afraid someone might see her. What a joke. Half the people at the fort had been gossiping about their year-long affair.

She gestured for him to come out. He needed a woman, and though he was tired of her, she was at least available. He went to the door. "Come in here before someone sees you."

She looked past him at the bearskin rug, frowned, and shook her head. *Ignorant savages.*

"All right then—meet you at the barn."

She nodded and fled. Had those been tears on her pretty face? He hoped she wasn't about to get emotional on him. He needed a woman, but he didn't have time to listen to some squaw cry. He was weaving only slightly as he walked to the barn.

Inside, out of the bright sun, it was cooler and the place smelled of horses and hay.

"Damn, you're pretty with that flower in your hair and those gold earrings." He lurched toward her and tried to take her in his arms.

"You're drunk," she said in disgust, pushing him away.

"Not as drunk as I'd like to be." He laughed.

She wiped away tears and sniffled. "You never think about my feelings."

"Okay, so what's the matter?" He didn't really care, but he had to make the gesture to get her clothes off.

"Dandy Jim's wife hanged herself a few minutes ago down in the scout's quarters."

"Who?" He wasn't quite sure who they were talking about or how it related to the well-being of Phillip Van Harrington.

"You know, one of the scouts they hanged this morning."

"Oh." Phillip blinked. "You mean she committed suicide? Why'd she do that? Probably another buck would have taken her—"

"Don't you understand?" Shashké screamed at him. "He's dead and she loved him and wanted to go with him."

"Okay, so she's dead, so what?" Phillip shrugged. He was beginning to get a bad headache.

"You don't care about anything," she stormed and slapped him. "Not me, not anything."

He slapped her back, hard. "You stupid squaw! Who do you think you are?"

She stumbled backward, weeping. "I thought you cared about me. I thought you were going to take me away from here. I have taken great risk in becoming your lover."

"I've got to go," Phillip said, yawning. In the mood she was in, she wasn't going to pleasure him.

"Is that all you've got to say?"

"I don't know what you expect from me." He was angry now as he shoved her aside and headed toward the barn door. "I'm going to marry Elizabeth Winters, not you."

"That terrible white girl? She won't even let you touch her—"

"Aw, she's not so bad," Phillip blurted before he thought. "She gave you those nice earrings . . ." His voice trailed off as he realized what he'd just revealed.

Shashké's hand came up slowly and touched one of the gold earrings as a light of understanding seemed to break across her face. *"She* gave them to me? You lied to me. You said *you*—"

"What difference does it make? Look, you stupid tart, don't bother me anymore. I'm sick of you!"

As he staggered away from the barn, there was a commotion out on the parade ground with men hurrying and shouting. *Ye gods. What now?*

For a moment, his blood froze in his veins and he wondered if the fort were indeed under attack. Then he realized it was a lone rider on a lathered old chestnut horse that still wore the remnants of a buggy harness.

Soldiers were running from every direction, and the bugle blew an alarm.

Phillip held back a moment, not wanting to take the responsibility of being the senior officer at the scene. Then curiosity got the better of him, and he strode over to the crowd. "What's going on here?"

The rough frontiersman had slid from the horse, breathing hard. He smelled as if he might have wet his pants, and his eyes were wide with terror. "Apaches!" he gasped, "took after me a few miles outta Willcox!"

Phillip recognized him now as a sometime stage driver.

"They follow you here?" He looked toward the distance in a panic.

"No, I came for help. When I looked back, they was coming hard toward the lady—"

"Lady?" another soldier asked. "You left a woman out there?"

"Well, there was only one horse, so I come for help."

Phillip was cold sober now. "What kind of a lady would make a trip on such a dangerous route on the day of the hanging?"

The other shook his head and leaned against the horse. "Dunno. Real looker, red hair. Said she was comin' to see her fiancé, a lieutenant. Said he'd give me somethin' for bringin' her."

"Red hair?" Phillip had a sudden premonition.

The other looked at the insignia on Phillip's uniform. "You Phillip Van Harrington?"

Elizabeth. Phillip grabbed the man by the front of his dirty shirt. "You left my fiancée to the mercy of a bunch of savages?"

"Like I said, there was only one horse and I come for help."

Elizabeth had been on her way to see him. Maybe she had planned to tell Phillip that his being penniless didn't matter, that she still wanted to marry him. He would have both her money and her virginity after all. But now the Apaches had her. "Someone get the colonel!" he barked. A private took off at a run toward the colonel's quarters.

Phillip confronted the shaking rider. "How many Apaches were there?"

"Could I have a little whiskey?" the man asked, "I'm a mite thirsty—"

"The devil'll give you a drink in hell!" Phillip shoved the man back against the lathered horse. "How many were there?"

"I dunno, a war party. Who stops to count in a spot like that? They was led by a big Injun on a fine paint stallion, though."

Cougar. Phillip didn't hear anything else in all the shouts and confusion around him. The damned scout hadn't died from his wounds after all, and he wanted revenge. Elizabeth had been on her way to Phillip and had been abandoned to Cougar. She might be dead, or at least raped and tortured by now. If anyone was going to rape Elizabeth Winters, he wanted to be the man to do it. Besides, if she was dead, Phillip could kiss her rich dowry good-bye.

The colonel strode to the scene just then. "Lieutenant, what is going on?"

Phillip gestured toward the rider and the lathered horse. "Apache raiders, sir."

"Damn!" The colonel took off his hat and ran his hand through his gray hair in frustration. "I just knew hanging those scouts was going to set this Territory ablaze! What happened?"

The rider filled him in.

"You abandoned a woman to the Apache?" The colonel was aghast.

"Like I told the lieutenant," the man whined, "there was only one horse, and I come for help."

"Anyone know who the woman is?"

Phillip sighed. "I think it might be my fiancée, sir, on her way to visit me."

"On the day of the hanging?" The older man looked incredulous.

Phillip shrugged helplessly. "I think there was an emergency."

The rider nodded. "Yeah, I think that's what she said, all right. Kept askin' me if I couldn't drive faster."

The colonel scowled at the rider. "Throw this cowardly bastard in jail until I see if there's something the sheriff can charge him with.'' Then he turned to Phillip as soldiers led the protesting man away. ''Lieutenant, get a patrol together.''

''Yes, sir.'' He snapped a salute and took off running toward the stable for his horse. Phillip was as furious with Cougar as he was worried about Elizabeth. How dared that half-breed take Phillip's woman? He'd make the Injun pay for that!

Phillip picked some of his best men, and in thirty minutes the patrol was riding out of the fort in the midday sun. He was cold sober now, his head aching, but he was eager for revenge. *Cougar.* Phillip recalled now the way the arrogant scout had looked at Elizabeth that time she came to the fort last August, as if he wanted her as no man should ever need a woman.

It was still cool for March, he thought grimly as he led the patrol away from Fort Grant, headed south. Along the road to the fort, they found the wrecked buggy and a woman's clothes scattered everywhere. Phillip dismounted and picked up a lacy corset cover. It smelled faintly of lilac perfume, the scent that Elizabeth favored. Except for her scattered things, there was no sign of her.

They had a white tracker with them, and Phillip noticed the man walking around the wreckage and then walking farther out. The tracker knelt and studied some tracks, then yelled to Phillip. ''Hey, Lieutenant, come here.''

Phillip strode to the tracker's side. ''What did you find? I don't see anything.''

The other pointed. ''Here's a woman's footprints; I can just make them out in the rocks. Looks like she tried to run and then got ridden down. See? The footprints end where a horse galloped up beside them. I'd say the rider swung her up on his horse.''

Cougar. Phillip seethed with the knowledge. Only Cougar would be strong enough to lift a running woman to a horse from a mounted position. In his mind, he saw Elizabeth fighting and Cougar holding her close, maybe putting his hands on her, maybe . . . No, the Apache raiders wouldn't stop for that right now. They'd be too afraid the escaping driver would bring help from the fort. "Which way are they going?"

The tracker walked in a circle, staring at the churned-up ground. "They're headed south, sir; probably runnin' for the border."

"South? Into Mexico?"

The other man nodded, and Phillip saw him exchange glances with some of the soldiers. They figured she was as good as dead by now. "How much of a head start have they got?"

The soldiers looked at him and each other uneasily.

The tracker spat in the dust. "Lieutenant, you ain't planning on riding off down toward Mexico with just this small patrol?"

"Oh, hell, I don't know." Phillip swore in frustration, then pulled at his wispy mustache and looked south. All his life, his mother had told him what to do, but Henrietta Van Harrington wasn't here right now. Phillip ground his teeth with rage. *Cougar.* This was just the kind of arrogant gesture the half-breed bastard would make, stealing Phillip's woman. Hanging was too good for him. In the silence, a buzzard glided on air currents overhead, throwing shadows across the men below.

The tracker said, "Lieutenant, there's no tellin' how many Apaches are up ahead of us, joinin' up as this group crosses the country. We might wanta report back to the colonel and get more men and supplies if you're going after them."

"Yes, of course." Phillip swung into the saddle and wheeled his horse back toward the fort. "When we catch up to them, I've got a personal grudge to settle with the leader.''

The others fell into formation and rode along behind him. The buzzard threw a shadow across Phillip, and he glanced up. *Oh, he'd feed Cougar to the buzzards all right, preferably alive.* They said a buzzard always tore a man's eyes out first and then started on his belly. Phillip grinned. *That might be even better than hanging that Injun bastard.* ''How far can they get before sundown?''

The tracker, riding alongside him, thought a minute. ''Ridin' hard, Apaches can cover a hundred miles a day, but that's a war party. Their women and young'uns'll slow them down a little, but Apache women are tough, used to hardship. A white woman isn't up to that.''

He didn't say anything else; he didn't need to. If Elizabeth became a liability, they might kill her. Otherwise, when they camped tonight, they would probably amuse themselves with her. In his mind, Phillip saw her in a circle of warriors, her clothes torn away as Cougar dragged her into the firelit circle and took her. He could imagine the tumble of red hair and the creamy skin as the dark, muscular savage spread her out and enjoyed her. Then he'd share her with the others.

Phillip swore and spurred his horse into a gallop, heading back to the fort. The army would catch up to those Apaches, all right. If anyone was going to take Elizabeth Winter's virginity, it was going to be Phillip!

It had been both a torment and a pleasure to ride holding Libbie Winters in his arms, Cougar thought as the shadows lengthened and the day passed and the little band headed south.

Libbie had been so warm and soft against him, and he was keenly aware that her torn bodice was barely held together by her makeshift fastenings. Holding onto her trim waist, her bosom kept brushing against the backs of his hands. It took all his willpower not to cup those fine breasts with his hands and stroke them. No, he must not touch her as long as she wore his necklace. He had given her his word, as she had reminded him, and he was a warrior of honor. He glanced down now at the necklace lying against her throat and the torn pink velvet, resisting the urge to take it off her.

He had been loco to kidnap her, but his passion had overcome his reason the moment he had seen her in that buggy. What was she doing in Arizona? But he knew why. She had come for the hanging and maybe to marry Phillip while she was here. She was his enemy's woman—and now she was at Cougar's mercy.

The Apache raiders reined in near a creek, and a warrior rode back to him, looking over the tousled girl with interest until Cougar frowned at him. "What say you? Shall we camp for the night?"

Cougar nodded. "We must have food and rest. Our old ones cannot take this very long." In truth, there weren't very many old ones along; Cougar had asked Beaver Skin and many of the others to stay in their village near the fort. The army wouldn't bother them, and they would pick up much information.

The warrior frowned at the girl in his arms. "The soldiers will come after us because of her and she slows us down. Better you should kill her."

"I will kill the man who even thinks that!" Cougar snapped in their language, and his tone brooked no argument.

The warrior acted as if he might argue the point, seemed to see the anger in Cougar's eyes, wheeled his horse, and rode off.

Libbie stirred in his arms and moaned softly. She was

spoiled and soft, he thought, not used to this kind of pace. And then he remembered her laughing at him and her cold-blooded design in wearing the necklace for protection, and he hardened his heart against his pity. Why had Phillip told him she had thrown it away? But they had laughed at him; Cougar had seen them at the stagecoach's departure. Now he was torn between desire and hatred for the lieutenant's woman.

"What's happening?" she asked.

He swung down off the horse and held his arms up for her. "We're camping for the night."

She ignored his outstretched arms and slid from the horse. However, she had been on the horse too long and her legs buckled. Instantly, Cougar caught her to keep her from falling, but she jerked away from him. "Don't you touch me, you—you—"

"Savage?" he suggested with a thin smile.

She must not show fear, she thought, and leaned against the horse to keep from falling. Sooner or later, the cavalry would be coming to her rescue. "I would like a bath and some food and water," she said, drawing herself up proudly. "The lieutenant will reward you handsomely for taking good care of me."

Cougar threw back his head and laughed. "We're counting on it! His money will buy a lot of ammunition and supplies for us." He caught her arm and propelled her along, leading his stallion with his free hand.

"You're holding me for ransom?"

"Of course. Can you think of any other reason for me to drag you along?" He sounded angry, which mystified Libbie.

Oh, God, suppose he found out Phillip is penniless? With no ransom forthcoming, what would they do with her? She didn't even want to think about it.

Women were hurrying about, building fires, unpacking

blankets and food. Several of the pretty young women
smiled at Cougar invitingly. He didn't even seem to notice.
"So, Blaze, can you do anything useful like build a fire or
cook?"

She decided she would not answer. She was Elizabeth
Winters, lately of Boston, and she would not answer to a
savage's name for her.

"Are you hard of hearing?" he snapped.

"No."

"All right, be stubborn. Here"—he gestured—"you can
help Owl Woman put up a wickiup."

"I will not!" Libbie was enraged. "You kidnap me and
then expect me to work?"

"All right. Sit there then and watch the old woman do
it all." He dismissed her with a curt nod and walked away.

Libbie tossed her hair and sat down on a rock, watching
the wrinkled Apache woman put up the temporary shelter
of sticks covered with brush. She felt guilty because the
gray-haired woman looked weary, but she only smiled at
Libbie as she worked. In less than a hour, the camp was
settled in around a big campfire, horses staked out and
women nursing babies while others cooked.

Libbie took a deep breath and smelled cooking meat.
She was hungry and thirsty, too, but she would die before
she asked for a drink of water. She licked her cracked lips.

Cougar walked up just then. He must have noticed her
licking her lips because he pulled out a canteen. "I'm not
stupid enough to hand it to you this time," he said. "Water
in these parts is too precious to waste."

She didn't want to pour it out, she wanted to drink it,
but she wasn't going to beg.

"Here," Cougar said. He poured some of the water into
his cupped hand and held it out to her.

Libbie hesitated. *Damn him for his arrogance!* He was determined to break her, but she was too thirsty to argue the

point now. She caught his big hand to steady it and drank the water from his palm. It was cold and good.

Then he turned his wet hand and wiped it across her hot, dusty face. It felt so soothing, she closed her eyes and let him stroke her face.

"You're becoming a very obedient little pet," he said as his hand slipped around the back of her neck.

"I'm nobody's pet." Before he realized what she was up to, she turned her head and sank her sharp little teeth into his wrist.

He jerked back, rubbing his arm and swearing Apache curses. "Damn you, Blaze, I ought to strip you down and take a quirt to you for that."

"You wouldn't dare!" She was scared but defiant.

He didn't answer, favoring his injured wrist as she glowered at him. He'd kill the man who tried to put one mark on that soft skin of hers. He took a deep breath to control his temper. "If I scar you up, the lieutenant might not pay a big ransom to get you back."

"Besides that," she said, and tangled her fingers in the necklace she wore, "I am under your protection, remember?"

"So you keep reminding me!" He glared down at her, favoring his bitten wrist. He had the most overwhelming urge to tangle his fingers in that necklace and tear it from her pretty throat, even if to do so would sully his honor as a warrior. "Blaze, don't push me!" he warned. He turned on his heel and strode away.

Libbie heard smothered laughter and looked up. The old woman had seen it all, and now she laughed and nodded as if pleased to see a woman give the big warrior as good as he got. Then the old woman returned to her work.

Libbie glanced around. There were no Apaches close to her now, everyone being preoccupied with their tasks.

Cougar had tied his stallion to a tree branch as he left. This was the best horse in the camp. No doubt it could outrun anything else in the Apaches' herd. Libbie was an expert rider, even though she had always used a sidesaddle. Did she have a chance at mounting up and getting away, taking them all by surprise? They wouldn't be expecting such a bold move. Well, nothing ventured . . .

She looked around again. No one was paying her the slightest heed. In a heartbeat, Libbie jerked the reins free, swung up on the stallion, and turned to ride out.

The old woman shouted the alarm as Libbie took off. Behind her, people were shouting and gesturing. Libbie looked back over her shoulder and saw the black thunder on Cougar's face as she started away at a gallop. She was going to make it!

Abruptly, behind her, she heard Cougar's sudden sharp whistle. The big paint slid to a halt, and she fought to keep her balance, but she managed to stay mounted. Oh, damn! Libbie could hear Cougar's moccasins coming at a run as she kicked the horse in the sides, urging it forward. It didn't budge, obeying its master's command.

Cougar reached out and caught her trim ankle. "You conniving little bitch! Get off that horse!" He pulled and she came off in a tumble into his arms. Her torn bodice had come open and there she was, fighting and kicking to get out of his arms with her naked breasts pressed against his massive bare body.

"Let go of me, damn you!" She pounded on his chest, but he ignored her as he turned and strode back to the wickiup that the old woman had almost completed.

"Blaze, I guess I will just have to stake you out like a pet dog."

Libbie bit and scratched, but he knelt and held her down while he tied a length of rawhide around one of her ankles. Then he tied the other end to a stake he drove in the ground before the new wickiup. "You can't treat me like this!" She shrieked and yanked hard on the stake, "I am Elizabeth Winters, not some stray dog—"

"You are my slave," he returned coldly, "and you will stay where you are tied."

She eyed the stake. Maybe when he left, she could pull the stake up and . . .

"Don't try it," he said. "You haven't got a chance of escaping, so save your energy."

"You bastard!" She came to the end of the tether and lunged at him, but he stepped backward and the stake held her just out of reach.

"I am that." He didn't smile. "And you are a spoiled, uppity, and annoying girl. Now shut up and sit down. Maybe if you're good, I'll feed you."

"I don't want your damned food!"

"Think twice about that, Spoiled One. It may be a long time before we eat again. We'll be riding hard tomorrow. The army's probably hot on our trail." Cougar turned and sauntered away.

Phillip. Yes, if that cowardly driver made it to the fort, Phillip would come to her rescue and bring soldiers. That thought gave her some comfort. But would he come because he loved her or because he might still think she was rich or simply because he hated Cougar? There was no way to know. What difference did it make anyway? And to think she'd come all the way to Arizona with some fool notion of saving Cougar from the hangman. Of course, if she told him that, he'd never believe her.

Twilight fell on the camp. Libbie retreated the length of her tether inside the wickiup to escape the curious stares of the passing women and children. She noted that they looked thin and weary. Through the opening of the wick-iup, Libbie could see the men gathered around the fire.

Occasionally, one of them glanced toward the wickiup. Cougar was frowning. *Were they discussing her?*

Out by the fire, Cougar listened patiently to the others.

"The army will come after us because of the white girl," one said. "Better we should kill her and hide the body."

"She is too valuable to kill," Cougar argued. "The whites will pay ransom to get her back unharmed. We can use the gold to buy rifles and supplies."

Geronimo frowned. "All Apaches know gold is sacred to Ussen and we are forbidden to dig in Mother Earth's body and violate her to get it. The whites care little for our sacred ways."

"True," Cougar agreed, "but we have violated no taboos in taking what the whites have dug. We can trade it to the Mexican traders and some of the white gunrunners for supplies."

"Will they pay so much for one small woman?" an elder asked.

Another laughed. "Have you seen the woman? They will pay."

"Who is her man?" Geronimo asked.

"The lieutenant who kills bears," Cougar said.

A murmur of disapproval went around the circle that anyone would do such a forbidden thing.

An elder shook his head. "Does he not know bears carry the spirits of our Apache dead?"

Cougar shrugged. "He does not care; he hates the Apache because of his father."

The warriors exchanged glances. Many of the old ones had known the major.

"Does the lieutenant know—?" Geronimo asked.

Cougar shook his head. "I doubt it. He would not believe it anyway."

A rider came into camp, dismounted, and hurried to the fire. Geronimo looked up. "You come from the fort?"

The other nodded and sat down cross-legged before the fire. "It was hard to sneak away. Dandy Jim's woman has killed herself from grief."

A murmur went around the circle, and Cougar gritted his teeth. It had been a sad day. "What will become of Dandy Jim's sons?"

The new man shook his head. "No one knows. One of the soldiers says he might take them to raise."

Geronimo rolled a smoke in a corn husk, lit it with a burning twig from the campfire, took a long puff, then passed it around the circle. "The Apache have lost three good men to a terrible, shameful death today."

The others nodded.

"There will be no peace for us until the white men are driven out," said one.

Cougar shook his head. "I have lived among the whites. We cannot win a war against them. They are as many as the needles on the cactus. But if they force us into it, we will have no choice."

"We will reach decisions later," Geronimo said. "We ride out before dawn. Maybe the soldiers will lose our trail, give up, and not follow."

"Won't they come after the woman?" another asked.

"Will the lieutenant pay gold to get her back?" another queried Cougar.

Cougar looked toward the wickiup. From here, he could see the occasional shine of her fiery hair when she moved, and he blurted out his thoughts. "If you owned a woman like that, would you not ransom her, no matter what it cost?"

The others nodded in agreement. She was indeed a very beautiful woman who would give a man fine, strong sons.

Gray Sky poked up the fire. "If the Long Knife does not

ransom her, she could be sold to Coyote Johnson. He could get a good price for her from a Mexican whorehouse."

Cougar winced at the thought of turning her over to the white gunrunner, but he said nothing. He hated her, he thought, and he should be pleased to think that the spoiled, arrogant white girl might end up servicing any man who wanted her. But he was not pleased. The thought made him set his teeth. "She is mine," he reminded them, "I captured her."

The others nodded. Geronimo said, "So she is. Very well, Cougar, you may do with her as you will—as long as she does not slow us down."

"She will not slow us down," Cougar said. He stood up.

"Will you pleasure yourself with her tonight?" Gray Sky said thoughtfully as he smoked.

"She wears my necklace. I promised her its protection." *By Ussen, why had he done that?*

Another warrior laughed and rubbed his groin. "For a woman like that, a warrior might forget his honor."

Cougar shook his head, even though he felt the hardening of his own manhood. It had been a long time since he lay with a woman. "My honor means much to me. I will not sully it for the pleasure of her body."

Geronimo frowned. "You made your promise to a white. Perhaps you need not—"

"I will think on it." Cougar's voice was gruff, mirroring his annoyance with both himself for making the promise and the arrogant white woman for expecting him to keep it. He had an urge to stride into that wickiup and rip the Apache Tears from her neck. No, of course he could not do that. But if she took it off of her own free will . . .

Cougar only half listened to the final discussions, his attention on the wickiup. It was dark now and it was going to be a long night. His groin throbbed at the thought of the fiery, desirable girl staked out like a wild bobcat kitten in his wickiup. Right now, he'd better feed her. After that, he wasn't sure he had what it took to stay in the same place with her all night without taking her with the same impassioned frenzy he'd felt from the first moment he'd saw her. Uppity Miss Elizabeth Winters didn't know just how much her virginity depended on his honor!

Chapter Thirteen

Libbie sat hunched inside the wickiup, watching the proceedings at the fireside with a mixture of fear and fascination. Every once in a while, one of the braves would look her way. *Was her fate being decided out there?* She reached up to touch the Apache Tears necklace for reassurance. Cougar had promised her his protection, but what if the council decided otherwise? In the meantime, she was tired, hungry, and cold and staked out like a naughty puppy inside this brush shelter. How dared that savage do this to her!

As she watched, Cougar stood up, walked over to the fire, and filled two gourds from a kettle hanging over the flames. Then he strode toward the wickiup, stooped, and came inside. "You hungry?"

"I might be." She wasn't going to beg if she starved to death.

He snorted. "Your pride gets in your way, my pet. Here."

He thrust one gourd at her and knelt, putting the other one next to his knee as he began to build a small fire.

She resisted the urge to throw the food back at him. It smelled good, and who knew when he would offer her food again? "You didn't give me any silverware. How do you expect me to eat this?"

He looked up from the fire he was building. "I'm not loco enough to give you a knife."

"If I had a knife, I would stick it between your ribs."

He turned his head, smiling ever so slightly. "You think I don't know that?" He returned to piling twigs on the tiny flame.

Libbie watched him. Maybe she could slam the gourd across the back of his arrogant head. No, it wasn't heavy enough to do any damage; she'd just make him mad. She had a feeling that when Cougar was angry, his mood could turn as black and dangerous as a thunderstorm. "I'm not sure I want to eat this—"

"Hush and eat it!" he ordered.

Hurriedly, she picked up the gourd. No wonder he was a leader, Libbie thought; no one would dare argue with him.

He had the fire going now. He sat down across from her cross-legged, picked up his food, and began to eat with his fingers.

Anyway, she decided there was nothing to be gained by fussing with him now. She hesitated, then began to eat with her fingers. It was a steaming hot and tasty stew. "What is this?"

He shrugged and finished his. "Ground maize and some beef we took from a rich rancher. I don't suppose you can cook?"

She looked down her nose at him. "Ladies have servants to do their work."

He scowled at her. "Then what do ladies do besides sit

about on pillows like small dogs, waiting for a rich husband to snap his fingers?''

A lap dog. She hadn't thought of it before, but yes, that was what she would be for some wealthy man. "You wouldn't understand. Ladies do watercolors and embroidery. They host club meetings and play the violin.''

"Sounds dull. *Our* women will teach you something useful, like cooking and weaving baskets.''

"Ha! I don't expect to be here that long.'' She finished her food and tossed the gourd to one side, passing up the temptation to throw it at him. She suspected he could be a dangerous man if pushed too far. "If you think you're going to turn me into a slave—''

"You are already my slave,'' he answered coldly. "The Apache life is a hard one. Each must work and help or we can't survive.''

"You think that bothers me?'' she sniffed. "I don't intend to learn to do lowly work—''

"It is not your fault you are useless except to amuse a rich man,'' he said calmly. "You will soon adjust.''

"Adjust!'' she screamed at him. "You don't understand, you—you savage! I will be returning to civilization, and Lieutenant Van Harrington will hunt all of you down and kill you.''

Cougar grinned. "He'll have to catch us first and the lieutenant is a greenhorn. We aren't worried.''

"You can't treat me like a common servant!'' Libbie fumed, forgetting that only moments ago, she had feared him. Obviously he didn't intend to kill her, or he would already have done so.

"There is much work in an Apache camp,'' he said as he rolled a cigarette and lit it with a burning twig from the fire. "All share the work and the food.''

"Do you know who I am?'' she announced loftily. "I am

Elizabeth Winters, lately of Miss Priddy's Female Academy and a debutante—''

"And were you happy, Blaze?"

Libbie hesitated, caught off guard. She'd never given that much thought. It was the only life she had ever known—the spoiled rich girl. And now that she had no money, what would her life be like?

"You do not answer, so you are not sure." He shook his head and smoked, frowning at her. "Think on this; you came out here to see the army hang the scouts. My friends are dead, and your fiancé's testimony helped hang them."

She saw the anger and the pain in his blue eyes and was angry herself that she had been accused so unjustly when she had come to try to save him from the gallows. He wouldn't believe that if she told him, and after all, she had her pride. "I wish you *had* been one of those they hanged!"

He scowled at her and blew smoke into the air. "Maybe you'll get your wish, but in the meantime, the army will think twice about attacking us because we've got you."

She was a hostage and when they didn't need her anymore . . . Libbie trembled at the thought.

Cougar looked over at her a long moment. "Are you cold?"

Was she shivering that badly? "No, I—I'm fine."

He tossed his cigarette into the fire. "You're not much of a liar and a little too delicate for this life." He stood up and came toward her.

She glared up at him. "What—what do you plan to do?"

He reached behind her, got a fur robe, and put it around her shoulders. He held on to the edges of the fur so that his hands were close to her face. He looked down into her eyes for a long moment as if deciding whether to cover her lips with his own; then the muscles in his jaw tightened. "Don't worry; your honor is safe . . . for now." His fingers trailed across the fur and touched the necklace at her throat. "In a couple of days, we'll meet some white gunrunners at a rendezvous. We're desperate for weapons and supplies."

She was only too aware of the touch of his fingers on the necklace and tracing along the swell of her breasts beneath it. If she pulled away, he would think she was afraid and she would not give him that satisfaction. She glared at him and gritted her teeth as his big hand trailed along her throat. "What is that to me?"

He did not move his fingers. "Do you know what gunrunners would give for a beautiful woman they can use for their pleasure or sell in Mexico City?"

She felt herself blanche at the thought. "I will hold you to your promise."

"Ahh!" He nodded. "One minute I am a savage, the next you expect me to behave like a knight in shining armor."

She didn't answer, surprised herself at how much she had come to depend on him for protection.

Cougar let go of her and reached out and caught her trim ankle.

"What are you doing?" His hand was big enough that it encircled her small ankle.

"Checking to make sure your leash is secure, my little dog. She tried to pull out of his grip, but he held on to her ankle while he checked the rope that tethered her. Then he sat down across the fire from her. "You underestimate your value on the open market, Blaze. A beautiful, desirable white girl is worth much in guns and supplies."

The thought of being handed over to a bunch of cutthroats and renegades made her swallow hard.

"So that thought gives you pause?" He looked deep into her eyes. "As well it should. I can assure you, renegade gunrunners will not treat you like a high-born lady."

"I thought I had the protection of your necklace?" She reached up to touch it.

"From me and other Apaches." He smiled wryly. "But I am not responsible for how your next owners treat you."

"You're trying to get around your oath." She licked her lips nervously. "Anyway, the question is moot. Phillip will pay much ransom to get me back."

Cougar only grinned ever so slightly. "I'm sure he will. I would if your body was promised to me and I had the gold."

Oh, God. Phillip had no money; what was going to happen if the Indians found out?

"You don't dare do anything to harm me," she shot back, "the army will destroy you for that."

He nodded. "Maybe, but right now, we know this country better than they do, and they've got to find us to destroy us." He stretched and yawned. "I'm tired."

Maybe she could escape while he slept.

"Come here," he commanded.

"What are you going to do?"

"I'm going to make sure you don't stab me or do some other mischief as I sleep." He stood up, reached out and caught her, then twisted her arms behind her.

Libbie struggled as he put her wrists together and began to tie them. "I promise I won't try to escape."

"You're not Apache," he said, "your promises are no good."

She fought to get away, but with his great strength, he held her, tying her hands behind her back, then whirled her around, pulling the fur closer around her. "Be a good slave, Blaze, and lie close and warm your master."

"I will not! If you think you're going to—"

"No, tonight I'm just going to use you for warmth." He pulled her toward him, then jerked her down on a pile of furs near the fire.

"Phillip will be furious."

"Phillip isn't here," he said and pulled her close against him, "so he won't know if you don't tell him. Besides, it will keep you warm, too."

"I'm not cold! Besides, you promised!"

"Blaze," he said patiently, "I haven't killed you, raped you, or hurt you. You strain my patience. Now shut up and go to sleep. We've got a long day ahead of us tomorrow."

He pulled her into his embrace, and with her hands tied behind her, there wasn't much Libbie could do except let him mold her slight body against his big, muscular one. Her head was on his shoulder, his face in her tousled hair, his arm thrown across her slim waist.

She hadn't realized how cold she was or how much heat his big body gave off. She tried to keep her body stiff and unyielding as he dropped off to sleep. The warmth of him was a temptation and besides, he was asleep; he wouldn't know. Libbie curled into the protective curve of him and stopped shivering as he drew her even closer. The curve of his muscular body almost seemed to have been made for her small one to fit into.

Libbie relaxed and watched him sleep. The small fire gave off enough light to see his face. If he weren't a savage and her captor, she would think him handsome. Yet how dared he lie with his arm across her so possessively? She looked down at the black gemstones lying against the creamy swell of her breasts. Cougar's honor was the only thing holding his tumultuous passions in check; she could sense that. If he changed his mind, he could use her for something more than just a bed warmer. He could . . . No, she must not think of that.

Finally, she curled up against his warmth and slept, dreaming of getting her hands free and stabbing him with his own knife.

Libbie awakened just before dawn and wondered for a

long moment where she was. The glowing coals of a small
fire illuminated the area, and when she tried to move,
she realized her hands were tied behind her and she was
tethered by one ankle. Then abruptly, she became aware
of something else. A dark, half-naked man lay with her,
his head against the swell of her breasts. She took a deep
breath to scream, then remembered. She must not bring
the other Apaches down on her. As it was, Cougar's face
was pillowed on her almost naked breasts. She could feel
his warm breath on her skin as he breathed. One of his
arms held her to him; the other hand was hot and possessive on her bare thigh, since the torn pink dress had worked
its way up her body. She lay there a long moment, gathering
her wits, then slowly wiggled until she was out from under
him.

At that point, he awakened, looked puzzled, then sat up
and smiled. "Did you sleep well? I did."

"Damn you! Phillip will kill you for this." She sat up,
too, and shook back her tangled hair.

"Maybe it was worth it. Here, let me untie your hands."
He reached around her, his bare chest brushing against
her breasts as he untied her.

Libbie held her breath as he worked on the ropes, only
too aware of his massive chest pressed against her.

"There," he said, "I hope today you'll behave a little
better."

Her arms were asleep, and she moaned when she tried
to move them forward.

Sympathy crossed his rugged face, only to be replaced
with a look as hard as blue glass. He caught first one of
her arms and then the other, rubbing them. "If I could
trust you, I wouldn't tie you up."

"Some night," she said coldly, "you'll forget and I'll
cut your throat with your own blade, steal your horse, and
escape."

"Don't count on it, Blaze." He stood up, hauling her to her feet. "I had thought you would become more reasonable and obedient."

"Never!" She screamed it at him.

"Then today I shall teach you that you must obey me." He untied her ankle, too, his hands lingering too long on her slim calf and she saw the need in his eyes. It would be so easy to push her over on her back, mount her, and enjoy her. Instead, he stood up, pulled her to her feet, and pushed her out of the wickiup ahead of him. "Perhaps today you shall walk beside my horse instead of riding."

She spat at him like a ruffled kitten, but he paid her no heed. The old woman came out of a nearby wickiup.

"Here," Cougar said, "this is Owl Woman who wet-nursed me and raised me when my mother died."

He said something to the woman in her own language, and she nodded and led Libbie into the brush to relieve herself, then gave her a bit of gruel in a small bowl. It tasted like ground acorns, Libbie decided. She started to complain that this wasn't nearly enough food, then noted the other women and children didn't have as much in their bowls as she did, but no one was complaining. Perhaps she was a tiny bit spoiled, Libbie conceded.

Now as the sun rose over the rim of the hill to the east, the Apaches finished tearing down the camp, and mounted up. She stood and waited, hoping Cougar had forgotten about her, but he came, caught her arm, and started to swing her up in his arms, but she resisted.

"I will not ride with you!" she taunted as she fought him.

"As you wish." His voice was as cold as his blue eyes as he dumped her on the ground beside the big paint. "Today you will walk until you are a more obedient slave."

"Damn you, I'm not used to walking."

"I know that, Blaze." He looked down at her as he

looped a rope around her trim waist and tied it to his saddle. "You give me no choice but to teach you who is master here. I am going to break you as I would a wild filly."

"I will not be broken, and I will not walk." She sat down in the middle of the path as the Apaches fell into line and began to ride out.

"Very well, then I shall drag you."

"You wouldn't dare!"

"Try me!" His blue eyes flashed glacier fire and that square chin was set.

This was not a man who could be pushed around by any woman.

"You dirty rogue!" She scrambled to her feet and began to walk.

He rode alongside her. "When you decide you are going to behave yourself, I will let you ride."

"You'll wait a helluva long time!" She struck him on the leg, making the horse snort and dance about.

"Such language for a lady," Cougar chided, "you may have more starch to you than I give you credit for, Blaze."

"My name is not Blaze!" Libbie screamed at him.

He looked down at her. "No, maybe you don't deserve that name. It is a good name for an Apache woman, not a spoiled, weak white girl." He nudged his horse on and didn't look back at her.

What to do? Libbie wavered. If she sat down, she had no doubt that she had challenged him to the point that he would indeed drag her. On the other hand, if she behaved herself, he was going to put her on the saddle before him so he could put his big hands on her waist again and pull her up against his virile body. *What to do?*

She would show him she was not a mare to be broken obediently to a man's will.

"Okay, I'll show you! I will walk!" She put her nose in the air and lifted her skirts, striding along.

He looked back over his shoulder and nodded. "That's a good slave. Remember, all you have to do is ask politely and I'll let you ride."

"I'll crawl first."

He smiled thinly and clucked to his horse. "Suit yourself, stubborn one."

Libbie took a deep breath and began to stride after his horse, tied by the leash around her waist like a disobedient puppy. She who had been willful and full of pride was now being treated like this man's pet, and he had full control over her destiny. She could not bear it!

All around her, quiet Apache women rode along, looking back at her. Why had she never noticed how thin and tired these women and children were? Phillip had said Indian agent Tiffany was taking good care of his wards, but they certainly didn't look like it. No wonder he and his partner, elderly Ebenezer Higginbottom, were getting rich; they must be cheating the Indians out of most of their government supplies.

Don't be an idiot, Libbie, she scolded herself. *Why should you worry about the welfare of a bunch of savages that have kidnapped you?*

Her little handmade shoes were going to be worn through by these rocks and cockleburs, but there was no help for it. She gritted her teeth, stared straight ahead, and walked. She knew that Cougar glanced back at her frequently, his face troubled, but she ignored him and kept moving.

The sun was beginning to climb in the March sky, and the day got warmer as the little group headed south. At least she was holding the tribe up with her slow walk. Maybe she could delay them until the army caught them.

After a while, the Indians stopped to rest by a small

creek. She waited for Cougar to offer her a drink, but he only nodded toward the water as he filled his canteen. She knelt next to his horse and drank her fill, trying not to think what the girls back at Miss Priddy's would think if they could see her on her knees. In the meantime, he had remounted. She could feel his gaze on her back. Libbie whirled and glared at him. "I can hardly wait to see you hang!"

He grinned. "Phillip is probably having to use a white or a Zuni tracker, and he'll find they aren't as good as Apache scouts. He'll never catch us. Let me know when you're tired enough to ride."

Libbie hesitated. Her feet were sore and aching. "And beg for it? I think not!"

He shifted his weight in his saddle. "Suit yourself, spoiled white girl."

Damn him. She was so very, very tired, but she wasn't going to admit it if she laid down on the trail and died right there. "I'm feeling very refreshed, thank you."

He chewed his lip as if fighting a battle with himself. "All right, then. Everyone else has already pulled out. Get moving!"

With her head high in the air, Libbie followed after him and his big stallion. Her feet were getting blisters on them and her legs were so weary, she wasn't sure she could keep moving. He glanced back over his shoulder and tugged on the line around her waist. "Hurry it up. You're slowing the march down."

Which was precisely the idea, Libbie reminded herself. In the distance, she could see low-lying purple hills. If she could slow the Apaches, maybe the army could catch up to them.

It was past midday and warm. She felt perspiration running down her breasts as she walked, and she wondered if she were getting sunburned. The thought made her smile. Mrs. Everett had been so concerned about her ruining her pale skin. She wondered where her plump guardian was right now. That thief! Without Libbie as a meal ticket, the woman was going to have to go to work in a shop or as a maid. The thought cheered Libbie considerably. Having stolen Libbie's inheritance and wasted it, it was all the snooty dowager deserved.

Cougar looked over his shoulder again and tugged on the line. "You'll have to walk faster than that. We can't get left behind the line of march."

"So drag me." She stumbled, righted herself, and kept walking.

"Libbie—Blaze—if you'd beg me, I might give you a ride."

"Not if my life depended on it." She took a deep breath and kept walking toward him.

"We've got a long way to go," he warned. "You can't possibly walk that far."

She shrugged and kept moving, stumbled, went to one knee.

In a flash, he was off his horse, catching her. "You little fool! Will you let your pride kill you?"

"I will not beg," she said and struggled to get out of his arms.

"You're the damndest woman I ever met." He gathered her into his arms and carried her to his horse. "I always said you were too much woman for the lieutenant."

"Let me be the judge of that, you savage."

He reached and pulled the canteen off his saddle horn, then held it to her lips. She hesitated.

"Libbie, don't tell me you'll turn down water?"

She thought about it a minute. "I suppose not."

He looked relieved as she drank; then he poured a little in his hand and wiped it on her face. "Now you're going to ride."

"I don't think so." She struggled to stand up, but he caught her, hoisted her up on the stallion, and remounted behind her.

"We'll have to hurry to catch up to the others." He nudged his stallion into a lope.

Libbie took a deep breath and leaned back against his massive chest, ignoring the arm that went around her waist even though her breasts rested against the heat of that muscular arm. The truth was, she could not have walked much farther.

Cougar was both ashamed of himself for what he'd put her through and angry with her for not giving in.

"Stubborn woman," he grumbled and held her close as he rode. He was both exasperated and proud of her. She was made of better stuff than he had imagined. He was only too aware of the soft heat of her in his embrace, the weight of her breasts against his arm, and the tangle of red curls falling against his bare chest. He had never wanted a woman as much as he wanted this one—both wanted and hated her.

He vowed then that he would have Libbie Winters in his blankets, even with Lieutenant Van Harrington coming hard on his trail. The only problem now was how to get that necklace off her without force and what to do with her once he'd had his fill of her charms!

Libbie said, "Since I'm slowing you down, you might as well turn me loose. The army is bound to be gaining on us."

He resisted an urge to tangle his fingers in those fiery locks and see if they were as soft as they looked. "We've sent back a little welcoming party for the lieutenant."

Libbie sat up stiff and straight and tried to look past his wide shoulder. "An ambush! You've set up an ambush!"

Cougar nodded and hung on to her. "The lieutenant

doesn't know much about Apaches or this country. He'll lead his men right into our trap."

She must warn them. Libbie opened her mouth and screamed.

"Damn you, Blaze!" He clapped his big hand over her mouth, and they struggled as she tried to break free and get off the horse. The stallion snorted and reared as she sank her teeth into Cougar's hand and tried to scratch his face. He began to swear and she could taste his blood, but she didn't stop fighting. She managed to fall from the horse, biting and clawing. Her ripped dress came open, and he grabbed a handful of the soft lace of her bodice and tore it away, then stuffed it in her mouth while she gagged and fought him. "You fiery bitch, let's see you warn the soldiers now!"

She was both angry and terrified as she fought him, but he was much stronger than she was and he had both her small wrists in one big hand. Abruptly, he stopped, staring. She followed his gaze downward. Her breasts were completely bare, with the black gemstones resting against them. He reached out very slowly and paused uncertainly, his big hand only inches from her bare breast.

She froze and stopped fighting, looking up at him with wide green eyes, then down at his poised hand. She couldn't get the gag out of her mouth to scream or curse or protest.

He pulled back, his voice was a hushed whisper of awe. "No man has ever touched these, have they, Blaze?"

Oh, if she could get loose, she would sink her teeth in his arm so deep, he would bleed to death! She glanced down, frozen by the image of his big dark hand so near her naked breast. Her nipple went taut and swollen.

"Just what I thought," he whispered, and his eyes were hot with need. "You could be a passionate woman, Blaze. You just need the right man to teach you how."

She tried to twist out of his grasp, tried to tell him through the gag how much she hated him and how she could hardly wait to see Phillip shoot him or hang him, but her words were unintelligible. With his big hand holding both her small wrists, she couldn't do much of anything, but she made sure her eyes flashed green sparks of warning.

Now he cupped her chin in that free hand and turned her face up to look into her eyes. "Sooner or later, I intend to have you, Blaze," he promised softly. "You were meant to warm a man's blankets and give him sons, and I intend to be that man, necklace or no necklace."

She glared up at him, struggled to get away from his hand, and tried to tell him through the gag how much she hated him and what would happen if she ever got loose and got her hands on a knife or gun.

Cougar smiled. "Well, we'll see, Blaze. It may be a long time before the army ever tracks us down. In the meantime, we'll be camping in another hour or so, and we still have tonight to finish this conversation." He reached into his saddlebags for a scrap of rawhide to tie her wrists together, then threw her up on his stallion and mounted behind her. He nudged his horse into a lope to catch up to the others.

If she could only get this gag out of her mouth! She tried to rub it against his bare chest, hoping to dislodge it, but he only laughed, a touch of anger in his tone. "Behave yourself, Blaze. I promise I'll give you the attention you deserve once we get camped."

His words struck fear in her heart. Tonight, when he felt safe from pursuit, would he use her for his pleasure?

Behind them, in the distance, she heard the sudden echo of rifle fire. Cougar glanced over his shoulder. "Looks like our green lieutenant and his men have ridden into our trap. I'll secure you and then I'll go back and help."

With that, Cougar nudged his horse into a lope and rode along a narrow trail to a stronghold high in the rocks. Behind them in the distance, she heard the rattle of gunfire.

He was off the stallion before it was even stopped, lifting her effortlessly and carrying her to a place in the rocks. Her bare breasts were against his naked chest, but Cougar seemed to pay no attention. He made sure she was tied securely, said something to the old woman, then checked his rifle and remounted. He took off back up the trail toward the sounds of battle.

Libbie struggled with her bonds, but they held firm. It was only a couple of hours until dusk, and she could only guess where she might be in the wild, rugged countryside. *Mexico?*

No one paid any attention to her, not even Owl Woman. Libbie was a prize that belonged to Cougar, she realized. If he didn't come back, what would happen to her? And if he did come back, had he decided to use her for his pleasure and his vengeance and forget the promise he had made her?

Chapter Fourteen

Libbie watched Cougar ride out with most of the other warriors to fight the soldiers who had been hot on their trail. Everyone seemed busy; no one was paying any attention to her. Maybe now was the time to escape. She rubbed her gag against a rock until she freed her mouth; then she began to work on the ropes that bound her with her teeth. Minutes seemed to race by as fast as the beat of her heart as she struggled with the ropes. Finally, she had them loose enough to slip her hands free.

She glanced around furtively. The children were running and playing, the women busy setting up camp. In the distance, she could see the horses grazing on the sparse desert vegetation. From over the rise, the firing still echoed through the canyons. She looked for old Owl Woman, but she was busy setting up a wickiup. Libbie made her plans. Maybe if she made her escape and worked her way back toward the soldiers, they might find her before it got dark.

Very quietly, she sneaked through the chaparral toward

the horses, her heart pumping with danger and excitement. If anyone spotted her trying to escape, there was no telling what they would do to her. She hesitated, then decided she had to take that chance before Cougar returned to claim his prize. From the way he had looked at her and everything he'd said, she had a feeling that tonight he might ignore the promise of the necklace and take her. The thought scared her, but it was also oddly exciting. He was big and powerful and primitive, with only a razor-thin veneer of civilization. She had a feeling that what he laid claim to, he took.

Of one thing she was certain—the snooty lieutenant would no longer be interested in her if another man had her first. And if Phillip weren't interested in her, he wouldn't be so eager to rescue her.

A dark gray mare grazed at the edge of the herd. Libbie looked around again to make sure no one noticed her movement. Everyone was too busy with children or setting up camp. She didn't even have a saddle. Could she ride bareback? Of course she could, but what would she do for a bridle?

Taking two long hair ribbons from her fiery locks, she tied them together and moved closer to the mare. Very slowly, Libbie approached, thinking that if it bolted and fled, the others might stampede. "Hey, girl, whoa there; don't move," she crooned, moving closer.

Then she felt silly, thinking the horse only understood Apache. The mare raised her head and snorted, but allowed Libbie to walk up to her and pat the dark velvet nose. Quickly, Libbie looped the pink hair ribbons around the mare's lower jaw in a makeshift bridle. It wasn't the best, but it would have to do. Taking a deep breath for courage, Libbie stepped up on a rock and climbed up bareback. For a long moment, she waited for some Apache to shout a warning, but there was no sound save the distant gunfire. It took all Libbie's self-control not to panic and do something rash, but she nudged the mare into a slow walk away from the camp and through the chaparral.

She didn't dare breathe or look back as she walked the mare away from the herd, expecting to hear a shout of alarm or worse yet, feel a bullet's sting as she rode out. Unconsciously, she reached up to touch the string of Apache Tears, thinking how angry Cougar would be when he returned to discover she had escaped.

What to do now? She wasn't sure from the confusing echoes of gunfire in just which direction the army patrol was holed up. If she weren't careful, she would ride right into the fighting. She decided she would just ride north until she ran onto some white civilization.

The sun had disappeared behind heavy banks of clouds, and the wind had picked up and changed direction. Libbie paused, no longer certain which direction to ride. The shifting pattern of the wind had muffled the gunfire so that she was no longer sure exactly where the soldiers were, and she dared not ride right into the Apache warriors. Perhaps if she swung in a wide circle, she could miss the Apaches and still find the soldiers. That decided, she rode cautiously, stopping now and then to listen, but the echoes through the canyons were blurred and confusing. *Suppose she didn't find the soldiers and ended up out in the night alone?*

The thought made her shiver. There were bears, bobcats, and rattlesnakes out here in this rugged country, and it was only a few hours until dark. No, she must not think of that, she must think about how nice it would be to return to civilization and . . . what? There wasn't anything waiting back there for her except a greedy young officer who was after her money or a cranky old geezer who wanted to trade his gold for her body. *Well, maybe she could find a job. Doing what?* Speaking French and playing the piano hardly qualified Libbie to make her own way in the world.

That wasn't the problem of the moment, she thought as she rode on. Getting back to white civilization was what mattered now.

Cougar was going to be so angry! Libbie smiled with satisfaction at the thought. He was the most arrogant, insolent male she had ever encountered, and he hated her with a passion that mystified her. For a moment, her memory lingered on the way he had held her against him, the heat of his big body cradling her as they slept, the hunger in his eyes when he looked at her. No man had ever looked at Libbie that way before, as if possessing her meant more than anything in the world to him.

"Are you crazy?" she scolded herself as she rode through the yucca and cactus. "He didn't care about you. He only saw you as a commodity to be traded for rifles and supplies."

And yet, the way he had looked at her lingered in her mind still. Why, tonight he had probably planned to . . . Her pulse quickened at the images that came unbidden to her mind when she thought about Cougar and the way his big hand had trembled as it hovered close to her breast. She didn't know whether she feared or anticipated his caress. *You were meant to pleasure a man and give him sons.*

"You arrogant bastard!" she said under her breath, "you won't be the man I'll pleasure. I'll teach you to kidnap me! I'll see you hang!"

If she'd been paying more attention to the trail ahead rather than thinking about Cougar, she might have seen the rattlesnake lying coiled up on a rock near the trail sooner than she did, but she barely got a glimpse of it before her mare whinnied and reared.

"Whoa, girl!" Libbie fought to hang onto the mare's neck, but with no more than a ribbon for a bridle and no saddle, Libbie flew off in a tumble of torn pink velvet and tousled red hair before the mare took off at a gallop. The snake promptly scurried away into the rocks.

"Damn it, now what do I do?" Libbie stood up and brushed herself off. She was sore and limping from her tumble, her ankle possibly sprained. She paused and looked around, realizing with sudden clarity that she was a long way from either white civilization or the Apache camp. This was rough country, with little water and no food. With the sun behind heavy clouds, she wasn't even sure which direction to begin to walk. She paused and listened.

From a distant hilltop, a wolf howled. That and the beating of her own heart were the only sounds she heard. The gunfire had ceased. *Was the battle over or were both sides taking a rest while they reloaded their weapons?* There was no way to know.

Libbie licked her dry lips and wished she had grabbed a canteen as she left. She could do without food for a day or two, but she had to have water. Well, she would just have to walk until she found some. She squared her small shoulders and set off with a determined step, limping in the direction that might take her toward the army patrol. Damn. Her ankle was beginning to swell and she wondered just how far she could go. The wolf howled again; it sounded closer now.

She might be spoiled and sheltered, but she could be resourceful, too. She picked up a stick to use as a weapon and kept limping along. It would soon be dark, and who knew then what wild animals, snakes, tarantulas, and Apaches would be out there in her path? No, she would not think about any of that. Libbie stuck her chin out with stubborn determination and kept walking, using the stick as a cane.

* * *

"Retreat! Sound retreat!" Phillip shouted as he waved frantically at his men scattered through the rocks. All around him, soldiers were pinned down by deadly Apache gunfire, the shots ricocheting off the boulders.

Damn those Injuns! Phillip stumbled backward, running for his horse. In the confusion of retreat, men shouted and screamed as they fell wounded. So this was what war was really like; not parades and medals, but men dying, all sweaty and bloody. Was this the way his father had died, terrified and sweating, screaming as Phillip was screaming deep inside?

Ye gods! He must get hold of himself! Phillip struggled to mount his rearing, snorting horse. He felt cold sweat running down his back, although the day was not that warm.

"Lieutenant!" Phillip turned in his saddle as a grizzled old sergeant rose up out of nearby rocks. "What's your orders, sir?"

"Orders?" Phillip was intent on saving himself, he wasn't thinking of command.

"Shall I sound recall, sir? Try to get the wounded out?"

"Yes, of course. I—I'm headed back to the fort for reinforcements!" And with that, Phillip spurred his horse into a gallop and headed away from the battleground.

Damn those Apaches! He'd sworn he'd seen Cougar in the midst of the fighting. Too bad he hadn't managed to get that half-breed in his gunsights. Phillip was miles away from the fighting when it dawned on him that in his panic, he hadn't given much thought to Elizabeth Winters. Phillip shrugged. She might be dead anyway, or even worse, raped by those savages, so she might as well be dead. He didn't want a wife who'd been had by Injuns, no matter how rich and beautiful she was.

Once safely away from the battle site, he slowed his lathered horse to a walk and glanced back over his shoulder. Behind him, the men had regrouped. Wounded and weary, they slumped on exhausted horses as they followed him toward the fort. Phillip wheeled his horse to ride back to the grizzled old sergeant. "We rode into an ambush, bad business."

The old sergeant wiped blood from a cut on his forehead. "Yes, sir." He didn't say anything else; he didn't need to. The sergeant had warned him they were riding into a canyon that would make a great place for an ambush, but Phillip, eager to catch up with the Apache and slaughter them, hadn't listened.

Now that he realized he was in no immediate danger, Phillip calmed down. He might still figure out a way to get a medal out of this and make Mama proud. "Sergeant, we'll report in, muster a larger force, and go after them again."

"Begging your pardon, sir, but my men have been hit pretty hard."

Phillip shrugged and tried to look concerned. "Anybody killed?"

"No, sir, but some of them hurt bad and we've lost a horse or two as well as a pack mule loaded with ammunition."

"Damn!" Phillip wiped sweat from his mustache with the back of his blue-clad arm. "Now they'll be shooting at us with our own bullets."

"Apaches are pretty good at that, sir—that is, if we find them again. We're not too far from the border. Once they're across that and reach the Sierra Madre we can forget about chasing them."

Elizabeth. That half-breed bastard, Cougar, had Elizabeth. Tonight, he would be using her for his pleasure, something Phillip had never gotten to do. The thought made him so angry, he clenched his teeth until his jaw hurt. "Sergeant, we've got to go after them again. They've got a white woman with them, and we all know what that means."

"Yes, sir." The old sergeant looked sympathetic. Everyone in the outfit knew by now that the abducted girl was Phillip Van Harrington's fiancée.

It was dark before the remnants of the patrol stumbled into the fort. Phillip was more than a little aware of the soldiers gathering silently as his defeated men rode toward the barn.

He might as well get it over with. With a sigh, Phillip turned his horse toward the colonel's office and dismounted, then went inside. "Lieutenant Van Harrington reporting in."

The pimply-faced young private at the front desk hopped up and gave him a quick salute and a curious stare before retreating into the inner office to announce him. Then he held the door open. "The colonel will see you now, sir."

The colonel's expression grew as black as a thunderstorm as Phillip limped in and saluted. "At ease, Lieutenant. You look like you could use a drink."

"Yes, sir." He sank gratefully into a chair. "We ran into an ambush."

The colonel handed him a whiskey and frowned. "Ambush? You had some experienced men with you— didn't they warn you?"

Of course they had, and Phillip had ignored them. He was, after all, a major's son and part of the aristocracy of Philadelphia which made him too superior to listen to common scouts and soldiers. "Perhaps I was too intent on rescuing Miss Winters."

"Oh, yes, I had forgotten your fiancée." The officer

hesitated, running his hand through his gray hair. "I don't know how to broach this delicately, Lieutenant, but you must realize that by the time you get her back, the warriors may, well . . . have had their way with her."

Rape. He meant rape.

"They wouldn't dare!" Phillip was seething as he threw the drink down the back of his throat. But he knew Cougar. Cougar would do anything he damn well pleased. "What I meant to say, sir, is that I expect they will hold her for ransom and won't harm her; she's an heiress, you know."

"I doubt the Apache know that—"

"Excuse me, sir, but Cougar's leading them; I think he knows."

"Hmm. Ransom." The colonel didn't look too certain. "Army policy wouldn't allow us to give them weapons, no matter how much danger the girl is in."

"But we could give them money, couldn't we, sir, for food and supplies? Of course, I intend to attack the camp and wipe them out before they could ever spend a dime of it."

"Excuse me for pointing this out, Lieutenant, but from what I saw from my window as your outfit rode in, I'd say the Apache are the ones who are doing the wiping out."

Phillip felt his face burn with humiliation and anger. Damn the old man for that observation. "I—I may not be as good a soldier as my father, sir, but—"

"Oh, yes, Bill Van Harrington." The colonel nodded. "Good man. Even the Apache respected him."

"Sir? The Apaches murdered him."

"Oh, yes, I'm sure that rumor . . ." The older man cleared his throat. "Of course. So what are your observations, Lieutenant?"

Phillip leaned forward. "If I can have more troopers, sir, and start tomorrow—"

"Unless you get a good scout, you're wasting your time,

Lieutenant." The colonel's voice was curt. "Washington won't stand for another ambush like this one. I'll have to give this some thought."

"Thought?" Phillip's voice rose in disbelief. "Ye gods, sir! Miss Winters—"

"I know, and I'm sorry if something happens to the young lady, but we need someone who knows both the country and the Apaches before I send out more troops. You're dismissed, Lieutenant."

"Yes, sir." Phillip came to his feet and saluted smartly. There went his newest medal. He wasn't going to get to be a hero and have his picture in the Philadelphia newspapers. Mama would have been so proud that he was following in Father's footsteps, killing Apaches. By the stern set of the colonel's face, there obviously wasn't much use in arguing with his commander. Phillip started to say something else, but the colonel was already digging through the papers on the desk.

Phillip turned and went out. *Damn the old man and damn those Injuns.* He smiled, imagining how it would feel to get Cougar in his rifle sights. It would be more satisfying than killing big game. By fair or foul means, he intended to see that half-breed dead!

What he needed now was another drink! Phillip limped back to his quarters and opened a fresh bottle of whiskey. It was late afternoon and would soon be dark. After dark, would Cougar use Libbie for his pleasure? Maybe he had already done so? He gritted his teeth in frustration and gulped another drink. Obviously it was going to be a day or two before the colonel authorized another patrol. Phillip knew he should go down to the base infirmary and check on the welfare of his men, but it was comfortable here in his room and he was tired and annoyed.

The bear's head over the fireplace seemed to glare down at him in a way that made him uneasy, as if it were still alive. "Damned Apache superstitions!" He threw the whiskey bottle at the mounted head and caught it across the snout before the glass crashed into the stone fireplace and shattered in a tinkle of shards.

A knock sounded at the door. Phillip reached to open another bottle. Maybe if he ignored the knock, whoever it was would go away. He didn't feel like talking to anyone right now; he only wanted to plan his revenge and drink.

Again the knock, more insistent this time.

"Go away! Damn it!"

"Lieutenant, it's me!" Shashké's plaintive voice called.

Phillip grinned. He'd sworn he was not going to bother with the sultry Apache bitch again, but he needed a woman and if she was willing . . . or even if she weren't . . .

"Just a minute, I'm coming!" He staggered to the door and threw it open. She stood on the step, her face buried in her hands, her shoulders shaking with sobs. Libbie's gold earrings flashed in the dim light and a pathetic, wilted flower drooped in her hair. "Come on in, you pretty little—"

Very slowly, she moved her hands, and he noticed the red on them and wondered about it even as she raised her head.

"My God!" Phillip stumbled backward in horrified shock as he got a good look at her face. It was slashed and bloody, and part of her nose was gone. "What the hell—?"

She burst into sobs, holding bloody, entreating hands out to him. "My old husband found out about us! But you still care about me, don't you? Remember how much pleasure I've—"

He retreated in horror from her bloody, outstretched hands, shaking his head at her. "Get away from me! You look like a monster! Get the hell out of my sight, you ugly—"

"But Phillip, I have no one, no place to turn—"

"You think I give a damn? You knew what you were

doing when you took that chance." He shook off her bloody hand that grasped his arm as she begged and pleaded.

"My beauty was all I had to offer. Where shall I go now? What shall I do?"

"Honey, that's not my problem." He shoved her off the doorstep, slammed the door, and locked it, then stood there a moment shaking as she pounded against the door and cried. After a moment, there was only silence outside.

"God, I need another drink!" He staggered over to wash her blood from his hands and open another bottle. When he looked up, all the dead bears in his room seemed to be glaring at him.

Shashké slumped in the dirt in front of the lieutenant's quarters, staring at the door that had just been slammed in her face. She was in pain and distraught and now her last hope had vanished. The penalty among Apaches for an unfaithful wife was disfigurement, and her beauty had been all she had to offer.

Very slowly, she rose and walked away from his door, weeping with anguish. The area was deserted as she walked across the parade ground and faded into the desert beyond. She had held the slightest hope that the lieutenant had actually cared a little about her and would take her in or at least give her a little money. She had nowhere to turn now. No Apache would befriend her, with her scarred face betraying her guilt at breaking the old taboo. In her heart began to burn a fierce hatred for the white soldier who had used her and tossed her aside.

What to do now? She was in pain, distraught, and homeless. Surely there must be someone who would help her. Shashké stopped weeping and thought about it. The desert chill had descended on the area when darkness fell, and she shivered with the cold. Shashké thought a moment, then smiled. Yes, there was someone who cared about the Apaches. Hadn't he once taken in another Apache girl who was suddenly alone? Yes, she knew who might help her without judging, without asking any questions; a kind, gentle man.

Shashké began to walk, and as she walked, she planned her revenge.

Cougar had aimed his rifle at Lieutenant Van Harrington as that officer began his pell-mell retreat from the battle site. Just as he started to squeeze the trigger, he remembered. He must not, could not, spill Phillip's blood. Regretfully, he lowered his rifle. Too bad the lieutenant had no such qualms about shooting at Cougar!

He watched with satisfaction as the lieutenant and his patrol retreated in confusion and disarray. It would be a long time before the army got on their trail again. Once they reached the stronghold high in the mountains of Mexico, the Apache could live happily again.

Blaze. What was he to do about her? He frowned as he thought about that vexing problem. Cougar mounted up and signaled his warriors to ride out and rejoin the camp a few miles to the south. No doubt tonight the council would insist he send a messenger to the fort with their terms of ransom. Yes, they needed the food and supplies, all right, but the trouble was, Cougar did not want to give up the girl.

Damn her. He told himself she was his enemy's woman and that he hated her, but yet she drew him to her in a way that no other woman ever had, a way that made him weak and willing to do anything if she would only send a smile his way. After the way she had humiliated and spurned him, he had not meant to grow attached to the fiesty white girl, and yet his attachment grew with each passing hour.

He glanced down at his bitten hand as he headed back to camp. He had to admire her spunk, even though she had journeyed to Arizona to see him hang. Maybe if he enjoyed her once, he would lose interest and realize that she was just a woman like a hundred others, even with that fiery mane of hair that she tossed like a wild mustang filly. He both desired and hated her—hated her because she made him want her so badly when a dozen pretty Apache girls would be happy to warm his blankets. But for him, there was only Blaze, and he was certain there would never be another he wanted so badly.

And she hated him with a passion that made it certain she'd kill him with his own weapon if she ever got the chance. He'd be smart to let the lieutenant ransom her and get the redhead out of the Apache camp. She was born to be in Phillip's bed, not Cougar's. Still, the thought of the other man holding her close, kissing her, stroking her, and finally mating with her, drove him into an anguished rage. He could not use her for his pleasure because of his honor, and yet he decided at that moment that he would not give her up without a fight, no matter how much gold the proud lieutenant offered.

Cougar rode into camp, dismounted, and tossed his paint's reins over a bush.

The Apache women began a chant to welcome their triumphant warriors' return. Someone had started a big fire for the dancing. Cougar smiled. He was looking forward to the feasting and the repartee with the fiery white girl. He strode toward his wickiup.

At that moment, Owl Woman ran toward him, wringing her weathered hands. "She is gone! Your captive has escaped!"

Chapter Fifteen

Cougar dismounted and gently comforted the hysterical Owl Woman. "It is not your fault. How did this happen?"

Quickly, she filled him in, wringing her hands. "I hardly took my eyes off her."

"I know." Cougar nodded. He couldn't help admiring Libbie's resourcefulness and daring. "She's not your average, whimpering white girl."

"I should have watched her better. I know the council has great need of the ransom she would bring."

"No one could have done better," he assured her, laying a gentle hand on her stooped shoulder. "The girl is as ornery and slippery as any Apache."

"What will you do?"

Cougar glanced toward the dark sky. "There are many dangers out there for a woman alone in this rough country. I'd better find her fast or . . ." He didn't even want to think of the things that could happen to the red-haired vixen.

Cougar swung back up on his horse, his worry making him increasingly annoyed with Blaze. He had counted on taking his ease by the fire all evening, feasting his eyes on the flame-haired beauty. But now, like the unpredictable little wench she was, she had taken off, trying to find her way back to civilization. Damn her for her foolishness! She had a better chance of crossing the trail of wild animals or dying of hunger or thirst, and it would be his fault. He had to find her.

Leaving the others dancing and smoking around the big fire, he rode around the camp, asking if any horses were missing. A woman complained that she had checked the herd and her sleek gray mare was gone. Cougar rode out to inspect the herd, knowing he couldn't tell much in the dark. As he looked, his keen vision spotted a lathered gray mare standing quietly, and when she moved, she limped. Then Cougar noticed the length of pink ribbon tied as a makeshift bridle and now dragging along the grass.

Cougar took a deep breath of relief and dismounted to inspect the mare. He took the hair ribbon and held it a long moment, remembering how it had tied back Blaze's long locks. What could have happened? Evidently she had taken the mare and something terrible had happened. Perhaps she had been thrown. He felt sudden alarm as he pictured her lying dead or injured somewhere in the wilderness at night.

Why couldn't Blaze behave herself and do as she was told? And yet, he knew she wouldn't have been half so intriguing if she'd been a conventional, obedient woman. She was a challenge for any man, and the one who finally tamed her would have a superior mate. Mate? She hated the sight of him, and right now, if he had her in his grasp, he would shake her until her teeth rattled and she yelled for mercy.

He grinned at the thought in spite of himself. Libbie Winters wouldn't beg for mercy if he spanked her little bottom until she was so sore, she couldn't sit down. At this point, that was a very tempting thought.

The moon came out then, round and full. Cougar rode away from the herd, following the limping tracks of the gray mare. However, the ground was rocky, and sometimes it took all his tracking skills to follow the trail. Now and then, he dismounted to take a closer look at the faint prints in the moonlight. The desert night had turned chill. He was a hardened warrior, used to the worst of elements, but Blaze was inexperienced. She probably had no food or water, and if she were hurt and afoot ... He must not think about that, and yet he worried, knowing he could never forgive himself if something had happened to her.

Patiently, he followed the faint tracks, stopping now and then to listen. Somewhere in the distance, a wolf howled and Cougar automatically reached for his rifle, making sure it was loaded. Besides wild animals, there could be other enemies in the open country, Mexican troops or renegade whites, or tribes that were enemies of the Apache.

He dismounted again, peering at the ground in the moonlight, reading the sign. Here was where she had been thrown from the horse and it had gotten away from her. At least Blaze could walk, although she now appeared to be limping. Cougar followed her small footprints across rocky soil, saw a place where she had fallen, gotten up, and walked on. Here she had lost a shoe. He picked it up, noted how small it was, and tucked it in his saddlebag.

Up ahead, a movement caught his eye and his heart quickened. But when he investigated, it was only a torn bit of pink fabric caught in a cholla cactus. He picked it up, running his fingers over it, thinking it was not half so soft as her skin. He had a sudden image of her, all silken and soft and yielding in his arms, and the terrible need made him angry with her all over again. No man should feel such a hunger for one woman; it put him at her mercy.

Cougar gritted his teeth and refused to acknowledge that need. He was angry, he told himself, because Blaze was so disobedient and had caused him so much trouble. If he were going to keep her, he needed to teach her obedience. No; he shook his head. Of course he could not keep her. He must trade her for guns and supplies. Rich young Lieutenant Van Harrington was going to pay a fortune to get her returned to his bed. That thought made him even angrier. She was too much woman for the prissy officer.

He began to walk again, leading his horse and watching for Blaze's tracks. Then he saw a faint print that made his heart almost stop, and his horse snorted and stamped uneasily. Cougar knelt and examined it, hoping it was an old track, but his keen senses told him it was fresh. A bear, a big bear by the look of the footprint, was on Blaze's trail, too. Bears were coming out of hibernation at this time of the year and they would be hungry and cantankerous.

Did Blaze know she was being followed by a bear? Probably not. Her tracks were moving at a limping walk, not a run, and bears could move silently if need be. The bear would have the advantage over both the humans. Every one of Cougar's sharp senses was heightened as he followed the trail, pausing to smell the wind and listen for the slightest sound.

Was that the scent of her perfume? Of course he must be imagining that. For a moment, he remembered the clean scent of her hair against his chest as he had held her. She had been so warm and soft in his embrace, and he had yearned to cup her naked breasts in his hands, kiss and caress them. If he had touched those, he would not have been able to stop himself from giving in to his passion. He had fought a terrible need to hold her close, to kiss and protect her. Now she was out here with no protection. If anything happened to her because he had carried her off, Cougar would never forgive himself.

Yet to care too much was a weakness he couldn't allow himself. Cougar shook his head. It wasn't that he cared about the girl, he told himself stubbornly, it was that she was such a valuable hostage for the Apaches—too valuable to lose.

Cougar took the scrap of pink fabric and tied it around his paint's muzzle so it would not whinny and alert the bear, although the scent was blowing toward the horse and rider. Then he paused, listening. Nothing but the wind and, somewhere, a coyote yipping at the coming night. Impulsively, he called out, "Blaze? Blaze, are you out here?"

No answer. Of course it had been stupid for him to yell her name. Even if she were within range of his voice, Blaze was too ornery to answer and make it easy to find her. In some spots now, the brush was so thick that he might walk right past her without seeing her if she hunkered down and kept quiet.

Where was the bear? He wasn't sure, and he dared not call out a warning about her danger. The knowledge that a bear was also on her trail might cause her to panic and go running blindly through the brush and over a cliff in these rough hills. On the other hand, he thought with grudging admiration, Blaze was not the typical white woman. She'd probably be as brave and resourceful as any Apache girl. He paused and considered. She couldn't be that far ahead of him. Maybe if he swung in a wide circle, he could come up on her other side and get between her and the bear.

Quiet as a shadow, Cougar moved off the trail, trying to judge just how far ahead of him she might be. If that bear caught up with her before he got there, Blaze didn't stand a chance. At that moment, his stallion got a scent of the bear and bolted, tearing the reins from Cougar's hands and galloping away, his rifle hanging on his saddle. Well, damn, now he was without a weapon except for a knife in his belt; not much use against a bear.

Libbie had paused and listened to Cougar's voice calling, "Blaze? Blaze, are you out here?"

Oh, damn! He was somewhere behind her, but she didn't intend to be recaptured. She quickened her step, not about to answer and lead him to her. She'd lost one shoe, and her ankle was swollen from the fall. Her dress was also badly torn from catching on passing cactus. Maybe the chances of walking until she found the soldiers was slim, but she had to try. Libbie kept moving, trying to be very quiet. Behind her, she heard a crashing sound through the brush and looked back, breathing hard. Cougar was usually as silent as a ghost, but maybe his big horse was making the noise. Yes, it did sound like a horse galloping away. Maybe he was afoot, too.

Could she outrun him? She shook her head as she considered. Not a chance, but she might outsmart him and still get away. It would be dark soon; maybe she could lose him in the darkness. She realized that was a small chance, too; Cougar was one of the army's best scouts and trackers. Still, what other option did she have? Even if she eluded him, it meant spending the night out here alone in this rough country with no food or water. Yet tomorrow she might run into an army patrol; all she had to do was be brave and resourceful tonight.

Libbie moved on, limping even more. Behind her, the crashing sounds through the brush sounded even closer. It couldn't be the horse again. Then the thought came to her: *What or who had made the stallion panic?* Cougar wouldn't make that much noise. She took a deep breath for courage and picked a small limb off a stunted tree. She wasn't even certain whether what she heard was real or a figment of her vivid imagination, but right now she was scared. She braced herself against a tree stump with her club raised and watched a clearing a few hundred feet away as the crashing sound grew louder and another sound was carried on the breeze, a sound that was half snarl, half roar.

Abruptly, something big and black loomed up out of the brush. Libbie bit her lip to hold back a scream and gripped her club tighter as a giant bear reared up out of the shadows, roaring and raking the air with powerful claws.

Now she did scream long and loud. The bear was close enough that she could feel the heat of its big body, smell the fetid scent of it, see the gleam of its teeth. Libbie screamed again, stumbled backward, and went down, the bear lumbering toward her.

At that moment, a form stepped out of the woods behind her and stood straddling her prone body as he faced the beast, unarmed but holding up his hands toward the bear.

Cougar. She could only lie there watching, too terrified to even scream as he faced the giant animal unarmed.

The bear hesitated even as Cougar said something to it in his native language. At that, the bear reared up again, hesitating uncertainly. Again Cougar spoke to it in Apache, his tone soothing.

The big bear paused, swaying on its hind legs, looked at him a long moment, then went to all fours and ambled away through the brush.

"Blaze, are you all right?" He turned and held out his hand.

Libbie was crying and shaking so badly, she could barely grasp his hand, and as he pulled her to her feet, she went impulsively into the safety of his big arms.

He held her very close, stroking her hair. "It's all right. I won't let anything hurt you."

She couldn't stop crying, and now he was kissing the tears from her face. "Shh, Blaze, dear one, you're all right."

She realized suddenly that she was in his embrace, her arms around his neck, trembling and seeking the shelter of his muscular arms. *Was she out of her mind?*

Libbie pulled away from him awkwardly, embarrassed. He was her captor, yet she had gone unthinking into his embrace. "What—what did you say to it?"

He let her move away from him. "I simply said, 'it is me, Grandfather,' and the bear, knowing who I am, did not attack."

"That's crazy." She shook her head.

"So the whites tell me, but you saw what happened. It is forbidden to kill bears; Apaches think our ancestors' spirits reside in them until they go to the Happy Place."

"But Phillip killed bears," she blurted, remembering how he had bragged about his hunting trophies. She was still staring after the disappearing bear, thunderstruck with awe.

Cougar shrugged. "He who kills the bear will feel the bear's wrath. Can you walk?"

Libbie took a step and winced. "Damn you, I thought I was about to get away."

"You were about to become my ancestor's dinner," he snapped. "Now Grandfather's spirit has spooked my horse and we're stranded out here until daylight. I don't want to risk running into that bear again in the dark. Next time, I might not have time to speak to him."

"I'm not returning to the Apaches."

"But of course you are."

She was tired, her ankle hurt, and she was discouraged at being recaptured. "I can't walk."

He looked around at the growing darkness. "I think we'll camp here until sunup. Maybe by then my horse will have come back."

"Fine. Have you got any food?" Maybe by morning, the soldiers would show up or she could outfox Cougar and lose him in this rough country.

"I've got my knife and maybe a match or two hidden in its sheath. If I can find a barrel cactus, that gives us water and we can peel and eat some prickly pear fruit. In the meantime, you could be at least a little grateful for my saving you."

"Grateful!" she snorted. "I wouldn't be in this fix if it weren't for you."

He looked annoyed as he began to build a small fire. "We'll make out all right until morning, and the fire will keep the animals away."

There went her idea for sneaking away into the darkness while he slept. There was nothing she could do but settle down by the small fire and wait while he went off into the darkness and came back in moments with part of a barrel cactus and some red prickly-pear fruit. It tasted good and she noticed he gave her his share. She started to say something, then decided he deserved to go hungry for getting her into this mess.

Now he took her other shoe off and examined her feet. "I'll have to get you some soft deerskin moccasins."

His big hands felt good massaging her instep. "I don't intend to be here that long."

"We'll see how fast the lieutenant comes up with the ransom." He rubbed each of her feet gently. "If the horse doesn't come back, I'll have to carry you."

"Don't you dare touch me!"

He glared at her, sighed heavily, and settled down before the fire. "Blaze, I'll touch you anytime I feel like it. As your captor, it's my privilege."

There was no point in arguing that. "So we're just going to sit here all night?"

He fumbled in his belt and came up with a small pouch of tobacco and papers. "Unless you want to take a chance on running into Grandfather bear."

"What—what would it take to get you to turn me loose?"

He raised one eyebrow at her, then returned to rolling a smoke.

She rushed on. "Suppose I—suppose I let you make love to me in exchange for freeing me?"

He threw back his head and laughed. "Have you ever had a man before?"

She felt her face flame. "You know I haven't!"

"Then you might not be skilled enough to make it enjoyable."

She was incensed. "You're turning me down?"

He seemed to be enjoying her confusion. "Let's just say the pleasure might not be worth the amount of ransom I'd have to forego. Besides, this isn't a very comfortable place for that, although I will admit your body would make a soft mattress."

"Oh, you half-breed bastard!" Libbie lunged at him, scratching and clawing. If she could sink her nails into those arrogant blue eyes . . . !

Cougar dropped the cigarette, threw up his hands to protect his face, then caught her wrists. They went down in a heap while they struggled. "You little wildcat! Stop that!"

"I am going to claw you to death!" Libbie fought to reach his face as they tumbled and rolled near the fire.

He came up on top. He lay there on her, both of them breathing hard as he pinned her hands above her head. "You little vixen! I ought to—"

He bent his head suddenly before she realized his intent, covering her mouth with his. He was too heavy for her to move as he pinned her down and kissed her deeply, thoroughly. His tongue invaded her mouth, ravaging it as he explored her lips, tasting and teasing, probing deeply with his tongue. No man had ever kissed her like this before. For a long moment, she surrendered to his seeking mouth, her body molding itself against the hard planes of his. She could feel his throbbing maleness through her torn dress and his skimpy loincloth. He was breathing hard, kissing her lips, her eyes, her throat as he murmured soft words she did not understand even as his mouth claimed hers again and his free hand moved down past the Apache Tears necklace to stroke her naked breasts.

Oh, God, no man had ever touched her like this, and the way her eager body responded scared her, arching up against his seeking fingers as the kiss deepened. At this point, she came to her senses and bit him.

Cougar pulled away from her with an oath, wiping one hand across his bloody mouth. "You are like embracing a viper!"

She sat up, pulling away from him, breathing hard, angry with him that she had momentarily surrendered with eagerness to the touch and taste of him. "Must I remind you that I am under the protection of your necklace?"

He paused and glared at her blackly, still wiping blood from his sensual mouth. "Don't push me, Blaze. It's already all I can do to keep from ripping it off your neck and taking you like you ought to be taken."

"Don't you touch me!" She knew her voice rose shakily as she backed away, knowing this was a big, virile stallion of a man. If he decided to throw her down and take her, she wouldn't be able to stop him, and from the look in his eyes, that was what he was thinking of at this very moment.

He took a deep breath and moved away from her. His hands were shaking as he rolled a cigarette. "The faster your lieutenant comes up with the money, the better it will be for all of us. You've been nothing but trouble from the first moment I laid eyes on you."

She realized that she was not in any immediate danger and pulled her knees up before her, resting her chin on them. Her dress was so torn, her bare legs were visible and he was staring at them, but she couldn't do anything about that. She wondered what it would be like to have the big savage make love to her. Would it be violent and exciting? Tender and gentle? "Have you made love to Shashké?"

He laughed without humor and continued to smoke. "What brought that on?"

"I saw you two outside the window the night of the dance."

Cougar shrugged. "Shashké's too ambitious to pick an Apache as her lover. She wants . . . anyway, she is a married woman. It would not be honorable for a warrior to take her." Even though he had told her once before that Shashké was not his woman, she was surprised to realize she was relieved that Cougar had never been the greedy girl's lover. *Who* would *an ambitious girl choose*? "Are you telling me she's got a white lover?"

He started to speak, then shrugged. "You wouldn't believe me if I told you. Now settle down and let's get some sleep."

Did he know something he wasn't telling? No matter. Libbie looked around at the darkness uncertainly. "You think the bear will come back?"

He shrugged again, obviously enjoying her uneasiness. "Who knows?"

A coyote howled in the distance, and the sound echoed across the hills.

"Can you build the fire bigger?" She hunched closer to it, shivering a little. The desert night was growing chill.

"Not without either setting the whole desert afire or

alerting every enemy for miles. Settle down and get some sleep, Blaze.''

If the army were near, that wouldn't be a bad idea, she thought, but he was too smart for that. "I will never answer to Blaze," she said as she rolled up before the fire.

He shrugged, his face immobile. "You're right. It is not a proper name for a white girl; it is too fiery and free for anyone less than an Apache."

"Aren't you going to sleep?"

He didn't look at her, but stared into the fire and smoked. "Someone has to keep watch; you're under my protection."

Libbie settled down and closed her eyes. Somehow, she took comfort in the fact that he was watching over her. Libbie drifted off to sleep.

Just before dawn, Libbie awakened to a gentle touch on her shoulder. She opened her eyes and looked up into Cougar's blue ones. For a moment, she was puzzled, and then she remembered. She was still a captive; she hadn't escaped.

"My horse came back," Cougar said. "Are you ready?"

She sat up and groaned. Her body was stiff and sore from yesterday's adventure. "I'm not sure I can move."

"Then I'll carry you." Before she could protest, he swung her up in his big arms easily.

She started to struggle, but decided it was a waste of time. Cougar was the most stubborn, determined male she had ever met, and he would have his way. She let her face rest against his wide chest as he put her up on the paint stallion and swung up behind her. He held her against him and nudged the horse into a walk back toward the Apache camp. "The Apaches should have moved out before dawn. You have held us up," he scolded. "I hope you've given up trying to escape."

She couldn't help but smile up at him. "You know me better than that."

And now he actually grinned. She had forgotten how handsome he was when he smiled. "Blaze, I'd be disappointed in you if you gave up."

They rode back to the Apache camp. There were heavily ladened packhorses tied in the middle of the camp, and Libbie almost shouted with relief at the sight of white men sitting around the fire. She was saved!

Cougar frowned and helped her to dismount, then held up his hand by way of greeting. "I thought we would meet you on the other side of the border."

"Hello, Cougar." The men smiled and nodded. They were a scruffy-looking bunch, Libbie thought with sudden alarm, and she pulled her torn bodice closed. The lustful way the five white renegades looked her over made her very nervous. She found herself moving closer to Cougar, and he put an arm around her. This time, she welcomed the feel of that protective embrace. She almost shuddered as she looked over the leader. He was dirty and bearded with tangled hair. One of his eye sockets was empty.

The one-eyed one stepped forward and offered his hand to Cougar. Cougar hesitated a long moment before he shook it. "Hello, Coyote Johnson."

As close as he stood, she could smell him now and drew back from the rank scent of dried blood and whiskey. Johnson's good eye roamed over Libbie freely and he leered at her, showing broken yellow teeth.

"Cougar, the council did not lie when they told me of your captive. The woman is beautiful and worth much, and I know where I can sell her. Whatever ransom her man offers, I will pay more to own this white captive!"

Chapter Sixteen

Libbie shuddered and instinctively crept closer to Cougar's protective arm.

Johnson turned his empty eye socket toward her and grinned with jagged yellow teeth. "What's the matter, girlie? Scare you? Sheriff shot my eye out while I was escapin', and now I shoot every lawman I see."

She didn't say anything, horrified by the filthy, tangled beard and the smell of him.

Johnson laughed. "I hate women like you—dainty, high-class bitches who wouldn't spit on me." He looked at Cougar. "They tell me she's yours. What do you say, Cougar? We got a deal?"

"No!" Libbie shouted, her anger overcoming her horror. "I'm not his woman and I won't be yours, either!"

Johnson winked at her with his one good eye. "Spirited! I like that. Where'd you get her?"

Libbie interrupted. "I've been stolen from near Fort Grant. My fiancé is an officer there." She started to say more, but Cougar gave her a warning look and she lapsed into silence.

"An officer's woman?" Johnson rubbed his dirty, calloused hands together. "That makes it even better."

Cougar frowned. "The girl is a captive, that's all. I expect the rich lieutenant to pay plenty for her safe return."

Johnson looked over his shoulder at the grave Apache warriors sitting around the campfire. "Why don't we sit and smoke and talk a deal?"

"Why doesn't anyone ask me?" Libbie fumed.

"Hush up, girl," Johnson said. "You got no say in this."

"That's right," Cougar said, "but I don't want to sell her."

Johnson rubbed his mouth. Libbie noted that his rawhide vest was as filthy as his beard. "I got a good bottle of liquor and a wagonload of food and supplies to trade. Let's parlay."

Cougar hesitated, looking toward the supplies and then back toward the hungry, silent women and children standing in the shadows. "Maybe we might trade you a few good horses for flour and blankets."

Johnson grinned. "That ain't the filly I had in mind." He gestured toward Cougar's wickiup. "We'll drink and talk. Maybe we can work something out."

Cougar took Libbie's arm, pulling her with him as he led Johnson into the wickiup past the four other gunrunners who were eyeing her with lust as they sat around the campfire.

She started to say something, but Cougar motioned for her to sit by the fire and be silent. Then the two men sat down cross-legged by the fire and Johnson pulled out a bottle, took a long swig, and handed it to Cougar. Cougar barely took a sip, but Johnson didn't seem to notice. His evil gaze was on Libbie as he took out a small sack and began to roll a smoke. "I've got some prime weapons, blankets, and plenty of dried beef and flour."

"No doubt our own supplies stolen from the shipment by the Indian agent." Cougar frowned.

Johnson laughed. "I didn't ask him where he got the stuff; I just bought it."

"Look," Cougar said, "we need those supplies. We've got a few good horses to trade, and if you'll trust us for the rest—"

"Trust you? I wouldn't trust my own mother," Johnson snorted as he lit his smoke.

Cougar watched him thoughtfully. "Later, when the girl is ransomed, we'll have gold. We could pay you then."

Johnson looked at Libbie again with his one good eye, bright with lust. "I don't do business on credit, you know that."

"But those are our own supplies, stolen from us, and we need them."

Johnson spat to one side and grinned at Libbie. "You can't prove that, Injun. You know the kind of trade I want."

Libbie realized in growing horror that he was talking about her as he ran his tongue along his lower lip.

Cougar shook his head, watching the fear on her lovely face. He didn't want her to hear this discussion, so he spoke now in border Spanish. "Don't even think it, *hombre*. Her rich officer is going to give us plenty of gold and then we can buy supplies."

She looked at him curiously, but he ignored her.

Johnson laughed and said in Spanish, "Don't want her to know, huh? *Bueno*. We'll discuss the terms so she won't understand. Women have a tendency to get hysterical about such things."

"I told you no, *hombre*," Cougar said. "I'll wait for the gold from the officer."

"*Sí*, but that may take weeks," Johnson said, "and in

the meantime, you've got hungry children in this camp. I would buy the girl from you, for—oh, let's say, one thousand dollars worth of flour and blankets?"

Cougar could see by Libbie's face that she was about to demand an explanation, so he silenced her with a stern shake of his head and replied in Spanish. "You could buy a dozen Indian or Mexican girls for that much."

Johnson nodded in agreement. "*Sí*, but they don't have red hair and green eyes. There's a whorehouse in a port on the Mexican coast that caters to rich travelers. They would give twice that for a girl like this one, provided she could please at least a dozen men a night."

Cougar closed his eyes for a long moment as if he were thinking. In his mind, he saw dozens of men lining up to take their turn rutting on the delicate body of the girl sitting by the fire. An anger began to grow in him.

Johnson took another gulp of the liquor. "Think about it, *compadre*. There's a ship I know sailing in a couple of weeks. Some Oriental potentate or Arab sheik would pay plenty for a beauty like this for his harem."

Cougar frowned. "I told you, I don't want to sell her. She's too fiery for most men; no one could ever tame her."

"I could have a helluva good time myself tryin'," Johnson said good-naturedly. "I tell you what, *hombre*. If you don't want to sell her, maybe I could pay you just to enjoy her the rest of the day until we pull out."

The fury in Cougar's heart became almost uncontrollable. "I told you no. The white officer won't pay if she's returned dishonored."

"She's a virgin?" The trader rubbed his groin and licked his lips. "I'll up the ante then. I ain't never had me no virgin. What do you say, Injun? Her man will never know the difference if she don't tell him. You'll get my gold and what he's willin' to pay, too." He gestured toward Libbie and said in English, "Stand up and let me get a look at you, honey. I wanta see what I'm buyin'."

She turned horrified green eyes on Cougar. "You've sold me? You rotten bastard—"

Before Cougar could answer, Johnson reached out and caught her arm. "Stand up, honey. I want to see if you're worth the money—"

"Enough!" Cougar thundered, and his big hand shot out, caught Johnson's arm, and twisted it, freeing Libbie, who backed away.

The ugly gunrunner shrieked in pain as Cougar twisted so that the man was on his face in the dirt. "You're breakin' it off! My God! you're breakin' my arm!"

Libbie shrank against the side of the wickiup, terrified of the look on Cougar's face. She had heard of murderous rage, but this was the first time she had ever seen it in a man's eyes. Cougar kept the other man pinned, groveling and twisting with pain. "I'm going to let you up, Johnson. If you know what's good for you, you'll get out of here and take your men with you!"

He let go of the man's arm and Johnson stumbled to his feet, favoring his arm and sobbing. "I'll get you for this! I'll see your people never get another side of beef or even a measly blanket!"

Cougar grabbed the man and pitched him headlong out of the wickiup. "Get out of here, you carrion! Your money's no good here!"

Libbie ran to the door and looked out. Johnson was rounding up his men, swearing and still favoring his injured arm.

Cougar looked at her. "Are you all right?"

"You were going to sell me?" She glared up at him, shaking with the realization.

"You know better than that," he answered softly.

She didn't mean to cry; she intended to put up a hard

facade, but she couldn't keep the tears from beginning to overflow.

"You're all right; he won't get you." He pulled her into his arms and she let him. It felt so safe and reassuring in the circle of his powerful embrace. "Shush, Blaze, everything's all right now." He held her tightly against him, stroking her hair, while she clung to him, sobbing.

He didn't mean to, but he leaned over and kissed the top of her head, wanting to reassure her, wanting to protect her. If she noticed, she gave no sign, only clung to him, all soft and yielding and trembling. He wanted to tell her at that moment that he had tried to hate her for who she was, but he knew now that he had loved her from the first moment he saw her step off that stagecoach wearing a green dress with the sunlight reflecting off that fiery hair. No one would ever harm her as long as he had breath enough to lift a hand in her defense. He kissed the top of her head again. "Blaze," he murmured. "Oh, Blaze . . ."

She managed to get control of herself. *What was she doing, going into the arms of her kidnapper?* She wouldn't even be facing danger from men like Johnson if it weren't for Cougar. "Yes," she remarked suddenly, pulling away from him, "of course I'm safe. After all, I had forgotten you expect to get a big ransom for my return."

He turned away with a resigned sigh. "That's right. If I let Johnson take your virginity, you would be of much less value—even to our prissy lieutenant!"

"Why didn't I realize that you were thinking of the money, you—you savage!" She lashed out at him with both small fists, angry and confused, unsure of her own emotions.

Cougar threw up his hands to protect his face from her ridiculous attack as she pummeled him. She was so small, he was capable of breaking her back across his knee, but he could not hurt her. He only waited until she exhausted herself hitting against his massive chest; then she turned away, sobbing.

He watched silently, feasting his gaze upon her beauty. Each time she moved near him, he came closer to losing control of his passions. Just now, with her so warm and trembling in his arms, he had been torn between two emotions; he wanted to comfort and protect her, yet he yearned to pull her down on that pile of furs by the fire and take her with the need that had been building in him ever since the first moment he saw her. In his heart, he knew now that there would never, never be another woman for him.

And in that moment, he knew something else, something he had realized just now as he held her. No matter what he had told her, he couldn't give her up, not for any amount of gold. He could not bear the thought that the white man would be the first to take her, that Phillip's lips would be the first to taste those breasts. At this moment, as he watched her, he knew that no man would ever touch her but Cougar. He would kill the man who even looked at her with lust as he had just come close to killing Coyote Johnson.

Yes, he was going to keep her for his own if he had to keep her against her will. There was not money enough in all the world to free Cougar's slave. To hell with Lieutenant Van Harrington's gold!

He made his decision in that split second as he watched the firelight play on her fiery hair. And at that moment, he knew that eventually he would have her body, if not her love. It was only a matter of time. His obsession with her would not be denied. Once Cougar had put his son in her belly, no doubt the lieutenant would not want her returned. Not that it mattered, because Cougar was not ever going to let her go.

Now she seemed to gain control of herself and cleared her throat. "You've sent the ransom message to the army?"

"Yes." He didn't look at her. "Yesterday. We're waiting for a reply. Maybe tomorrow or the next day." His friend Turtle had left with the message, all right, but no matter how much the lieutenant offered, Cougar would not accept it. Maybe if he hurried the tribe, the Apache could be safely in a hideaway near the border before Phillip's troops could find them again. No white man save trusted Mac McGuire knew the location of that place. From there, it was only a couple of miles across the border and to their old stronghold in the mountains. Once there, the Apaches were safe from pursuit.

He wanted to reach out and gather her into his arms again, tell her how much he cared about her, but of course, he could not do that. She was awaiting rescue and escape from him, the uncivilized half-breed. He would have to lie to her, impugn his honor, but all he could think of now as he watched the firelight play on that fiery hair was how she had felt in his arms and how it would feel to make love to her. Maybe after he had put a fine, strong son at her breast, she would forget about escaping and resign herself to being Cougar's woman. His passion and need for the flame-haired temptress overruled everything else.

She looked up at him, wondering about the emotion on his rugged face. "What are you thinking?"

"Nothing," he snapped, avoiding her gaze. "Let's go outside and make sure the gunrunners are out of the camp."

"All right." *There was something wrong.* She had gotten to know him too well over the past several days, better than she had ever known anyone in her whole life. They went outside.

The dirty renegades were just riding out of the camp.

The one called Johnson looked back at her with a gaze that made her shiver.

When Cougar saw the way Coyote Johnson looked at her, he put a protective arm around her. She stiffened for a long moment, then let him pull her close against him. She trusted him, he realized, and here he was planning how to foil Phillip's rescue efforts. Cougar felt guilty, but he could not help his hunger for this woman.

Geronimo came over and said to him in Apache, "You did not sell her?"

Cougar shook his head. "I have decided I want to keep her for my own."

Geronimo scowled. "She will bring you much trouble."

Cougar sighed. "She already has, and yet I would do it a thousand times and count it worth it."

The other shook his head. "No man should be such a fool for a woman."

"I admit I am a fool," Cougar said. He wanted his green-eyed beauty in his blankets where he could make love to her night after night, teaching her about passion.

The other considered. "Warriors tell me there is a white officer who will stop at nothing to get her returned."

"That is true," Cougar admitted with a shrug, "but if we pull out in the morning and hurry our pace, we can be safely away from here and the army will never find her."

"Does she understand?" Geronimo asked.

Cougar glanced down into her trusting green eyes, then looked away and shook his head. "No, she thinks she is to be ransomed and returned to white civilization. But once her belly is heavy with my son, what other choice will she have? The rich white man won't want her then, and I'll make sure she'll never have a chance to escape."

"She will hate you for it."

Cougar sighed. "My need for her is so great, I am past caring about that."

"Women!" Geronimo made a sound of disgust and walked away.

Libbie looked after the other man, then up at Cougar. "What is being said? Are you discussing me?"

"Yes." He didn't look at her. "We will ride on to a secret hiding place just this side of the border. There we will wait for Turtle to bring us information to arrange your return."

"But why don't we just wait here?"

Cougar shook his head. "The army knows this place; they might plan an ambush. Trust me, Blaze. You are going to end up where you belong."

She looked relieved and smiled. "I was beginning to fear ... but of course I know I am safe because of the necklace and the promise you made me."

He didn't answer, only nodded and avoided her gaze, which puzzled her. No matter. What was really worrying her was whether Phillip might be able to come up with the ransom money. If he were penniless and she was, too, where could the gold possibly come from?

Cougar seemed to sigh with relief as the renegades rode out. "There goes supplies that are rightfully ours. We need to get them back." They returned to the wickiup.

"Tell me what is bothering you," she said.

He shrugged. "Nothing. Tell me again why you returned to Arizona. Did you come to see me hang?"

He probably wasn't going to believe her, but she would tell him anyway. "I wasn't sure you were one of the condemned. I hoped to be able to talk the commander into delaying the sentence, or at the very least giving me a chance to say good-bye to you."

She wasn't certain he believed her, but what did it matter? She was only now admitting to herself that she had been attracted to the big scout the moment she saw him leaning against the corner of that adobe building as she got off that stage.

"Let us not talk of this," he said briskly, "or your ransom." He looked her over critically. "That pink dress is ragged. Maybe old Owl Woman can come up with something better."

"I'd also like a bath if I had any soap," Libbie agreed. "I don't want to look too terrible in front of all those troops at the exchange."

"Of course." He avoided her gaze. "I'll be leaving on a hunt later this morning with the other warriors, since we failed to get supplies from Coyote Johnson and his gunrunners."

They went outside, where he spoke to the old woman in Apache and she smiled, nodded, and disappeared into her wickiup. When she returned, she held up a soft doeskin dress, a pair of moccasins, and some yucca root.

Libbie looked at Cougar, a question in her eyes.

He said, "Yucca root makes good soap; you'll like it."

She had a sudden suspicion. "You aren't going to watch?"

"Are you inviting me?" He smiled and she realized again how handsome he was.

"You know I'm not!"

"Good thing," he said. "I might not be able to stop myself from joining you in the water—and I wouldn't want to bathe."

"You're terrible!" She found herself bantering with him; not really afraid anymore.

"No, I just want you, Blaze." The need for her burned in those startling blue eyes for all to see.

She reached up and touched the necklace automatically.

"You don't need to remind me; I know," he said.

"I trust your honor," Libbie said and turned to Owl Woman. The two women started for the nearby creek. While Owl Woman stood guard, Libbie scrubbed herself thoroughly with the yucca soap and washed her tangled mop of hair. Soon all her problems would be behind her if Phillip could find the money to ransom her. If he contacted her old governess, maybe she would be smart enough to borrow the money from crooked old Mr. Higginbottom. Mrs. Everett would probably lie to the old geezer and tell him Libbie had changed her mind about marrying him.

Libbie returned to her wickiup and was sitting inside before the fire in the doeskin dress, moccasins, and his necklace, drying her hair on a scrap of her old petticoat, when Cougar entered suddenly.

"You look beautiful," he blurted and she saw the passion for her in his eyes. "Here, let me help you put your hair up."

"That's not necessary," she said.

"But I insist." He sat down cross-legged, reached for a porcupine-tail brush, and pulled her between his thighs. "You have beautiful hair." He began to brush her long locks.

She started to protest that she could do it herself, but his stroking felt good and she closed her eyes and enjoyed it.

Behind her, Cougar brushed her hair slowly, breathing in the clean scent of it and feeling the softness. So much taller than she was, he could look down over her shoulder and saw she wore nothing under the doeskin dress. He could see the naked swell of her breasts, and he yearned to reach under her arms and cup those breasts, pull her against him so he could kiss the back of her damp neck, but he dared not do that. He did not want her to know how much he cared. The white girl would exploit his weakness. He wasn't sure he believed her explanation of why she had returned to Arizona, but he wanted to believe it.

One of the men yelled at him from outside.

Cougar stood up and began to gather his weapons and

canteen. "We'll return after dark from our hunt," he said. "Am I going to have to tie you up to make sure you don't run away?"

Libbie laughed, feeling lighthearted as she looked up at him. "Why should I go to all that trouble when I'll be ransomed any day now?"

He only nodded, not meeting her eyes as he turned and strode outside. Libbie followed him and stood with Owl Woman, watching the warriors mount up. She had forgotten how graceful he looked on a horse, big and masculine. She noted several pretty young Apache girls smiling at him as he rode out. Somehow that annoyed her, although she wasn't sure why. Sooner or later, he would take a wife and she'd be back in white civilization, so what did it matter? Still, for some reason, it bothered her.

Now that the warriors had left, Libbie found herself helping around the camp under Owl Woman's guidance. Some of the women smiled at her with encouragement as she used the one or two Apache words she had learned. Small brown children ran about the camp, and she found herself laughing at their antics and playing with them. Libbie loved children and had always regretted that she was an only child.

The old woman showed her how to cook over a campfire, how to grind corn with a pestle, and how to stretch and cure a deerskin. For the first time in her life, Libbie felt useful, and she realized that people were pretty much the same everywhere, whether they be brown or white. Life in an Apache camp was not so bad after all, and the Apache clothing was much more comfortable than the tight stays and bustle she'd been used to wearing.

The camp settled down quickly after sunset. The landscape was alive with the coming spring. Libbie helped Owl Woman with chores such as carrying water and banking the campfire so that the coals would make it through the night. There were few men left in the camp, mostly old warriors. Soon she would be returning to civilization. And to what? Now Libbie faced cold reality. She didn't want to marry Phillip, and he had no money anyway. Life could be hard and lonely for a penniless spinster.

She loved the West. Maybe she could stay and open a little shop of some kind. *How could she do that with no money?* Maybe she could get a job teaching on the reservation. She'd grown to respect and understand the Apache people the last few days and she'd learned a few words in their language. Well, what she would do with the rest of her life wasn't today's problem, she thought with a sleepy yawn as she settled down in her wickiup. In another day or two, she would have seen the last of Cougar. Funny, she should be glad, but she felt a little empty at the thought; she'd grown to depend on him so much. Gradually, she dropped off to sleep, still thinking about him.

She awakened with a start. What was it? She rose on one elbow, straining to hear, but the camp was quiet. *There was someone in the wickiup with her.* For a moment, she thought it was her imagination; then she heard a slight sound and smiled, wondering if the warriors had returned early. "Cougar?"

She smelled the rank scent as she drew a breath and abruptly she knew! As she opened her mouth to scream, a hand reached out and clapped over her mouth. "Be quiet, bitch! He won't sell you, so I'll have to steal you!"

Coyote Johnson. For a split second, Libbie was frozen with horror. Then she came to life and began to fight him.

Chapter Seventeen

She fought her assailant in the dark wickiup, but she was a petite woman and Coyote Johnson was strong. The small campfire flared abruptly, and she could see the gleam of triumph on his bearded, dirty face as he stuffed a scrap of blanket in her mouth, tied her hands, and threw her across his shoulder. Now he put his hand up and patted her bottom familiarly. "You just behave yourself, girlie, till we get out of this camp. You ought to be glad I'm rescuin' you from these Injuns."

He chuckled and carried her out of the wickiup and across the sleeping camp.

Was there any chance he was really taking her back to civilization? Maybe Mrs. Everett had come up with the ransom after all. Libbie was paralyzed with fear and indecision, but there was nothing she could do to stop him at the moment anyway.

He carried her out beyond the edge of the camp and threw her up on his horse. "Yesirree." He grinned at her.

"And maybe when I get tired of you, I might even let your fancy officer ransom you."

Oh, damn, she was in more trouble now than she had been as a captive in the Indian camp. If she could just get the gag out of her mouth and scream, Apaches would come running from everywhere to help her. It surprised her that she was now thinking of the Indians as friends and allies against renegades like Coyote. She tried to break free, but he had tied her securely. He mounted up behind her. "Just riding with you, girlie, is gonna be fun."

He put his arms around her, pawing her breasts and thighs as he clucked to his horse and they rode away from the camp at a walk. She tried to jerk away from his hot, grimy hands, but he only laughed, his mouth close to her ear. "You uppity little bitch! As soon as I get you back at my place, I'm gonna do more than just handle you!"

Oh, God. Libbie almost retched at the thought. Of course that was what he intended to do to her—probably share her with the other gunrunners once he'd satisfied his own lust.

Cougar, where are you? She hadn't realized until this moment how much she depended on the big half-breed and how much she trusted him to always be there for her.

Johnson rode slowly away from the Indian camp. "Don't want to wake anyone by hearin' a horse gallop." He ran his hands up and down her body as they rode and laughed close to her ear. "Honey, by the time those Injuns find out you're gone, I'll have you under me a long ways from here, and are we gonna have some fun!"

She shuddered at the images that came to her mind.

"Now, honey, don't be like that! I'm gonna teach you how to please a man, and if you please me enough, maybe you can just please me and my buddies, not get yourself sold to that Mexican whorehouse on the coast."

She didn't know which sounded worse—ending up in

an untraceable bordello or having to be the whore for the slimy renegades.

She stopped fighting her bonds, realizing she must not waste her strength, but must think of a plan. Libbie decided to stay calm and wait for her opportunity to escape . . . if there was one. Maybe once he took the gag out of her mouth, she could talk Coyote Johnson into letting down his guard. Yes, that was what she would do. She stopped struggling and didn't react when he squeezed her breasts and ran his dirty hands down her thighs.

"Honey, you learn fast. Now, that's more like it! And if'en you think that Injun cares enough about you to ride into my camp, you don't know Injuns very well. One woman is as good as another to them. I reckon Cougar will just go out and steal another girl."

She shook her head violently, and Johnson snickered again as they rode through the night. "Don't believe that, huh? You ain't gettin' sweet on that brave, are you now, girl?"

She shook her head again. Of course it wasn't that, it was just that every time she'd run into trouble lately, Cougar had been there for her, rescuing her, comforting her. The thought surprised her.

Or was Johnson right? Maybe Cougar wouldn't care enough to come; or maybe he wouldn't be able to track them.

Well, she'd deal with that when she got to it. Libbie took a deep breath and began to think of ways to escape or get her hands on a weapon. She listened in vain for the sound of horses' hooves, hoping rescue was on the way. Once she even imagined she heard a horse, but decided it was only her wistful imagination.

Several hours passed as they rode. The night was cloudy, hiding the moon, and she had no idea which way they were going. Even if she did escape, would she be able to find her way back to the fort or even to the Apache camp?

Finally, Johnson reined in near a brushy canyon. "Hello the camp!"

"Coyote, that you?"

"Damn right, and if I'd of been an Apache, I'd have cut your throat by now! Bif, you ain't keepin' much of a watch."

"Against what?" grumbled the other, walking out to meet him. "You ain't seen anyone, have you?"

Johnson shook his head and rode into the circle of tents. "Look, Bif, I brought us a play-pretty."

She could see the other man in the firelight. She remembered him now from the circle around the fire at the Apache camp, one of the gunrunners. He was short and stocky and looked like he needed a good bath. "Oh, Holy Christ, Coyote! You went back and stole that girl that belongs to that Apache brave?"

"He's not there. He don't know the difference." Johnson dismounted by the small fire and pulled Libbie from the horse.

The other man squatted down and spat tobacco into the fire, peering at Libbie with lust. "That's a fancy necklace she's wearin.' Worth anything?"

Coyote laughed. "Shows she's owned by that big Apache. We'll try to sell it down in Mexico."

Bif stared at her. "We all gonna get a chance at her?"

"Sure." Johnson nodded. "Share and share alike, remember? Now, you go on to bed. I'm gonna enjoy this sassy little bitch a while, and when it's your turn, I'll wake you up."

The other rubbed his groin. "Okay. Just make sure I'm next. I don't want to wait until the rest of them get through with her."

Johnson guffawed as he threw Libbie across his shoulder. "Don't worry. I'll wake you first."

Libbie's heart was pounding so hard, she was sure Coyote Johnson could feel it through her doeskin dress. The other man yawned and disappeared into his tent. Johnson carried her into another tent and dumped her, still bound, on a pile of blankets next to a small fire.

She looked up at him, asking for mercy with her eyes, but he only appraised her as if she were a toy he'd just purchased. "Yes sir, honey, I'm gonna find out if that big buck knew what he was talkin' about when he told me you was a virgin." He reached out, ripped open the doeskin dress with his dirty hand, and licked his lips as he looked at her exposed breasts. "I can hardly wait to get my mouth on these."

She closed her eyes against the lust in his one good eye and tried to keep her wits about her.

Coyote reached out and pulled the gag from her mouth. "Now, honey, it won't do you any good to scream. All that will do is wake the others. Since I stole you, I want to be first."

Libbie licked her dry lips, trying to think of ways to stall him or outwit him. "I—I won't be of much worth if you take my virginity."

He laughed, reached out, and squeezed her left breast hard. "Would you believe I don't care? To top a gal like you is worth whatever gold you lose in value. Now you behave yourself, since you can't get away nohow." He reached down and untied her hands.

Instead, Libbie suddenly came alive, scratching and biting. If she could get out of this tent and into the darkness, he and his friends might have to spend hours searching for her while she slipped away.

"Why, you ornery little bitch!" He was angry as he tried to corner her, but Libbie's desperation made her strong. If she could just get her hands on a knife or gun, she'd make him wish he'd never stolen her.

However, Johnson must have read her mind, because he jumped in front of his stash of weapons. "No, you don't, you little slut!"

The tent opening was off to his left. If she could get through that . . . Libbie tried to run past him, but he reached out and caught her dress, ripping it almost off as they fell to the ground. He was half on top of her as she struggled to get out from under him, but he was a big man, and he jerked her arms up above her head and paused, leering down at her bare breasts.

"Honey, I'm gonna give you a pokin' you'll never forget!"

"I'll die first!" Libbie was fighting him with sheer desperation. She might not be able to escape from his slimy hands, but she wasn't going to be raped quietly and without a struggle.

"Gal, stop this! I'm gonna have you, and you might as well let me before I knock you senseless and take you anyways!"

In answer, she jerked one hand free, reached up, and stuck her finger in his one good eye. He cried out, cursed, and struck her across the face.

She lay there, temporarily stunned, tasting the blood from her cut lip. "No!" she protested. "No!" She began to fight again as he struggled to get between her thighs.

A shadow loomed over them suddenly, and Johnson jerked up. "What the hell—?"

One of the other renegades, Libbie thought in terror, and then she saw the sudden glint of the firelight on the steel blade coming down as a big hand clapped over Johnson's mouth. The renegade made a strange gurgling sound, jerked, and went limp. Libbie opened her mouth to scream, but a terse voice ordered, "Blaze, keep quiet!"

"Cougar! Oh, Cougar!" Even as she began to sob, he dragged the dead renegade off her and tossed him to one side. She went into Cougar's arms, weeping. "Oh, I knew you'd come. He said you wouldn't, but I knew you'd come!"

He held her against him and kissed her hair again and again. "It's okay, Blaze. Are you all right?"

She managed to nod. "The others," she gulped, "the others—"

There was a sound and a muffled scream from somewhere outside.

"My warriors are taking care of them right now. Did he hurt you?"

"Just a little. I'm all right now that you're here."

He swore under his breath. "If I'd known that, I'd have kept him alive and tortured him."

She shuddered, thinking sometimes he was more Apache than white. She clung to him, still shaking, her doeskin dress torn to pieces as Cougar lifted her and carried her easily across the camp to his horse.

"Blaze, dearest, can you stand up?"

She nodded, but when he tried to stand her on her feet, her legs collapsed under her and she had to grab the paint's saddle to keep from falling. Cougar caught her in his arms, kissing her face, her eyes, her lips. "Take it easy. You're all right, Blaze—you'll always be all right as long as you're with me!"

She began to cry with sheer relief, comforted by his feverish kisses. "Oh, Cougar, I knew you'd come!"

He was still kissing her cheeks and eyes as he dragged her to him and held her tightly, his mouth covering hers in a possessive hunger. His lips teased hers apart, and he thrust his tongue inside. She surrendered, letting him taste and explore her mouth. She made a little whimpering sound and threw back her head as his lips moved down her throat.

"My Blaze, how I've yearned for you to let me touch

you!" He bent his head, his mouth seeking her breast, and she arched her back, offering up her nipples for his eager lips. He held her close, his hands caressing her.

"Yes," she whispered. "Yes!"

"Not here," he murmured against her throat. "Not here." He swung her up on his horse and mounted behind her, his big hands reaching out to protect her, to hold her close against him.

She was safe now, she knew that. She would always be safe from anything and anyone who would harm her as long as she was within the circle of Cougar's powerful arms. She leaned back against him, feeling the hardness of his rigid maleness. She knew she should stop him, but the sensations his skillful fingers evoked as he stroked and caressed her skin were making her tremble all over.

Apache warriors came running out of the shadows of the camp. Turtle came to Cougar. "We have killed the others. Now we will take back the supplies and the guns."

Cougar nodded. "I will meet you back at the camp."

At that, he wheeled his horse and cantered away, holding Libbie close, one hand cupping her breast in a gesture of ownership, the other on her bare thigh where her dress had pushed up. The touch of his fingers on her bare flesh sent a thrill up her body that she had never felt before.

"No man but me is ever going to touch you again!" he murmured under his breath.

Had he forgotten his vow? Surely he would not break it. She reached up to touch her necklace. As long as she wore this, her life and her virtue were safe.

The camp was still dark when they rode in, everyone sleeping except a few sentries. Libbie clung to Cougar as he dismounted and took her from the stallion. He carried her across the camp and into his wickiup, where he sat her down gently on a pile of furs and looked into her face. In the faint firelight, she could see the concern in his blue eyes. "Are you sure you're all right? I couldn't stand it if he'd—"

"No, you got there in time." She had to swallow hard to keep from sobbing, but she was shaking.

He took her in his arms. "Blaze, don't be afraid. I'll always look out for you; you know that."

"I know that, Cougar." She turned her face up to him, tears on her cheeks, and he kissed them off. She didn't pull away as his lips moved to her mouth.

He was kissing her feverishly now, as if he couldn't get enough of the taste of her lips. She threw back her head, and he tangled his fingers in her hair, kissing his way down her neck. She went slowly to the blankets and let him kiss her throat and the hollows above her collarbones. She had never felt this way before and she wanted him to continue. She arched her back and offered him her bare breasts.

Cougar groaned aloud as his mouth went to the hollow between her breasts. "If you only knew how I've dreamed of this, how I've hungered to taste these." And then his warm mouth covered her breast.

For a moment, she could only gasp at the sensation; then she caught his head between her two small hands, guiding him to her nipple. He caught it gently between his teeth, and she forgot that she was saving her virginity, that no white man would want to marry her if a half-breed Apache had been with her. Nothing else mattered but that she wanted him, too.

He pulled her to him, kissing her lips, her eyes, her breasts. "I'm going to love you the way no other man ever could, Blaze, my dearest one," he whispered as he reached out and threw open her torn dress. She lay there looking up at him, wearing nothing but the black and silver necklace that nestled against her breasts. He began to kiss his way down her belly.

Her pulse seemed to be beating in her head like a drum. Libbie closed her eyes and lay back, letting his hot mouth tease its way down her belly. Then he moved to her thighs. Libbie stiffened. Surely he wasn't going to . . . ?

"Relax, my darling," he whispered against her bare thigh. "Relax . . ." And with those words, his mouth found the bud of her womanhood, tasting and teasing there, thrusting into her with his tongue until she was wild with desire.

She gave a little cry and let her thighs fall apart, holding his face against her, pleading—no, demanding—that he satisfy her own hungers.

His skillful mouth obliged until she was crazy with her need, pressing him against her, wanting him to drive her to new heights of excitement. She reached out and touched his throbbing manhood.

"Yes, Blaze, I want to give you that," he promised, moving back up her body to kiss her mouth. "I want to join with you and turn you into a woman! Tell me you want me! Tell me!"

She hesitated. Her emotions were thrilling and new, but now that she had a moment to think, she hesitated. A woman could only give her virginity once. Her heart and soul cried out that this was that special man, worthy of that gift, but her head warned her what an impossible union this was. Only the greatest of loves could transcend the differences between two cultures, two races.

In that split second that she hesitated, he pulled away from her and sat up. "I am a fool to think you cared! Worse yet, I dishonor my vow!"

What on earth had she been thinking? She had been about to give away her most precious asset to this penniless half-breed on a blanket in an Indian camp, and yet . . .

Libbie wasn't sure whether she was relieved or saddened by his reluctance to continue. "You could take me anyway."

"Take you? You stupid little fool!" He reached out and caught the necklace, pulling her to him as he twisted his fingers in it. "What I wanted was to share this ecstasy with you, not use you like a whore!"

With a terrible oath, he stood up and stalked out of the wickiup, leaving her puzzled and trembling, struggling with emotions that she didn't understand herself. She hadn't wanted him to stop until he'd brought her down from the emotional peak she'd just ascended. She felt angry and frustrated as she pulled the furs over her naked body and waited for the coming dawn. Maybe she was a stupid little fool, to almost give herself to her half-breed kidnapper out of sheer . . . gratitude? *Was it nothing more than that?* Libbie didn't want to think about it. Instead, she would concentrate on being rescued.

Yes, that was what she would think about—her future life. Maybe today or tomorrow, the soldiers would meet with the Apaches and ransom her if Phillip could get the money together. Now that she was cool-headed and logical, she realized she'd almost done something very, very foolish. No high-born white girl would waste her virginity on a half-breed scout who had nothing in the world to offer her. Nothing but his love and a way of making her feel that if he would only take her and make her his own in the universal way a man possesses a woman, she could count herself the luckiest woman in the world.

Phillip hadn't been able to sleep all night. He had paced his quarters, throwing things at the mounted bear head's baleful eyes and thinking about what might be happening in the Apache camp. He wondered if Cougar had enjoyed Elizabeth yet. Every time Phillip closed his eyes, he could see them together. Sometimes he even imagined that she made love to the warrior eagerly, welcoming his touch.

Ye gods! No, of course the frosty Miss Elizabeth Winters wouldn't enjoy passion. Like most women of her class, she would only endure it as her duty. Still, the thought that Cougar had probably already taken her virginity drove Phillip nearly crazy with jealous rage. He paused in his pacing and considered. No, Cougar was a reasonable man. He'd know that no white man would pay ransom to get Libbie back if the breed had been using her for his pleasure. And the Apache did want ransom. A young warrior named Turtle had come with Cougar's demands and conditions yesterday.

Phillip had promised to meet the demands and sent the messenger on his way, when what Phillip really yearned to do was hang the man. He had telegraphed Mama, who was trying to connect with Mrs. Everett. The plump guardian had indicated she would send the ransom. Of course, Phillip had no intention of paying it.

He paused and grinned, pulling at his mustache. Somehow, he intended to come out of this with the girl and the money, too—and Cougar's neck in a noose. He hoped he got the privilege of putting the rope around Cougar's thick neck himself.

It was almost dawn. Phillip went to the window and peered out. *How was he going to make all this happen?* Cougar would be too smart to walk into a trap. The Apache held all the cards. He'd make the arrangements to meet someplace where he couldn't be ambushed.

Phillip walked across his room and kicked the bearskin rug. "Taboo, ha! I'll show these stupid Injuns what I think of their ignorant beliefs! I'll take my revenge for my father's murder yet!"

To get to Cougar, he was either going to have to outsmart him or trick him. Either would be hard to do because

Cougar was such a cunning rascal. No, the only way to get to Cougar was through someone the Injun trusted.

Mac McGuire. Phillip paused and smiled to himself. Mac surely knew where the Apaches were; they all trusted the old man. Maybe Phillip could trick Mac into leading him and a troop to the Apache stronghold. He'd have to lie to Mac to do that, but what the hell? Lies didn't count if you were dealing with an Injun lover, even if the old man had been his father's best friend.

At dawn, Phillip saddled up and rode out to the ranch. The barking dogs brought Mac onto the porch as Phillip reined in. The old man was yawning and his hair was mussed as if he hadn't been awake long.

"Hello, Lieutenant. I'm just barely out of bed." He did not smile.

"Well, you might at least ask me in for a cup of coffee." Phillip dismounted.

Mac nodded. "Out of respect for your father, I'll do that." He led the way inside the cabin and back to the kitchen.

Phillip looked around. "Honestly, Mac, I don't know how you stand it out here alone in this solitary place; it would drive me crazy."

Mac indicated a chair at the rough table and checked the fire under the coffee pot in the old stove. "I'm not alone; I've got a lot of critters and my memories. Sometimes friends drop by."

"Speaking of which"—Phillip pulled at his wispy mustache—"I don't suppose you've heard anything from your son?"

"Cougar?" Mac paused in getting two mugs out of the cabinet. "You wouldn't expect me to tell you that if I had."

Phillip scowled and took a deep sniff of the aroma of coffee drifting through the small kitchen. "Now and then, you might remember you're on *our* side."

"I'm on humanity's side," Mac snapped and poured the coffee. "By the way, it wasn't right, the way you treated Shashké."

"That's hardly any of your business." Phillip shrugged and accepted the steaming cup. "She was just an Injun slut; that's all."

Mac looked as if he were having a hard time holding his temper. His jaw worked a long moment before he spoke. "I took her in because she had noplace else to go. She's horrible to look at, and she'll never be accepted back into her tribe."

"She knew what chance she was taking." Phillip sipped the strong brew gratefully and warmed his hands around the mug. Then he paused and looked around uneasily. "Is she here?"

"I checked the spare room as I walked to the door; she's gone, along with her things. Don't know where the poor thing thinks she can go."

"Who cares?" Phillip shrugged. "Maybe her husband will take her back."

"What?"

"I said, who cares?" Phillip raised his voice. "Let her go home to her husband."

Mac's hand tightened around his coffee cup so hard, his gnarled knuckles turned white. "Ye haven't heard then. Old Beaver Skin has died—the Apache say of a broken heart, for hurting her. He loved her, but she had dishonored him."

"Too bad; but that's not my problem." Phillip sipped his coffee, savoring the strong, hot flavor.

"You're at the bottom of this tragedy, and we all know it."

Phillip shrugged. "I was like most soldiers, just looking for amusement to pass the time. Shashké shouldn't have been so greedy and naive."

"Your father would turn over in his grave because of this." Mac glared at him. "Bill was very sympathetic to the Apache."

"And look what it got him!" Phillip snapped. "The savages killed him for it."

The old man looked as if he would say something more, then paused and took a deep breath, as if reconsidering. Then he leaned against the cabinet and pulled out his pipe. "So what is it you want, Phillip?"

Phillip finished his coffee; wondering how to bring up the question he really wanted answered. "You knew Cougar kidnapped Miss Winters?"

"Aye, I've heard; bad business." He filled his pipe and lit it.

Phillip leaned closer. "I thought you might help get her back."

Mac frowned and puffed his pipe, scenting the rough-hewn room with the sweet smell. "It's a bad business, him taking her, but he's wanted the girl from the first moment he saw her."

"You know this is crazy." Phillip frowned. "He can't just pick out a woman, steal her like he'd steal a mare, and keep her."

Mac smiled ever so slightly. "Looks like he's done just that."

"Yes, and got the whole United States Army on him. We'll hunt him down if we have to chase him clear across Mexico."

Mac blew a cloud of fragrant smoke. "Maybe the girl's with him because she wants to be."

"That's impossible!" Phillip sneered. "Miss Winters is an elegant aristocrat from the finest family. She couldn't possibly be happy out there in the wilderness with that— that savage."

"Sometimes love can bridge anything."

Phillip stood up, scowling. "Just because you took up with an Apache doesn't mean other whites could do it."

"No, you're right," Mac said. "It takes a very great love to bridge a chasm like that, but it can be done." He turned and looked out the window toward a distant hill.

What in the world was the old fool looking at? Phillip took a deep breath and decided to try a different tactic. "Mr. McGuire, you were my father's dearest friend. For that reason, I came to you."

Mac turned and looked at him. "Yes?"

"You know that the army will hunt those Apaches ruthlessly until we get Miss Winters returned?"

"You'll have to find them first, and the army will never find them."

"But you know where they are?" Phillip waited, but Mac only stood and smoked. "Look, in the name of my father, I'm asking for your help."

"You're asking me to turn in Cougar—?"

"No, I'm asking you to lead me out to talk to him, to reason with him," Phillip said earnestly. "Maybe you could convince your son to let her go."

"And suppose she's happy with him and doesn't want to leave the Apaches?" Mac looked at him intently.

Phillip sighed. "Well, I guess I'd just have to accept that, but I want to know."

Mac smoked, thinking. "Are you saying just you and me would ride out and meet with the Apaches?"

Phillip nodded. "I give you my word as an officer and a gentleman." He held up his hand as if he were taking a solemn oath. "If she wants to stay with him, that's one thing. But if she's being held against her will, I'm duty bound to try to rescue her."

"Your father was a great one for honor and duty," Mac said.

There was no sound for a long moment. Then abruptly, up in the nearby hills, a coyote began howling.

Mac jerked around at the sudden sound and peered out the window. "Lieutenant, I—I've got to go."

Damned old Injun lover. Probably an Apache out there bringing him a message from his renegade son. "If I give you my word, would you take me out to meet with Cougar and Miss Winters, see what the situation is?"

Mac hesitated. "It would take an awfully brave man to ride out and face up to all those Apaches."

"My father would have done it." Phillip drew himself up proudly. "I am, after all, William Van Harrington's son."

"Aye."

The coyote howled again.

Mac fidgeted, then seemed to come to a decision. "All right, Lieutenant. I'll lead you out to meet with Cougar and find out what the young lady wants to do. You swear it's going to be just you and me, no tricks?"

Phillip held up his hand solemnly again. "My only concern is Miss Winters' welfare."

The coyote howled, louder and more insistent.

Mac went to the back door and peered out. "All right, Lieutenant, I'll send you word where to meet me—tomorrow, maybe, or the next day. Now I've got to go. I—I think maybe my horses have gotten out of the corral."

"That's all right, I can let myself out," Phillip said, standing up. "I'll be awaiting word then."

Mac nodded as if he hardly heard him before heading out the back door and up the hill.

Damned old Injun lover! Mac wasn't fooling Phillip. He was meeting some messenger out there by the corral. Well, Phillip couldn't do anything about that right now. His biggest problem now was setting up a meeting with Cougar face-to-face. Phillip turned and strode back through the house toward the front porch.

Mac met with the young Apache messenger, Turtle, and told him to pass the word to Cougar that Mac would be coming for a meeting and bringing the lieutenant with him.

"Is this wise?" asked the Apache in his own language.

Mac sighed. "That girl doesn't belong with Cougar, no matter how much he wants her. If he doesn't give her up, the lieutenant will never quit until one of them is dead. Tell Cougar I'll be careful. The lieutenant has promised me on his father's honor that this is no trick, and surely even the worst of villains would not sully such a fine man's memory."

Turtle looked dubious.

"Tell Cougar I will bring the lieutenant to the secret place just this side of the border. If he is indeed holding the girl against her will, he needs to consider what ends the army will go to to rescue her."

The young Apache nodded, swung up on his bay pony, and disappeared into the brush.

Mac stood looking after him a long moment, then returned to the house. *Was he doing the right thing?* There was no way to know, but if the girl were being held against her will, it was only right that she be returned to her fiancé, no matter how dislikable Phillip was.

And poor little Bear Tracks; what would become of the disfigured Shashké? Ostracized by other Apaches and too ugly now to be a soldier's whore, she was a walking dead person running out of time and alternatives.

Still deep in thought, Mac walked into the living room, puffing on his pipe. The lieutenant had left the front door open. Out of habit, Mac shuffled over to close it. As he turned away, his straining old eyes focused on the gun cabinet. One of its doors hung open. Now why—?

He limped over to close it. Something was different. For a long moment, it did not register, and then he realized that the major's pistol was missing from the cabinet.

Mac ran out the door onto the porch. "Lieutenant?"

His voice was getting as weak as the rest of his senses, Mac thought, peering into the distance. Phillip was only a moving dot on the horizon, headed back to the fort. Would Phillip have taken that Colt? Surely Bill's boy wouldn't stoop to thievery. *But if not Phillip, who?* Then Mac remembered how annoyed the young officer had been when Mac refused to give him his father's pistol. Mac couldn't tell him the Colt's history or that he'd felt it would bring Phillip bad medicine. Good Lord, he was thinking more and more like an Indian.

Mac closed the gun cabinet and went back to the kitchen for more coffee as he considered his dilemma. He would ask Phillip about the pistol tomorrow when he saw him again. Despite all his misgivings, Mac felt he had no alternative but to take Phillip out to meet with Cougar. It was ironic that the two were such enemies, considering . . . ah, well.

He wasn't at all sure he could trust Phillip, even with the snooty officer swearing on his father's honor. Yet Mac must bring about the meeting to protect the Apaches. Phillip Van Harrington bore them, and particularly Cougar, such hatred that they would never be safe as long as he was alive to pursue them. Mac could only hope that the lieutenant would be transferred back east before he found out things he would not want to know.

And what had happened to Shashké? Poor thing, she would have been welcome to stay, but she had been terribly distraught. He hoped she hadn't killed herself the way Dandy Jim's wife had done.

Well, it would all come to a finale tomorrow or the next day. Mac wasn't looking forward to it; he sensed events were headed for a terrible tragedy!

Chapter Eighteen

Once Cougar stalked from their wickiup after he had rescued her from Coyote Johnson and returned her to the Apache camp, Libbie was so weary that she dropped off into a heavy sleep. In the middle of the night, she awakened, chilled from the desert air. As she lay there, she heard a noise and tensed. However, she couldn't stop shivering. With eyes half closed, she saw Cougar looming over her.

Had he returned to take that which she had so foolishly almost given him only hours ago—her innocence? Even as she wondered and tried to plan a course of action, he leaned to pull a blanket over her and tucked it in. Then he brushed a lock of hair from her forehead and sighed. As she watched, he returned to his place on the other side of the small fire and lay down. Libbie was touched by his tender gesture, only one of many over the last few days. Then she remembered that she must not let her heart soften toward her half-breed kidnapper. Sooner or later, the army would be coming to rescue her and probably kill him. Somehow, that thought didn't bring her the pleasure it once had.

Dawn came. When Libbie awakened, Cougar's blankets were empty. Across the foot of her blankets lay a magnificent beaded doeskin dress and fancy moccasins to replace the torn clothes she wore. It was so beautiful, she realized it must be very fine and expensive. It was also very soft and comfortable. Thrilled, she put the dress on and went outside, thinking she had never realized how beautiful sunrise could be when she lived in a house and hardly ever saw the dawn.

The Apache were up and taking care of simple tasks, getting ready to move the camp to another, safer location nearer the border. The women smiled and nodded to Libbie as she walked among them. Funny, she no longer saw them as red-skinned monsters; they were just people, after all. The Apache lived such simple, peaceful lives . . . as long as the soldiers weren't chasing them. With a start, Libbie realized how relaxed and carefree she felt. It was exhilarating not to have to wear a corset, worry about attending dull social events, or wonder if there was going to be enough money for carriages and fancy teas. Of course, when she returned to civilization, she'd have to deal with all that again. She found the prospect depressed her.

The camp was alive with women preparing food and children running between the wickiups. Libbie found herself smiling when she spotted Cougar's tall, lithe form walking through the camp toward her.

"Ah, Blaze! So you are finally up."

"Where did you get this lovely outfit you left me?" She indicated the fancy dress and moccasins she wore.

He shrugged. "You needed something to put on; it's not important. Look"—he dug in the pouch hanging over his shoulder—"I've shot a rabbit. If you can get some coffee going, we'll have a nice breakfast."

She started to tell him that she was a society girl and had never cooked in her life and wasn't about to for him, but then she looked around and realized that everyone else was sharing the work. "All right. I'll have to get some water."

She took a big copper pot and walked down to the stream to fill it. Returning, she was struggling to carry it when Cougar hurried toward her. "Here, let me. That's too heavy for you."

He took it from her hand and they walked back to the camp, others greeting them cheerily as they passed.

Libbie nodded to them. To Cougar, she said, "I'm surprised they seem to accept me."

Cougar laughed. "They think you have shown great heart."

"Oh?" She didn't want to ask, but her curiosity got the better of her. "What else do they say?"

"They think Blaze would be a good name for a red-haired woman of the Apache."

"I'm not Apache," she reminded him.

"They say you have enough courage to be one. You surprise them; they expect white women to be weak and whining."

She couldn't help but laugh. "Even you said I was spoiled."

He nodded as they approached the wickiup. "Spoiled, yes, but you couldn't help the way you were raised. You're a strong woman, Blaze. The lieutenant is no match for you."

She agreed silently, but she said nothing. Whatever happened, she didn't intend to marry Phillip, even if he took her back to civilization. However, the thought of being her own woman, making her own choices and decisions didn't scare her as it once had.

They came to the wickiup and he set the kettle down. "Blaze, you make the coffee, and I'll skin the rabbit."

She started to remind him again that her name was not Blaze as he walked away, decided he was as stubborn as she was, and shrugged. Old Owl Woman came into the wickiup, smiling and nodding. She gestured, showing Libbie how to put the water on to boil and make the coffee.

Libbie went to the wickiup door, wondering what was keeping Cougar. He stood in the center of the camp circle, the rabbit hanging from his hand, talking to a very pretty Apache girl. The girl was flirting shamelessly with him, and he was nodding and smiling. An unfamiliar emotion rose in Libbie's heart. "Hey," she called, "I have the coffee ready."

Cougar nodded to the girl and came over, handing Libbie the skinned rabbit.

"Who was that?" Libbie demanded.

Cougar shrugged. "Little Fawn. I had once thought of asking for her in marriage. Pretty, isn't she?"

"Some might think so." Libbie bristled. "She's also a shameless flirt!"

"What do you care? You're engaged to the lieutenant, remember?"

Libbie felt her face go hot. "I—I don't care. She's just very bold, if you ask me."

"I didn't ask you," Cougar said. He turned and looked after the girl's shapely form as she walked through the camp. "A man needs sons and a woman. After you're gone, maybe I'll think about her again."

Libbie didn't like the emotions she felt at the way his frank appraisal took in the disappearing Apache girl. Libbie jerked the skinned rabbit from his hand, took it back inside, and the old woman helped her cut it up and cook it. "Little Fawn," she muttered through clenched teeth, "thinks she can have Cougar any time she wants him!"

Owl Woman said in English, "If you don't want him, why should you care?"

Libbie gasped. "You speak English! Why have you never told me?"

The other shrugged. "To what purpose? You would have bothered me with questions I might not want to answer."

"Where did this dress I'm wearing come from?" Libbie indicated the fine doeskin outfit.

"He paid much for it, five horses, but he was determined to give it to you. It is the finest dress in the whole tribe."

Libbie felt flattered. "Why would he do that?"

"You do not look into his heart and see why?" Owl Woman left the wickiup abruptly before Libbie could ask more.

Libbie puzzled over the answer while she finished cooking the rabbit. Later, Libbie served it to Cougar as he sat cross-legged before the fire. He took a bite. "Very good. You do have some talents besides your beauty, it seems."

"I suppose it's edible," Libbie admitted, trying not to blush at his praise. Then she was annoyed with herself that his compliments had pleased her. *What was wrong with her?* This half-breed savage was holding her hostage, and soon she would be leaving here. Yet she was beginning to admire Cougar for his bravery and the decisions he was making in leading this little band. This was a man in every sense of the word—brave, strong, yet gentle when need be. "Thank you for this fine dress," she said. "Owl Woman told me."

He scowled. "She talks too much; it was nothing."

"No one woman among all the Apaches has anything so fine; I know this."

"I would not have any say I do not dress my woman in

a manner which shows my status as a warrior." He made
a gesture of dismissal and returned to his food.

His woman? The nerve of him! She must remember that
she hated him, she reminded herself as she got herself a
tin cup of coffee and a portion of roasted rabbit. It was
more delicious than any pheasant or squab in cream sauce
that she had ever eaten at fancy parties.

Before the dew was off the stubby grass, the Apache were
mounted, moving south. *We must be moving closer to the
border,* Libbie thought, but she asked no questions as she
unpacked her travois and, with Owl Woman's help, began
to build a new wickiup.

About midday, a young Apache she recognized as the
one called Turtle came galloping into the camp and dismounted. Libbie watched Cougar stride out to meet the
young man. They engaged in very animated conversation,
both occasionally turning to look toward the wickiup. They
must be talking about her, Libbie decided.

Cougar finally dismissed the messenger and strode over
to the wickiup.

Libbie said, "Well?"

"Well, what?" He poured himself some coffee.

"Don't evade the question," Libbie said. "That was
about me, wasn't it?"

"White women are very spoiled and think the whole
world revolves around them," he said coldly, not looking
at her.

"Is Phillip bringing the ransom?"

He frowned. "Do you really intend to marry that prissy
officer if I free you?"

"That's hardly your concern, now is it?" She had already
decided she wouldn't marry Phillip even if he were rich,
but she didn't want to give Cougar the satisfaction of know-

ing that. Maybe Mrs. Everett had talked crooked old Ebenezer Higginbottom into providing the ransom.

"I don't want to talk about this now," Cougar said finally. "I have some thinking to do."

"If he's not offering enough money—"

"It's not about the money!" he snapped at her and strode away.

What was eating him? This was what he wanted, wasn't it? Trading her for a lot of gold so the Apaches could buy supplies? The black expression on his face as Cougar walked away warned her not to bring the subject up again.

The day passed slowly, with the women cleaning up the camp and settling in. Libbie helped Owl Woman arrange her few belongings in her wickiup, but the old woman stubbornly refused to speak English to her again.

To pass the time, Libbie played with some of the Apache children. She loved children and had always hoped, as a lonely only child, to have a large brood of her own someday. She realized now that her attitude toward the Apache had changed over the last several days. After living with them, she really didn't hate them anymore, and she didn't want the army to hurt them. They were just people, after all, even though they spoke a different language.

She was picking up a few of the words herself from the children. *At this rate,* she thought, *in a few weeks, I could speak to them in their own language.* Of course, she wouldn't be here in a few weeks; she'd be somewhere among the whites, dealing with all the problems and complications that went with that civilization. The thought depressed her.

And when she was gone, Cougar would pick a mate, someone like Little Fawn, and sire children by her. The thought of him in the arms of that dark beauty made Libbie swallow hard. He deserved better than that. *Was she out of her mind?* What he deserved was to be strung up by his thumbs and whipped for kidnapping, that's what he deserved!

Evening came. Cougar sat in the wickiup, staring into the fire. Why was he so preoccupied? *What decision was he struggling with?* Libbie had let the smiling Owl Woman teach her how to grind maize and put together a stew from the leftover rabbit. Cougar nodded appreciatively as she handed him a bowl.

Outside, dust painted the sky with hues of purple and pale pink. Cougar ate and stared at the sinking sun. "Soon we will be moving across the border and into Mexico."

"How soon?"

"A day, or maybe two. There we'll be safe from the soldiers."

A day or two. The thought sent a chill up her back. If he didn't free her before then, she would be many miles away in the mountains, where the soldiers would never find the Apache. Well, of course Cougar had sent a message back to Phillip concerning the ransom; she had seen Turtle ride out. Any time now, she would be free. She was startled to find that she wasn't terribly excited about the prospect of leaving these people.

As darkness fell, the people had built up the campfire and were dancing.

Cougar looked at her a long moment. "Would you like to go out by the fire?"

She wanted to ask him about the messenger, about her future, about what was worrying him, but noting his moody expression, decided now was not the time. "Sure, why not?"

They went out by the firelit circle. The old mother brought them each a gourd.

Libbie sipped it. "What is that?"

"Tiswin—Apache beer," Cougar said. "Drink up or you'll insult her."

Libbie drank. It warmed her and she felt more relaxed standing here by the fire, watching the dancers. The drum rhythm seemed to move through her and she swayed to it.

"Here"—Cougar motioned—"dance with me."

"Oh, I couldn't!" Libbie protested.

He shrugged. "I could ask Little Fawn."

Libbie looked over at the Apache girl, who was smiling invitingly at Cougar from across the circle.

"On second thought, I've changed my mind." Libbie let Cougar lead her out into the circle. "I—I don't know the steps."

"Just do what everyone else is doing," Cougar said. "Let the drum tell you."

Libbie closed her eyes and began to move to the hypnotic beat. When she opened them, Cougar was dancing, watching her as they stepped rhythmically around the big fire. She caught her breath at the lithe sensuality of his muscular, half-naked body swaying to the drumbeat. When his blue eyes looked deep into hers, they seemed to be asking a question.

She found herself looking back at him, her heart beating faster, her mind a little foggy from the beer. She shook her hair loose so that it fell around her shoulders as she swayed to the music. *Blaze.* Yes, she was beginning to feel that maybe the name did fit her. His eyes were hot with desire as he looked deep into hers, and then she realized that it wasn't the money Cougar wanted for ransom. He wanted her body; every heated glance he sent her way betrayed that. Could she trade her virginity for her freedom? Did he want her badly enough that he would free her if she went into his arms willingly tonight? She was torn between two emotions and two civilizations.

Libbie danced, swaying close to him so that their bodies brushed against each other. Around them, more *tiswin* was passed around and people laughed and men pulled women into the shadows. Cougar's blue eyes were even more intense as he stared down into hers. Libbie made her decision then. Even if she returned to white civilization, she wanted to spend one night in this man's arms and see if it was as wonderful as his passionate gaze promised. With her eyes, she told him so.

He hesitated, as if wondering if the unspoken message might be a mistake. Libbie smiled at him again.

Hesitantly, he reached out and pulled her to him.

"Yes," she whispered, "yes!"

He gave a low sigh and swung her up into his strong arms. "Are you—are you sure?"

In answer, she put her arms around his neck as she hung there. "I am very, very sure!" she whispered and reached up to kiss him.

He was tense against her as he turned and strode away from the fire, carrying her against his bare chest. "You don't know how long I've waited for this."

She ought to be terrified, or at least dreading it, but she wasn't; she was as tense as he was, her heart pounding with anticipation. "If I leave here, never having experienced this, I know I will regret it the rest of my life!"

He carried her in and laid her very gently on the furs, as if afraid she might break. "Making love to you has meant everything to me from the first moment I saw you stepping off that stagecoach," he confessed.

"And I have wondered what it would be like ever since the night you put your necklace on me and touched me with your hands." Very slowly, Libbie reached up and unhooked the silver chain, laying the Apache Tears necklace to one side.

"Blaze, are you sure?"

In answer, she took off the soft doeskin dress and threw it to one side so that she lay naked in the glow of the firelight.

His look swept over her, hot with desire. "Just let me look at you a moment; I have waited for this a long, long time."

"And I am only just now admitting to myself how much I have wanted you," she sighed.

No man could have wanted her so much, she thought as his fingers traced a path down the valley between her breasts. Even Phillip or Mr. Higginbottom had never looked at her with such intense passion. In answer to Cougar's caress, she arched her back, offering him the feast of her breasts.

With a heated sigh, Cougar bent to nuzzle them, playing with her nipples with his hot mouth, sending unexpected spasms of pleasure through her body as his big hands stroked her thighs. She caught his head between her two hands, directing his face against her breasts, urging him to suckle harder still as his hand crept up her thigh and touched her most sacred place.

Instinctively, Libbie let her thighs fall apart so that he could stroke and tease her with his fingers.

"You're wet," he murmured, "eager for me to take you."

She knew this night could only lead to sorrow, yet her body was responding to his mouth and skillful hands in ways that both thrilled and frightened her.

"I—I didn't know women could want this," she confessed, and then his mouth cut off her words as his lips covered hers, tasting the velvet depths of her mouth, sucking her tongue into his. Her pulse pounded even harder as she responded to his kisses and his stroking. She tried to think rationally, but her pulse was beating in her ears like the loud drums outside the wickiup, and there was no time for clear thinking; there was only the emotion of desire so long denied.

He caught her hand and brought it to clasp his rigid maleness.

He was so big, Libbie thought with awe as she stroked and explored him. She wasn't certain how she could take all that great length, but then he kissed her again, caressing her breasts with his skillful hands, and none of that seemed to matter anymore.

Cougar stood up suddenly and stripped off his skimpy loincloth and moccasins. "Look at me," he whispered.

She studied his magnificent body in the glow of the fire. He was scarred and well muscled, every bit a stallion of a man, and he was rigid and ready to mate with her. Libbie's heart pounded harder at the thought, and she felt her body thrill with anticipation as old as time itself. She lay there, slowly holding out her arms to him.

He lay down on the furs, pulling her so that she was lying half on top of him. "Now, my beautiful one, you make love to me," he whispered.

She nodded, breathing hard. Her heart seemed to be pounding louder than the drums outside. "I—I don't know how."

"Listen to your heart, Blaze, my love, and follow it."

Tentatively, she closed her eyes and slowly lowered her face to brush her lips across his. Her heart was pounding so hard, she no longer heard the drums outside. There was nothing else in the universe but this man and this moment. She kissed him; awkwardly at first; then he opened his lips and she forgot everything except that his lips were so warm and hungry for her own. Very slowly, she probed his lips with her tongue as she pressed her naked breasts against his hard chest and his hands came up to caress her hair as it fell around his face.

At that moment, he opened his mouth to accept her

tongue and she became the aggressor, plunging her tongue inside, tasting and caressing his mouth. His hand caught the back of her neck, pulling her mouth down on his, still deeper, as his other hand played up and down her bare back. His hand was big and rough; possessive yet protective. And she felt goosebumps on her naked skin as his fingers seemed to touch every nerve, as his hand moved up and down her back, then settled on her bottom.

She moaned aloud against his mouth and moved restlessly, but he only lay there, letting her lead the way, although she could feel his manhood, hard and insistent against her body. "I—I don't know what to do," she whispered.

"Yes, you do, my Blaze," he said against her mouth, "yes, you do."

Libbie gasped and half moved on top of him, supporting her weight with her elbows so that her breasts were above his face. He reached out and caught her breast with one hand, moving her so that she was more convenient for his mouth to reach and suck her nipples, playing with her breasts.

Libbie threw back her head, breathing hard. *Blaze.* Yes, she felt as if she were on fire when this man touched and caressed her. She felt his turgid manhood against her body and she wanted him, wanted him with an urgent need that surprised her. *This is crazy,* she thought, *tomorrow or the next day, you'll be leaving this man forever, yet you're giving yourself to him freely.* Then she knew that there was no man in this universe that she wanted to share this with more, and her own need could not be denied.

Then he raked his teeth gently across her swollen nipple, and she forgot everything but cooling this fever that seemed to be about to burst into an uncontrolled fire.

"Make love to me, Blaze," he commanded. "Make love to me."

This wasn't the way she had pictured this seduction at all. She had imagined he would throw her down across the blankets and take her hard and fast. When he satisfied himself, it would be over in only a few seconds. Yet this gentle teasing and touching seemed to go on and on and was driving her wild with a desire she hadn't realized she was capable of. Parting her thighs, she sat atop his thighs and surveyed his manhood. "I—I can't. You're too big for me."

"No, your body wants me; it will be all right. Make love to me, Blaze, mount me and ride me."

And, abruptly, she wanted that more than she wanted anything else in the world—the feeling of being one with this magnificent stallion of a man. Hesitantly, she came up on her knees over him, then came down very slowly on the hard dagger of his manhood. She didn't take it all, but paused while he breathed hard and seemed to be fighting to control himself. "Take it, Blaze, take every inch of it!"

She could feel him throbbing hot and hard inside her as she tried to come down on him, but the thin silk of her virginity held her back. "I—I can't. You'll have to help me. . . ."

His big hands reached out and caught her small waist, almost encircling it with his strong fingers. He was trembling, his sinewy muscles shiny with perspiration. "This may hurt."

She threw back her head, her fiery hair going everywhere, her eyes half closed, wanting the completion, hungering for the sensation of him totally buried in her depths. "It doesn't matter. Do it. Do it!"

In answer, he arched his muscular hips while holding onto her trim waist and ground her down on his body hard. Libbie felt his turgid maleness tear through the silk of her virginity and then he plunged deep inside her. She bit her lip to keep from crying out as he ground her down on him, impaling her on his throbbing manhood.

He reached up and caught both her breasts in his two big hands, running his thumbs across her nipples as she began to grow accustomed to the sensation of having him inside her. Slowly she began to move in a timeless, erotic rhythm. She had never imagined that mating could create this kind of pulse-pounding need.

"I love you," he whispered. "I've loved you since the first moment I saw you!"

And she loved him, she realized; it was crazy, it could never be, but she loved this man as she could never hope to love another. She could not think; she could only feel, reveling in the sensation of his body inside hers as he throbbed and stroked her breasts into a mounting excitement that she could not control. She leaned over and kissed him, touching his tongue with her own as she rode him hard. She had not expected it to be like this, and now nothing else mattered but this man and this moment.

"Blaze, I don't know how much longer I can hold back," he gasped against her mouth. "I'm waiting for you. . . ."

She didn't know what he was talking about, but she didn't stop riding him harder and faster, driven by her own wild need. It felt as if she had climbed to the top of a summit and was about to fall over the edge of the precipice. "Cougar, I—I don't know how—"

"Relax and let it happen," he whispered fiercely as he reached for her. "Trust me, Blaze, trust me to love you."

And at that moment, she stopped fighting her desires and let them sweep her along as she moved on his body. She felt his hand catch her waist again, grinding her down on him so that she could feel every inch of him throbbing deep within her and she was swept up in an unfamiliar emotion that she had never known before. She gasped aloud.

"That's it!" he murmured. "Come with me. Come with me, Blaze, my dear one."

At that moment, his virile body began to convulse under her. It seemed she could almost feel the heat of his seed surging deep within her. Then she thought no more because her own body began to tremble and she wanted nothing more than to fall into the rhythm of giving and taking as they meshed and strained together.

For a long moment, she seemed to be floating in the most delicious blackness. When she opened her eyes, her head was on his wide chest as she still lay on him and he was tenderly stroking her hair. "Did I—did I do it right?"

He laughed gently and kissed her forehead. "It was more wonderful even than in my dreams over these past few months."

He sounded relaxed and sleepy. Funny, she felt the same way. She lifted her body from his, noting the smear of her virginity on her thighs, and settled down into his embrace, her head on his shoulder. He reached to pull a blanket up over them both. She felt safe here in the circle of his strong arms.

I have just sacrificed my virginity, she thought, but she didn't regret it. Cougar reached to cover her breast with one big hand, and his touch made her gasp with new need. She turned her face and kissed him.

The kiss lengthened and deepened until he took a deep breath and rose on one elbow, looking down at her. "You want me again as much as I want you." It wasn't a question; it was a simple fact.

And now, looking up into his honest blue eyes, she had to be truthful even with herself. "Yes, I want you," she admitted. "I didn't know it could be like this."

In answer, he rolled over on top of her, tangling his fingers in her fiery hair as he pushed between her thighs. "I'm going to love you all night; I've waited so very long for this." He bent his head to her breasts and her own urgent desire surprised her.

"I will never get enough of you, never! Not if I loved you a dozen times a night, my darling," he whispered as he stroked her face. "You are mine in a way you can never belong to anyone else because you gave me your virginity."

A dozen times a night. With his hot mouth on her breast and his virile manhood hot and hard deep inside her, she thought a dozen times might not be enough for her newly discovered desire. She forgot about white civilization and the consequences of what she'd just done; at this moment, she forgot everything except tilting up her body so she could take him even deeper. She dug her nails into his hard hips, locking her long slim legs around him, holding him to her so that he couldn't escape until her hungry body was satisfied. She panted aloud and clawed his muscular back, pulling him down into her, meeting him thrust for thrust until they both reached that pinnacle of pleasure and plunged over the edge.

They lay there breathing hard only a few minutes before Cougar began to ride her again, teasing her nipples into two swollen points of desire with his demanding mouth, and she climaxed under him even harder, clawing at his back while he smothered her face with kisses.

It was nearly dawn when they finished their night of frenzied mating. Then they dropped off to sleep, wrapped in each other's arms. Libbie had never slept so soundly or so dreamlessly. *Tomorrow could take care of itself,* she thought. This love might be forbidden, but she had never known such passion and pleasure as she had found in this man's arms!

Chapter Nineteen

Libbie awakened, smiling at her memories of last night's lovemaking. In the early dawn light, she found herself snuggled down in Cougar's protective embrace. Then reality struck. *What in God's name had she done?*

Libbie sat up, thunderstruck. She had surrendered her virginity like some wanton woman. No, not surrendered— *given* him her innocence and enjoyed doing so. Even now, her face burned at the pleasure he had given her.

"It wasn't my fault," she whispered, "I didn't know it could be like that."

Her whisper apparently awakened Cougar, and he smiled and pulled her down to him. "I didn't know it could be like that, either."

He kissed her and snuggled her against him for warmth, stroking her hair. "I love you, Blaze."

Love? No, this hadn't been love. It had been—what had it been? She had never unleashed her emotions like that before. Last night, she had felt wild and alive and free.

Now in the cold light of dawn's reality, she had second thoughts and misgivings. She was a captive in a savage's camp and today or tomorrow at the latest, she would be returning to her own people.

And yet, when he began to stroke her body with one big hand, she shivered at his touch and the anticipation of what might come. The touch of his fingers ever so gently on her skin wiped out all her guilty feelings.

In turn, her fingers reached up and traced his high cheekbone. "You're very, very good at that," she admitted softly. "I had no idea it could be so—"

"And will be again." He cut off her words with his kiss and began to make love to her all over again.

Libbie tried to remember that this was crazy, that such a love could never surmount all the obstacles that lay between their two peoples, but the way his hands were cupping her breasts, the way his lips were tracing a path down her belly, made her lose her reason. She forgot everything except how pleasurable it was to lie in this man's arms and let him touch and tease and thrill her into whimpering submission so that she wanted nothing so much as she wanted him between her thighs, putting his hard maleness within her, making her gasp and pull him to her, urging him deeper still.

"I love you, Blaze," he said again as he began to make love to her.

Love? No, this could not be love. Yet at this moment, there was no place in the world she would rather be than in this man's arms as his lips moved gently down her throat, and no one she would rather be with.

He had taught her something last night—taught her to want him, to burn for him with an overwhelming need that seemed to sweep through her very core like a forest fire. She must not let him do this to her again; it made her feel defenseless. Libbie tried to think, but all that mattered was the way his hot mouth caressed her breast, making her arch up and hold his face against her.

She must not let him stroke down her thighs with his skilled fingers, touching her deeply where no man save he had ever touched. And when his mouth went to kiss her there, she forgot what she must not want because she was swept up in an overwhelming need to be one with this man.

Then he meshed with her, and all she could think of was the sensation of him taking her, the emotion of taking and giving of her deepest self as she surrendered to that need. "Cougar. Cougar!"

"Yes, my love, yes, my Blaze, go with me," he urged. "Trust me enough to go with me."

He was holding back, waiting for her. She could feel his great effort as he thrust deeper still. She clawed his back, pulling him even closer as they went into a frenzied rhythm of love, bare flesh slamming hard against bare flesh as she rose up to meet each thrust, wanting him, urging him to go deeper still.

At the precise moment when she had reached a pinnacle of need, he wrapped his arms around her and they were only one person as he carried her far away into a place where there was no time and nothing save being together in a half-conscious world of mutual need and desire.

Afterwards, he lay holding her, kissing her face. "And to think I ever considered letting you go."

Libbie stiffened. "I thought that was the bargain; I would let you pleasure yourself with me, and you would let me go free."

He sat up suddenly, his dark, handsome face turned ugly with anger. "You bargain with your body like a whore? I thought you wanted me, too."

She had needed him so badly, she had lost all sense of shame or reason. Her face burned with the knowledge, but she would not admit to that. "You—you had been wanting my body. I thought if I submitted, you would lose your obsession with me and—"

"Submitted?" His blue eyes were so full of fury, she was afraid. "If I had known that—"

"Would you have turned the offer down?" she challenged. "I think not!"

With an oath, he stood up. "You plot to take advantage of my love for you."

She didn't want to think about love, or about last night, about how it had felt to lie in his arms. She felt angry with herself that it had meant so much to her that she had thrown reason to the wind. "Why are you so angry? I thought it a fair trade."

His features turned as dark as thunder. "Your little trick of playing the whore has done you no good, Blaze. I don't intend to let you go!"

With that, he dressed and stalked out.

He had enjoyed her body, so why did he care whether it had meant anything to her or not? And yet she was ashamed as she remembered the deep hurt in his eyes. He was not only hurt, he was furious, and he did not intend to let her go. She rolled that thought over in her mind and was not as devastated as she expected. After all, what did she have waiting for her in white civilization? Only everything she had ever known. And yet, those moments in Cougar's strong arms had made her forget her own heritage, forget everything and yearn to go with him, wherever that journey might lead.

Was she out of her mind? The canyon between their two civilizations was too wide to bridge; their union could never work. However, soon the Apache would be pulling out, headed deep into Mexico, and once there, her chance of returning to the whites was gone forever.

Apache Tears. Libbie picked up the necklace, touching each stone, remembering the legend of the warriors and the women who loved them. He had given her the necklace as a symbol of his love and protection. Very slowly, she fastened it around her throat. It was like feeling his fingers touching her neck, gentle and strong.

What he had given was more than mere sex, and he wanted the same from her. Well, he wanted too much, she thought with a determined shake of her head. She wasn't Blaze of the Apache, she was Elizabeth Winters, a refined debutante lately of Boston, and after Cougar cooled off and thought it over, she would be turning her back on this wild and dangerous life to return to the more sedate and safe life she had always had. *Safe? Dull was more like it.*

Her emotions in confusion, Libbie went to the door of the wickiup and looked out. Cougar was sitting by the fire with several other men, making arrows. When she looked at him, she wasn't sure about the emotion that coursed through her. This was the man to whom she had given her virginity, and she was surprised to find herself smiling when she thought of last night. She didn't regret it at all, which shocked her into scolding herself silently: *Libbie Winters, you shameless hussy!*

Of course Cougar would change his mind, once he thought it over, and free her. After all, the Apaches did need the food and supplies the ransom would bring. If Phillip were going to meet with Cougar, he had come up with the money somehow. As she watched, Cougar gathered up his weapons and swung up on his big paint stallion, obviously going off to hunt. She had no doubt he would bring in enough meat for his lodge and many of the others.

She went outside and began to grind maize to make bread, smiling and nodding to the women who passed.

When Little Fawn walked past on her way to the creek, Libbie gave her a satisfied, contented smile that told the girl how pleased she had been with Cougar's lovemaking last night. The girl looked resigned to defeat and shrugged as she passed.

Several hours later, Libbie and Owl Woman baked some flat bread in the primitive stone oven. It tasted better than the most delicious white rolls Libbie had ever eaten at fine dinners.

"Owl Woman, why won't you talk to me?" she demanded.

The other shrugged and gave her a stony stare. "You break his heart," she answered, "and even now, he struggles with his choices."

No more than she, Libbie thought in surprise, but did not answer.

She was playing with one of the toddlers when Cougar rode back in. Sure enough, he had a fat deer slung across the back of his horse. He rode up to her and dismounted. "There will be plenty to go around," he said. "I'll skin it and cut it up. The woman and children of Cougar need never go hungry."

But she was not going to be that woman. She found herself feeling empty at that thought. Little Fawn hurried up, smiling and making much of the deer he had brought in. Libbie found herself bristling at the girl. *Yet why should she care?*

She deliberately looked away. When Libbie glanced up, Cougar watched her and frowned. Then he strung the deer carcass up in a tree and began to skin it. After a while, he brought her some of the meat. "Cook it!" he ordered.

She had a million things to say to him, and yet nothing seemed adequate, so she kept silent. After she cooked the venison, she handed him a gourd full of the corn tortillas and roasted meat and their hands brushed and he looked away. She felt troubled by the way he looked at her, and by the touch of his hand, remembering last night and this morning. She knew deep in her heart that no other man would ever be able to arouse such a frenzy of passion in her very soul.

Finally, he said to her, "The arrangements have been made; the exchange will take place about sundown tonight."

"How—?"

"Hush!" he thundered. "Isn't it enough that you are returning to your lieutenant?"

"Oh, yes, the gold." She felt a slight disappointment that his desire for the ransom was winning out after all.

He swore under his breath. "You look but you do not see!" he thundered. "It is not the money I want; it was you, from the first moment I saw you stepping off that stage. I remember every small detail. You wore a green dress and carried a parasol, but the sunlight reflected off that fiery hair and from that moment on, I wanted no other woman but you!"

"But after last night, wasn't that enough?"

Cougar shook his head, reached out, and touched the necklace at her throat. "No, last night only made me want you by my side forever."

"But this could never work out," she protested and reached up to unclasp the necklace, but he caught her hand.

"No," he said, "don't take it off. I want you to have it as my mother gave it to my father—as a symbol of my undying love."

Why was her throat choking up? She should be thrilled and relieved that she was going to be ransomed at last. She could only nod at him. "I—I'll never forget you, Cougar."

He swallowed hard, turned, and strode away.

She watched him a long moment, remembering last

night, then turned and went back in the wickiup. It was about midday. At dusk, unless Cougar changed his mind, she would be rescued and returned to white civilization. From the tortured expression on his dark face, she wondered if he might not change his mind again and hurry the little band across the border to safety. She knew that should worry her, but it didn't.

Phillip looked at the sun, high in the midday sky. By sunset, he hoped to see Cougar dead and Elizabeth Winters riding beside him, on her way back to the fort. The more he thought of her, the more desirable she became. He had been sent the money for the ransom, but he didn't intend that the damned savages should get one penny of it. And Elizabeth would marry him, all right, if he had to rape her to get her. Once dishonored, she wouldn't have much choice in the matter, and Phillip would not only have her ripe body for his pleasure, but her wealth as well. All he had to do was rescue her from that damned half-breed.

Now he remembered how he had plotted with the other officers about how this campaign would be conducted. He glanced sideways at old Mac McGuire as they rode, remembering. The others had not been in favor of tricking the trusting old man, but Phillip had insisted.

"He's getting old," Phillip had said, dismissing their doubts, "and his hearing and eyesight aren't all that good anymore. If we're careful, he'll never know until it's too late."

Sergeant Tribby had rubbed his hands together nervously. "Sir, beggin' your pardon, but this plan of yours is putting people in danger. Why don't you just go out there under a flag of truce, give them the money, and get Miss Winters released?"

"You expect to deal with a bunch of savages with honor?" Phillip had scoffed. "No, I've okayed it with the colonel; he told me to do whatever I deemed necessary, so I'll handle this my way," Phillip said coldly.

"Beggin' your pardon, sir," the sergeant had said again, "don't you suppose by now she's already been . . . well, you know, outraged?"

Outraged. Phillip ground his teeth together now at the thought as he and old McGuire rode along across the rough desert. In his mind, he saw that big, virile half-breed lying between Libbie's shapely thighs, his hot mouth on her fine breasts. His groin went hard just thinking about it. Even with her lying there, frigid and ladylike, she'd be enjoyable. He could hardly wait to outrage her himself. But he only shook his head. *That damned Injun wouldn't dare touch her! If nothing else, he'd be afraid he wouldn't get paid the ransom.*

Old Mac peered at him. "Carryin' on a dialogue with yourself now, are ye, Lieutenant?"

He felt like a fool. "Just thinking. I've got ten thousand dollars in gold in my saddlebags that was just brought by train from a Mr. Higginbottom—Miss Winters's lawyer, no doubt. You don't think Cougar would try to double-cross us and steal the money—?"

"Cougar is a man of honor," Mac said coldly, "and he knows the Apaches need that money to buy food and supplies. They're starving, since that crooked Indian agent steals most of their supplies."

Phillip made a gesture of dismissal. He didn't want to hear all that. Right now, as the pair rode, he amused himself with thoughts of the trap he was setting up to kill as many Apaches as possible. His father was finally going to be avenged after all. Better than that, with any luck, Phillip could keep the ransom money and have Elizabeth Winters, too. So what if he'd given trusting old Mac

McGuire his word of honor? Honor didn't count when dealing with savages. Tonight he hoped to be the one to put a bullet in Cougar's brain. He reached out and patted the rifle hanging from his saddle. No, not in the brain—in the gut, so the half-breed would die a slow, agonizing death. Phillip grinned at the thought.

It had been a long, troubled day for Cougar. Every time he looked up, the white girl was looking at him. He both loved and hated her at the same moment. Damn her for letting him make love to her! Now she was a fever raging in his blood that he never wanted to recover from. Yet she did not share his affection; she had cold-bloodedly bartered her innocence for her freedom and was now looking forward to being free of him. Well, it couldn't come soon enough for him.

Young Turtle had brought him word late last night about how the exchange would work. The trusted old white man would be bringing Phillip with the gold. Yet Cougar did not want to let her go; he loved her too much. It would be a simple choice if she loved him, too, but she had made it very clear that all she wanted was to be returned to the whites. *Why was he even puzzling over this?* She was his captive; he needn't meet with Phillip at all. Cougar could just throw her across his horse and take her up into the mountains of Mexico, where he could sleep with her in his arms every night and never, never let her return to her old life. She would produce fine, strong sons for him, and after a while, maybe she would stop yearning to return across the border.

When he glanced at Blaze as he went about his chores, she was looking at him. He couldn't read her expression. No doubt she was regretting giving herself to him. Truly, making love to the fire-haired girl had brought him more ecstasy than he had ever thought possible, and now he was

going to lose her forever to a man who was his own ...
no, he must not think about that; it was too ironic.

Libbie watched Cougar, wondering what he was thinking. Her own thoughts were troubled and confusing. After
last night in his arms, she was no longer certain what she
wanted to do. But of course there was only one choice for
her.

She reached up and touched the Apache Tears necklace
she wore, remembering last night, remembering Cougar.
It reminded her of him, all right, his strength and his
honor and the way he had held her close and made love
to her. She did not ever want to lose that memory. She
knew then that she was no longer a spoiled, whining girl;
she was a woman. And like an Apache woman, she could
be strong and independent, make her own choices, chart
her own path. Being with these people, and most of all,
last night in Cougar's arms had changed her in many ways.
She was not afraid of what the future might bring; she
could handle whatever Fate threw at her.

She had had one night of ecstasy, and she never expected
to find such passion and fulfillment in another man's arms.
Yet tonight she would be leaving this man and returning
to her own civilization. It was the sensible thing to do; the
only thing to do. *Then why did she feel so empty inside?*

As the sun crept closer to the western horizon and the
Apaches began to pack up their camp to cross the border,
Libbie made ready for the exchange and would not allow
herself to think of anything else. By tomorrow, she would
once again be the very civilized Miss Elizabeth Winters!

Chapter Twenty

It would soon be dusk. Young Turtle had ridden in at a gallop and was now jabbering excitedly to Cougar. Libbie watched them, feeling almost detached as she fixed food, while around her the small band was gathering up the last of their things and making ready to leave this place.

Cougar came over to her. "Phillip and old Mac have been seen several miles away. This will all be over for you soon." He started to say something else, hesitated, but looked troubled.

What was bothering him? He would get a lot of gold for her and now the starving Apaches would have supplies, probably bought with Mr. Higginbottom's dishonest loot.

"I have food ready," she said softly and held out a gourd.

"Did you not hear me?" He was testy, knocking the gourd from her hand. "In an hour or so, you can ride away with Phillip and never see me again!"

"I heard." She nodded.

"I expected you to dance with joy at that news."

Damn, she had expected that also! "Cougar"—she put her small hand on his arm—"I want you to know that even if I do go back with Phillip, I'm not going to marry him. You've taught me I can be a self-sufficent, independent woman."

He shook her hand off. "So what will you do?"

She shrugged. "I don't know for sure; maybe get a job out West someplace."

He looked at her for a long moment, his gaze softening. "The white civilization is a scary place for a lone woman."

"I know that; but I've grown up quite a bit lately. I can make my own decisions."

"I've half a mind to throw you across my horse and take you across the border with me."

"You wouldn't want me under those circumstances," she said calmly.

He chuckled, a forced laugh because his eyes were grim. "You know me too well. Besides, it would be asking too much of a white girl, asking her to turn her back on everything she knows when I have nothing to offer but danger, hardship, and sometimes hunger."

And love, she thought, but she said nothing, watching the people gathering their few possessions, loading them on horses and making ready to ride out the minute the exchange was finished. They depended on their leader to keep them safe and see that they were led into good hunting areas. Cougar's responsibilities were great. *He can handle it,* she thought to herself and was surprised at how confident she was in his abilities.

When she looked at him, he was watching her, a slight smile on his sensual lips.

"What is it?" she asked.

Cougar shrugged. "I just like to watch the sunlight reflect on your hair. It is the first thing I ever noticed about you; that day I decided I must have you for my own."

His own. The gentle tone sent a shiver up her back. She had reveled in the ecstasy of him possessing her body and soul last night.

"What are you thinking, Blaze?"

Blaze. She liked the image now, it brought to mind her time with the Apache band—wild, free, and defiant. "I am not an Apache woman," she reminded him. "I am Miss Elizabeth Winters, a very ordinary and compliant white girl."

He shook his head. "Nothing about you is ordinary. That's why I desired you as I never wanted another."

She must not let him talk like this; this all must end in an hour, and then she would put these moments with him behind her forever. Except for the necklace.

He stood up, staring at the sun moving closer to the Western horizon. "I will make ready. By sunset, my people will be safely across the border; it's only a couple of miles and then we're headed up into the Sierra Madre."

Before she could say anything else, he strode away.

She watched his broad shoulders as he walked toward his horse and tried to get excited about being freed. Just before sunset, she would no longer be a prisoner. She would be headed back to civilization to join her own people.

Very slowly, she finished packing up the few things from Cougar's wickiup. Penniless, she thought; he owned nothing more than some weapons and a few horses, and he had traded five of them for a pretty dress for her.

Libbie nodded to old Owl Woman as she gathered up the last of the stuff and placed it on Owl Woman's travois.

"He will never forget you," the old woman said in English, frowning at her.

"Nor I him," Libbie whispered, "but he'll find another woman."

The other shook her gray-streaked head. "Cougar is like

his father. He gave his heart completely, and he could not live without her.''

''What are you talking about?'' Libbie asked, ''Mac—''

''Not Mac McGuire.'' Owl Woman shook her gray head. ''What?''

Ignoring Libbie's questions, the Apache woman walked away to finish her packing.

Mac McGuire reined in his horse and peered at the sun now low on the horizon. It had been a long day, and he was weary and eager for this to be over. He glanced over at the young officer who rode with him. ''Lieutenant, I reckon we ought to meet up with the Apache in less than an hour.''

Phillip grinned. ''Good. I had begun to despair of ever getting Miss Winters returned.''

Mac sighed. ''Aye. I reckon Cougar's good sense has prevailed, from what Turtle said. The Apaches really need the supplies that gold can buy. You bring it?''

The lieutenant reached back and patted his saddlebags. ''Right here. I'll hand it over at the same time Miss Winters is freed.''

Mac stood up in his stirrups and looked around. ''You hear anything?''

Phillip shook his head. ''No. You're imagining things, old man.''

''Aye, that's probably true; my hearing and sight aren't what they used to be.'' Yes, he must be imagining things; there were only the two of them riding through these rugged canyons toward the secret camping place near the border. Phillip had agreed to that condition. Certainly Bill Van Harrington's son might be dislikable and snooty, but he was a gentleman and wouldn't go back on his word.

Mac nudged his horse into a walk again, and he and the

young officer rode across the rough terrain. "I've got to hand it to ye, Phillip, you're braver than I thought ye were, coming alone out here with me, just the two of us to meet all those Apaches."

Phillip nodded. "I'm my father's son after all."

Which reminded Mac. He couldn't think of a polite way to ask. "Lieutenant, when you came out to my ranch—"

"Yes?"

"It wasn't good manners to help yourself to my belongings."

Phillip looked blank. "What?"

Was he going to lie about the pistol? Well, maybe Phillip thought he had a right to take it from the gun cabinet, since it had belonged to his father. "You know what I mean."

The lieutenant shrugged. "I don't think I do."

Mac stuck his pipe between his teeth, considering. This was not the time to get into a fuss with the lieutenant; not when they were on their way to ransom Miss Winters. *Should Mac tell him the terrible secret behind that Colt?* No, of course not. Mac had helped Bill's commanding officer hide that truth for more than a quarter of a century; it would serve no purpose to tell the son now. In fact, if the young officer returned to Philadelphia soon with his rescued fiancée, there was no need for him to ever learn how his father had died. "So Phillip, as soon as you retrieve Miss Winters, you'll be returning East?"

Phillip ceased puzzling over the old man's queries and nodded. "My mother has pulled some strings in Washington; we'll be returning almost immediately." Funny old codger looked positively relieved. *Ye gods, what did the old man think Phillip had taken from his house?* Mac was not only getting a little blind and deaf, his mind must be going.

"Good. This is no place for ye." The old rancher looked relieved.

Doesn't want me killing his half-breed son, Phillip thought with annoyance, wondering when he would get a chance to double-cross and kill Cougar, as well as any other Apaches. He owed it to his murdered father.

As far as the gold . . . Phillip glanced back over his shoulder at the saddlebags. He had no intention of letting the Apaches get away with that money, although he might tell Mr. Higginbottom they had. If he could manage it, Phillip planned to end up with Elizabeth Winters, her inheritance, and all this ransom, too. He smiled at his own cleverness and kept riding, thinking how easy it had been to fool old Mac merely by giving his word of honor. Lying to the crazy old Injun lover didn't count.

Phillip glanced at the sun. In less than an hour, it would be sundown, and he and Mac would be meeting with the Apaches in a secret canyon that could never be found without the old man's help. Mac was too naive to realize Phillip planned to turn this canyon into a trap. Phillip smiled, thinking that, with any luck, not a single Apache would escape. Thank God the old man's sight and hearing were bad, so he couldn't know soldiers were riding just out of sight behind them. Certainly Phillip wasn't crazy or brave enough to ride into a meeting with Cougar all alone. He hummed to himself as he rode. A canyon was a great place for an ambush. After Libbie was safely out of the Apache's hands, he'd instructed the soldiers to turn their guns on the little band from their superior positions along the canyon rim. Phillip didn't intend that Cougar should escape alive!

The Apache camp was packed up and ready to move out. Libbie went into the wickiup one last time and stood there, loath to let go of last night's memories.

Before she could go outside, Cougar came into the wickiup. "Are you ready to go? Mac and Phillip have been sighted."

She turned to him. There was so much to say, yet nothing to say. "Once you hand me over and get the gold, you'll cross the border?"

He nodded. "In a couple of hours, the Apache will be safe in the Sierra Madre, where bluecoats cannot find us."

"I—I see." She had expected to be thrilled at the thought of returning to white civilization. Instead, she remembered the love she had shared in this man's arms. "Cougar, thank you."

He swallowed hard and shrugged. "I want you to be happy, Blaze. No, I guess you were never Blaze; you are Miss Elizabeth Winters after all."

She reached out and put her hand on his arm. "I will never forget you."

"Don't do that!" He scowled and shook her hand off. "It's going to be hard enough to give you up."

"That's it, then? After all we've been through together, we're just supposed to shake hands and walk away?"

With a strangled sound, he enveloped her in his strong arms, kissing her in a way she could only have imagined, as if he were putting a lifetime of love in that kiss. She was lost in his powerful embrace, the passionate domination of his lips. She didn't intend to, but she was so shaken by his ardor, by the strength of his big body, that she clung to him, returning his kiss with all the feelings that were in her. When she finally pulled away, she was not sure she could speak. It was relief, she told herself, relief at finally being rescued, returning to civilization. "I'll never forget you," she said again.

He blinked rapidly, his voice unusually gruff. "Forget me, Miss Winters, forget you were ever stolen and loved by a savage! Return to your safe, ordinary existence, marry

Phillip or someone just like him, and spend your life as you were supposed to do."

Her safe, ordinary life seemed to stretch ahead of her like a prison sentence. She had gotten used to the free, roaming life of the Apache, but most of all, she had been introduced to love by this man, and she knew she would never find ecstasy like that again.

Outside, a warrior shouted something.

Cougar took a deep breath. "It's time to go now; they're waiting out in the canyon."

"Yes, of course." Libbie swallowed hard. She would do the safe, sensible thing. To do otherwise was unthinkable. She followed him out of the wickiup. Outside, the Apache were mounted up, some horses hooked to travoises. Libbie nodded and smiled at the Owl Woman who looked sad, but nodded in return.

She followed Cougar to the paint stallion. Her throat had grown so thick, it seemed to be choking off her breath. She looked up at Cougar a long moment, thinking how handsome and magnificent he was, wearing only a breechcloth on his muscled body. A thought occurred to her and she reached up and touched the necklace of Apache Tears she wore. "Oh, I can't keep this; it's your most precious possession."

"*You* were my most precious possession." He made a gesture to stop her. "Keep it and wear it until you are out of Apache country; it will protect you. After that, you can throw it away or keep it as a souvenir. Maybe your friends back East will be amused by it."

The bitterness in his eyes told her there was no point in telling him she would treasure the necklace forever. It would be a souvenir, all right, the only remembrance she had of the greatest moments of ecstasy she would ever experience. She fought to keep her eyes from tearing up. "I guess I'm ready."

His strong, square jaw worked a long moment. "All right; let's not drag this out. Will you ride with me one last time?"

She nodded. "One last time."

He swung up on the big stallion and held out his hand to her. Libbie hesitated only a moment before she took it. His hand was as big and strong as she remembered as he lifted her up behind him. She had meant to sit stiff and remote, but she couldn't stop herself from putting her arms around his lean waist, laying her face against his muscular brown back. She was weeping, but she wasn't sure why. Today should be the happiest day of her life; she was being rescued. Rescued from a people she had grown to love, a savage she had come to trust and depend on.

"Miss Winters, are you sure you're all right?"

"Y—yes, of course." She realized then that she was trembling against him.

She felt him sigh, and then he signaled to the others and the small band rode out of the old camp, headed for the big clearing in the canyon.

She was about to be freed and returned to civilization. By this time tomorrow, she would be back in stiff corsets and many petticoats with everyone supervising her life for her. She was Miss Elizabeth Winters, soon to be sent back east and putting all that had happened in the last several weeks behind her. But one thing she would never forget— the way Cougar had held her, the way he had taught her passion. Without meaning to, she tightened her hold on his waist. In turn, his big hand reached down and gently covered her small one, patting it as if offering reassurance. He was right; it was all for the best; to think otherwise was foolish.

Silently, the little band of Apaches rode toward the meadow. She craned her neck to see around Cougar's big body. From this angle, she could see two men on horseback out in the clearing. There was Phillip, all right—Phillip and old Mac sitting their horses all alone out in that vast meadow, the red walls of the steep canyon rising about them. The late rays of the sun reflected off Phillip's brass buttons. He looked very stiff and ill at ease; so very, very civilized.

He was braver than she had realized, Libbie would have to give him that. She would not have believed Phillip would have the courage to ride out and face Apaches alone, with no one but old Mac as an interpreter. Perhaps she had underestimated him; perhaps she should reconsider. Given half a chance, he might make a good husband after all. She thought about letting him make love to her and winced, remembering the passion she had shared in Cougar's arms. Well, Phillip need never know about that.

Around them, the Apaches reined in their horses. Cougar kept riding, moving toward the pair. They reined in a few hundred feet apart. Cougar swung down off the stallion, as graceful as the big cat whose name he bore. He reached up for her. She had never seen such pain in a man's eyes.

She went into his arms, let him lift her down. He was so very strong, and she always felt so safe and protected with him. He was looking down into her eyes with those startling blue ones and she noted with alarm that there were tears in those eyes; Apache tears. "Good-bye, Miss Winters."

"Good-bye, Cougar."

Now he turned toward the pair of white men, took a deep breath, and shouted, "Did you bring the ransom?"

Phillip nodded and shouted back. "A Mr. Higginbottom sent it. Libbie, are you all right?"

She nodded, thinking. Crooked old Mr. Higginbottom, the cheater of Indians. Well, it was only right that his ill-

gotten gains should be given to these hungry Apaches. She
wondered if Phillip had found out yet that she was broke.

"All right," Phillip yelled, "then we'll get off our horses
and make this trade in the middle."

He was so much braver than she had given him credit
for, Libbie thought, with this little band of armed warriors
watching this exchange.

Cougar nodded, but he said nothing. She looked over
at him. One look into his eyes told her everything she
needed to know. This man was dying inside, his agony at
losing her apparent in his face. "Always remember I love
you," he whispered.

She nodded, her throat too thick to speak. "If—if you
care so much, why are you letting me go?"

"I want you to be happy," he said under his breath.
Now he took her arm. "Are you ready to return to civilization, Miss Winters?"

She didn't answer, her eyes suddenly blinded by tears
as she let him guide her. Phillip would think they were
tears of relief, and he need never know the difference.
"Let's go."

Behind them, the little band of Apaches watched silently.
Libbie and Cougar began to walk toward the pair standing
alone out in the meadow, Phillip with his saddlebags
thrown across his arm. It seemed a million miles across
that grass with the late afternoon sun throwing long shadows. She could see Phillip closely now, his handsome face
triumphant, satisfied. She felt Cougar's strong arm tremble
as he held hers.

The four were only a few feet apart now. In only a couple
of minutes, Cougar would be just a memory, and she would
be watching him ride away into Mexico with the other
Apaches, riding away from her forever.

Abruptly, she made her decision, hesitated, and stopped.

"Phillip, I think you should know I don't have any money. I'm as penniless as you are."

"What kind of joke is this?" Phillip shook his head. "You're hysterical from terror."

"I have never been more decided in my whole life. I'm penniless, do you hear me? Mr. Higginbottom probably sent the money because he hopes to marry me."

Phillip looked stricken. "But you've got all that wealth—"

"No, I don't, Phillip." Now it was her turn to shake her head. "We're two of a kind!"

"That's not true. I still want you. We've got the ransom—we'll still be rich!"

So he had never intended to give the gold to the Apaches. "You don't understand, Phillip. I—I've made my decision. I'm not returning with you. I'm going with the Apaches!"

"What?"

All three of the men looked at her, thunderstruck.

Cougar appeared confused, startled. "Think hard, dear one—don't make a choice that you'll regret later."

"Miss Winters," Mac began.

"I am no longer Elizabeth Winters." She said it with conviction now, her chin coming up. Yes, this was right, she could feel it in her heart. "I am Blaze of the Apache, and I am now and forever Cougar's woman!"

Phillip swore a murderous oath and threw the saddlebags aside. "You dirty Injun! What have you done to make her say that!"

"Nothing, Phillip, he hasn't done anything!" she protested.

However, Phillip was staring into her eyes, screaming. "He's had you! I can tell by your face! The dirty bastard has had you!"

She threw up her hands in an appeasing gesture. "He didn't force me. I wanted him. I—"

"You dirty Injun! I'll kill you for this! I'll kill you!" With a maddened shriek, Phillip charged at Cougar, and they went down, meshed into a fight, tumbling over and over.

"Stop them!" Blaze screamed. "Oh, for God's sake, someone stop them!"

But there was no one to stop them. Old Mac stood by helplessly while Libbie wrung her hands. The Apaches did not move, stoically watching the two men battle.

Cougar came out on top, his rage uncontrollable as he slugged Phillip. "You rotten no-good! I've ached to do this since the first time I saw you!"

Phillip reached up abruptly and hit Cougar at the base of the nose with the heel of his hand.

Cougar gasped at the pain, temporarily helpless. Phillip pushed him away and scrambled to his feet. He grabbed up a rock and ran at Cougar.

"Cougar, look out!" Blaze screamed.

As fast as his namesake, Cougar dodged to one side. Phillip, still charging, could not stop his momentum and went down, rolled over, and came to his feet as Cougar attacked again. The two went down in a jumble of flying fists, their shadows long and grotesque in the last rays of the sun.

What could she do to help? Nothing. The two men were in a life and death battle while everyone else watched silently. They rolled over and over, each trying to gain the momentum, tumbling under the hooves of Phillip's horse, which whinnied and reared, its hooves narrowly missing the fighting pair as they struggled in the dirt beneath it.

Phillip had his hands on Cougar's throat. "I've hated you since the first minute I saw you! Now you've dishonored my fiancée and I will kill you for that!"

The saddlebags. Phillip had dropped them when he

charged Cougar. Blaze ran for them, struggled to lift them. They were full of gold, all right. She charged, swinging them at Phillip, and caught him across the shoulder, knocking him off Cougar.

With a curse, Phillip stumbled to his feet. "You slut!" He slapped her hard. Blaze stumbled backward, tasting blood from her cut lip as she fell.

Cougar's eyes turned as cold as blue ice as he came to his feet in a crouch. "For hurting my woman, I will kill you!"

Mac shouted, "No, Cougar! Remember the taboo!"

But Cougar already had his hands on Phillip's throat, throttling his breath away. Arms flaying wildly, Phillip's hands went to his uniform and pulled out a hidden knife.

"Cougar, look out!" Libbie screamed, but Cougar, as quick as a mountain cat, caught Phillip's knife hand, twisting his wrist until the officer screamed in pain and dropped the blade.

It fell with a clatter onto rocks, and now Cougar reached for the gleaming dagger, murder in his eyes as he brought it up for the death blow.

"Cougar!" Mac implored, "remember the taboo! You can't kill your own brother!"

His words seem to bring the half-breed back to reality. With a shuddering sigh as he seemed to fight for self-control, he stood up and tossed away the knife. "He's right," he said. "It's taboo to kill my own brother."

"No!" Phillip stumbled to his feet. "You're crazy! What does he mean?"

And then Libbie looked from one to the other and she could only wonder why she had never noticed it before—the same wide shoulders, strong jaw, and startling blue eyes. And in that moment, she understood what Owl Woman had hinted at. "Oh, my God, Phillip, he's right. You two look alike!"

"No!" Phillip shook his head violently, turning to old Mac. "Tell her she doesn't know what she's talking about! Tell her—!"

"It's true." Mac nodded. "Your father fell in love with an Apache girl and she was expecting his child. But he was being transferred back East."

"No!" Phillip shouted violently as if shouting could change that. "No, my father was murdered by Apaches—"

"Lieutenant," Mac said, "Bill killed himself because he could not bear to leave her, but his honor was sending him back to a loveless marriage. Your father put his own Colt in his mouth and pulled the trigger!"

"No!" Phillip shouted in denial, but even in his desperate eyes, Libbie could see he knew it was true.

"I'm sorry if I've hurt you, Phillip," she said gently and, picking up the saddlebags, started walking back toward the Apache lines.

"No, Libbie, you can't go," Phillip yelled after her. "Don't you see? This is madness! You can't give up everything the civilized world has to offer and run away with some penniless, half-breed scout. You are Miss Elizabeth Winters—you can't do this!"

She paused only once and looked back at him. "I am no longer Elizabeth Winters," she said. "I am Blaze of the Apache and I am Cougar's woman! Are you ready, my love?"

Cougar looked at her as if he could not believe her words. "I am ready."

Then he swung her up in his big arms and walked back toward the Apache with powerful strides.

Her heart was so full that she could hardly stop herself from weeping as Cougar set her on the ground, mounted, and held out his hand. She handed him the saddlebags full of gold, Ebenezer Higginbottom's crooked gains stolen from the Apaches. He tossed the saddlebags across the cantle of his saddle and reached for her. Everything in this world that meant anything was there in his eyes to read. This man would die for her. A love like that was worth whatever it took to keep it.

"I love you," she said and swung up behind him, slipping her arms around his lean waist and laying her face against his back.

"No," Phillip protested again. "No, I can't let you do this!"

Blaze looked back as old Mac shouted a warning. Phillip had run to his horse and grabbed his rifle from the scabbard. "I'll kill you!" he screamed, aiming at them. "I won't let you take her!"

It happened in a split second, Phillip aiming the rifle and Blaze throwing herself against Cougar's back, intending to take the bullet meant for him.

And in that split second, from the cliff, a woman's voice called. "Phillip! Phillip, beware of the bear!"

They all turned to look, Blaze straining against the setting sun to see who was calling. She saw the glint of sun on a pistol, and a pair of gold earrings. Shashké, Blaze thought in horror—Shashké with her torn, ruined face up there in the rocks. And in that split second, Blaze knew with a terrible certainty who had been the Apache girl's white lover.

Phillip had turned at the shout, swinging his rifle around. "Who—?"

Shashké. For a moment, he saw a flash of a scarlet cactus flower, the glint of earrings, and the reflection of the setting sun on a pistol.

"Look out!" he heard Mac shout. "She's got the major's old Colt!"

And then Phillip didn't see a girl anymore; instead, there was a shadowy apparition that slowly took form—the spirit of a bear. *Beware the bear spirit when you break an Apache taboo.* Phillip screamed once in terror and denial as the pistol fired.

Blaze gasped and put her hand over her lips to hold back her cry as Phillip crumpled to the ground. When she glanced up toward the rocks again, she saw nothing at all. Had it only been an illusion, a trick of the setting sun?

Mac ran to Phillip and took him in his arms. He looked up at Cougar and Blaze. "She's had her revenge," he said. "She took the gun from my house."

Abruptly, a line of soldiers appeared around the canyon rim, the last dying rays of the sun reflecting off their brass buttons and rifles.

With horror, Blaze looked at the many soldiers. The outnumbered Apaches had no chance to escape now. Phillip had had no honor after all.

A sergeant called from the troops on the hillside. "Mr. McGuire, I don't know what to do—"

"Let them go," Mac said. "They've done nothing wrong, and she's leaving with him of her own free will."

"That's right." Blaze reached up to touch her necklace, then put her arms around Cougar's waist and laid her face against his back.

His hand reached down and covered hers. "Blaze, my love, are you sure?"

"I'm very, very sure. Everything important to me I hold within the circle of my arms. Let's go to Mexico!"

The setting sun threw blue and purple shadows across the canyon as old Mac waved farewell. While he and the soldiers watched, the little band of Apaches turned and rode out, Cougar and Blaze in the lead. The old man blinked away tears as the little group grew smaller and smaller against the setting sun. "Good luck to ye!" Mac shouted and waved again.

The pair paused once on the rim of the horizon, silhouetted against the orange sun. *Love that's great enough can overcome any obstacle.* Mac looked after the pair of lovers, his old eyes blinded by tears. "Ah, Bill," he whispered, "I did the best I could to keep your secrets and look out for your two sons. I hope you know that."

The sun made one final burst of light, as if in answer to his words, before it slid behind the horizon. The pair in the distance waved one more time, then turned and galloped south toward the safety of the Mexican border. Mac smiled through his tears and watched until they disappeared from view. Cougar and Blaze had their freedom and each other's love. No one could ask for more!

Epilogue

Immediately after Cougar, Blaze, and the warriors galloped away toward the safety of the Sierra Madre, the soldiers, accompanied by a few Apache scouts, rode up to the rocks to arrest Shashké. However, the girl had disappeared as though she had been swallowed up by the lengthening shadows and lavender twilight. They found nothing but an old ivory-handled Colt pistol, a pair of gold earrings, and a wilted scarlet cactus bloom lying in the dust. There was no trace of a woman's moccasin tracks—only the print of a bear's paws.

The soldiers scratched their heads in puzzlement and wondered how this could be. A pistol couldn't possibly shoot such a great distance. The Apaches watched and said nothing, but they looked at each other and nodded silently and knowingly. All knew the bear spirit had returned to take its revenge on the hated lieutenant. One did not kill the bear and escape unpunished in Apache country!

One more thing: many years later, sometime around the turn of the century, whites and Indians alike began to report a young and unusual warrior leading an occasional Apache war party riding out of Mexico to bedevil outlying army posts and steal livestock from rich ranchers along the border.

They say he was a magnificent, broad-shouldered specimen, riding half-naked on a great paint stallion as he came charging down out of the Sierra Madre, leading his men to hit and harry and then disappear back across the border. However, what was most unusual about this young chieftain was that while his skin was darkly tan with Apache features, his long hair was the color of fire. The few who saw him up close and lived to tell about it swore that he had green eyes, a strong, square jaw, and that around his sinewy neck he wore an ancient silver necklace of turquoise and Apache Tears.

TO MY READERS

The tragic events at Cibecue Creek, on August 30, 1881, happened almost exactly as I told it, except that the actual officer in charge of scouts was Second Lieutenant Thomas Cruse, not the fictional Phillip Van Harrington. Lieutenant Cruse would later write a classic book called *Apache Days and After*.

As ironic as it may seem, Major General Willcox had sent Colonel Carr a telegraph message to use his own discretion and not take the Apache scouts if he questioned their loyalty. As I told you in my story, unfortunately, the wires were cut so the message never got through to Carr. If it had, no doubt the Cibecue incident need never have happened.

For those who ask if there ever actually was a half-breed Apache who rode as an army scout, the answer is yes. His real name was Mickey Free.

You might also be amazed to know that among the Apache, there is an old legend of a red-haired warrior who led the warriors sometime around the turn of the century. No one has ever given a plausible explanation of who he was or where he came from. I like to think he might have been the son of Blaze and Cougar.

At Cibecue, only one Apache scout, Sergeant Mose, fought on the cavalry's side. All the others, because of tribal loyalties or confusion, turned and fought the army. Unfortunately, eight white soldiers were killed or mortally wounded, including Captain Edmund Hentig.

Immediately after the Cibecue battle, the Apache put Fort Apache under siege, and the garrison had to send for help. The first rider didn't make it; the second, Sergeant Will C. Barnes, outrode the Apache war parties to reach Fort Thomas for help. Barnes, for his heroism, was awarded the Congressional Medal of Honor and later wrote a popular book called *Arizona Place Names*.

The Cibecue incident reignited the Apache wars that burned across the Territory for another five years until Geronimo and most of his followers were exiled to Florida in 1886.

While eleven of the sixteen Congressional Medals of Honor awarded to Native American scouts during the Indian Wars were given to Apaches, that group is better known as the only Indian scouts to ever mutiny against the army. However, after Cibecue, they served honorably for the many years of their remaining service, as did the other Indian scouts.

Dandy Jim, Skippy, and Dead Shot were hanged at Fort Grant on March 3, 1882, as I told you, while others were sent to Alcatraz. Dead Shot's wife then committed suicide, leaving two orphaned little boys. Dead Shot's sons were raised by Will Barnes, who became a rancher in the area after he left the army. Those sons became army scouts themselves, as did Dandy Jim's son. The final detachments of Indian scouts were disbanded in 1943, the remnants transferred to Fort Huachuca, and the last three sergeants were retired in 1948.

One more thing: in 1890 the Indian scouts had been given their own special insignia, "U.S.S." over crossed arrows. In 1942, when the army was looking for an image for their tough, elite combat unit, the Special Forces, some-

one remembered the bravery and the heritage of the
Indian scouts and paid homage in an unusual way. America's best, the Special Forces, were given as their insignia
the old Indian scout emblem, crossed arrows. Perhaps it
is as fitting and just a tribute as the Indian scouts will ever
get.

I made two trips to Arizona to walk the historic ground
where this story takes place. I spent two days with my San
Carlos Apache friend, Irma Kitcheyan, who owns Moccasin
Track Tours in Phoenix. She took me to places few white
people ever see and shared much of the authentic tribal
lore that is found in this story.

Fort Grant is now inactive and used as a correctional
facility. However, the Apache tribe now controls Fort
Apache and is restoring it for visitors with a wonderful
museum and General Crook's headquarters. Also, at Fort
Huachuca which is still an active fort, there is a good
museum with displays of the Apache scouts and the Tenth
Cavalry, the black regiment known as the Buffalo Soldiers,
who served out of that post. Both groups are also honored
with large statues. Fort Huachuca is located southwest of
Tombstone.

Near the town of Superior, Arizona, are found deposits
of the obsidian stone known as Apache Tears. In this area,
at a cliff called Apache Leap, legend says the warriors
jumped to their deaths rather than surrender, and their
women's tears turned into the jet-black stones.

As always, I'm providing a list of research books that you
might find at your local bookstore or library for further
reading: *The Red-Bluecoats,* by Fairfax Downey & J.N. Jacobsen, published by the Old Army Press; *Wolves for the Blue
Soldiers,* by Thomas W. Dunlay, University of Nebraska
Press; *Apache Days and After,* by Thomas Cruse, the Caxton
Press; *The Conquest of Apacheria,* by Dan L. Thrapp, University of Oklahoma Press; *Once They Moved Like the Wind:*

Cochise, Geronimo, and the Apache Wars, by David Roberts, a Touchstone Book (Simon & Schuster); *Indeh: An Apache Odyssey,* by Eve Ball, University of Oklahoma Press; *The Great Escape: The Apache Outbreak of 1881,* by Charles Collins, Westernlore Press; and *Western Apache Raiding and Warfare,* from the notes of Grenville Goodwin, edited by Keith Basso, the University of Arizona Press.

I will close this story with a quote on display in the Fort Huachuca museum:

> *We were recruited from the warriors of many famous nations; we are the last of the army's Indian scouts. In a few years, we shall go to join our comrades in the Great Hunting Grounds beyond the sunset, for our need here is no more. There we shall always remain very proud of our Indian people and the United States army, for we were truly the First Americans, and you in the army are now our warriors.*
>
> *—Sinew Riley*
> *Apache Scout*
> *Fort Huachuca*

The display says Sinew Riley was Dandy Jim's son.

* * *

Apache Tears is the eighteenth novel in my ongoing Panorama of the Old West series in which I am gradually telling you many of the historic events of America's Western heritage. All my stories connect in some manner, so my regular readers should remember Cougar's friend and fellow scout, Cholla, as the hero of his own book, *Apache Caress.*

My series is written in such a way that you do not have to read the stories in order. In fact, that would be almost impossible since some are written out of sequence and many are out of print. Ask your local bookstore which ones they can still order or check Zebra's ordering service. However, those of you who have been searching for my most scarce and beloved book, *Comanche Cowboy*, will be delighted to know it was reprinted in May, 1999.

If you would like a newsletter and an autographed bookmark explaining how all the stories fit together, please send a letter-size, stamped, self-addressed envelope to: Georgina Gentry, P.O. Box 162, Edmond, OK 73083-0162. Also, if you have a computer you may read my Internet Web Page at: http://www.nettrends.com/georginagentry.

> Wishing you much love
> and few tears
> Georgina Gentry

Put a Little Romance in Your Life with
Georgina Gentry

__Cheyenne Song   0-8217-5844-6 $5.99US/$7.99CAN

__Comanche Cowboy   0-8217-6211-7 $5.99US/$7.99CAN

__Eternal Outlaw   0-8217-6212-5 $5.99US/$7.99CAN

__Apache Tears   0-8217-6435-7 $5.99US/$7.99CAN

__Warrior's Honor   0-8217-6726-7 $5.99US/$7.99CAN

__Warrior's Heart   0-8217-7076-4 $5.99US/$7.99CAN

__To Tame a Savage   0-8217-7077-2 $5.99US/$7.99CAN

Available Wherever Books Are Sold!

Visit our website at **www.kensingtonbooks.com**.